SHADES
OF GRAY

MAYA BANKS

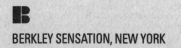

BERKLEY SENSATION, NEW YORK

THE BERKLEY PUBLISHING GROUP
Published by the Penguin Group
Penguin Group (USA) Inc.
375 Hudson Street, New York, New York 10014, USA

Penguin Group (Canada), 90 Eglinton Avenue East, Suite 700, Toronto, Ontario M4P 2Y3, Canada
(a division of Pearson Penguin Canada Inc.) • Penguin Books Ltd., 80 Strand, London WC2R 0RL,
England • Penguin Group Ireland, 25 St. Stephen's Green, Dublin 2, Ireland (a division of Penguin
Books Ltd.) • Penguin Group (Australia), 250 Camberwell Road, Camberwell, Victoria 3124, Australia
(a division of Pearson Australia Group Pty. Ltd.) • Penguin Books India Pvt. Ltd., 11 Community
Centre, Panchsheel Park, New Delhi—110 017, India • Penguin Group (NZ), 67 Apollo Drive,
Rosedale, Auckland 0632, New Zealand (a division of Pearson New Zealand Ltd.) • Penguin Books
South Africa) (Pty.) Ltd., 24 Sturdee Avenue, Rosebank, Johannesburg 2196, South Africa

Penguin Books Ltd., Registered Offices: 80 Strand, London WC2R 0RL, England

SHADES OF GRAY

A Berkley Sensation Book / published by arrangement with the author

PUBLISHING HISTORY
Berkley Sensation mass-market edition / January 2013

ISBN: 978-0-425-25112-6

BERKLEY SENSATION®
Berkley Sensation Books are published by The Berkley Publishing Group,
a division of Penguin Group (USA) Inc.,
375 Hudson Street, New York, New York 10014.
BERKLEY SENSATION® is a registered trademark of Penguin Group (USA) Inc.
The "B" design is a trademark of Penguin Group (USA) Inc.

PRINTED IN THE UNITED STATES OF AMERICA

10 9 8 7 6 5 4 3 2 1

ALWAYS LEARNING   **PEARSON**

For my babies. Love you all to pieces.

WHISPERS IN THE DARK

"A must-read for . . . Christine Feehan and Lora Leigh fans. The nonstop action and sensuality is a treat not to be missed. I can't wait for the next installment of the KGI series."　　　　　　　　　　　　　　　　　 —*Fresh Fiction*

"A deeply emotional, highly satisfying, edge-of-your-seat read . . . Compelling and cutting-edge romance."
　　　　　　　　　　　　　　　　　　　　　 —*Joyfully Reviewed*

"Maya—FREAKING—Banks . . . can do it all. Absolutely nothing is out of this author's reach."
　　　　　　　　　　　　　　　　　　　　　 —*RT Book Reviews*

"You'll be on the edge of your seat with this one . . . and it's so worth the ride."　　　　　　　　 —*Night Owl Reviews*

HIDDEN AWAY

"If I ever wanted to be adopted into a fictional family, it would be the Kellys . . . I am devoted to the Kelly brothers."
　　　　　　　　　　　　　　　　 —*Fiction Vixen Book Reviews*

"[An] action-packed story."　　　　　　 —*The Mystery Gazette*

continued . . .

NO PLACE TO RUN

"Fast action is the name of the game . . . If you're looking for a sexual, sensual, romantic suspense story, look no further." —*Night Owl Reviews*

"Great twists and turns." —*CK²S Kwips and Kritiques*

THE DARKEST HOUR

"An intriguing mix of military action and sizzling romance." —*Publishers Weekly*

"Suspenseful, sinfully sensuous and straight-up awesome" —*Joyfully Reviewed*

"Wrought with a sensual tension." —*Romance Junkies*

SWEET TEMPTATION

"Sizzle, sex appeal and sensuality! Maya Banks has it all . . . This book is on the inferno side of hot, and it shows on every page." —*Romance Junkies*

"An enjoyable tale of [a] second chance at life." —*Genre Go Round Reviews*

SWEET SEDUCTION

"Maya Banks never fails to tell compelling tales that evoke an emotional reaction in readers . . . Kept me on the edge of my seat." —*Romance Junkies*

CHAPTER 1

P.J. Rutherford cocked back her chair and flung her boot on top of the table in front of her. She adjusted her straw cowboy hat so her eyes were barely visible and stared over the smoke-filled room to the band setting up along the far wall.

The waitress thumped a bottle of beer on the table next to P.J.'s boot and then sashayed away, her attention reserved for the male customers she flirted with and chatted up.

P.J. wasn't a chatter. She'd never spoken to anyone in all the time she'd been coming here. She couldn't be called a regular, but yet, in all her irregularity, she was.

This was her place to unwind between missions. It wasn't what most would consider a place of rest and relaxation, but for P.J. it worked to throw back a few beers, inhale some secondhand smoke, go deaf from listening to bad cover songs and watch a few bar fights.

She winced when the guitarist riffed a particularly bad chord and then ground her teeth together when the mike squealed. These guys were amateurs. Hell, it was probably their first live gig, which meant she was going home tone-deaf and popping ibuprofen for the headache she'd be sure to have.

But it beat spending the evening alone in her apartment with jet lag. Although she wasn't even sure it could be considered jet lag. She'd been three days without sleep, so truly she could sleep at any time, but she was wired and still buzzed from adrenaline the last mission had wrought.

She was wound tighter than a rusted spring and there was no give in her muscles tonight.

The big, happy mush fest that had gone on at the Kelly compound, complete with double weddings and enough true love and babies and bullshit to make her green around the gills, hadn't helped.

Not that she was a cynic when it came to romance. She had her romance novels and she was fiercely protective of them and against anyone giving her shit over reading them.

But sometimes the Kelly clan was a little overbearing in the sheer sugary sweetness of all that unconditional love and support. Did no one ever get pissed off and start a fight?

The truth was, she just felt out of place, which was why she'd rather stick to her own team, let Steele take the orders from Sam or Garrett Kelly and she'd follow her team leader. The day Steele became embroiled in all that happy, bubbly shit was the day she hung up her rifle and called it quits.

She liked Steele. She knew where she stood with Steele. Always. He didn't sugarcoat shit. If you fucked up, he called you on it. If you did your job, you didn't get any special accolades. Not for doing your fucking job, as he put it.

And she liked her team, even if Coletrane was one giant pain in her ass. But he was a cute pain in the ass and he was harmless. Plus he was a perfect target for cutting jokes and egging on. Easy. Too easy. He rose to the bait on too many occasions for her to count.

She was the better marksman. She knew that without false modesty. But it didn't stop a healthy rivalry between her and Cole when it came to sniper duty.

It pushed them both, made them better at their jobs and made the relationship between them easygoing and casual. Just the way she liked it.

The current song ended, and she sighed in relief. The

band looked to be taking a short break, but her ears were still roaring from the deafening sounds of just moments earlier.

She was reaching for her beer when she saw a group of three men walk through the door. Her hand shook, nearly knocking the bottle over. Her stomach plummeted like a rock, and she briefly considered making a break for the restroom.

Just as quickly, anger replaced the sudden panic. What the hell was she contemplating hiding for? She hadn't done anything wrong. Her ex-lover and his buddies had hung her out to dry. Not the other way around.

She forced her gaze away, pretended interest in an object across the room and hoped they wouldn't notice her. From her periphery, she saw the moment Derek looked her way and recognized her.

He went completely still and then he nudged Jimmy and Mike and pointed in her direction.

Fuck. They were walking this way. Just what she god-damn needed on a night she just wanted to be left alone.

She was still staring ahead when Derek stepped in front of her, blocking her vision. She slowly looked up, making sure her expression was cool and unruffled.

"So is this where you're hanging out now, P.J.?" Derek drawled. "Didn't figure you one for trolling this kind of place."

The insulting tone grated on her nerves.

"Get out of my space, Derek."

He lifted an eyebrow and quirked the corner of his mouth up in a sneer. "That's not what you used to say. Of course that was before you decided to shit on your team. Where are you working these days, P.J.? Surely not here. You don't quite have the body to pull this gig off."

The old P.J. would already be in his face and would have knocked him on his ass. The new P.J. . . .

Fuck it. There was nothing wrong with the old P.J.

She rose from her chair, tipped back her hat and leveled a cold stare at the three. Back in the day they'd been tight. All four of them. She and Derek had been lovers for two years. They'd hooked up almost immediately after P.J. had joined the S.W.A.T. team and they'd managed to keep their relationship a secret, hiding behind friendship. Friendship they genuinely shared with Jimmy and Mike.

Derek smirked, almost as if he figured she'd turn and walk out. Because that's what she was good at. Running.

Not this time.

She pulled her hand back and slugged him right in the nose.

His hand flew up as his head whipped back and he staggered backward several steps.

His fingers came away bloody and he charged forward. She held her ground, refusing to be intimidated by the asshole.

"What the fuck was that?" he roared.

"Something I should have done a hell of a long time ago," she said calmly. "Listen up, pencil dick. I don't have time for your bullshit. I don't give a shit about you or your lame sidekicks, so do us both a favor and leave me the fuck alone."

"Once a bitch always a bitch, huh, P.J.?" Mike said with curled lips.

"You think what you want, Mike," she said in a calm, measured voice. "I walked away with a clear conscience. Can you say the same?"

He flushed red, and anger bristled visibly from him. He started toward her but Jimmy stuck out his arm.

"What the fuck, Mike? You going to start a fight in a public bar with a woman?"

"Feel free," P.J. said sweetly. "I'm more than happy to kick his ass."

"What happened to you?" Derek demanded. "You didn't used to be so cold."

"Forgive me for not rolling over and taking the ass fucking you gave me so well. I wasn't the one who was dirty. That's on you and your buddies. You expected me to look the other way, and when I didn't, you hung me out to dry. Fuck that and fuck you. Now get the hell out of my space."

She was so focused on her former teammates that she

didn't notice the newcomer until a strong arm wrapped around her waist and hauled her up against his side.

"Sorry I'm late, darlin'," Cole drawled. "Who are your little friends?"

She stiffened in shock, her mouth falling open. Cole covered her lapse by pressing his lips to hers and giving her a long, lingering, toe-curling kiss.

She was so flustered and flabbergasted over his sudden appearance that she could do little more than stand there while he ravished her mouth.

What a silly word. She'd read the word a lot in her old-school romances, and when she was a teenager, she'd giggled over the idea of being ravished, but holy hell, there was no other word that came to mind as he thoroughly tasted every inch of her mouth.

He drew away, amusement sparkling in his blue eyes. His hair had gotten a little longer than his normal neat cut, so it was spiky on top, aided no doubt by what looked like hair gel. She'd have to give him shit over that later. Right after she found out what the hell he was doing here in her bar when he was supposed to be across the country in Tennessee.

When he pulled away, she got a better look at him and nearly laughed out loud. He was still dressed in fatigues, black shirt and his combat boots. He looked like he'd come here straight from the last mission, and, well, she supposed he had, since he was here and not in Tennessee.

She had to admit, he looked like a total badass. He dwarfed her and was a good two inches taller than Derek, who was the tallest of his trio. And his biceps bulged and strained against the tight short sleeves of the T-shirt.

She couldn't have planned this any better. His timing was impeccable.

"Cole, this is asshole number one, two and three."

Cole lifted his brow and his eyes gleamed with amusement. "Is there a problem, gentlemen? Because the way I saw it across the room, you didn't look friendly. In fact, it looked very much to me like you were trying to intimidate someone much smaller than yourselves, and a woman, to boot."

"Fuck this," Derek snarled. "You're welcome to the fucking ice queen. She nearly froze my dick off."

"What dick?" she asked, crossing her arms over her chest.

Cole's arm was still around her and he didn't seem inclined to remove it anytime soon.

"Fuck you," Derek said rudely. "Come on. Let's get out of here. I can't stomach being around a rat fink."

The three men headed for the door and P.J. blew out a deep breath. That could have gotten ugly, and in this joint, there wasn't much in the way of security. The one bouncer was balding, middle aged and had a beer gut that made him slow and clumsy. He wouldn't be much help in an altercation.

"You can let go now," she muttered.

Cole let his arm fall and then pulled a chair out at her table and sprawled into it, waving to the waitress at the same time.

The waitress wasted no time hurrying over. She gifted Cole with her best flirtatious smile and hovered a lot closer than necessary, affording him a prime view of her cleavage.

"Bring me whatever you have on tap, sugar," Cole said with a wink.

P.J. rolled her eyes as the waitress all but fell for that fake charm. Cole was easy on the eyes for sure. Muddy blond hair, a newly grown goatee, which P.J. had to admit looked damn good on him. Blue eyes that could be mean as hell one moment and twinkling and carefree the next.

He was the total package, not that she'd ever tell him so. It suited her purposes to keep him down a few notches. Wouldn't do to have his ego blow up on her. She did have to work with him, after all.

"What the hell are you doing here, Coletrane?" she demanded after the waitress had left. "This isn't exactly your neighborhood."

He shrugged. "Can't a guy come in and check on a team-mate?"

Her gaze narrowed. "Sure. There's Dolphin, Baker and

Renshaw, and you could always look in on Steele. I'm sure he'd loooooove the company."

"Maybe you're just special," he said with a grin.

"Lucky me," she muttered.

But she couldn't control the peculiar butterflies floating around her belly when he turned all that charm on her. Hell, she was acting like a damn girl.

The waitress returned and he tipped back his drink, taking a big gulp before he thumped it back down on the table. Behind him, the band struck up another ear-piercing song and Cole visibly winced.

"Holy shit, Rutherford. I thought you had better taste than this. What the hell are you doing in this shit hole anyway? Shouldn't you be at home catching some R and R? You haven't slept in what, three days?"

She cast a baleful look in his direction. "I could ask you the same question. At least I'm within a few blocks of my bed. Last time I checked you still resided in the great state of Tennessee. That's a long-ass way from Denver."

"Maybe I like your company."

P.J. snorted.

For a long moment they sipped their beer in silence while the music clanged and more smoke filled the air. Cole's eyes suddenly widened when two girls in either corner hopped up on an elevated step and began to do a slow striptease.

"Rutherford, are you a lesbian?"

She choked on her beer and then sat forward, letting her feet drop off the table and onto the floor with a clunk. She tipped back her hat so she could look him square in the eyes.

"What the hell kind of question is that?"

He gave her a quelling stare. "You're in a strip joint. What else am I supposed to think?"

"You're an idiot."

He gave her a mock wounded look. "Come on, P.J. Throw me a bone here. Tell me you aren't a lesbian. Or at least crush me gently."

"You're ruining my downtime."

"Well, if this is downtime, let's do it up right. Want to do some shots? Or are you afraid I'll drink you under the table?"

Her brows went up. "You did *not* just challenge me."

He gave her a smug smile. "I believe I did. First round's on me."

"They're *all* on you since this is your idea."

"Okay, but I'm guessing you can't get past three."

"Blah, blah. I'm hearing a lot of talk and no action."

Cole held up his hand again and the waitress walked up to the table.

"Can you set us up with some shots?" He turned to P.J. "You got anything against tequila?"

"I've only got something against bad tequila. Don't cheap out on me, Cole. You better get the good stuff."

"You heard the lady," Cole drawled. "Give us a setup of the best tequila you have."

The waitress looked dubious but she nodded and headed in the direction of the bar.

P.J. studied him from underneath her eyelashes. Despite her initial annoyance, Cole was intriguing her. What was he doing here? And why? She could swear he was flirting with her, and the weird thing was, it was a rather delicious sensation.

A guy like Cole wouldn't have to look far to get laid. No way he came all the way to Denver just for a piece of ass.

"So who were the clowns giving you a hard time?" he asked, breaking the silence.

P.J. grimaced. "Just some people I used to know. A long time ago."

"Apparently they aren't as taken with your charm as I am."

She sputtered and choked on her laughter. She missed the camaraderie and constant ribbing when she was away from her team. It used to be like that on the S.W.A.T. team before Derek had to fuck it all up. P.J. had been certain she'd never find another position that was better than the early days with S.W.A.T. when she'd still been riding high on landing the gig as a female and had been wrapped up in her relationship with Derek.

But she'd been wrong. Going to KGI had opened her eyes to what loyalty to the team and one another was all about. The men she worked for were deeply honorable, but she'd always been careful to keep her distance. Especially from Cole. After Derek, she'd sworn off ever getting involved with someone she worked with.

The waitress returned, carrying a long board that had ten shot glasses. She set it on the table, took Cole's credit card and then looked at them both as if to say have at it.

Cole picked up one glass, handed it to P.J. and then took another for himself. Then he held it up in a toast.

"To another successful mission."

P.J. could drink to that. She tipped her shot glass against his and then they both downed the alcohol.

She nearly coughed as fire burned down her throat. Hell, it had been a good while since she'd had anything stronger than beer. She'd sworn off the hard stuff after her stint with S.W.A.T. and the aftermath of her leaving the unit.

She brought her glass down on the table with a thump and then stared challengingly at Cole. He grinned in return and then scooped up another glass. She leaned forward to take her own, but this time they were a bit slower to down them.

The music seemed to grow louder and the smoke got thicker. Her eyes watered, whether from the tequila or the smoke she wasn't sure. Cole was right about one thing. This was a sucky place to spend her first evening back home.

"What do you say we finish up our five shots and head to my place?" she said before she could change her mind.

She couldn't believe she'd taken the plunge after being so set on never allowing this sort of thing to happen. Chalk it up to the alcohol or her shitty evening. Either reason constituted one mistake, right? She just knew she suddenly didn't want to be alone.

He frowned, and her heart sank. She hadn't read him right at all, and now she was going to make a giant fool of herself. She was already preparing to excuse the invitation away with casual indifference when he spoke.

"If we're going back to your place, one or both of us needs to stop drinking now. How about I get us a bottle and we'll finish up there."

She let out a sigh of relief that she hadn't even realized had welled up in her chest. She stood, pushing back from the table.

"You get the bottle. I'll meet you in the parking lot. You can follow me back to my place."

COLE went to the bar, motioned for the bartender and, a few moments later, left with a bottle and two shot glasses. Not that he intended on needing or wanting either, but he was going to make it look good.

He sauntered out to the parking lot, wondering if P.J. would even be there as she'd promised or whether she'd taken off.

She was a hard-ass. Hard to get close to. Hard to get any information from. He knew next to nothing about her personal life. She never slipped up and dropped hints. When they were on a mission, she had single-minded focus. And when the mission was over, she was always the first to bug out. No chitchat or social hour for her.

It had been surprising as hell to discover that she hung out in this joint. He would have guessed she hated people and that she'd never go out of her way to actually hang out in a place infested by them.

He didn't feel one iota of guilt over slipping the GPS chip into her backpack before she'd left Tennessee. She carried that damn thing with her everywhere, and it had led him to the parking lot of the bar.

To his surprise she was standing by her jeep, leaned back with a cool expression on her face. Her eyes were unreadable as she stared up at him.

He held up the bottle and flashed a grin in her direction.

She gave a half smile in return then threw her thumb over her shoulder. "Follow me and try to keep up."

Saucy little heifer. She had to make everything a challenge or a dare. It was okay, though. It wasn't worth it if it was easy.

He climbed into his truck and quickly maneuvered onto the highway behind her, making sure she didn't lose him. After a mile, she turned right into an apartment complex that looked like it dated back to the seventies. It was clean and seemed quiet, but Cole didn't like how dark it was and that there were no security gates.

How the hell did a woman whose job was all about security and protection live in a place like this?

He pulled into the parking spot beside her and slid out. She was already on the sidewalk waiting for him, and before he could catch up to her, she turned and walked up the pathway to her front door.

He grimly surveyed the area, and when she opened the door, he frowned harder because the door wouldn't withstand a simple kick. He walked through and then paused as she closed and secured the door. Not that it would do any good if someone really wanted in.

When she turned back to where he was standing, she frowned as she stared down at his hands.

"You forgot the tequila."

"I didn't forget anything."

Before she could react, he backed her up against her door, his body pressing in close, and he did what he'd been dying to do ever since the day he'd first laid eyes on her.

He kissed her.

And this time it wasn't some act he was putting on for the assholes giving P.J. a hard time, nor was he stopping anytime soon.

CHAPTER 2

FOR the second time that evening, P.J. found herself completely flustered and unable to think straight. Damn but the man could kiss like a dream.

She hated a man who was hesitant and unsure in his movements, and Cole was anything but. She loved strength. Confidence. But not an arrogant asshole.

Cole had the perfect combination. Confident. Convinced. He came across absolutely certain of himself.

She ran her hands up his chest between them and splayed her fingers out over the rippling muscles of his chest. Hard and so drool worthy. He'd starred in more than one of her erotic dreams, and now she had the real thing standing in her apartment, his mouth fused to hers like they were permanently attached.

His tongue swept sensuously over hers, stroking with velvety softness. She could taste the tequila they'd both consumed, but it was mixed with the strong, masculine taste of him as well.

She slid her hands back down and tugged impatiently at

his shirt to free it from his pants. Then she placed her palms over his abdomen and he sucked in his breath, breaking raggedly away.

"Bed or couch?" she asked huskily.

He stared down at her, his eyes glittering hungrily. "Depends. How big is your bed?"

"King."

"Perfect."

He kissed her again, backing her away from the door as he did and farther into the living room. She was pulling at his shirt and he was yanking at hers.

"You got condoms?" she asked.

"Does it make me an asshole if I say yes?"

She laughed softly. So he *had* been planning to get into her pants. "Aren't you military boys supposed to be prepared for anything? You never know when you'll need to have end-of-the-world sex."

"Hmm, now there's an idea. Let's have sex like the world's going to end tomorrow."

She pulled him down in a hot, mind-numbing kiss. "You talk too much."

Her fingers were working the fly of his pants, and he was making quick work of her shirt. She pulled her hands away long enough for Cole to pull her shirt over her head, and then she unzipped him while he unzipped her.

"Bedroom," he rasped out. "And be getting out of those jeans on the way."

Clad in her bra and jeans that had the fly wide open, she led the way to the bedroom, working her pants down her hips as she went.

As soon as they entered the bedroom, she heard the clunk of one boot. She turned to see him hopping on one foot while he was taking the other boot off. They'd left a trail of clothing all the way from the living room, and now he was making fast work of his pants.

"Get the light," he said.

"I like the dark."

"Hell no, I'm not missing a single moment of this. Do you know how long I've fantasized about seeing you naked? That's like denying a dying man his last wish."

She smiled and reached for the light switch. When the room flooded with light, she saw that Cole was completely naked and she sucked in her breath, holding it until she was light-headed.

Holy crap. The man was gorgeous. Absolutely lickable. Broad shoulders, muscled biceps, a lean, very toned abdomen and my oh my was he stacked in all the right places.

"Jesus, P.J., quit staring. You're going to give me a complex."

She barely managed to drag her gaze upward to meet his. Unable to resist, she moved forward and pressed her hand to his bare chest, enjoying the feel of the light smattering of hair right over his heart. Then she let her fingers glide downward until they touched the tip of his cock.

Her fingertips danced along the length, teasing as he grew harder beneath her touch. Oh yes, there was no doubt this man was going to satisfy her.

"A man who looks as good as you do should never get a complex," she murmured.

Satisfaction burned in his eyes, and then he surprised her by sweeping her into his arms. He carried her over to the bed and dropped her onto the mattress. She bounced once and then he yanked her jeans down her legs, tossing them over his shoulder.

"I would have never imagined you in this kind of lingerie," he breathed.

She arched one eyebrow and sent him a quick frown. "What do you mean by that?"

"It's positively sinful. Black, lacy. *Girly*."

He said the last almost accusingly.

"I wear it on all my missions. Not that I'm superstitious or anything, but if it works I'm leaving it alone. I consider them my good luck undies."

She grinned because now he'd never be able to go on a

mission with her without thinking of what she had on underneath.

He leaned down and she immediately went quiet, breath held in anticipation of what he'd do. When he'd touch her. *How* he'd touch her.

He slid his palms up her legs to rest possessively on her hips and then he bent lower to press his mouth over her navel.

The simple action sent a cascade of chill bumps dancing across her skin. The crisp hairs of his goatee brushed over sensitive flesh and heightened her awareness even further.

Such a simple gesture, but it was like opening the flood gates. Every nerve ending in her body was on high alert.

Then he hooked his thumbs in the band of her panties and pulled down, untangling them from her feet and tossing the wispy piece of lace in the direction her jeans had gone.

"No tan line," he murmured. "Oh, the images that conjures for me. I'd love to know where the hell you sunbathe in the nude. I think I need a membership."

He parted her legs then lowered his head. He nipped at the inside of her thigh, barely grazing the flesh with his teeth. It sent a delicious shiver all the way up her spine.

Using his thumb and index finger, he spread the lips of her vagina. His hot breath blew over the exposed skin, and she closed her eyes just as his tongue made contact with her clit.

It was like a sudden surge of electricity.

Her legs shook and her nerves tingled from head to toe. The man was an expert at going down on a woman. He wasn't rough or in a hurry. He knew just how much pressure to apply and just where to touch.

He alternated pressing delicate kisses and stronger swipes of his tongue. The lighter touches were driving her insane. She was balanced on a razor-sharp edge ready to plummet at any second. Just a little more . . .

He lifted his head, and the breath she'd been holding escaped in a long sigh. If he'd touched her one more time with that delicious mouth, she would have gone off like a rocket.

"Can you get your bra off or do you need my help?"

She reached for the clasp in front and grinned as she unhooked it. A moment later she angled so she could get it all the way off and then sent it flying toward the pile of clothes on her floor.

Cole climbed up her body, sliding between her legs until their noses were a breath apart. His body was pressed to hers, his heat enough to scorch her.

"Damn but you have a gorgeous body, P.J. I could look at you for hours."

"I'd much rather you touch," she said impatiently.

He grinned and lowered his mouth to hers, kissing hard and deep until she forgot everything but him and this moment. Their tongues met and tangled. She returned his passion in equal measure. Never before had she felt such an urgency when having sex. She couldn't wait for him to get inside her, to feel his strength in the very heart of her.

"I'm planning to do a lot of touching," he murmured as he pulled away.

His mouth slid warmly down her neck and then to her chest. Her breasts were small, but he didn't seem to mind. He palmed one soft mound, caressing and molding until her nipple was turgid and straining upward.

Finally he lowered his mouth and licked a circle around the puckered nub. She let out a long sigh of appreciation. This man seemed to know all her sweet spots. Knew just how to pleasure her. He couldn't have done better if she'd given him a handwritten manual on what did it for her.

"You like that?"

"Mmm hmmm."

He sucked the peak between his lips and applied rhythmic pressure until she was squirming beneath his body, restless and aching.

His hands were everywhere. He stroked and caressed her body like he was appreciating something of great beauty. She was no less enthralled. Her hands slid over every inch of his skin she could reach, exploring the contours, the hard muscles and the feel of his hair-roughened flesh, so different from her own.

When was the last time she'd been in such heaven over a sexual partner? Or maybe she and Cole had just let the tension between them go on for too long. Maybe they should have blown off some steam and had hot monkey sex long before now.

Maybe now they could stop driving each other crazy all the time. Or maybe this would make things a lot worse.

She refused to dwell on the future now. Not when she wanted him with every breath. It was stupid and irresponsible to give in to the growing attraction between them, but she wasn't about to call a halt at this point. Whatever happened afterward, they'd just have to deal with it like adults and not let it interfere in their jobs.

"I don't know if I can wait this first time," he said hoarsely. "I've got to have you, P.J. I'm dying here."

She smiled and tugged him upward for a long, breathless kiss. "What do you need, an engraved invitation? Fuck me, Coletrane. Foreplay is nice, but sometimes it's overrated. Let's get to the good part."

"I love a woman who knows what she wants."

He rolled off her long enough to get a condom and within seconds he was back, sliding up her body to position himself.

"You want top or bottom?" he asked.

She reached down to grasp his erection and positioned him at her opening. "I want both, but right now, I like you just where you are."

"Oh hell, so do I," he groaned.

"Take me, Cole," she said. "I want it hard and fast."

The muscles in his arms and shoulders coiled and bunched. His jaw was tightly clenched as he pushed into her.

They both let out a slow moan when he was all the way in. For a long moment he rested there, his eyes closed as if he were trying to retain what little control he had left.

She slid her hands down his back to his ass and wrapped

her legs around him, trapping him against her. Then she lifted her head, hungrily meeting his mouth.

He growled and she swallowed up the sound as he pulled back and thrust hard.

"Yes," she whispered. "That. Just like that. Please, Cole."

He needed no further urging. He began thrusting harder and faster until the entire bed shook with the force of his movements.

Their mouths and bodies were fused. There was such a sense of rightness that it overwhelmed P.J.

He gathered her in his arms, buried himself deep and then rolled, taking her atop him as he landed on his back.

"Now this is a fantasy that's haunted my dreams a lot of nights," he said as he stared up at her. "You, on top of me, having your wicked way with me. It's your turn, P.J. You fuck me now."

She leaned forward, allowing his hands access to her breasts. He rolled the nipples between his fingers and caressed the soft flesh.

She rocked forward, lifting and then coming down hard, taking him deeply. Her knees dug into the mattress and she braced her hands on his broad shoulders, fingers digging into his flesh.

She alternated rhythm, slowing and then speeding up. She'd feel him swell and tighten, knowing he was close, and then she'd slow again, not wanting it to end just yet.

Leaning lower, she licked over his chest, eliciting another strangled sound from him. Then she nipped and bit at his flesh. The urge to mark him was strong. She liked the idea of him having bruises where she'd sucked at his skin. Something to remind him that she'd owned him every bit as much as he'd owned her tonight.

He gripped her hips, his fingers as hard against her skin as hers were against his. She'd probably wear those fingerprints for days to come. Then he started to take more control, holding her in place while he arched his hips to push farther into her.

She was nearly to the very edge of her own release when

he shifted again, rolling her underneath him once more. But this time, he turned her with rough, impatient hands and she found herself facedown on the bed.

He spread her legs, lifted her hips just enough to get the right angle and thrust into her from behind.

It was like he couldn't get enough of her or her of him. Their breathing was harsh and erratic and the sound of skin against skin was loud in her ears.

Harder and harder, he pounded into her until she was screaming his name. Her orgasm wasn't a sweet, pleasurable thing. It was more like a grenade going off. Explosive. Volatile. Nothing like she'd ever experienced before, and she had no way to stop it, not that she would in a million years.

It was frightening in its intensity. Never before had she been so out of control. Never had she allowed someone else as much control. It should have scared her, but she trusted Cole. With him she could be herself. She could let go.

She heard Cole's hoarse cry through the fog of her own release and then felt him lower himself, covering her body with his. He was still buried deep inside her as they both lay, chests heaving, desperately trying to catch their breaths.

Then he kissed her shoulder. A soft, affectionate kiss that sent butterflies through her chest.

He laid his cheek over her back and they rested that way, him blanketing her, their legs tangled and his cock still swollen and hard inside her.

CHAPTER 3

P.J. lay in the hollow of Cole's arm, her head rested on his chest. Lethargy had her in its firm grip and she was okay with that. She was loose and limber and extremely satisfied. She hadn't felt this good in a long time.

His fingers stroked idly up and down her arm and she liked the sensation of those light touches.

Never in a million years would she have guessed when she got up this morning that she would have had mind-blowing sex with Cole and then be snuggling with him afterward like an old married couple.

It defied logic.

"Why didn't we do this a long time ago?" she asked.

Cole's grip on her arm temporarily tightened. "It certainly wasn't for lack of desire on my part. I figured you'd have my balls if I ever suggested it."

She pushed upward so she could face him, and his hand fell down her back to rest possessively on her ass.

"So why now? You didn't come all the way to Denver just to say hello, so you obviously planned this."

"I wouldn't say I planned it," he corrected. "I hoped. I was tired of wondering whether this preoccupation was one-sided. I finally said fuck it and got on the plane. The worst you could do is tell me to fuck off and mock me for the rest of my life."

She laughed. "Would I do that?"

He cupped her breast with his other hand and rubbed his thumb across her nipple. "You most certainly would."

Her breath hitched as he continued to toy with her nipple. It was a stiff peak straining toward him, begging for his touch. Her entire body was begging. It scared her because this was one man she would never be able to get enough of.

It was like putting a ten-pound Hershey bar in front of a chocolate addict and expecting the person to stop after one bite.

"So who were the guys at the bar?" Cole asked.

She went from being deliciously mellow to instant agitation at the mention of Derek and company.

"That bad?"

She glanced at Cole, who was studying her curiously.

"Not people I really want to talk about."

"Throw me a bone here, P.J. I know next to nothing about you and I have to admit, I'm not in the habit of going to bed with women I barely know."

She lifted an eyebrow.

"You don't believe me? Do you think I'm some kind of man whore?"

She smiled at that. "Maybe not a man whore, but I'm sure you get your share of action from the ladies. There's not a whole lot wrong with you."

"Somehow you make what seems like a compliment sound more like an insult."

She sighed and sat up, crossing her legs so she could sit next to him. He remained lying down so that she was looking down at him, her knees just touching his side.

"It's complicated."

"Aren't most things?"

She couldn't argue with that.

"They're from the S.W.A.T. team I was on. I was . . . involved with Derek."

"Is that the guy you decked?"

She winced. "Saw that much, huh?"

"Kind of hard to miss. Pretty impressive swing, by the way. He's much bigger than you and you nearly flattened him."

That made her grin. Cole was just . . . comfortable. She liked being around him. He was easy to talk to even if she rarely talked about anything personal. Maybe it was why she was careful not to broach those kinds of topics with him, because he was so easy to talk to that she'd no doubt find herself blurting out everything.

"Yeah, that was Derek."

"So I take it the breakup wasn't exactly amicable."

She sobered. "Not at all."

She closed her eyes and took a deep breath. She'd never told anyone about what had happened, even though she knew her current teammates were curious as to why she left S.W.A.T.

"Derek was dirty and I refused to look the other way. He was stealing drug money and later even drugs themselves when S.W.A.T. was called in to assist in drug busts. Instead of logging everything, he'd pocket stuff from the scene when things were still chaotic. I don't know how long it had been going on. But one night I saw him pocket cash along with a bag of marijuana. When I called him on it, he basically told me to shut the fuck up and forget I ever saw it."

"Upstanding guy," Cole said in disgust.

"Maybe I am naive and too idealistic. I mean, to me, when I took the oath as a police officer and when I joined the S.W.A.T. team, it meant something to me. I had a very clear vision of right and wrong. Everything was very black-and-white to me with no gray area. But even being that way, I wanted to give Derek the benefit of the doubt and I was reluctant to turn him in because, like an idiot, I thought I was in love with him and I felt loyalty to him because we were lovers."

Cole frowned.

"Yeah, tell me about it," she muttered. "You aren't thinking anything I haven't said to myself countless times since. I was young and an idiot. To make a long story short, I confronted him and told him that if I ever caught him doing it again I'd turn him in."

"I'm guessing that probably didn't go over too well. Is that what caused the breakup?"

Her lips tightened. "No. And no, he didn't take it well. Told me he didn't take threats and that I needed to butt out. At that point our relationship cooled in a major way, but I figured he'd get over it and that my threat would dissuade him from doing it again. I'm still pissed at myself that I even gave him that second chance. It wasn't the right thing to do, but I was thinking with my heart and so I went against everything I believed in. I hated myself for that."

"Damn," Cole murmured. "Don't you think you're being a little too hard on yourself?"

"No," she said bluntly. "I wish I would have been harder. Two months later, we assisted in another drug raid. This was a big one. Several police officers went down, and Derek, the asshole, instead of worrying over his fellow officers, was more concerned with taking money from the scene. I went to my commander the next day and told him what I saw."

"Oh shit."

"Yeah, exactly. Internal Affairs got involved. It was a big, messy investigation. Derek was smart, though, and he didn't leave any sort of trail. No deposits to a bank account. No change in spending habits. He'd planned long term and was apparently stashing the money where it couldn't be found and was going to use it at a later date or maybe quit and then move off somewhere and spend the cash. I don't really know what his plan was, but whatever it was, it certainly didn't include me in the picture."

"So they didn't have any evidence on him?"

"No," she said softly.

"Is that why you left then? Because you couldn't work with him any longer?"

She hated this part. It still had the power to unravel her even after all this time.

"P.J.?"

She looked up, not really wanting to continue the conversation at this point.

His gaze was intense. Peeling back layer after layer until she felt bare and vulnerable under his scrutiny.

"What aren't you telling me?"

She drew in a long breath and then let it out. "What I left out is the fact that my two best friends, or rather Derek's best friends who I thought were my friends too, along with Derek hung me out to dry."

Cole slipped his hand over the knee closest to his reach and squeezed gently. "What happened?"

"Up to this point, Derek and I had kept our relationship secret. It was against policy for members on the same team to fraternize, a rule, mind you, that didn't exist before I joined because I was the first female on that team. But Derek went to our commander, along with Jimmy and Mike to corroborate his story, and told him that Derek and I were lovers and that he broke things off with me and that I'd launched my accusations out of revenge. Jimmy and Mike backed up his story by telling him a bunch of made-up shit, like that I'd threatened to ruin him when he broke up with me. And then they leaked that story far and wide until there wasn't a police officer in the precinct who didn't know that I was a crazy ex-girlfriend who'd tried to fuck over a fellow officer."

"What a dickhead," Cole said in disgust.

"I didn't have a friend left in that department or on my team. No one *wanted* to believe that one of their own could be dirty, so it was far easier to believe his made-up bullshit. And there was also the fact that not everyone on S.W.A.T. was overjoyed that a woman had joined their ranks anyway, so Derek didn't have to work hard to discredit me in their eyes."

"Wow," Cole said, shaking his head. "That is some fucked-up shit."

"So I walked away, and I still hate myself for giving up that easily. I was devastated because I honestly didn't see that coming. I did what I thought was the right thing and it was the hardest decision I've ever made in my life. But I couldn't just stand by and let him continue what he was doing, because it was wrong, and I thought it would be as simple as telling the commander what I knew to be true and that the situation would be resolved. I learned the hard way that sometimes it is the wisest choice to just sit back and say nothing at all."

"Bullshit," Cole said.

She looked up in surprise at the explosive outburst.

"You did the right thing, P.J. Don't ever doubt yourself on that count. You did the right thing and they didn't. That's on them. Not you."

"But I'm the one who lost," she said in a bitter tone.

"I'm sorry for the way it went down, but I'm not sorry you walked away, because it brought you to our team. To me."

She was startled by the hint of emotion she heard in his voice. He levered up on one elbow, turned so they were much closer now and reached up to cup her cheek. He pulled her down into a tender kiss, and this time he took his time exploring, slowing the pace from their earlier reckless haste.

Slowly but with a firm hand, he nudged her over onto her back, his mouth never leaving hers.

Where before they'd been impatient and eager, now he seemed determined to be patient and gradual.

"I'm glad you came to KGI," he murmured into her mouth. "I can't imagine the team without you."

She felt him reaching toward the nightstand, and then a moment later he rose up just enough that he could roll on the condom, and a bare second after, he slid into her in one firm push.

She closed her eyes and wrapped her arms around his body, pulling him even closer until they were molded against each other, flesh on flesh, no part of their bodies not touching in some way.

He rocked and undulated his hips, leisurely drawing out their pleasure, all the while making love to her with his mouth. Covering her face and neck with tender kisses.

It was a complete change from earlier when every kiss, every touch had been hot and frantic, almost a race to completion. That had been sex. Pure, unadulterated, hot sex.

But this?

This was different, and it unsettled her even as she allowed herself to fall over the edge with him. Because this wasn't just sex. It felt a hell of a lot like making love. And she hadn't reached that point with Derek even after two years of being with him.

CHAPTER 4

THE peal of an obnoxious cell phone ringtone startled P.J. into wakefulness. She'd been having the most awesome, erotic dream, and it irritated her to be so rudely yanked from it.

She stretched and yawned, feeling oddly rested, and promptly bumped into a hard male body.

Her eyes flew open. Oh shit.

David Coletrane was in her bed.

She'd had hot monkey sex with Cole.

They'd also made tender, sweet love, and maybe that was what bothered her the most, because she couldn't just brush it aside as a one-night stand. Couldn't chalk it up to blowing off some steam and walk away from it, pretending it never happened.

She was so fucked and now she had to face the awkward morning-after stage.

The phone quit a moment and then started up again as she lay there admiring Cole's beautiful physique. He muttered something and then promptly leaned over, blindly grabbing for his fatigues that had been discarded the night before.

She got a prime view of his ass, and oh Lord, what an ass it was. Every part of him was delicious, and she continued to stare dumbly as he grabbed the phone and put it to his ear.

Reality had a way of dumping a cold bucket of water over her head. She was positively numb over what she'd done. What *they'd* done. It was quite possibly the dumbest thing she'd ever done, and she'd made some pretty stupid decisions in her life.

This was going to fuck up everything.

"Cole," he said shortly. "Yeah, Steele, what's up?"

P.J. froze. Goddamn it. They were being called out on a mission. Today of all days? The one time she'd given in to temptation and had crazy, insane, all-night sex with her teammate, not to mention pouring her guts out to him, and they had to be called out now?

Cole's expression was grim, and then he said simply, "I'll be there."

He ended the call and then turned slowly to meet P.J.'s gaze. On cue, her cell started ringing and she was contemplating the most modest way to sprawl over his body to reach her phone when Cole reached down and snagged it for her.

"P.J.," she said crisply, not wanting even a hint of what she'd spent the night doing to come through that phone call.

"P.J., this is Steele. We've been called up. How fast can you make it back out to Tennessee?"

She glanced over at her clock to see it was quite early. "I'll head to the airport and see what I can get standby on. Should be able to get out this afternoon."

"Let me know fast. If you can't get on the first flight, we'll send a Kelly jet for you."

"Will do," she murmured, peeking at Cole from the corner of her eye.

She hung up and then took a deep breath, preparing to deal with the awkwardness.

"Guess we should go," she said lamely.

"Yeah, we can hop a ride to the airport together," Cole said.

He lay there completely unbothered by his nudity while she was sitting up, covers pulled to her chin as mortification swept over her.

She shook her head forcefully. "No. We go separate."

Cole frowned. "That's stupid, P.J. We're here together. Why on earth should we leave separately when we're going to the same damn place?"

"I don't want anyone to know we were together."

His frown deepened.

"Look Cole," she said before he could protest further. "We have to work together. I don't want there to be any speculation on our . . ." She choked and almost said relationship. "Our association. This isn't some office job where we flirt and play cutesy. People's lives depend on our concentration and I don't want to become the butt of jokes by Dolphin or Renshaw or Baker and I don't even want to know what Steele would do if he found out we hooked up. He'd probably toss one or both of us off the team."

"Are you saying I'm a distraction?"

The smug look on his face made her want to hit him. He was grinning and he'd stretched out his considerable length and rolled to his side, propped up on his palm as he stared unabashedly at her. She could swear he was plotting to yank the sheets from her, so she tightened her grip just in case.

She closed her eyes and took in a deep breath. When she reopened them, Cole was still staring at her like he wanted to have her for breakfast. A flutter began deep in her belly and worked outward until her skin was warm and flushed. Damn but the man was good. Everything about him was good. His mouth, his tongue, his hands and his cock. Most definitely his cock.

"Look, can we just agree that last night was a mistake? A huge mistake. One we need to promise never happens again. We can't afford to fuck up our jobs or the team. It's best we go our separate ways and pretend this never happened."

Suddenly he loomed over her, big, all badass. She hated

how small she felt beneath him, and she loved it all at the same time.

With a low-sounding growl, he pressed her down to the bed and covered her mouth with his, kissing her until she was panting for breath.

Even as he was pressing her downward, his hand tugged at the sheet until it slid to her waist. One hand came up to cup her breast, his thumb rolling over the rigid peak of her nipple.

God, she loved his hands on her.

His tongue slid past her lips and filled her mouth, tasting her, rubbing over her tongue and exploring every inch. He had a mouth made for sin, and she wasn't a good girl by far. She'd done her share of sinning. If last night didn't send her to hell, she didn't know what would.

When he pulled away, her lips were swollen and her entire body was tingling and alive with lust and desire.

His hand stayed intimately cupped around her breast as if he had no desire to break the contact between them. His eyes were hard and piercing, anger and lust all rolled into those blue orbs.

"If you think I'm going to pretend this never happened, you're out of your goddamn mind. Now stop being silly and let's get our asses to the airport. If it bothers you that much, you can get a different ride from Nashville. But there's no reason we can't take the same plane back."

Her heart stutter-stepped and she swallowed hard.

Finally his hand slipped away from her breast, leaving her instantly cold and still aching for his touch.

"I have to get my rental back to the airport, so you can ride with me," he said as he rolled out of bed.

Her lips tightened at how readily he'd taken over and started dictating the action. Then she sighed. He was right. She was being stupid and shrill. But the very last thing she wanted was for her team to know she and Cole had just spent a hot night together under the sheets. Or rather on top of the sheets. Twisted in the sheets . . .

Her face bloomed with heat. She had to stop. She was

the one harping about concentration and focus and hers
was shot straight to hell because all she could remember
was how good Cole felt sliding in and out of her body.

THE fates were kind and at least she didn't find herself seated
next to Cole when the plane lifted off four hours later. The
two had packed, or rather Cole had watched as P.J. threw a
few changes of clothes into an overnight bag. Most of her
gear was stowed with KGI. She had plenty of backup at her
apartment, but when she had to take a commercial flight, she
was SOL for bringing anything but the bare essentials.

There had been plenty of times the Kelly jet had flown
in for her, making a quick stop to get her and her gear
before heading out for the latest mission. Steele had mentioned the possibility of her moving closer to the KGI base
in Tennessee, but so far she'd hesitated, not willing to make
the final break from her past.

Maybe it was time to move forward. It would make things
a lot easier if she were in closer proximity to the rest of the
team. Hell, she lived, ate and breathed with them seventy-
five percent of her time anyway. The other twenty-five percent she spent in her tiny apartment on the outskirts of
Denver, and she spent nights in a hole-in-the-wall bar and
strip joint. Yeah, that was the kind of life she'd always
imagined having.

Steele lived just outside of Nashville, a little less than
two hours' drive away from the Kelly stronghold on Kentucky Lake. He was a loner, and maybe that was why she
liked and respected him so much. He didn't want to be
intruded on, so he rarely intruded on his team members.

Nashville was far enough away that she wouldn't be
covered up by the team all the time, but close enough that
for missions they had to act fast on, she wasn't stuck traveling from Denver or having the team come to her en route to
the eventual location.

But now she had a complication she hadn't envisioned.
Cole.

Cole lived between Nashville and the KGI compound. Moving to Nashville would mean being a lot closer to him, and she wasn't sure how she felt about that now. He was a distraction she didn't need.

The person sitting next to her in the middle seat got up and headed for the lavatory, and P.J. leaned into the window, hoping to get an hour nap before they landed in Nashville. Out of the corner of her eye she saw Cole also head in the direction of the bathroom from several rows behind her.

When the woman who'd been sitting next to P.J. came out, Cole stopped her and the two spoke a moment. Cole turned on that infectious charm with the suave smile, and in disgust, P.J. watched as the woman became putty in his hands.

She frowned even harder when the woman returned but didn't stop at her seat and instead continued on. Then Cole started back down the aisle without going into the bathroom and she groaned when he stepped over the person in the aisle seat and plunked down beside P.J.

"Oh come on, Cole," P.J. muttered. "Was that really necessary?"

He grinned. "I just told her that we're traveling together and couldn't get seat assignments and then offered her my aisle seat a few rows back. She was happy to accommodate us."

"And again, why?"

"Loosen up, Rutherford. You're way too uptight. You act like last night was the end of the world."

"Shut up!" she hissed out between her teeth. "I'm not having this conversation with you on a crowded plane."

He turned and leaned in so he was close, and he murmured in a low voice, "It happened, P.J. Nothing you say or do changes that fact, so get over it."

"It doesn't mean you have to act like we're a freaking couple now."

"Why are you so prickly?" he asked.

There was no censure or condemnation, just honest curiosity.

"You've been standoffish since day one. No one can get close to you. No one can ask you questions. Hell, you know all there is to know about me, Dolphin, Renshaw and Baker. Not so much Steele, but then who does? But you act like it's a cardinal sin for us to know a damn thing about you. What happened with S.W.A.T. sucks, but do you honestly think the team would judge you if they knew? Or is it that you don't trust us because your last team let you down?"

She sighed and banged her head against the window. They still had two more hours and now Cole was right up in her space. No escaping. Unless she wanted to hang out in the cramped lavatory for the rest of the flight.

He shifted closer to her until his shoulder rested against hers and she could smell him. Her soap on him, since he'd used her shower. But she used plain soap, so that wasn't what she was smelling. It was him. Clean, delicious male.

It was too easy to remember how much time she'd spent up close and personal to all that wonderful male flesh. She'd licked him and he'd licked her in return. Oh yes, he had.

She shivered.

"You cold?" he asked. "I can adjust your vent."

She shook her head and wondered how she was going to survive the next two hours.

CHAPTER 5

WHEN P.J. and Cole left the security gate in Nashville, P.J. groaned when she saw Dolphin standing a short distance away holding a sign that said P.J. in big letters. Smart-ass. She'd usually have fun with it and give him some shit, but not today.

He grinned when he saw both her and Cole and then started in their direction. He was the epitome of cocky good ole boy. He was originally from Texas and he had the worn cowboy look down without actually looking like he was right off the ranch.

More often than not he wore jeans with at least half a dozen holes, flip-flops that made him look like he was heading to the beach and a T-shirt, usually with a snarky saying. Today's offering was "Heavily armed, easily pissed."

Damn but she wanted that T-shirt.

He, like Cole, was a former navy SEAL, and he'd been called Dolphin since BUD/S training, because he swam like one. The man was more at-home in the water than on land. P.J. half expected she'd find gills in his rib cage somewhere.

"Fancy meeting you here, Cole," Dolphin said with a sly grin.

Before P.J. could contemplate removing Cole's testicles—she knew this was going to happen!—he responded so casually that *she* even believed him.

"I tagged P.J. coming out of one of the gates. Figured we were going the same place so we may as well hitch a ride together."

Dolphin frowned. "You went out of town?"

Cole snorted. "I do have a life, you know. We were supposed to be up for some extended R and R."

P.J. cut in, relieved that Dolphin seemed to accept Cole's explanation. "So what's up anyway, Dolphin? Steele was as closed mouthed as ever when he called me up."

Dolphin shrugged as he motioned them toward the doorway leading to the parking garage. "Got me. You know him. We'll know all when Steele deems it appropriate. Me, I'm just the errand boy sent to provide P.J. a ride."

Just then Cole's phone went off. He glanced down and frowned as he read the message.

"What's up?" P.J. asked and then realized how nosy she sounded.

But Cole didn't seem bothered.

"Looks like a text that just got through. Steele says we're meeting at his house, not the compound."

"Oh yeah," Dolphin said. "You didn't know? I figure the world's coming to an end. Us seeing Steele's inner sanctum? This must be some pretty heavy-duty shit. I just hope to hell my OnStar can find it. Knowing him, it's probably not on any official GPS map."

P.J. and Cole exchanged a look. Dolphin was being a smart-ass but he wasn't far off the mark. Suddenly she was anxious to get the hell where they were going so she could find out what sort of mission they'd been called up on.

When they arrived at Dolphin's truck, he grabbed P.J.'s pack before she could toss it in the back herself. She climbed into the extra cab, leaving the front for Cole. She only hoped he took the hint. She found herself holding her breath as he walked around the other side.

To her relief, he climbed in the front just as Dolphin slid behind the wheel.

"You get any rest at all, P.J.?" Dolphin asked as he glanced in the rearview mirror.

It took everything she had not to blush. Cole made a noise that sounded like a cross between a cough and a laugh. She wanted to stick her knife right through the back of his neck. Asshole was enjoying this.

"Slept like a baby," she said in a silky voice.

Dolphin shook his head. "I wish I had. I thought we were in for a long layoff so I went out. Hell, my head is *still* hurting."

P.J. rolled her eyes. Dolphin's nights out were legendary. He always had a new story about all the crap he got into. At least it passed the time during transit and when they were stuck in some shit hole awaiting orders or for the enemy to make their move.

"I didn't get much sleep," Cole said slyly.

Dolphin guffawed. "You finally get laid, dude? I was beginning to think you were considering monkhood."

P.J. wanted to crawl under the seat. It wasn't that the discussion was anything out of the ordinary. When she was working, she was just one of the guys. She didn't get a pass because she was female, and she liked it that way. No way she wanted them acting all weird around her, afraid to say anything for fear of offending her.

What surprised her even more was that if Dolphin's words were to be taken to heart, Cole had told the truth about not hopping into bed with just anyone.

"Monkhood? Nah. Just needed to meet the right woman."

Dolphin made an exaggerated rear back with his head. "Dude! Don't tell me you're off the market! I knew the damn Kellys were bad influences. If we aren't careful, we're all going to be domesticated and ball-less before it's over with."

P.J. closed her eyes and willed Dolphin to drive faster.

"Nothing wrong with one woman," Cole drawled. "As long as it's the right one."

"So, do tell," Dolphin urged. "What's she like?"

Cole grinned. "A gentleman doesn't kiss and tell."

Thank God.

"So that's why you were out of town, then," Dolphin mused. "How she feel about you being yanked out of her bed so abruptly?"

Cole cut a glance over his shoulder in P.J.'s direction, and she shot him a murderous glare that said *If you don't shut up, I'll kill you.*

He chuckled and drummed his fingers on the dashboard. "She was remarkably understanding. Of course, I promised her I'd be back as soon as I possibly could."

P.J. choked and then coughed to cover the sound. She was so going to kick his damn ass over this. He was going to torture her endlessly, and there wasn't a damn thing she could do about it without letting everyone else know they'd slept together.

"When was the last time you got laid, P.J.?"

Her eyes widened as she stared back at Dolphin, who was peering at her in the rearview mirror. It wasn't as if it was an out-of-the-ordinary question, especially coming from Dolphin, who had no couth. The whole "one of the guys" thing. But his timing sucked ass.

Cole turned in his seat and sent her a wicked grin. "Yeah, P.J., when was the last time you got nasty between the sheets?"

She flipped them both off and turned her gaze out the window as they flew down the interstate.

She dozed on and off, trying to block out the memory of the night before. She was jerked awake when her head bumped the window, and she straightened to see they were driving down a long dirt driveway.

"Wow," she said.

"Yeah," Cole replied. "Impressive."

Acres of rolling pasture spread out on either side of the driveway. In the distance a huge pond glistened in the fading afternoon sun. Horses grazed sporadically. She hadn't imagined Steele to be a horse person.

A sprawling ranch house was situated in the middle of the small block of acreage that was cleared. Thick forest surrounded them on all sides, and knowing Steele, he likely owned it all and controlled access as tightly as they did Fort Knox.

"Hey, did you have to give a blood sample at the gate?" P.J. said as she leaned forward.

Dolphin chuckled. "He damn near made me get out and drop trou to give him a urine specimen."

P.J. grinned. They gave Steele shit privately, but to his face—and behind his back too—they gave him absolute respect. They might joke about how much of a hard-ass he was, but he had their unwavering loyalty.

Steele had given her a chance. Despite her past, her record. He'd looked beyond what was on paper and the fact that she'd walked away from a position on a S.W.A.T. team, and he'd believed in her.

In return she gave him one hundred and fifty percent every time.

Their team was kick-ass and she knew so without false modesty. They worked like a well-oiled machine. She and Cole were damn good snipers. Baker and Renshaw were the muscle and the brains behind explosives and tactical maneuvers. Dolphin was their utility man. He could do a little bit of everything, whatever the team needed. Steele was just one badass motherfucker and he could do it all.

Not that Cole wasn't just as much of a badass . . . But he, more often than not, was sniping with P.J. He'd actually scared her shitless when he'd taken a bullet when the teams had gone into Colombia to rescue Rachel Kelly from a fucked-up situation.

She'd never admit it. Not in a million years.

Now it made her think of Dolphin's own close call not so long ago.

"Hey man, you feeling okay?" she asked as they pulled to a stop behind the other parked vehicles.

Baker and Renshaw were obviously already there.

Dolphin turned with a lifted brow. "What's this? Concern from my teammate?"

She scowled. "Of course I'm concerned. Did you get clearance for this?"

He shook his head and got out of the truck and then politely opened her door for her.

"I'm fine," he said, when she stared up at him.

He held up his fist and she smiled and bumped it. Cole tossed her the bag that he got out of the bed of the truck, and they headed toward the doorway.

"About time you two got here," Steele said from the front porch. "Where you been, Coletrane? I figured you'd be here long before now."

"Was out of town," Cole said easily. "Thought we were getting some R and R. I caught up with P.J. at the airport and Dolphin gave us both a ride in."

Steele grimaced. "Yeah, sorry about having to call you up."

"So what's going on, boss man?" Dolphin asked. "Why did you call us up so quickly? Must be some heavy shit going down, right?"

Steele turned and motioned them inside. "I'll give you the report with the others. We don't have a lot of time."

CHAPTER 6

THEY stepped inside the spacious foyer of Steele's home, and P.J. curiously took in as much as possible as he walked the two steps down into the sunken living room.

It was all male, rugged and outdoorsy. It had the look of a hunting lodge. Rustic. Something you might find in the mountains alongside a trout stream.

Wood floor, cedar furniture, huge stone fireplace. There were several taxidermy pieces, from a huge elk over the fireplace to the mule deer mounted directly across the room facing the elk.

A bear rug covered the floor in front of the fireplace, and several other animal hides were either pinned to the walls or covering the backs of the furniture.

It looked like a hunter's paradise. And, well, Steele was essentially the biggest badass hunter there was. He just happened to hunt men along with what other big game he hunted.

To her surprise, when they entered the living room, Donovan Kelly was seated with Baker and Renshaw on one of the far couches.

Van, as he was called by those close to him, ran KGI with his brothers Sam and Garrett. More recently their younger brothers, Ethan, Nathan and Joe, had joined their ranks, but the three older Kellys essentially ran the show.

Donovan was the computer geek, and while some people would look at him compared to his hulking Neanderthals for brothers and immediately think *nerd*, Donovan was a badass through and through. P.J. had a lot of respect for him.

He was quiet. Didn't need to be loud to get his point across. Plus he was smart, and for P.J. there was nothing sexier than a smart man. And if he happened to be a complete badass too? The perfect package.

"Hey, there they are," Baker called out as he scrambled off the couch.

There was a moment of fist bumping and grasping of hands as the team reunited. One would think they'd been separated forever instead of just three days. But they also knew that in their line of work, there was always the possibility that one of them wouldn't come back from a mission.

It was a reality they lived with, and it made them closer. While P.J. might cringe at the thought of having people close to her, this was essentially her family. A whole bunch of big brothers. Well, except for Cole. She'd pretty much axed any chance she'd ever look at him as a sibling. Not that she ever had anyway.

Steele and Donovan were both looking at her oddly, and she couldn't shake the sensation that somehow everything she and Cole had done the night before was on her face for the world to see.

Donovan moved to her side, gave her a greeting, but it seemed grim. Alarm prickled up her spine. This had nothing to do with any silly self-consciousness she was feeling. Donovan wouldn't be here at all if this weren't a pretty damn important mission.

"Have a seat," Steele told everyone.

He and Donovan both remained standing as the others slouched on the couch and in the chairs. P.J. made sure to grab the only available spot left on the couch next to Baker and Renshaw, forcing Cole to take one of the unoccupied armchairs across from the sofa.

Steele took a deep breath. P.J. honed in on his mood with pinpoint accuracy. He was hesitant, which flabbergasted her, because he wasn't the hesitating type. Steele was nothing if not to the point.

"I apologize for calling all of you up after you were promised time off. Something came up, though. Something big."

P.J. and the others leaned forward. Everyone had gone completely still at his announcement, because, indeed, it would have to be big to elicit this kind of reaction.

Steele turned to Donovan, who stepped forward, his expression one of utter seriousness.

"Carter Brumley is one of the largest traffickers of children in the world. He likes them young, preferably in the range of eight to twelve, and he deals exclusively in females."

The hatred in Donovan's voice was evident to all, and now it made perfect sense to P.J. why he was here and why the team had been called up. Above all things, Donovan had a soft spot for children. Women and children, but particularly kids.

He had a hand in every single mission that dealt with children, whether they were missing, exploited or kidnapped.

"He's public enemy number one in a number of countries. Many agencies have gotten close, but no one has been able to take him down. He's smart, but he's also lucky and he has more lives than a cat."

"We going after him?" Dolphin asked.

Steele silenced him with a look.

"In a manner of speaking, yes," Donovan said grimly. "An opportunity has presented itself that we can't pass up. But in order to get close to him, we're going to have to use unorthodox means."

P.J.'s brow went up at that.

That was when both Steele and Donovan looked directly at her.

"Brumley's right-hand man has a predilection for petite brunettes with killer legs. He likes them toned, small busted. Not too small, but not overly endowed."

P.J. had the sudden urge to cover her chest with both arms as she stared at the men in mortification. They were all but assessing her charms in front of God and everyone.

Her lips curled in disgust. She was being such a goddamn girl. Here, she was one of the guys. Not a one of them would be so much as blinking an eye if they were talking about each other's dick size.

"He also has a big mouth," Donovan continued on. "We got a tip from a prostitute he had an association with that he's a talker. With enough alcohol and encouragement, he'll air damn near anything."

P.J. was starting to get a very bad feeling about this.

"Rumor is he's delivering girls to a buyer in Europe. American girls. The specific order is for blondes. Eight to ten years old. Blue eyes. Long hair. The buyer was very exacting."

"Jesus," Cole said in disgust.

"So how do we stop him?" P.J. asked evenly.

Donovan took a deep breath. "We know where he's going to be in three nights' time. There's a party he's attending in Vienna. Arthur Stromberg, one of Europe's biggest arms dealers, is hosting a soiree, and he and Brumley are good friends. And where Brumley goes, Gregory Nelson goes. That's where you come in, P.J."

Cole sat straight forward, a dark scowl savaging his face. "What do you mean that's where she comes in? What exactly are we talking here?"

Steele frowned and Donovan held up his hand. "Let me finish."

Cole didn't sit back and P.J. glared holes through him. The last thing she needed was him embarrassing her in front of her team.

"We want you to get close to Gregory Nelson at the party. Be friendly. Smile a lot. Wait for the invitation. Once you get him alone, try to get as much information out of him as possible."

P.J. blinked and stared back at Donovan, not at all sure what to say.

Cole didn't suffer any such problem, however. He was on his feet, his fists down at his sides clenched into balls.

"What the fuck, Van? You want her to prostitute herself for information?"

The other guys didn't look thrilled with the idea either.

"Why don't we just go into the party, take down Carter Brumley and rid the world of his filth?" Cole demanded.

"I don't like the idea any more than you do," Steele said in a terse voice. "But we can't just go in and take him down. For one, he's guarded to the teeth. We'd need a hell of a lot more manpower than one team or even Rio's team with us. Two, us taking him out doesn't help us free those girls. This mission requires finesse and patience."

"And where the fuck are we going to be while P.J.'s working Nelson over?" Cole demanded.

"We'll be close," Donovan said. "We aren't leaving her on her own and we'll provide the hotel room for their rendezvous. We'll take the room next door so if anything goes wrong, we'll be there in five seconds."

"I don't like it," Cole said stubbornly.

P.J. shot to her feet, determined to shut Cole up. "Hey, can everyone shut up a minute and let the person this actually involves ask a few questions?"

Cole reluctantly snapped his lips shut and then retook his seat, but he continued to stare belligerently at Donovan.

"This all sounds good on paper," P.J. said balefully. "But there are a damn lot of holes in this scheme. I'm not a party girl. I'm not some temptress or seductress. I can't walk three steps in heels and I damn sure don't have killer legs."

Cole's lips tightened further, and she could positively see the denial in his eyes. She shot daggers at him, a promise that if he so much as opened his mouth she'd remove his testicles. He seemed to get the hint because he remained silent.

"You clean up good, P.J.," Donovan said.

"And how the hell would you know this?"

He smiled. "I can see past all the camo and the bullshit. You'll look stunning in the right dress and the right shoes and with the right hair and makeup. I bet your own team won't recognize you when I'm done."

"Uh, Van? You're going to be my wardrobe advisor?"

He lifted a brow. "Why not? I know what looks good on a woman. I won't be much help with hair and makeup, but I'll make sure we have someone who can help with that. The important part is that you believe you can carry it off. You have the attitude and confidence. No doubt about that."

"And I'm going into this party alone?"

"I can procure invitations for you and myself. We'll go in together, but you'll need to drop me once we get inside so you can make contact with Nelson. Once the flirting is done and you have him on the hook, you tell him where you're staying and that you wouldn't be opposed to company. If everything works out the way we hope, he'll be putty in your hand."

She looked at Steele, her team leader, the man she put all her trust in.

"What do you think?" she asked softly.

She didn't care if it offended Donovan that she'd seek the opinion of Steele when in actuality Donovan signed all their paychecks. Donovan wasn't her team leader. Steele was. Donovan had been on plenty of missions with them. He had her respect. But Steele was the one she took orders from and no one else.

Steele was silent for a long time as if grappling with his thoughts. Then he glanced her way, meeting her gaze.

"I think it's probably our best option. I don't like it, but I think we can make it happen and make sure you're safe."

"This is fucking insane!" Cole exploded. "Since when do we pimp out our teammates for a mission? Do you even understand what could happen to her if the slightest thing goes wrong? She'll be helpless."

"That's enough, Cole," she said through her teeth. "You need to shut the fuck up and stand down. I'm not fucking helpless. I can defend myself and my team won't let me down."

Not like her last one had. It was left unspoken but she knew Cole got the meaning. She trusted her teammates. They weren't Derek, Jimmy and Mike.

"No, we won't," Baker said, his voice strained with utter seriousness.

Renshaw nodded his agreement.

"She has to go in wired," Dolphin said. "We have to know what's going on every step of the way so if things get out of hand, we can pull the plug damn fast."

Donovan made a sound of exasperation. "We aren't hanging her out to dry. This is a mission just like any other mission. We work as a team. We plan for any eventuality."

Then he turned to P.J.

"This mission isn't mandatory. It's completely your choice and it won't be held against you if you opt out. I'll understand entirely if you don't want to assume this kind of risk."

"Don't do it, P.J.," Cole bit out. "We'll find another way to save those girls."

But they wouldn't. Not these girls. It would be too late for them. Just babies. Taken from their mothers and their homes. Forced to endure nightmares no child should ever experience.

How could she say no when she had a chance to help them?

Her gaze swept the room. Her teammates were quiet, their expressions pensive. They all stared back at her, unwavering support reflected in their eyes.

Cole was furious. And worried. She could see the concern in those blue eyes a mile away and it pissed her off that he didn't have more confidence in her abilities. They had sex one time and he was already acting like an overprotective ninny. The next thing he'd want would be for her to stand behind him on their missions so she never got caught in the cross fire.

Then she glanced back at Steele and Donovan. She searched Steele's expression for some sign of what he was thinking. Finally she gave up and voiced her question aloud.

"Steele? Do you think this is what we need to do?"

"I can't make this decision for you, P.J. I'm not going to bring my opinions to the table on this. It's a righteous cause or I wouldn't have bothered to call you guys up when you just came off a mission where you got no sleep and you're badly in need of some downtime. But all I can do is call you up."

Steele surveyed the others and then looked back at P.J.

"Let's put it to a vote."

P.J. took a deep breath and swallowed some of the anxiety building in her chest. Give her a sniper rifle and tell her what target to take out and she could do it in her sleep. But this . . . This was so far outside her comfort zone that her mind was screaming *what the fuck* at her.

"I'm in," she said in a firm voice.

Steele looked to the others.

Dolphin blew out his breath. "Hell, I'm in. She's not going without her team."

"Ditto," Baker muttered.

"I'm there," Renshaw spoke up.

Which left Cole, who was still looking pissed. He glanced at P.J. then looked around at all the others.

"Goddamn it. I'm in but I don't like it and I'm going on record as saying so."

"Okay then, we're a go," Donovan said softly.

CHAPTER 7

COLE sat with the others while they waited for P.J. to make her appearance. She and Donovan and the woman he'd hired to make her over had been holed up in that damn hotel room for two hours and he was growing more irritable by the minute.

Every one of his gut instincts told him this was all wrong. He couldn't believe that Donovan and Steele had signed on to put P.J. in such a vulnerable position and he couldn't believe P.J. had agreed.

Well, maybe he wouldn't go that far. P.J. was hard-core. It was one of the things he admired about her. She did her job and she never complained. She kept up with the guys on their team, and if he were honest, he'd admit oftentimes she went above and beyond.

She was a damn good shot, and as much as it bruised his ego, he'd never engage her in an outright shoot-off. She'd probably smoke his ass and he'd never live it down.

He rubbed his hands down his jeans and drummed his thumb over his knee.

"How the fuck long does this take anyway?" he grumbled.

The door to the adjoining room opened, and Donovan stepped out adorned in a swanky tux and shiny, expensive-ass shoes, and his hair looked like it had some sort of gel in it.

Whistles went up and Donovan rolled his eyes.

"Damn man, you look good," Dolphin crowed.

"Where's P.J.?" Steele asked. "We need to move out in a few minutes if we're going to stay on schedule."

Donovan turned and reached behind him. A moment later, he pulled P.J. out to stand beside him. The entire room went dead silent.

Cole damn near swallowed his tongue. Ho-ly fuck.

P.J. looked like a goddamn million dollars. She was wearing a dress that gave a whole new definition to *little black dress*. And hell but it was little. Tiny!

It fit snugly at her hips and clung to her thighs, stopping several inches above her knees. The top had a scooped neck that gave an impressive glimpse of her cleavage. The soft mounds rose temptingly just at the neckline but gave enough mystery to make a man really want to tug just a little at that top.

Her hair was upswept and tendrils escaped down her cheeks and at her nape, giving her a soft, feminine look that had Cole groaning. Diamonds hung from her ears. Hell, he hadn't even known her ears were pierced. Around her neck was a simple diamond pendant that said expensive but elegant and not overstated.

Around her wrist she wore a dazzling bracelet that grabbed the light and bounced it back. Her nails. She even had fingernails for the occasion. Perfectly manicured and painted shiny red to match the splash of color on her lips.

Her eyelashes were long, accentuating startling green eyes, and he was gratified to see that other than lipstick and mascara, they hadn't done much else. She didn't need a lot of makeup. She was just fine the way she was.

But the pièce de résistance was her . . . legs.

Holy hell in a bucket. Donovan had said this Nelson guy went for killer legs, and Cole knew from personal experience that P.J. had a very nice set, but seeing her in heels and that short dress?

He wiped at his mouth to make sure there was no drool or that he wasn't gaping.

She was stacked. Toned from a strict exercise regimen. Her legs were a thing of beauty, and he didn't have to think hard to remember how they'd felt wrapped around him while he was sliding into her over and over.

Sweat beaded his brow just as the room erupted in reaction to seeing P.J.

"Dayum!" Baker exclaimed. "Holy shit, P.J., you're hot!"

She grimaced and Cole could see the nervousness in her eyes. Her discomfort was obvious. She didn't like being in the limelight.

Dolphin whistled and grinned. "Van was totally right. You clean up good, girl!"

Renshaw added a catcall of his own.

"You look beautiful, P.J.," Steele said in his calm, unruffled tone.

Beautiful? Hell, she was fucking gorgeous. But Cole liked her just fine in camo with face paint on. He'd fantasized more than a few times about taking her to bed, stripping off her fatigues and getting her face paint all over both of them.

"You got nothing to say, Cole?" Dolphin asked incredulously. "She looks sa-weet!"

Cole cleared his throat and then saw the desperate look in P.J.'s eyes. It annoyed him. She should know him better than to think he'd let on what had happened between them. Not that he gave a damn. Right about now, he'd like to have a stamp that said "Mine, stay the hell away" to put right on her forehead.

"You look killer, P.J."

"Thanks, guys," she said in a low voice.

"Okay, here's how it goes down," Steele said, snapping

everyone's attention back to him. "Donovan and P.J. will arrive together. We'll be monitoring P.J.'s every move as soon as she breaks away."

Cole's eyes narrowed. "Where the hell is her wire and how on earth is it going to hide in that getup? It doesn't even cover *her*, much less anything else."

P.J. scowled at him.

"Don't mess up that lipstick, darlin'," he drawled. "It looks too pretty on you."

She rolled her eyes and shook her head.

"Cut it out you two," Steele barked.

"P.J. is wearing the latest of my tech toys," Donovan said with a grin he reserved for any time he was talking about his high-tech playthings.

He lifted her arm and turned it slightly so the inside of her upper arm was visible.

"What you can't see is the flesh-colored patch. It's actually made from human skin and blends seamlessly with her own skin. Underneath is the chip that enables us to hear everything she hears."

"For real?" Dolphin asked.

He got up and moved closer. He reached out to touch her arm, running his finger up and down from her elbow to underneath her armpit. Cole wanted to tell him to keep his hands to himself, but that wouldn't go over well with P.J.

"I'll be damned," Dolphin said. "I can't tell it's there."

"That's the point," Steele said dryly.

Donovan continued. "I have flesh patches with GPS locators as well, but her bracelet has a minicam that displays images in real time in high definition. With a simple touch of her cheek or a casual brushing of a piece of her hair behind her ear, she can give us a good view of everything around her. And it has a GPS locator in case we need to find her fast, so it kills two birds with one stone."

Cole's gut tightened. He didn't want to think of worst-case scenarios.

"So let me get this straight," Cole cut in. "You and P.J. go to this highbrow party. She splits off from you, hones in on this Nelson guy and comes on to him, tells him where she's staying and then leaves and waits for him to come to her?"

The others looked at him oddly.

"We've been over this," Steele said impatiently.

"Yeah, well, I just want to make sure."

P.J. shrugged. "He may want to leave with me. Either way the result is the same. No one can predict what he'll want or if he'll even rise to the bait. But adapting to a changing situation is what we do and we're damn good at it."

"Hooyah," Dolphin crowed. "I say we make her an honorary SEAL."

Yeah, Cole knew he was being a total wuss about the whole thing. He just couldn't get rid of the knot in his gut. He just wanted the night to be over with and for P.J. to be back where she belonged. Safe. With her team. Preferably where he could see her at all times.

"And that's precisely why we have to stay on our guard," Steele said. "We don't know how it's going to go down."

He turned to P.J. "If you need out at any time, you know the word. Don't hesitate to use it. At the party, Cole, Dolphin, Baker, Renshaw and I will be outside spread out over the perimeter. Once you leave, we'll tag you and follow you back to the hotel. If anything changes, just make sure you're talking about it so we know what's going on."

Donovan touched her arm. "I'll be inside the entire time until you leave. Any problems, I'll be watching."

Then he turned to the others. "There's a lot riding on this. Aside from the obvious need to rid the world of this scumbag and get those girls back to their homes, there are three governments offering a huge bounty if we deliver this asshole. Dead or alive, they don't care. Resnick wants him alive because he wants information on his network. As much as our resident CIA contact has annoyed the shit out of me in recent times, I'm inclined to agree with him on this one. Brumley is just the supplier. There are a lot of sick sons of bitches who are buying these girls out there, and I want their asses too."

Everyone nodded their agreement, their expressions grim.

"Then let's go nail his ass to the wall," P.J. said. "I can flirt with the devil himself if it helps us save those babies."

Cole blew out his breath because she was right. If it were any other woman except P.J. he wouldn't be so pissed over her going into this kind of situation. This is what they did. Whatever it took to accomplish the mission.

He had to stop thinking of her as the woman he'd slept with, the woman he'd laid claim to, even if she had no idea that in his mind she was his.

She was just a teammate tonight. One he had to back up and make sure they got out safe and unhurt. It was nothing they hadn't done a hundred times before.

"Okay then, if there are no questions or concerns, let's move out," Steele said.

CHAPTER 8

THE residence wasn't what P.J. had been expecting. It was right in the heart of the city with off-street parking. Four men were performing valet duties and quickly moving along the line of cars waiting.

Donovan had opted to park a block away so he'd have access to a vehicle if necessary, and he and P.J. walked toward the gate, where two burly looking security men had been posted to check invitations.

Interestingly enough, there were several women, all decked out like Christmas trees scattered along the sidewalk. A stunning blonde was approached by one of the men getting out of his car. They conversed a moment and then the woman smiled and looped her arm through the man's and they walked to the gate where he flashed his invitation.

"Is that the European equivalent of a blind date?" P.J. murmured.

Donovan chuckled. "Working girls. Just more high-class. And a hell of a lot more expensive. They get wind of a party like tonight's and they know they can score a sugar daddy for the evening.

"Is that what you are tonight?" she asked mischievously. "My sugar daddy?"

"Hell no, I'm dumping your ass as soon as we get inside, remember?"

They both fell silent when they approached the gate. Donovan extended the ornately inscribed invitation and they were motioned inside where another man directed Donovan to hold his hands above his head while he patted Donovan down.

He glanced a moment at P.J. but then motioned her on after deciding there weren't a lot of options for her to be hiding a weapon.

It would make her feel a whole hell of a lot better if she had a handgun at least. Her rifle was an extension of herself. It was odd not to feel her hands around it when she was on a mission. But a pistol would do nicely for this occasion. Then maybe she wouldn't be so nervous.

Some women packed purses. P.J. packed heat.

The stairway of stone steps leading up to the front door was long, and P.J. prayed she wouldn't trip in her heels and break her neck before they ever got inside.

When they finally reached the top, she sighed in relief and then took a deep breath as they entered the house. They were directed through the foyer and then to where double doors were open wide.

Music and the din of conversation could be heard from within. Donovan didn't hesitate, but walked in as if he owned the place, arrogant and confident. Surprisingly, he fit right in among the glitz and the glam of all the attendees.

P.J. stopped in her tracks when she took in the glittering ballroom. Donovan's grip tightened on her hand as he tucked it underneath his arm.

"Don't slow now," he murmured. "Smile and look confident. Like you belong."

Easy for him to say. Places like this struck terror in her heart. It was filled with beautiful people. Beautiful rich people.

There was a sea of them.

She nearly laughed as Donovan expertly maneuvered them through the crowd toward the bar. She was here to garner the attention of one specific man. Gorgeous women were stacked wall to wall in this place. And she was supposed to stand out?

Donovan took two flutes of champagne and handed one to P.J. As he lifted one to his lips, he murmured to her.

"Okay, see the man on your far left? No, don't look. Gradually scan. He's in a group. Can't miss him. Tall blond. Laughs really loud. Likes to be the center of attention. Women surround him because they know he has money and power. They have no idea of his perversions or they'd run like hell."

A shiver raced down her spine.

Great.

She casually scanned the room until she found the man Donovan was referring to. Definitely couldn't miss him. The boom of his laughter was loud even over the rest of the two hundred plus people gathered.

"That's Brumley, and he's a man to avoid. Under no circumstances do you want to gain his notice. Nelson is across the room and is currently alone. He's surveying the crowd and, if I had to guess, looking to score. See him standing by the window? Shorter, stocky guy. Muscled, but he's not one of Brumley's bodyguards or he'd be hanging a hell of a lot closer to Brumley. He's Brumley's damage control. He's the guy Brumley sends to clean up his messes. Dark hair. Mustache. Fake tan."

"Yeah, I see him," she murmured, her lips barely moving.

"Now would be a very good time for you to make a pass by him. The ladies' room is beyond him so it's the perfect opportunity for you to walk by and it's likely why he's taken position there, because he knows he'll see the majority of the women at some point on their way to the powder room. Go reapply some lipstick and make eye contact on your way by. Give him a once-over, just enough to make him think you might be interested, but be subtle and don't tip your hand too early."

"Why Van, you sound like such an expert," she said mockingly. "However are you still single?"

"Smart-ass," he muttered.

She took a deep breath. "Okay, here I go."

"You'll be fine," he reassured. "We've all got your back."

She clutched the beaded handbag, wishing desperately it was the stock of a loaded pistol, and walked as gracefully as she was capable across the room.

As soon as she approached she could feel Nelson's gaze on her, all but peeling off her dress. She felt violated before she got within ten feet, just from the intensity of that lustful stare.

Even though Donovan had told her to make eye contact and to make that first move, her gut told her that obliviousness would serve her better. This was a guy who didn't like not to be noticed. He was someone used to garnering attention. He probably had any number of women clinging to him at any given time if for nothing else than his connection to Brumley.

She unzipped her bag and pretended to focus her concentration on finding the lipstick as she drew even with Nelson. As soon as she passed, she relaxed but could still feel the weight of his stare boring into her back. He'd definitely noticed her.

It appeared as though Donovan's intel was correct, because along with P.J. there had been two blondes and a stunning redhead walking in the direction of the ladies' room, but Nelson had zeroed in on her.

She positioned herself in front of the mirror and forced herself to calm the jitters. She was a professional, with a hand as steady under pressure as they came. She always made her shot. No sweating. No panicking.

This girl stuff was more terrifying than an entire company of gun-wielding terrorists, though.

She made a show of touching up her lipstick, made sure it was nice and shiny, and then after she rubbed her lips together, she slid the tube back into her clutch and squared her shoulders, ready to exit.

To her utter surprise, she nearly ran headlong into Nelson as she left the ladies' room. She stumbled back and her hand flew to the wall to regain her balance.

He grasped her arm and she managed a weak smile. "Thank you. You frightened me."

"You are American," he said in a heavily accented voice. A voice that was heavy with approval. His eyes gleamed, and she could almost see him rubbing his hands together like she was some choice steak he was about to devour.

"Y-yes," she stammered out.

She had no basis for her assumptions, but with the predilection for young girls his boss had, and that he likely had as well, she imagined him going for young and innocent. Even when he went for legal-aged women.

She stared up at him wide-eyed and nervous, and even as she did, his arm came around her protectively as he herded her back toward the ballroom.

They paused a moment as he collected drinks for them both. While she stood there, Nelson looked across the room. She followed his gaze to find Brumley staring intently at both of them. If Nelson's earlier frank assessment had made her uncomfortable, then Brumley's very blunt gaze made her feel naked in a room full of strangers. Then his eyes gleamed and he gave Nelson a short nod that made P.J. grow cold.

Nelson didn't give her time to ponder the meaning behind Brumley's acknowledgment. He urged her toward the patio doors and then out onto the terrace. The night air was chilly on her bare arms and legs. It was an excuse for him to get even closer to her, and he took it, wrapping a beefy arm around her, all but hauling her up to his side.

She positively itched to knee him in the balls and then kick his ass on the spot, but she managed to control those urges and instead glance shyly up at him.

"What's an American girl like you doing here?" he demanded.

She raised an eyebrow. "Are Americans not welcome?"

He chuckled. "No, of course they are welcome." He

stared at her a long moment, obviously studying her with avid curiosity. "You're different from the other girls. The man you came in with. You belong to him?"

"I don't belong to anyone," she said crisply. "I met him outside. I heard about the party and that it was a swanky affair. Thought it would be fun to crash. There were other women picking up dates at the gate." She shrugged. "I figured why not? I made him look good coming in and now I'm free to mingle, eat good food and have as much as I want to drink."

"You even sound American," Nelson said with a chuckle. "So independent. I like American girls. They have fire."

"DAMN, she even has me convinced," Dolphin muttered.

The rest of the team had gathered outside a bar just half a block from the house where the party was being hosted. They were dressed casually. Like a group of guys out for a good time.

"She's good," Renshaw said. "Thinks quick on her feet. Smart girl."

Steele held up his hand as the conversation between P.J. and Nelson resumed. Cole stood in the dark, hands shoved into his pockets as he listened in disgust while the creep came on to her with all the finesse of a rutting bull.

P.J. said and did all the appropriate things. She was believably hesitant and she sounded shy at his forceful proposition.

Nelson turned cajoling, seemingly more excited the more reluctant P.J. came across.

Finally, after what felt like an eternity, they came to an agreement that they would travel back to her hotel room.

"On my way out," Donovan said in a low voice they could hear from the transmitter he carried. "I'm giving them a head start, so you'll see them first. Tag them and make damn sure you keep on her tail. I don't want anything going wrong."

Cole swiveled sharply, looking for them to make their appearance.

"He's taking her out the back. He likely has a car parked behind the house," Donovan reported.

Cole started to clench his first, and as if sensing his agitation, Steele focused on him. "Stand down. We know where they're going. We have her on GPS. Get in your vehicles and make the block."

The others quickly spread out, fading into the evening crowds on the street as they went to their parked vehicles.

"I've got a visual," Donovan said over the wire.

"I wish she wasn't so damn quiet," Cole muttered to Dolphin, who was paired with him.

They slid into the BMW and Cole immediately pulled into traffic, looking for Donovan's car.

He executed a left turn and spotted Donovan's vehicle just ahead. Some of the tension left him. The hotel was at least a twenty-minute drive across town depending on traffic. Cole wanted to be there yesterday, because he damn sure didn't want P.J. alone with this asshole any longer than necessary.

As soon as she got him to talk, Cole was pulling the plug on this and he didn't give a fuck what Donovan or Steele had to say on the matter.

Ahead, traffic slowed and flashing lights illuminated the area. Cole slammed on the brakes and then pounded a frustrated hand on the steering wheel.

"Are they still talking?" he demanded. "Are they caught in this snarl too or are they still heading to the hotel?"

His pulse was racing too hard to get a handle on what was coming through his earpiece. They were all wearing a receiver so they all could hear what transpired with P.J.

"Calm down. They aren't saying much. Oh wait, okay, yeah, they must be ahead of it. P.J.'s doing good. She's keeping us posted on her whereabouts without being obvious. Sounds like they're just pulling into the hotel."

"Son of a bitch," Cole fumed. "Do your magic on this fucking GPS and find us a way around this goddamn traffic. I'm not leaving her alone with that slimy little bastard."

"Relax, Cole. Our P.J. can take out one guy with her hands tied behind her back. She's a badass."

"He's a hell of a lot bigger than her and he's trained too," Cole said gruffly.

"Yeah, well my money's still on our girl. Okay, make a U-turn and then take the next side street to the right. We can circle around by detouring four blocks. Will take a few extra minutes but we should be through."

Cole and Dolphin both strained to hear the conversation between P.J. and Nelson. It was obvious that she'd just let him into her room, and Cole was growing more nervous by the minute.

"I have a better idea," Nelson said smoothly. "I have a house not far from here. Every kind of wine you can imagine plus whatever your heart desires to eat."

"I'm more interested in something a little stronger," P.J. said coolly.

"Thata girl," Dolphin said approvingly. "Keep him there and keep him talking."

"Name your poison," Nelson said in an amused tone. He was likely thinking that a nice, young American girl had no chance of ever standing up after a few shots.

"Tequila, and I just happen to have a bottle in the liquor cabinet. This hotel is remarkably well stocked. Shall we have a drink to get . . . comfortable?"

"Damn she sounds sexy," Dolphin said as they flew down the city streets.

"Shut the fuck up," Cole growled.

Things went completely silent. Cole tapped his earpiece. "Hey, are you hearing anything, Dolphin? Things have gone too quiet."

Dolphin was silent a moment. "No, not hearing anything, but they might be making drinks."

Damn it. They were getting closer but the evening traffic sucked ass. Still too many damn pedestrians in the streets. Cole swerved to miss one crossing and kept going, bearing down on the hotel still eight blocks ahead.

He picked up his secure cell, planning to call Donovan or Steele, but he was likely ahead of them and would be on scene first anyway. No point in asking them what they were hearing, because he'd had enough of this bullshit.

He was going in and dragging P.J. out. He could claim to be a jealous boyfriend. Ex-boyfriend. Whatever didn't get her cover blown, but he was pulling the plug because his gut was screaming that this was all wrong and that P.J. was in serious danger.

Five minutes later, he finally screeched into the parking lot of the hotel and parked underneath the awning in front.

"Whoa, wait a minute, Cole, what the fuck are you doing?" Dolphin demanded.

Cole was already out and running into the lobby. Dolphin caught up to him at the elevator and pinned him against the wall while the elevator rose to the top floor.

"I'm going in and taking her out of there," Cole said. "She's gone radio silent. This mission is over."

Just then her voice slid like silk over Cole's ears.

"I much preferred my hotel," she said crossly. "I don't know why it was so important for you to take me somewhere else."

"Whoa, what?" Dolphin asked.

"Hell no. She's not leaving this hotel. Check your GPS. Give me her location."

Dolphin and Cole stepped off the elevator and quietly went to the room next to P.J.'s as Dolphin brought up the handheld GPS.

"It says she's right there. Next door."

"But she said why it *was* so important. Not is," Cole said as his gut tightened even more. "I don't like this, Dolphin."

"The city is beautiful," P.J. said, once more coming in clearly. "Even the bridge is quaint looking. What river are we crossing?"

Cole and Dolphin exchanged looks and then at the same time hit the adjoining door with enough force to knock it down. They rushed into the hotel room only to find it empty.

The liquor cabinet was open but everything else was exactly as P.J. had left it.

Their gazes tracked downward, and lying on the floor was the jewelry that P.J. had been wearing. The necklace was carelessly strewn and the earrings were scattered as if they'd been ripped off her and discarded. Just as they took in the glittering bracelet that was broken into three pieces, P.J.'s voice came over the wire once more.

"I still can't believe you broke my bracelet," she said in a pouty tone. "It was my favorite."

"It wasn't even real," Nelson said impatiently. "Besides, you won't need it. All you need to worry about is pleasing me."

The threat in his voice sent a hot flush down Cole's body. Rage. Anger that P.J. was vulnerable and as of now he didn't have a fucking clue where she was. She was trying to give them clues through the wire Donovan had planted on her.

Steele, Donovan, Baker and Renshaw burst into the room, their expressions grim. They'd heard everything he had.

Cole looked up as cold fear replaced the heated fury that had boiled in his veins. He held up the broken bracelet so the others could see it.

"We have a huge fucking problem here."

CHAPTER 9

P.J.'S nerves were shot to hell by the time they arrived at the looming stone house just a few miles from the city center. Though on the fringe of the hustle and bustle of downtown, it was a quiet neighborhood with much more space between the homes. And the one whose garage he'd driven into was huge.

She oohed and made the appropriate noises of appreciation all the while trying her best to convey enough information that her team could find her. She probably sounded like a complete airhead with the way she parroted information, but damn it, she was *scared*.

Never before on a mission had she felt fear like this. If someone handed her a rifle right now she couldn't hit the broad side of a barn. But then she'd never been separated from her team. She'd always had their backup and unwavering support.

Now? She was completely on her own.

She was convinced that the asshole had broken her bracelet on purpose, which meant she was in some pretty deep shit. If he suspected she wasn't who she said she was or even if he just wanted to play it safe, it still left her without a huge safety net. And it meant he had some not-so-nice plans for her.

At least she still had the patch on her arm so her teammates could hear her.

"You talk too damn much," Nelson snapped as he herded her toward the door.

She halted and made a show of getting huffy. "Then maybe you should just bring me back to my hotel."

His hand curled around her nape and he all but shoved her inside the house. "Not going to happen, princess."

"What the hell is wrong with you?" she demanded as she tried to wrench herself free from his grasp.

But his fingers pressed tighter into her flesh and he all but picked her up, dragging her into the spacious sitting room. He tossed her down onto the couch and then wrested the bottle of tequila from her hands.

"Don't even think about going anywhere," he threatened.

She held up her hands hoping to hell they weren't shaking.

"Hey, chill out. Pour us a drink. No need to get so damn rough. Are you into that kinky shit? Because let me say before things go too far that I'm not. And if you are, then let's just call it quits right now."

He gave her a look that told her without words to shut up. She went silent and waited, every single second agonizing.

He pulled out glasses that damn sure weren't shot glasses and he poured a liberal amount of tequila into both. A moment later he returned and shoved one of the glasses into her hand.

"Bottoms up," he said.

Maybe if she got him drunk enough she could toss his ass and be out of this. Or maybe she could at least buy enough time for her team to come get her. Either plan worked for her.

She gulped down half the contents of the tequila, stopping before she risked puking it all back up. She wiped the back of her mouth with her hand as he finished off his. To her surprise he didn't get angry that she hadn't drunk it all. He took the glass from her then touched her hair in a surprisingly gentle gesture.

He gave her a look that seemed regretful. "This isn't the way I wanted things to go down for the evening, but the boss saw you and he wanted you. Not much I could do after that."

Oh shit. Shit, shit, shit! Her adrenaline shot up and her pulse started pounding like a jackhammer.

Despite her heightened anxiety and her increased pulse rate, the room was moving in slow motion. She tried to lift one of her arms and it felt like it was encased in lead.

"You drugged me!" she accused, hoping she wasn't so garbled that her team heard and knew it was time to yank the plug for this mission.

Nelson grimaced. "I like my women to fight. Drugging is the coward's way out, but my boss gets off on knowing they're completely helpless." He shrugged as he made his way over to where P.J. was precariously sagging toward the couch. "I don't mind a few scratches. Makes it more exciting when I overpower them."

"You're sick. All of you. Sick bastards," she croaked.

He put his hands on her shoulders to guide her to the couch and she cringed, trying to fight him off. She was as ineffectual as a kitten batting at a lion.

He pushed her down to the couch and stuck his hand in the bodice of her dress, ripping downward.

"Nice lingerie," he murmured as he stared down at the black lace bra and panties she wore. "I'll leave them on for the boss. He likes black."

As he moved away she whispered brokenly, hoping her team would hear. "Please, please, you have to pull me out. I'm drugged. I can't fight him off. Please, he's going to rape me."

The sound of a door opening made her slowly move her head in that direction, hope alive that maybe they'd come for her. But when she met the satisfied gaze of Carter Brumley, her heart sank and she knew there was nothing anyone could do to save her now.

CHAPTER 10

THE entire van froze when P.J.'s broken plea came over the comm. Cole punched the back of the seat with enough force to knock the headrest loose.

"Goddamn it! Where is she? We have to find her now. Those assholes are going to fuck her over."

"I'm working on it, damn it!" Donovan shouted.

Every single one of the team members was tense. The van vibrated with rage, helplessness and dread.

"How did this happen? How the fuck did this happen?" Cole raged. He needed someone or something to blame. Hell, he blamed himself. He should never have allowed it. It didn't matter if P.J. never spoke to him again. At least she'd be safe and not in the hands of a monster.

"Shhh!" Steele snapped. "Brumley's there. Goddamn it. I hear him."

The tremble of emotion in the team leader's voice was uncharacteristic. He was generally cool under pressure but this had shaken him badly.

The van went silent as Donovan received more intel on

every residence that Brumley owned or was associated with in the area.

Even Donovan looked up, his expression tense when Carter Brumley's voice came over the wire again.

"I know you picked her out, Nelson, but there was something about this one that spoke to me. I had to have her. Did you make sure she was clean?"

"Yeah, boss. Only jewelry she was wearing was a necklace, earrings and a bracelet and I trashed them at her hotel room. She's an American bimbo who crashed the party looking for a good time."

Brumley chuckled. "Very nice. I'll do my very best to accommodate her."

They could hear his breathing, so they knew he was close to P.J., but she hadn't uttered a sound. Had the drug affected her so much that she could no longer speak? Was she rendered incapable of fighting back?

Then he prayed she wouldn't offer resistance. They'd likely kill her. Oh God. It made him nauseous that he actually wanted her to lie there and take it because he couldn't bear for her to be hurt even more if she fought back.

There was a peculiar popping sound. Metallic. Cole screwed up his forehead and looked at the others. "What the fuck was that?" he mouthed.

A moment later, P.J. screamed in pain and Brumley laughed.

"It sounded like a knife opening," Dolphin said hoarsely.

"Dear God," Renshaw whispered. "What is that sick fuck doing to her?"

"What have you got for us?" Cole asked Donovan in a desperate voice. "That son of a bitch is cutting her up."

Another scream rattled the entire team. Baker was driving and he slammed on the brakes, pulling to the curb. He stared back at Donovan, his eyes blazing with fury.

"You pick a location, Van. Use the info she gave us. There can't be that many that fit the bill. Get me a goddamn coordinate so we can go in and get our girl. This is bullshit!"

Two more screams sent the hairs on Cole's nape straight

up. And then complete silence followed by the unmistakable sound of thighs slapping against thighs. There was a quiet sound that Cole had to strain to catch amid the other noises, but he heard it.

It was soft weeping.

He buried his face in his hands, his own eyes burning with tears. Having to listen as P.J. was violated was the worst thing he'd ever endured in all his years in the military and in KGI. He'd never felt so helpless in his life.

Donovan thrust the map with shaking hands at Baker. "Here," he said hoarsely. "This has to be it. There are only two locations that work with the information she gave us, and given the time frame in which they arrived, this one has to be it."

Baker gunned the accelerator and roared into traffic, causing everyone to brace themselves as he swerved around cars.

Brumley let out a satisfied grunt, and then the sound of flesh being struck echoed over the comm. The bastard had slapped her. And then the unmistakable sound of pants being zipped back up.

Cole's stomach revolted. He punched the back of the seat again and then the window. Dolphin jumped on him, restraining him before he shattered the glass.

"Save it, man," Dolphin said quietly. "Save it for those assholes and save it for P.J. She's going to need us."

"She's all yours, Nelson," Brumley said, a clear smirk in his voice. "I know she's messier than you usually like them, but I don't think you'll have any complaints. She's a damn fine fuck. If I didn't have other matters to attend to, I'd take her along. She would have made a very good temporary mistress."

"Yes, sir," Nelson replied.

"Kill her when you're done. Make sure you clean up the mess. I need you for the exchange Sunday night. The girls are coming in on a plane at eight P.M. The buyer will be there to inspect the goods. I don't want any issues."

"Wainwright going to take possession then or are we

shipping to his choice of location?" Nelson asked gruffly. "Will I need to bring along extra firepower?"

"No, he's coming alone, except for his usual three who accompany him everywhere. He won't do a thing because he wants those girls very badly. We'll off-load the plane and he's going to have a truck parked at the airport that the girls will be herded onto. It all should take five minutes tops, and then we'll fly out on the plane the girls came in on. Easy transaction and I make another ten million."

"We could take this girl with us," Nelson hedged. "She's not so messed up I can't have her cleaned up in half an hour. I'll keep her drugged enough she won't be a problem."

"Get us the hell there, goddamn it," Cole barked to Baker. "This is bullshit!"

Brumley chuckled. "Have your fun with her then silence her for good. She saw your face and mine, not to mention Colin's and Isaac's. I don't take chances. Especially not over some two-bit whore."

Steele held up four fingers to signal the number of people in the room.

The sound of footsteps echoing through the comm and then the shutting of a door signaled Brumley's departure.

Son of a bitch!

"What's the ETA, Baker?" Cole demanded.

"Fucking traffic!" Baker snarled. "It's not far but this is balls, man. It's balls!"

They all went quiet again when more came through P.J.'s wire.

"Why the tears?" Nelson asked mockingly. "Surely he wasn't that bad. Most women fight over the honor to be his lover. But maybe you'll like me better."

Cole covered his ears, no longer able to bear to hear anything more. When he looked up, he could read the expressions of the others.

They'd gotten the information they'd needed after all. Brumley had spilled the details of the shipment of girls.

But at what cost? At what fucking cost? Something so

precious that it gutted Cole to even dwell on what the success of this mission had cost P.J.

As much as it shamed Cole, he'd give it all back and never know how to save those girls if he could take back what had just happened to P.J.

CHAPTER 11

P.J. lay sprawled on the couch, pain knifing through her body as surely as the blade had cut into her skin. Nelson loomed over her but he was frowning. He didn't like passive women. He'd said as much.

Well that was fine because the drug was starting to wear off and if the asshole gave her just a little more time, he was going to have one hell of a fight on his hands, because she wasn't going to lie here and take it like she'd been forced to do for Brumley.

Rage ate at her. It was acid in her blood, eating a hole in her very soul.

There was nothing more horrific than being so helpless that she hadn't been able to move. She could barely speak. And it hadn't been enough for the bastard to rape her. He'd gotten off on making her bleed.

The smell of her own blood gagged her. It was an assault to her senses. Smeared all over the front of her body where he made the jagged cuts. He hadn't minded the mess. He'd wallowed in it like a gluttonous pig.

Nelson left the room and P.J. immediately tested her

ability to move. Some of the lead had left her limbs and she could move both arms and legs. She looked around for something, anything, she could use as a weapon. She wasn't strong enough to get off the couch yet, but she could make the bastard sorry he'd ever touched her.

To her utter shock, the knife that Brumley had used on her was on the coffee table just a few inches from her grasp. She leaned as far as she could, straining and reaching for the blade.

She bumped it, sending it into a slight spin. Swearing mentally, she tried again, wincing when the edge sliced into her fingers. It was a small price to pay for pulling it closer.

She turned it so she could grasp the hilt and then she took it, transferring it to the hand closest to the inside of the couch, and then tucked her hand between the back of the couch and her side.

Nelson returned a moment later with a damp cloth and set about cleaning the smeared blood. He frowned when he realized she was still bleeding from the cuts.

He looked . . . pissed.

"There was no point in this," he muttered. "No need to cut you at all, much less so deep. You need stitches."

An odd thing to say when he planned to kill her. What the fuck did it matter if she was sliced open?

"Please," she rasped out, trying to buy more time. "I'm just an American college student. I was out for a good time. I don't even know who you are. I just want to go home. No one will ever know."

Nelson's lips thinned into a firm line. "I have orders."

He wiped at most of the blood and then finally gave up. He rose, and she was appalled to see the bulge at his groin. Despite his seeming disgust, he was certainly turned on, blood or not.

"I wanted you to be able to fight," he said in irritation. "It's not fun when you just lie there."

Come get some, bastard. You'll get your fight.

He unzipped his pants, not even bothering to remove

them. He shoved them down his hips and then he yanked her legs apart and was on her and inside her in a brutally painful thrust that momentarily paralyzed her in her shock.

"Come on, bitch, fight me," he snarled.

"Be careful what you ask for, asshole," she hissed.

His eyes widened in surprise just as she nailed him right in the jaw with enough force to break it. Pain lanced through her fingers, but she ignored it. Then she raised the hand holding the knife and plunged it into his back.

He howled in pain and immediately rolled off her, ripping himself from inside her. She struggled upward, fighting the effects of the drugs. Her weapon was gone and now it was up to her wits to escape alive.

And then the roar of an engine and bright headlights flooded the entire living room. It was obvious that whatever it was, it was coming straight for them.

Nelson scrambled away and bolted for the back, his hand reaching for the knife as he went. The knife clattered to the floor and P.J. lunged for it, prepared to defend herself however necessary.

A moment later the living room exploded in glass and debris as a utility van crashed through the front windows. She threw herself onto the floor and covered her head to protect herself.

"P.J.! P.J.! Goddamn it, where are you?" Cole roared.

She sagged in relief, her strength gone. Her team. It was her team. Finally here. She was safe. Nothing else would hurt her.

Suddenly Steele was over her, his eyes so intense and full of hatred that she flinched.

"He escaped out the back," she said hoarsely. "He's bleeding. Don't let him get away. Don't let that bastard get away."

Steele turned and barked to the others. "Stay with P.J. Van and I are going after Nelson."

Steele moved beyond her, Donovan on his heels. And then she found herself carefully enfolded in a strong pair of arms.

Cole.

She'd know him anywhere. Could smell him.

She buried her face in his chest as shame crashed over her.

"P.J., P.J., sweetheart. Oh my God, baby. Oh my God."

It seemed to be all he could say as he rocked her back and forth, his heart beating like a drum against her broken body.

"I'm so sorry," he said brokenly. "I'm so damn sorry."

Pain screamed through her system and she let out a whimper she could no longer call back. Now that she was safe, her barriers were down. The adrenaline rush was gone. She had nothing, no buffers to what had happened. She'd been raped by two men and sliced open like some piece of meat.

Where was there for her to go? To hide? They would all see her. Her shame. And know that she hadn't been able to prevent what had happened.

She wanted to crawl into a hole and die.

"I've got you," Cole whispered, his voice choked. It sounded like he had tears, but she was nearly unconscious now.

"Blood. All over you," she managed to whisper.

"I don't give a fuck," he said fiercely. "I'm getting you the hell out of here. You need medical attention."

She shook her head, trying to grasp his shirt to gain his attention. But there was something wrong with one of her hands, and in the other she still gripped the knife she'd plunged into Nelson's back.

Cole gently took hold of her hand and pried the knife away, closing it with a click.

"No!" she protested.

She struggled, trying to reach for the knife again. She wanted it, damn it.

Cole pressed the closed knife into her palm in an effort to soothe her and she gripped it until it left indentations in her skin.

She had to remain conscious. This was too important. It

could mean her life. It could mean the lives of those baby girls. She would do anything to spare them what she'd endured, and they'd fair much worse. They didn't have her team. They had no one. She had to save them or her very soul had been sacrificed for nothing.

"P.J. Ah hell, P.J. Talk to us. Don't go out. Not yet. Come on."

It was Dolphin. He'd hunkered down next to Cole. And Baker. She could hear him and Renshaw arguing over who stayed and who went to help Steele and Donovan go after the bastard who did this to her.

She smiled faintly, so in shock that it seemed appropriate to smile even amid all the blood and horror of what had happened.

But then she refocused and remembered the objective. She reached for Cole's shirt, shocked at how weak she was. Her fingers wouldn't curl and she ended up flailing uselessly at his neck.

He captured her hand and held it to his lips. He quivered beneath her touch and she realized how hard he was shaking. He was losing it. Right here in front of everyone.

"The girls," she said, rousing every ounce of her flagging strength. "He mentioned them. Said the pickup was tomorrow night."

"I know, baby. We heard. We heard every goddamn thing," he said in a tortured voice.

It was a reminder, a slap to her face. Yeah, she knew they'd heard, but his words just brought home how public her humiliation had been.

"Have to save them."

Tears of pain crowded her vision, and she hated that she couldn't be stronger. She hated that these sons of bitches had managed to subdue her and force her to submit to their depravities.

She was fading fast, and she had to make sure those girls would be taken care of. If she didn't, she'd see their faces right alongside the faces of her rapists every night in her dreams.

"Promise you'll save them," she whispered. "Promise me. No matter what happens to me. You can't let this happen to them. They're just babies. So scared."

She choked off before she said, "like I was." But she knew they'd heard the unspoken words. Could hear them in her tone.

A loud clatter from the direction where Donovan and Steele had run made her teammates draw their weapons and surround her. Cole's grip tightened on her and then Donovan was there, pressing in close.

"Talk to me, P.J.," Donovan said in a low voice. "How are you, sweetheart?"

"C-cold." She turned her face upward, her head so heavy she could barely manage the feat.

He all but pushed Cole out of the way and took P.J. into his own arms, lowering her to the floor.

"Get me something to wrap around her," he ordered.

"What about the cuts?" Cole asked hoarsely.

P.J. struggled not to succumb to the blackness surrounding her. "Where's Nelson? Did you get the bastard?"

She'd never forget the look on Donovan's face as long as she lived. It was full of regret, rage and guilt.

"He escaped. He had a car parked behind the house, and our first priority is you. We'll find him, P.J. I swear to you we'll make that son of a bitch pay."

She closed her eyes, tears leaking down her cheeks in hot trails.

"We'll get you to the hospital," Donovan said. "You won't hurt much longer."

He was wrong. So very wrong. She couldn't imagine ever not hurting. Some hurts were so deep, beneath the skin. Soul deep.

"Not here. Take me home. He owns this city. I don't trust anyone here. Just take me home and find those girls."

Cole leaned down as Donovan carefully arranged a blanket over her body. He smoothed her hair back and kissed her brow. "I'll do whatever you want, P.J. Whatever you need, baby. I swear it."

Steele knelt and framed her face in his strong hands. His blue eyes bore into her with burning intensity.

"We'll get the girls, P.J. But right now we're going to take care of you."

She nodded weakly and closed her eyes, welcoming the yawning abyss where she floated free of pain and shame.

CHAPTER 12

THEY bundled P.J. into the back of the van, and Baker hopped into the driver's seat while Cole and Donovan took positions by P.J.

Cole managed to pry the knife from her fingers without her protest this time, but he pocketed it because she'd been adamant about keeping it. Then he closed his hand around hers, unwilling to let her think even for a moment that he wasn't right here, by her side. That her entire team wasn't surrounding her.

"What do you think, Van?" Cole asked, trying to control the anxiety in his voice. "That bastard cut her up pretty bad. She's lost a lot of blood, not to mention that he . . ."

He closed his eyes and looked away, unable to say the word *rape*. The bastards had raped her. They'd put their hands on her. They'd *brutalized* her. And he hadn't been able to do a damn thing about it.

"I want to get her to the airfield," Donovan said grimly. "The sooner we get her loaded and take off, the better. I'll work on her while we're in the air."

"What about Sunday? What about those girls?"

"As soon as P.J. is stable, I'm putting a call in to Sam. He'll have to call in Rio and his team. They'll have to be briefed so they know what they're up against."

"I want those bastards," Cole said through gritted teeth.

Donovan leveled a stare at him as they raced down the highway. "Make a choice, Cole. I won't stop you. But you have to choose. You going to stay with P.J. or are you going in with the others?"

Put that way, it wasn't even a choice. He belonged at P.J.'s side. He'd never want her to feel like her team had abandoned her. He didn't want her to think *he'd* abandoned her.

Rio and Sam would exact justice. P.J. needed him.

"I'm not leaving her," Cole said.

From the seat just in front of them, Dolphin and Steele leaned over the top, closely monitoring the conversation.

"None of us are leaving her," Steele said tightly.

"Hell no," Dolphin muttered.

"We live as a team and we die as a team," Steele said. "I want to go kick the living shit out of those assholes too, but P.J. needs us more than we need revenge. We'll leave it to others in KGI to get justice for one of our own."

Donovan barked up to Baker, "ETA?"

"Two minutes. Pilot is on standby."

On time, the van pulled onto the dirt road to the airstrip on the periphery of the city. It was a regional airport, mostly used for cargo, and wasn't a hub for passengers.

The plane was parked at an angle, ready to roll onto the runway. Baker roared onto the paved tarmac and slammed on the brakes.

The team sprang into action, opening the cargo doors to the van and making sure the hatch to the jet was open.

Donovan started to reach for P.J., but Cole brushed him off and gently gathered her in his arms, careful to keep the blanket around her to shield her nudity.

He hurried to the plane, carrying her up the three steps into the cabin.

"Bring her to the back and lay her on the couch," Donovan said. "I'll get my med pack, give her something for pain and then see what I can do to suture the cuts until we get her to a hospital. Tell the pilot to get us off the ground."

To Steele, he gave a terse order. "Get on the horn with Sam and fill him in. Rio and his team need to be here in twenty-four hours and in position to intercept the shipment of girls."

Cole bore his precious burden to the back of the plane and gently arranged her on the sofa so that she was shielded from the view of others.

The slashes to her body were horrifying. Two were deep and the flesh lay raggedly open. One carved a path down her midline between her breasts. There were two just underneath her breasts and one across her flat, muscled belly. And another two on the insides of her thighs.

The son of a bitch had carved her up and then forced himself on her because that's how he got his rocks off.

"Damn," Donovan murmured.

Cole focused on Donovan, trying to calm his fury. Donovan was holding P.J.'s right hand. It was swollen and bruised. Cole hadn't noticed because it had been her left hand he'd clung to as they'd raced for the airport.

"Looks like she broke it," Donovan said grimly.

He turned it over carefully in his palm and examined the swelling before returning it to her side.

Dolphin brought back the med pack and then took a seat across from the couch, his eyes burning with concern.

"Is she going to be all right, Van? How bad is it? Level with us. We're going crazy up there."

Donovan took in a deep breath. "Physically? She's going to be okay. Eventually. The cuts are bad but not life threatening. Emotionally? I can't say. What she went through was horrific. P.J.'s strong, but I don't know of any woman who can escape what she suffered unscathed."

Cole scrubbed his hands over his face and then through his hair. "This shouldn't have happened. I should never have let it happen. Goddamn it, I knew it was wrong. My gut was screaming at me that it was all wrong, and I let her walk into that situation."

Donovan sighed. "It was her decision, Cole. You can't make those for her. It was a team decision."

"It was bullshit," Cole spat. "It was a coward's move, using a woman to draw out a monster. There was another way. There's always another way, but we were too anxious and lazy to find it."

"Try telling that to the mothers of the girls we'll send home," Dolphin said quietly. "And then ask P.J. if she thinks it was worth it. Knowing her as I do, I know which way she'll go. Do you?"

Donovan gave P.J. an injection of pain medication and then numbed the area around her wounds. Afterward he began the meticulous task of stitching the wounds closed.

"This is beyond my scope," he admitted. "There is tissue damage that needs to be repaired, but my main concern is to get the wounds closed so infection doesn't set in."

He checked the pulse in her injured wrist and then did another perusal of the swelling. Then he wrapped an ice pack around it and secured it so she couldn't move it if she awakened.

Steele ducked into the back. "How is she?"

Donovan's shoulders heaved. "I've patched her up. She needs care more advanced than I can provide, but she'll do until we get to Fort Campbell. Have you gotten us clearance to land there instead of Henry County? Will sure as hell save us some time."

Steele nodded. "Sam's getting it worked out now. They're pretty pissed and they want blood. He's called up Rio and his team. This could get messy. I told him we were staying with P.J. unless he absolutely needed us. I don't want to leave her, but I don't want any member of KGI getting killed either."

Cole studied his team leader for a long moment. Steele wasn't much of a talker. He rarely volunteered more than a terse order or a very cut-and-dried summary of a situation.

But this had shaken that legendary composure of his and melted some of the rigid ice that seemed to encase him. Anger—no, *fury*—burned in his eyes, making them colder than ever. His jaw was set in a permanent bulge, and he looked like he wanted to physically put his hands on someone—anyone—and make them suffer a long, painful death.

But then Steele was all about the team. The team was it for him. He lived it, breathed it. He performed his duties, and he'd never failed in a mission.

Until now.

It was a weight they all had to bear. They weren't used to failing. They always did whatever it took and they accomplished their goal.

Well, they'd accomplished what they set out to do, but one of their own had paid a very dear price, and for Cole, that was unacceptable. It was an epic fail on their part that they couldn't keep P.J. from harm and succeed in their mission.

It was a truth they'd all have to confront, live with and deal with in their own way, but Cole knew his team and he knew this weighed heavy on their minds and would for a long damn time.

WHEN they landed at Fort Campbell, they were met by Sam and Garrett along with the base commander who'd given permission for the jet to land. A medical team hurried in with a stretcher, and P.J. was loaded and quickly hustled away.

Cole put up a fight when they wouldn't allow him in the transport with P.J. She was still out. Donovan had kept her medicated during the flight so she'd be pain free, but Cole didn't want her to wake up and feel like she was back in that nightmare.

Dolphin, Baker and Renshaw restrained him, pushing him back against one of the vehicles parked nearby.

Sam and Garrett both wore fierce expressions.

"What the fuck happened, Steele? What went wrong?" Sam demanded.

Steele's demeanor was normal for him. Cold and formidable. But his eyes told another story. Usually cool, icy even, they blazed with a fury Cole hadn't seen in all the time he'd worked for his team leader.

Steele met Sam's gaze unflinchingly. "I failed my team."

Garrett swore. "Bullshit." He glanced around at all the members of Steele's team, almost as if he could see the same thought in all their heads. "Look, I get that you're all feeling shitty over this but you can't get so down on yourselves. We need facts. Not guilt."

Steele's lip curled but he gave the report, not leaving a single detail out. Cole closed his eyes as Steele repeated what Brumley and Nelson had done to P.J. The rest of the team stood stiffly. Dolphin looked down as if he didn't want anyone to see his eyes or expression.

Cole just wanted to get all the chitchat over with so he could go to P.J.

"Son of a bitch," Sam swore, closing his eyes momentarily.

"What are you doing for the shipment of girls?" Steele demanded. "We belong here, with P.J. She needs her team right now."

"Rio and his team are already en route, and Nathan, Joe and Swanny are meeting them in Vienna. They've been briefed. Resnick wants Brumley alive, and he might very well get him that way, but after Rio and his team heard what the son of a bitch did to P.J., I think he may be missing a few body parts when he's delivered."

Cole curled his hand into a fist. He wanted to be there when Brumley was taken down. He wanted it badly. He'd never wanted to hurt someone as much as he wanted to make Brumley pay.

He'd killed people when he was a SEAL and then in his time with KGI. He was a sniper. It was his job to take people out effectively. Quickly. Quietly. But it had never been personal. He did his job without emotion because it was what he was paid to do. The people he dispatched were the bad guys. He didn't need to justify his actions, but the world was a better place without the people KGI went up against.

But with Brumley, rage was a living, breathing fireball inside him. Cole wanted to make him suffer many times over what he'd made P.J. suffer.

"If everyone's been briefed then can we get on with this and get back to P.J.?" Cole snapped.

"Hooyah," Dolphin said, his lips thin.

Even Steele looked impatiently at Sam and Garrett.

"Yeah, let's go," Sam said, motioning toward the two parked SUVs.

CHAPTER 13

P.J. opened her eyes to find her hospital room mostly dark. There was a beam of light emanating from the bathroom where the door was barely open a crack.

She glanced to the side of the bed to find Cole as he'd been for the last two days. Propped in an uncomfortable-looking chair that had been pulled up as close to her bed as it could go.

He was sleeping, a fact she was grateful for. She'd purposely taken refuge in the pain medication, not wanting to deal with her team, all gathered in her room, sympathy and anger in their eyes.

And when she was lulled into oblivion by the medication, she didn't have to remember the leering faces of Brumley and Nelson. Didn't have to hear their grunts, feel their bodies pressed against hers.

She closed her eyes, unable to prevent the physical reaction the memory caused.

She'd have permanent reminders of Brumley's violation. Scars she'd wear for the rest of her life. The doctor had gently explained that some of the cuts had been too deep, too jagged, but that in time they would fade. But there would always be a mark there to signal the cuts the animal had made to her flesh.

The more she came to awareness, the more the memories crowded in until her jaw clenched and she valiantly tried to steel herself from the raw agony that clawed at her.

She stared down at her right hand, which was casted, and she was confused because she couldn't remember how she'd broken it. Clumsily, she reached for the nurse's call button with her left, hoping she wouldn't wake Cole. She didn't want to talk. Didn't want to deal with the torment in his eyes. She just wanted oblivion.

A few moments later, the nurse hurried in and spoke to P.J. in low tones. She left once more but was back in less than five minutes with a syringe. She injected the medication into the port and P.J. closed her eyes and waited for the comforting lull to claim her.

The next time she opened her eyes, sunlight had flooded the room and her entire team was slouched in chairs surrounding her bed. Her brow instantly went clammy and nervousness flooded her.

She made eye contact with Steele first. Steele she could deal with. He was professional. He wouldn't make her want to break down and weep like a damn crybaby.

"The girls," she croaked out.

She frowned, cleared her throat and then blinked in surprise when Dolphin was there with a cup of water. He held it to her lips and she gratefully gulped half the contents.

When she was done she whispered her thanks and then leaned back against the pillows again.

"The girls," she said again. "Did they get them out? Are they safe?"

Steele nodded, but his expression was still grim.

"Rio and his team went in with Nathan, Joe and Swanny. They intercepted the truck and brought down Wainwright and his entourage. The girls are on their way back stateside as we speak."

"And Brumley? Did you get him?"

She held her breath, hope billowing forcefully into her chest.

Steele looked away, his jaw bulging. She glanced sideways toward Cole, who looked so coldly furious that she shivered.

"He escaped with his men onto the plane and took off," Steele said in a quiet, pissed-off voice. "Rio had to make a choice between going after Brumley or saving the girls. They went after the girls."

P.J. closed her eyes. She had no right to feel angry. The girls were more important than any sense of justice she felt needed to be exacted.

But the fact of the matter was she was gutted. Numb. While she lay in a hospital bed, Brumley and Nelson were out there. Free. Unpunished both for what they'd done to her and for what they'd done and planned to do to those babies.

She turned her face to the side, biting into her lower lip to keep her emotions in check. And then the soft brush of a caress glided over her cheek. Just one finger. The back of a knuckle. But she'd know that touch anywhere.

She should be angry with him for showing her any tenderness in front of the others. But they were all being gentle with her. Things had changed and she hated it all. How could anything ever be the same with her team?

This would always be between them. They'd treat her differently. Like she was fragile instead of a teammate capable of carrying her own weight and kicking ass with the rest of them. All because she'd failed a mission. She hadn't been able to protect herself and she'd been stupid enough and panicked enough to take a drink from a man she knew not to trust.

"P.J."

Cole's voice came out husky, riddled with emotion. It was there for everyone to hear.

"Look at me, please," he begged softly.

She turned, opening her eyes to see the tortured look in his own.

"We'll get him, P.J. I swear to you we'll nail his ass to the wall. He's not going to get away with this."

No one in the room denied Cole's terse vow. They all looked just as Cole did. Furious. Worried. Sick at heart.

Live as a team. Die as a team. She was bringing them down. They were dying with her.

She took a steadying breath, determined not to let her building rage overwhelm her. She had to stay calm and focused. One thing at a time.

"We're driving out to the compound to meet Rio and the others," Steele said. "Be gone several hours at the most. You need to rest. We need to know what went down in Vienna. We'll give you whatever intel we receive. I promise."

She nodded stiffly.

Cole was the last to stand. He was still holding her left hand, his fingers twined through hers. Then finally he rose and leaned over to brush his lips across her forehead.

"I'm going to kill that son of a bitch for you, P.J.," he whispered.

She watched him walk away to join the others as they left her room.

"No, you aren't," she said quietly as her door closed, leaving her alone in the room. "I am."

CHAPTER 14

P.J. rested for an hour after her team departed. She hadn't asked for pain meds and she wasn't going to. She was getting out of this place.

Hearing that Brumley had escaped had done something to her soul. It was like she'd become a different person at that point. Someone harder. Necessary to get her through the pain and shame of her ordeal.

Time to suck it up and deal. Nothing worthwhile came easy. She'd learned that early on. And she'd been down before. She would never have imagined she'd reach a lower point than when she'd walked away from S.W.A.T.

But here she was, stripped of who she was, what made her the woman she was. That bastard had stolen her confidence. Her arrogance. Her cocky demeanor that held her together on the tough missions. He'd made her doubt herself and everything about her.

She wasn't going to lie here a moment longer.

She pushed herself out of bed, going clammy as pain gripped her as soon as she put strain on the stitches. Holy hell, it hurt.

She was sore from head to toe, and the damn cuts on the insides of her thighs made standing and walking damn hard.

One of her teammates had brought a duffel bag and dropped it on the counter next to the sink. She slowly made her way to it and unzipped it to inspect the contents.

There were sweatpants, a large T-shirt that would swallow her, socks and a pair of scuffed tennis shoes.

Her chest softened when she realized that the clothing belonged to one of the guys.

But at the bottom was the knife. Brumley's knife. The knife she'd insisted on keeping. Cole had kept it for her.

It took her several long, agonizing minutes to dress. She made sure the bandages over the cuts stayed in place and then she put the socks and shoes on. When she was done, she slipped the knife into the pocket of the sweats.

She stared at herself for a long moment in the mirror, not liking what she saw. She saw someone . . . broken. And she'd be damned if she allowed those bastards that kind of power.

She'd hunt the motherfuckers down herself.

No one. No one would ever get away with making her feel the way she'd felt that horrible night.

Revenge wasn't just a concept, some fantasy she dreamed about. It had become her reason for being.

The longer she'd lain in this hospital room, the angrier she'd become and the more she fantasized about having the bastards at her mercy. Of making them beg for mercy. Mercy she wouldn't provide.

They would die.

They would die for what they'd done to her and for what they'd done to countless young girls and for what they'd tried to do to those babies Rio and his team had managed to rescue.

Thank God, they were on their way home, back to their mothers and fathers. Their families.

The only family P.J. had was her team, and she couldn't allow them to take on her vendetta. KGI wasn't a vigilante group. She wasn't about to turn them into one.

She walked out of her hospital room and down the hall in search of Cathy, one of the nurses P.J. had met during the countless times KGI had been through the hospital at Fort Campbell. Cathy was the closest to another female friend P.J. possessed, and it had been Cathy who'd swept in and taken charge of P.J.'s care.

Cathy was a retired naval nurse who'd moved to Kentucky with her husband, and they both worked on base. She was a brisk, no-nonsense woman whose bluntness had always been appreciated by P.J.

When she got close to the nurse's station, Cathy looked up and then did a double take. To her credit she didn't say anything, but she shot out of her chair and rushed around to meet P.J. in the hall.

She quickly drew P.J. into the family room where it was just the two of them and then lit into P.J. with both barrels.

"What the fuck are you doing up?" she demanded. "You should have your ass in bed. I was just preparing to bring you some pain medication."

"I need out of here," P.J. said in a low voice. "I can't stay here another day. I need your help."

Cathy's eyes widened. "You want to do *what*?"

"Your shift is almost over, right? Give me a ride out of here."

"And where the hell are you going to go? What you need is to stay your ass in bed and let me and the others take care of you for a while. It won't kill you to depend on others for once."

P.J. very much wanted to hug the older woman but wouldn't allow herself the weakness. "I have to do this, Cathy. I don't expect you to understand."

Her expression softened. "Honey, you're not just physically injured. You've got a lot to deal with that has nothing to do with stitches or a broken hand. You need to be surrounded by people who care for you right now. Not off on your own with whatever harebrained scheme you've concocted."

"I need to go," P.J. said in a quiet, determined voice. "Will you help me or do I have to go myself?"

Cathy made a sound of disgust. "You'll get that pretty ass of yourself shot up by the night guard. For the love of God, P.J., you're on a military base. You can't just waltz around like you own the place."

P.J. gave her a crooked grin. "I'm just a civilian, remember? I can't be expected to keep up with all those military rules."

"You're going to try sneaking out if I don't help you, aren't you?"

P.J. nodded, her expression growing somber.

"Fuck me," Cathy muttered. "Do you have any idea what those men of yours are going to do if they find out I was the one who aided and abetted you?"

"Just throw a hooyah in Cole and Dolphin's direction. It'll all be all right then."

"You're so damn irreverent," Cathy said in exasperation. "Navy sticks together, you know. I ought to turn your ass in and then cuff that good arm to the bed."

P.J. glanced down at the awkward cast. Her shooting hand. She needed those fingers steady.

"How long until this heals?" she asked seriously.

"Few weeks in that cast, and you should be good. Hairline fractures of three fingers. Once the swelling and bruising goes down, they should heal quickly, but only if you don't try to rush things. Give yourself the time you need and don't try anything stupid or you'll be sorry. I'm only going to help you if you swear to me that you'll take care of yourself and give yourself time to heal. Do we have a deal?"

P.J. slowly nodded. "Thanks, Cathy. I owe you."

"You don't owe me a damn thing," Cathy said, her voice thick with emotion. "I have a twelve-year-old niece. Those girls you saved. They could have been my niece. Any one of them. You did a good thing, P.J. You sacrificed too much, but you saved them."

P.J. blinked away the betraying moisture in her eyes. "How much longer until you get off?"

Cathy checked her watch. "Well now that I don't have to give you meds and take your vitals, give me five minutes and I'll be clocking out. Stay put and I'll come get you when it's time to go. We'll take the stairs down and hope to hell no one looks at us too closely."

She studied P.J. a little closer and then rubbed her chin. "Tell you what. I'll bring you some scrubs. It'll draw less attention than you walking down looking like some street urchin in those clothes."

P.J. smiled. "Thanks."

"Now sit and rest until I come get you," Cathy said with a scowl.

P.J. gratefully sank into a chair as she cemented her next course of action. The very first thing she needed was to go back to Denver and take care of a few things there and then take the time to heal. As much as it pained her, she knew Cathy was right. There was absolutely nothing she could do in her present state. And she needed the time alone to come to terms with what had happened. Without the smothering presence of her team members. They all had jobs to do, and as long as she was a weak link, they weren't going to be able to perform.

By the time Cathy made it back, P.J. knew exactly what she was going to do. With Cathy's help she changed into scrubs and the two took the stairs and ducked out of one of the personnel entrances.

The checkpoints were more challenging. But Cathy told the truth. Sort of. She dropped KGI's name, said that P.J. was being discharged and that she was giving her a ride out.

"You can drop me anywhere in Clarksville," P.J. said. "I can get a ride to the airport."

"Fuck you," Cathy said rudely. "I'll take you to the airport."

"But you just worked an entire shift. The airport is over two hours away."

"I can run you up to Paducah. Might take you a little

longer to get where you're going, but you know the minute the guys figure out you flew the coop, they're going to look at Nashville and Memphis."

P.J. sighed. "You're probably right. Paducah it is."

"You know you can stay with me as long as you like," Cathy added quietly.

"Thank you for being a friend," P.J. said, a knot growing in her throat. "It means a lot."

Cathy glanced over at her. "Just as long as you realize that you *do* have friends, P.J. And that you can lean on them from time to time. It's in the friend's codebook. Scout's honor."

P.J. smiled. "I'll remember that."

"Okay, well let's get you to that airport. You got money?"

"I have my ID and a credit card. That'll get me where I'm going."

"All right then. Let's hit the road."

CHAPTER 15

THE war room on the KGI compound was filled with a large group of very pissed-off men. Steele stood to one side with his team—minus one. Noticeably absent P.J. Cole stood shoulder to shoulder with his team leader as he surveyed the other occupants of the room.

Rio and his team, consisting of Terrence, Diego, Decker and Alton, stood looking haggard and tired. They too were down one man. Browning, who'd betrayed Rio's trust in a previous mission. Rio was a hard, unforgiving bastard and you only got one chance to fuck him over. Browning was lucky Rio hadn't killed him, but he'd cut him loose and walked away from him.

And then there were the Kellys: Sam, Garrett, Donovan, Ethan, Nathan and Joe. And Swanny, the newest recruit to KGI.

The room bristled with rage and testosterone overload. The silence was heavy but the undercurrents were electric. Cole knew what was on the minds of every single member of KGI.

Revenge.

Vengeance for one of their own.

"What happened, Steele?" Garrett asked, first to break the silence. "And I don't want any of that I failed my team bullshit. Just the facts."

"Why the fuck was she left alone?" Rio demanded.

His temper was on edge and he simmered with anger. Cole could see the fear in his eyes and knew he was thinking of Grace, and that once, Grace had been as helpless as P.J. had been.

He also knew that Rio and P.J. were friends of sorts. As much as P.J. allowed anyone to get close to her. She and Rio had hung out in that dive P.J. frequented. It had pissed him off that she'd made it obvious he wasn't welcome when apparently she and Rio had thrown back a few drinks together.

Sam held up his hands. "Enough. We need to figure out what the fuck went wrong so it never happens again."

"I should have stayed closer to her in the ballroom," Donovan said tightly. "I wanted her to get close to Nelson, but he took her out the back, and before I could get over to keep an eye on her, he'd gotten her into a car."

"It was the fucking traffic," Dolphin seethed. "We would have been able to intercept her at the hotel. They were there long enough that he took off her bracelet. If we hadn't gotten caught in the wreck, we would have tagged her leaving the hotel and we would have been in the house as soon as we knew Brumley was there."

Garrett frowned. "Do you think he made her? Is that why Nelson took the bracelet?"

Steele shook his head. "No, I think this was just routine. If it weren't for Brumley, Nelson would have just taken P.J. back to the hotel thinking he was going to get some action and we would have been there the whole time. But Brumley saw her and decided he wanted her. He's a cagey, paranoid bastard and he wanted Nelson to make sure she was clean before he brought her to Brumley's house."

"So what now?" Ethan asked, his tone somber.

His jaw was tight as well. His wife, Rachel, had been a

victim and had undergone an entire year of captivity in South America before Ethan was tipped off that she wasn't dead, like the entire family had thought.

They were all on edge. Nerves were frayed. The women that had married into the Kelly family, and the woman who'd married Rio, were all resilient women who'd all experienced tragedy in one shape or another.

Rachel, Sophie, Sarah, Shea and Grace were weighing heavily on all their minds. And now violence—*violation*—had touched P.J. Their teammate. Partner. A woman that had Cole's insides so twisted up that his stomach was one giant ball of anxiety.

"We go after those fuckers," Cole seethed. "That's what's now."

Dolphin, Renshaw and Baker nodded grimly. Even Steele looked like he was in total agreement.

Sam and Garrett exchanged uneasy glances.

Donovan's cell phone went off, breaking the awkward silence. He glanced down, frowned and then put it to his ear.

Cole didn't tune in until Donovan swore and said, "She did what? And you just let her walk out of there? What the hell happened? How did this happen? I want some damn answers."

Everyone focused intently on Donovan as he listened to the person on the other end of the line. Then he cursed again and shoved the phone back into the clip at his side.

"What the fuck is going on?" Cole demanded.

Donovan blew out his breath. "I don't even know how to say this. P.J. checked out. Or rather she didn't check out. She just walked out."

There was an explosion of what-the-fucks that echoed around the room.

"Where?" Cole bit out. He didn't care about the details. He just wanted to know where to find her.

Donovan looked like he'd just swallowed barbed wire. "No idea. She didn't exactly inform the on-duty people that she was planning to take off."

"Son of a bitch," Steele swore.

The others cast surprised glances in his direction. Garrett raised an eyebrow, but Cole wasn't as aghast as the others.

Steele may be a cold-blooded machine to some, but Cole knew his team leader was invested absolutely in his team. He considered each and every member his, and he was possessive and protective of them all. He didn't take shit from anyone, and he expected instant obedience when he gave an order, but everything he did, every decision he ever made, was for the good of the team, and he'd never do anything to compromise their safety.

"Where would she go?" Sam asked softly.

He directed the statement to Cole and his team members. They knew her best, but Cole wanted to laugh at that idea. Did anyone really know P.J.? Did anyone know what made her tick?

Renshaw shook his head. "She's private, man. She doesn't talk a lot about personal shit. I wouldn't have the first clue where to start looking."

"Get on the phone and start calling the airports. Every one in a hundred-mile radius," Sam said to Ethan. "See what you can find out. I don't care what kind of story you have to make up or what kind of strings you have to pull. Just get it done."

"I'm on it," Ethan said, striding toward the computer as he spoke.

"And what if we find her?" Nathan asked. "We can't make her stay where we put her. Or where we want her. We can't make her accept our . . . help. Or support, even as much as we want to give it."

No one had a ready answer for that. Cole didn't need to verbalize his intentions. P.J. needed them. She needed someone. He didn't give a shit about her lone-wolf status in life.

He wanted to be there for her, to help her get through this. God, he just wanted to make her smile. For things to go back to the way they were when they bantered back and forth, cut jokes and threw insults.

He didn't want to contemplate a world without P.J. He didn't want to be on a team where she wasn't an integral part. He didn't want to lose any of his team. They were a unit.

They were family.

"Let's find her first. Then we'll figure out our options," Steele said.

Everyone nodded, agreeing with Steele's assessment. The group broke and Cole headed in Rio's direction.

"Can I have a word?" he asked Rio quietly.

Rio stared back at him with dark eyes. "Yeah, let's step outside."

They left the war room and walked outside where dusk was gently falling over the lake. It was early fall and the evenings were already starting to cool. The wind hinted at impending brisker days. It was usually Cole's favorite time of year, except now he couldn't enjoy the changing season because the world—*his* world—was in complete turmoil.

"Is there anything you can tell me that would help?" Cole asked. "I know you spent some time with P.J. Did she ever say anything to you that would help us find her now?"

Rio looked regretful. "We had a few drinks. I was passing through Denver, looked her up and we had bar food and beer. We didn't do a whole hell of a lot of talking, and when we did, it was about work stuff. Past missions. Just shooting the shit."

Cole grimaced. "Yeah, she doesn't ever talk about herself."

Cole had a feeling that the one night he and P.J. had spent together had been the most she'd opened up to anyone. Ever. But even then, she hadn't given him enough to know what she'd be thinking right now.

Rio's lips turned up in a half smile. "Do any of us?"

Rio had him there. How much did he really know about any of his team? Yeah, they were family. No one would ever dispute that. But it didn't mean they were all touchy-feely and up in one another's business.

Cole was starting to regret that he hadn't tried harder in

the past. He'd always respected P.J.'s privacy. Hadn't pressed her for information she was reluctant to give. Being a good guy and teammate didn't mean shit now when they were so desperate for information.

"Look, I've pretty much seen it all. I'm sure you have too. It's hard when it's a teammate, but the fact is, she's like a wounded animal and it's likely she just wants to go off to heal on her own. You saw what Nathan was like when he got back from Afghanistan. You see how closed off Swanny is. Hell, we've all got our burdens to bear. We just do it differently. Maybe the best thing to do is just back off and give her some space. Let her deal with this in her own way."

Cole knew Rio was giving good advice but it pissed him off all the same. He stared hard at the other man.

"Tell me something, Rio. If it was Grace, would you be so willing to back off and give her space and not worry over where she is, if she's hurting or if she can make it on her own right now?"

Rio's brows lifted, his eyes widening. "So it's like that."

Cole swore. "Yes. No. Hell if I know. Look I'm making a point here. If it were any of the other women. What if it was Shea? Or Rachel? Would you be saying to back off and leave them alone to sort it out themselves?"

Rio sighed. "No. I wouldn't. But you have to remember, Cole. You can't treat P.J. like just any other woman. She's a warrior. A highly trained operative who goes into combat and deals with situations most other women don't. She's wired differently."

Cole took a step closer until he and Rio were just inches apart.

"All that may be true, and I certainly don't dispute it, but the fact of the matter is, she is still a woman and she was violated in the worst way a woman can be violated. And her team let her down. So you tell me. If she was on your team, would you be so willing to let her walk away and figure it all out on her own?"

Rio shook his head. "Hell, no. I wouldn't let one of my men do it. I'm just trying to offer some perspective."

"Well, I sure as hell don't have any," Cole said bluntly. "What I want is for her not to be alone to deal with this by herself. She has the team. And she has me. And she has no business being out of that hospital bed."

Rio put his hand on Cole's shoulder. "I get it, man. I understand when a mission becomes personal. I understand it all too well. My team will do whatever we can to help. We respect the hell out of P.J. She's one of us. Will always be one of us. If you need us, just say the word."

Some of the tension left Cole's shoulders, and suddenly he was weary beyond belief.

"I appreciate it. I'm sorry that our fuckup meant you had to be away from Grace and Elizabeth."

"You didn't fuck up," Rio said quietly. "Shit happens. There was nothing you could have done. And Grace and Elizabeth are fine. They're with Shea and the other women enjoying a visit. I don't let them out of the jungle often."

Cole grinned crookedly. "No, you don't. That's for sure."

"Keep me posted, okay?" Rio said as Cole turned to walk back into the war room. "I like P.J. a lot and this whole thing pisses me off. I want that bastard as much as you do."

Cole stared straight into Rio's eyes. "I doubt that."

CHAPTER 16

P.J. parked outside Steele's home, cut the ignition and then gripped the steering wheel with both hands. She closed her eyes and took a deep breath. This would be the hardest thing she'd ever done, but it was necessary.

She glanced at the huge duffel bag sitting in the passenger seat of the rental. Everything that belonged to KGI.

Getting out, she walked around to the other side to open the door. Bracing herself, she picked up the heavy bag and hoisted it over her shoulder.

Grimacing as her still-healing incisions protested, she started for the door only to see Steele standing in the doorway watching her progress.

His silence unnerved her, but only because she was nervous and she hated what she was about to say.

"Where the hell have you been?"

She blinked and drew up short on the top step. He looked angry when Steele usually looked unflappable. His gaze swept over her, top to bottom, as if examining her wellness for himself.

"Can I come in?" she asked. "I need to talk to you."

Steele reached for the bag and then scowled. "What the hell is this, P.J.?"

She sighed and brushed past him into the house. Her palms were sweaty and she rubbed them repeatedly down her pants legs.

This wasn't a social call, and he evidently picked up on that much. He didn't steer her toward the living room but instead walked her back to his office, which overlooked the expansive rear of his property.

She flopped gratefully into one of the armchairs in front of his desk and waited.

He dropped the bag on the other chair and then stalked around to sit behind the desk. And then he leveled a stare at her. One that would make a grown man quake in his boots.

"Care to explain why you bailed from the hospital, didn't let me or your team know where you were going, how you were doing or, hell, even if you were alive? Do you know how worried we've been for the last few weeks? You fell completely off the radar. No one's been able to get in touch with you. You didn't go home and you didn't check in. What the fuck, P.J.?"

She winced and closed her eyes. There was no easy way to do this, and a clean cut was always better than a jagged one. She ought to know.

"I'm turning in my gear."

Steele's lips tightened. "I can see that much."

"I quit," she said baldly. "I'm off the team."

"That's it?"

She nodded.

He swore through clenched teeth. "What the hell is going on in your head, P.J.?"

"This is something I need to do," she said, notching her chin upward. "It's what I have to do."

"I won't accept your resignation."

"You don't have a choice," she said softly. "I'm out."

"Look, take some time off. There was no way in hell you were going out with the team anytime soon anyway. Don't make an emotional decision you'll regret later. Your job will be waiting when you get yourself together."

She almost laughed. Get herself together? She'd done nothing but that for the last three weeks. Three agonizingly long weeks where she'd lain dreaming of revenge and of returning tenfold the hurt that had been done to her.

She rose, knowing nothing good could come of her continued presence here. Steele was pissed and she didn't want to waste time arguing with him.

"My decision is final."

Steele's jaw bulged and flexed. "Don't do anything stupid, P.J."

She turned back to face him and paused a long moment. And she lied.

"I need some downtime. I don't want my team worrying. I don't want to leave you a man short while I'm getting my shit together. It's not fair to you or my teammates. I should be replaced and you know it. I'm a liability, and you can't afford to take a mission short a man. Fill the spot, Steele."

"Just like that," he snapped.

She took a steadying breath and prayed she didn't lose her composure before she managed to get out.

"I can't do this, Steele. Just let me go."

He stared at her a long moment. And then he rose and walked around to stand just in front of her. He put his hand on her shoulder and gently squeezed. It was so out of character for him that she could only stand there in befuddlement.

"Take your time, P.J. Get your head straight and then you come back and talk to me. If you're still so determined to quit in a few months' time, then I'll accept your resignation. But until then, you're still a part of this team. *My* team."

She bit into her lip to keep the tears from crowding her vision.

"Thank you."

Then she turned and walked rapidly out of his office and back through the house. She strode blindly to her vehicle and got in before she could change her mind. She couldn't be weak. Not now.

What she had to do could in no way reflect on KGI or her team. She wouldn't drag them into the mire she was about to descend into herself.

CHAPTER 17

COLE knew whatever Steele had to say couldn't be good. He'd called everyone to his home. Not the KGI facilities where business was usually dealt with and missions were outlined.

They only waited for Baker to make an appearance, and the atmosphere was thick with tension and nobody was talking.

He clenched and unclenched his fists and then rose from the patio seat because he could no longer just sit there idly while waiting to hear what Steele had for them.

The last few weeks had been a fuck storm of frustration and it was wearing on him. He'd gone on his own to Denver, hoping that P.J. was holed up in her apartment. He respected the need for her privacy, but he hated that she was alone and had no one to lean on after what had happened. No one was that much of a hard-ass. She had to crack sooner or later, and he didn't want her alone with no one to help pick up the pieces.

And damn it, he wanted to be that person.

Sure he'd lusted after P.J. for a damn long time, but

things had changed between them that night they'd spent at her apartment. He'd known it and he damn well knew she knew it as well. It was why she shut him down so quickly and wanted to pretend like nothing had ever happened.

Well, he couldn't do that. No matter what she wanted, he couldn't go back to the easy camaraderie and bullshit of before. Maybe this was one-sided, but he was carrying around a pretty heavy obsession for her and it sucked.

If he closed his eyes, he could still smell her. Taste her. Could feel her skin against his. But it wasn't just sex. He could get that anywhere, and he'd gone a long time without because none of the women were P.J.

They just clicked. There was something indefinable about their connection, and he knew he couldn't have been the only one to have felt it.

There was an audible sigh of relief when Baker strode through the door a moment later. He looked tense, as if he were expecting the worst. His gaze automatically swept the room, and he frowned, almost as if he were doing a head count.

Yeah, they were down one and it sucked.

"What's up, Steele?" Baker asked.

"Take a seat," Steele ordered.

Baker slid into one of the chairs and Cole remained standing. Steele didn't even bark an order his way.

"P.J. came to see me two days ago," Steele began.

Cole surged forward. "What the fuck? And you're just now getting around to telling me—us? Where is she? How is she? Is she all right?"

Steele held up his hand. His expression was grim. "She quit the team."

The entire room exploded with what-the-fucks but Cole didn't say a word. His nostrils flared and he heaved several breaths through them, willing himself not to lose complete control.

"Where is she now?" Cole gritted out. Like hell she was quitting. Of all the things he thought Steele might say, that wasn't one of them.

Steele sighed. "I don't know."

Dolphin held up his hand, his head shaking in disbelief. But Cole beat him to the punch.

"Let me get this straight. P.J. came to you. She quit the team. And you just let her walk out of here and you have no idea where she is or where she was going?"

"I told her I wouldn't accept her resignation," Steele said. "She was adamant. She gave me this bullshit story about not wanting to bring the team down and that she needed time."

"And you bought that load of crap?" Cole asked incredulously.

Everyone else had quieted and looked between Steele and Cole with apprehension. Steele was their commander and he was afforded the respect due that position. Always. Until now. He wasn't ever questioned. Until now.

"I didn't say I bought anything, but I couldn't force her to stay. I can't force her to make decisions we think are for the best. She asked for time and space. I couldn't not give it to her."

"Jesus," Dolphin muttered. "You blew this one, Steele. It's fine to pull that ice man routine on the job and on a mission. But this is a goddamn teammate we're talking about here. No one gives a fuck about being fair and evenhanded in this situation. She needs us, and you let her walk away."

Steele rounded furiously on Dolphin. Before Cole could blink, he had Dolphin against the wall, his forearm across Dolphin's neck.

"Don't you fucking talk to me about being an ice man. I was *there*, remember? I heard every goddamn thing that happened to her. She's mine. Just like every one of you are mine. If you don't think I'm furious over the entire situation then fuck you."

Dolphin stared back unflinchingly, and finally Steele loosened his hold and stepped back. Just as quickly, Steele collected himself and the cool facade was back in place. But now they all knew just how close he was to the edge.

Cole turned and rammed his fist into the wall. He

couldn't even think for imagining P.J. alone, feeling God knows what. She'd quit the fucking team. They were family. And she walked away.

He drew back to hit the wall again and was nearly tackled by Baker and Renshaw. They took him down, pinning him to the floor.

"Get off me!" Cole roared.

"Chill your ass out," Renshaw barked. "None of this is helping."

"Enough!" Steele bellowed.

Cole flipped Baker off his chest and then swung at Renshaw. Renshaw ducked the punch, but it was enough to unbalance him, and Cole was back on his feet and staring a hole through Steele.

"I agree with Dolphin on this one, ice man. You blew it." He advanced on Steele until it was virtually only the two of them. The others faded into the background as Cole faced his team leader down.

"Goddamn you, Steele, you knew I was looking for her. You knew I'd been all over Denver. You knew how fucking worried I've been. And you just let her go and you get around to telling us two days later? What the fuck, man?"

Steele's jaw tightened. "I hoped she'd change her mind."

"Yeah, well, how did that work out for you? What the fuck are we supposed to do? Pretend nothing happened? Move on? Take another mission? Hell, why don't we just replace her since she's so goddamn expendable?"

"Enough, Cole," Steele said, his voice as cold as ice.

"Enough is right," Cole said, fury rising, sharper, harder with every breath.

He turned and stalked toward the door.

"Whoa, wait a minute," Dolphin said. "Where the hell are you going?"

Cole turned and looked at his team,that was no longer the same. It never would be. It wasn't a team without P.J.

"I'm out," he clipped out. "I'm going after P.J. I'm not leaving her to shoulder this alone. She needs us."

"Don't be so damn hotheaded," Steele growled.

Cole's lip curled in disgust. "Yeah? Why don't you stop being so fucking coldhearted. What you did was wrong and you damn well know it. You should have sat on her if you had to until we could hash this out as a team."

"She came to me," Steele snapped. "Not you. Not the team. She came to me, so I can only assume she wanted it that way."

Steele's words dug deep because he was right. It was obvious P.J. had no intention of facing Cole, and it gutted him.

"I don't give a damn what she thinks she wanted," Cole said softly. "She's not thinking straight and we all know it. Sometimes doing the right thing is all wrong. Giving her space and time and all that other bullshit is great on paper, but you and I both know that the very last thing she needs is to be alone. We're her family. Her only family. We're supposed to give a damn. We're supposed to stand up for her when no one else will. And we're damn sure supposed to call her out when she's making stupid choices and fucking up. That's what family does. Live and die as a team, right? Well, you hung her out to dry, Steele. And you hung the rest of us out right along with her, because now we all look like a bunch of uncaring assholes who just let her walk away without a fight."

"Hooyah," Dolphin said quietly.

Steele looked like he wanted to hit somebody. Cole stared challengingly at him because right now he'd love a good fight. Steele was rattled, and he didn't often get rattled, but Cole didn't give a shit.

"Her last team did the same goddamn thing we're doing," Cole said in disgust. He shouldn't break P.J.'s confidence. She'd opened up to him when she hadn't opened up to anyone else. But right now he'd fight dirty if that's what it took. Steele and the others needed to know what they were dealing with.

"You talking about S.W.A.T.?" Renshaw asked.

"Yeah. She walked away because they hung her out to dry. She did the right thing and turned in a dirty cop. They turned on her and made her look like a vindictive ex-lover out for revenge. Not one of them fought for her. Over my dead body is that going to happen this time. We're fighting for her. She deserves that much."

"I'm with Cole on this one," Baker said in a low voice.

"Me too," Dolphin said.

"And me," Renshaw echoed. "She's one of us. When she goes down, we go down. We're not picking up and moving on without her."

"Hell no," Cole snarled.

Cole stared at Steele for a long time before finally turning away. "I'm going to be gone. If you need me, I'll have my cell."

Then he turned back to Steele once more when he reached the doorway.

"Consider this my request for vacation time."

CHAPTER 18

SIX MONTHS LATER . . .

COLE stepped out of his truck and inhaled the crisp air, trying to shake some of the fog from his mind. Steele had called him and tersely told him to report to the KGI compound. He hadn't waited for confirmation. He'd just issued the order and hung up.

Given what little Cole had given his team since P.J.'s disappearance, Cole was surprised Steele bothered. He was even more surprised that he found himself here.

Cole had spent the winter alternating between searching for leads on P.J. and secluding himself at his home in Camden, just a short distance from the KGI compound.

P.J. had vanished. It frustrated him to no end. He'd spent a lot of time canvassing her neighborhood, talking to people about her. The problem was, no one really knew her. The bartender and waitress at the pub where he'd gone to see her that first night said she had been a regular but kept to herself and never talked to other customers.

Cole had even gone so far as to see the commander of her S.W.A.T. unit. It had taken all he had not to lose his temper and get some payback on P.J.'s behalf, but getting

information had been more important than his fury over
her betrayal.

It had been like hitting a brick wall, though. At the mention of P.J.'s name, the commander had clammed up and
refused to discuss anything having to do with her. Cole told
the asshole what he thought about him and his team of
dickheads before taking his leave.

Six months of no sleep and endless frustration were
catching up hard with him. He walked to the entrance to
the war room, punched in the pass code and then entered.
As he walked down the short corridor into the main room,
he rubbed at his eyes and then scuffed a hand over his
short-cut hair in an effort to look somewhat presentable.

Everyone was present and accounted for, which meant
Cole was late. Not that he gave a shit. He grunted in the
general direction of his teammates and slouched into a chair.

"Glad you could make it," Steele said, a hint of anger in
his voice.

"You said it was important. Otherwise I wouldn't be
here at all," Cole snapped.

He glanced around, frowning as he noticed new faces.
There was a guy standing close to Swanny and Joe, arms
crossed, his stance stiff, like he was expecting a fight at
any time. He was about Garrett's size with tattoos running
up both arms, disappearing behind the short sleeves of his
T-shirt.

He looked like he'd been in a few too many bar fights.
Cole pegged him as a boxer or perhaps a mixed martial
arts fighter because he had the telltale beginnings of the
cauliflower ears and his nose looked like it had been broken at least once.

Cole tensed when he noticed the female standing
between Nathan and Swanny. She was about P.J.'s size but
with honey blond hair and deep blue eyes. She looked
young. Far too young to be working on a mercenary team.

Then he was struck by a terrible thought. His stomach
churned and a knot formed in his gut.

What if they'd called him in to announce that they'd

hired someone to fill P.J.'s position on the team? What if this was some stupid meet and greet? A "let's make the new recruit feel welcome." Bullshit. He wasn't going there.

He glanced at Steele, looking for some clue, but Steele's expression was hard and cold. Cole could get a chill just from looking at his team leader.

"You didn't hire her to replace P.J."

He didn't make it a question, and his disgust was evident for everyone to hear. He didn't care. He was in a surly, piss-poor mood and he didn't really give a fuck who knew it.

He didn't want to be here. Especially if he was going to be told he had a new teammate. This chick couldn't hold a candle to P.J. Cole didn't care what her qualifications were.

Steele's eyes narrowed, and then he glanced back at the woman before turning back to Cole.

"She's a recruit for the new team," Steele said.

Cole's eyebrow went up. "What new team?"

"If you'd spent any time with *your* team over the last few months, you'd know that KGI has formed a third team comprised of Nathan, Joe and Swanny and two new recruits, Skylar Watkins and Zane Edgerton."

Cole dismissed them in a glance. He wanted to know what the big, hairy deal was that made Steele call him up. Two new recruits for a team that wasn't his own couldn't have been what made Steele call him in.

Donovan, who'd been on the phone in the corner, stuffed the cell back into his pocket and then walked over to where everyone else was gathered.

"We have a lead on Brumley," he said. "We know where he'll be in three days' time. He has another deal going down, one important enough for him to resurface." Donovan took a breath and leveled a serious stare at the others. "This one's big. Much bigger than past ones. He's gotten a hell of a lot bolder. It's thought he has well over thirty girls. A mixture of nationalities and all under the age of fifteen."

There were grimaces and noises of disgust. Skylar's nostrils flared and her eyes burned with anger.

Cole's pulse accelerated, and his stomach churned. He'd

dreamed of having that son of a bitch at his mercy. He'd conjured up some pretty harsh images of all the ways Brumley would die a long, painful death.

He glanced up at Steele, noticing the savage glint in his eyes.

Cole sat forward, propping his elbows on his knees. Yeah, he wanted in, but his first priority was finding P.J. He couldn't afford to be distracted by revenge. Killing Brumley wouldn't bring P.J. back, as satisfying as seeing the bastard die would be.

He started to get up, his intention to leave. Being here with all the members of KGI just highlighted P.J.'s absence even more.

The entire idea of a mercenary group was to be detached. Do the job. Don't get emotionally involved. Their success hinged on being able to turn off their emotions.

But KGI—his team, headed by Steele—was different. It was a hokey bunch of bullshit, but the entire KGI organization wasn't the average gun-for-hire group. They had a conscience. Their missions were righteous. At least from their perspective, and that was all that was important. At the end of the day, if they could look at themselves in the mirror and not flinch away, it was all good.

"Sit down, Cole," Steele said. "You need to hear this."

Cole's jaw tightened, but then he saw the glint in Steele's eyes. It wasn't anger over the fact that Cole had been about to walk out. There was keen interest. Anticipation. Like something big was about to go down.

It made Cole stop in his tracks.

Donovan picked up a folder from the table and opened it before addressing the occupants of the room.

"We've been looking for Brumley for months. He disappeared, and it seems he's been hiding. Which is interesting enough—given his arrogance and the fact that he has so many connections, he's never concerned himself with being too obscure."

"He's got a damn horseshoe stuck up his ass," Garrett bit out. "The son of a bitch is lucky."

"Yeah, well when you add the kind of money and power he has to luck, you get someone damn near invincible," Sam said.

"He's scared," Donovan said.

He got everyone's attention with those words.

"Two members of his personal security team, men he's never without, have turned up dead," Donovan continued. "Brumley doesn't take a shit without them, so the fact that someone got close enough to kill his guards is enough to make him spooky. It's probably why he's gone to ground for these past months. He's been quiet, but the magnitude of this new deal apparently was enough to flush him out of his dark hole."

Donovan pulled out a stack of enlarged photos and then carefully laid them out on the table.

Curiosity got the better of Cole, and he moved so he could see the pictures.

Several whistles and exclamations echoed through the room as everyone crowded around the table.

"Holy shit," Dolphin said. "Whoever killed these dudes harbored some serious animosity. This isn't a simple execution. This is personal."

Cole stared down, frozen, as he took in the cuts on the men's bodies. One vertically down the midline of their chest. Two more above the ribs. Two on the insides of their thighs. And each one had his throat slashed. In one instance, the head looked to only be barely attached to the rest of his body.

Ice crept through his veins until he felt incapable of moving or reacting. Fear clutched his insides.

"Sweet Jesus," he finally whispered.

His hands shook as he picked up one of the pictures. Then he looked first at Donovan and then at Steele. Both had the same recognition in their eyes.

Cole let the picture fall from his fingers to the table. "P.J. went after them."

"We believe so, yes," Donovan said grimly.

Cole picked up the picture again, held it up and pointed

to the knife wounds. "Believe? This is pretty conclusive evidence. These wounds are identical to the ones that bastard put on P.J. You were there. The only people who saw them were us and the assholes responsible for it happening to her. We're supposed to believe it's a coincidence P.J. quits her team, disappears and then guys who have ties to Brumley start showing up dead?"

"It's why we want to get to Brumley before she does," Steele said.

"Hell yes we have to get to him before she does," Cole bit out. "I don't want her near that bastard ever again."

Dear God. The idea of P.J. going vigilante filled him with gut-wrenching fear he hadn't felt since he was a brand-new navy recruit back in the day.

She could be dead even now. What if she'd attempted to get to Brumley and the bastard had her right now? Nelson had wanted her as a plaything and would have kept her if Brumley had allowed it. If they ever got their hands on her again, there was no telling what they'd do to her.

"She started with the two men who were there but didn't participate in the attack on her," Donovan said in a quiet voice. "There were only four men there when she was raped. Two are dead, which leaves Nelson and Brumley. I think we can assume she has plans to go after both of them. Our intel says that Brumley and Nelson both will be present for this deal to go down. If you want my opinion, I think Brumley knows P.J. is after him and he's scared because she managed to get to his men without anyone discovering her. But he's also a greedy bastard, and if he thinks he can surface to make a deal, he'll do it. He'll just beef up security."

"Or he could be fucking with her," Dolphin said grimly. "He's the type whose ego wouldn't allow him to hide from a woman. I'm with Cole. I don't want that bastard anywhere near her, or rather her anywhere near *him*."

The others nodded their agreement.

Cole didn't want to even think of P.J. falling into Brumley's hands again. He couldn't go there or he'd lose his damn mind. He glanced up at the others, resolve etched in every word. "Nothing we can't handle, right?"

Steele lifted an eyebrow. "That mean you in or you still plan to fuck around solo."

"Oh, I'm in," Cole said. "I want to take out both those bastards before P.J. has a chance to get to them. I don't want her to go through what she did all over again."

Dolphin, Baker and Renshaw closed in around Steele and Cole. They exchanged fierce looks, their intentions made without ever uttering a word.

"I'm in too," Donovan said.

Steele frowned. "This is my mission, Van. You're not taking over. This involves my team. My teammates."

Sam started to open his mouth, but Donovan shot him a stare that had him backing down. Garrett frowned but didn't intervene. The rest of the members of KGI looked on with abject interest.

"You've got the lead, Steele," Donovan said calmly. "But I'm along for the ride. I was there. I may not be a member of your team, but I was there with P.J. I heard every god-damn thing you did. I'm the one who let her get away at the party. I have as much a stake in this as you and your team do. P.J. is KGI. You're all KGI. I'd feel the same if it was any other person."

Garrett couldn't contain his silence any longer. "I think we should send at least two teams."

"Who are you going to send?" Cole demanded. "No way a new team can handle this." He sent an apologetic look in Nathan and Joe's direction. "No offense to your team, but this is too important to fuck up."

He turned his stare back to Sam, Garrett and Donovan. Yeah, technically they ran the show, but everyone knew the teams operated independently.

Donovan stared intently at his two older brothers. "Steele's team goes and I go with them. You can help by providing intel. But we do this Steele's way."

"Then let's get it done," Cole cut in impatiently.

He was tired of talking. He was tired of arguing. He just

wanted to get moving so he could get to Brumley before P.J. did. If she hadn't already.

There was a murmur of conversation, mostly between Sam, Garrett and Donovan. Cole's thoughts had drifted to P.J., wondering if he should have been focusing his search internationally. He would never have dreamed P.J. would have gone after them herself, but it all suddenly made sense.

Why she'd left. Why she'd been so adamant that she cut all ties with her team. It wasn't that she wanted to. She'd done it because she hadn't wanted to involve them.

He wanted to strangle her. Anything that happened to her involved the team whether she liked it or not. Just as had been the case when Cole and then Dolphin had taken a bullet while on a mission.

She hadn't minded butting in then to boss them around and make sure they were resting. But then they hadn't planned a vigilante mission to go track down scumbags on their own either.

"Cole, a word," Steele said tersely.

Cole turned and met his team leader's gaze. Steele motioned toward the door and then left the war room. Cole followed him outside and then a short distance away before they both halted.

"What's so top secret?" Cole asked.

"Don't be a smart-ass," Steele said sharply. "I need you to have your head on straight if you're going to be a part of this."

Cole frowned. "Wait just a damn minute."

Steele pinned him with his forceful gaze. "No, *you* wait a minute. Don't act like you haven't gone to shit in the last months. You look like something the cat dragged in. You've lost weight. You look like you haven't slept in a month. You won't do P.J. a damn bit of good if you can't perform your function within the team. We don't need a goddamn hero, Cole. What we need is an efficient team to go in and take care of business without allowing our emotions to rule."

Cole wanted to argue. Damn but he wanted to tell Steele

to shove it up his ass, but his team leader was right and Cole knew it.

"I get it," Cole said gruffly. "I'm in. You aren't doing this without me."

Steele held up a finger. "The only reason I'm letting you in on this is because I know if I sideline you, you'll only go off on your own and then you'll get in the way. I'm not losing P.J. and I'm damn well not losing you either. I'm keeping this team together if it kills me."

Cole sobered and then turned away to stare over the lake. "I hope we're not too late, Steele."

Steele sighed. "Yeah, me too."

"I want this bastard. I want him to pay for what he did to P.J. But more than that, I just want her back home, with us. With the team."

"I get it," Steele said quietly. "And she will be. I told her what she could do with her resignation."

Cole chuckled. And then he glanced Steele's way. "You're not the robot everyone accuses you of, you know."

Steele's expression could have frozen lava. "Don't start thinking I have a heart, Coletrane. I just don't want to have to start over and train a new recruit."

Cole stifled a smile. Yeah. Whatever.

CHAPTER 19

SLOVAKIA, SURVEILLANCE DAY TWO

SWEAT rolled down P.J.'s sides, making the thin camo shirt she wore cling to her flesh. She was absolutely still, barely breathing as she waited, just as she'd waited for the last twenty-four hours, for the right opportunity to present itself.

She was patient. She'd often spent long hours in the field on sniper watch. Some missions had been drawn out for days, and she and Cole had been partners in the silence. Unable to communicate or even acknowledge the other's presence in any way, but it had been comforting to know she wasn't alone.

That wasn't the case now. She didn't have Cole as her partner. She didn't have her team to back her up. She was flying solo straight into the lion's den.

She was smart enough to be scared, but she refused to allow that fear to paralyze her and make her helpless and weak. Never again.

She held her breath as she stared through the binoculars to the residence below. Two armored cars had arrived, and she watched as Brumley got out on one side. Nelson got out

on the other and looked around, his gaze obviously searching for any threat.

You won't find me, bastard. Not until I'm ready.

Brumley went in, surrounded by his guards. It would be
so easy to pick the asshole off with her sniper rifle. But it
was too easy. She wanted him to suffer, and she wanted her
face to be the last he saw right before he died. So he'd know
it was her and that she'd made him pay for his sins.

Nelson lagged behind, lighting a cigarette as Brumley
entered the house.

P.J. smiled. Arrogant assholes. They thought the high
fence and million-dollar security and surveillance protected them from the outside world. That she couldn't come
in. That they were safe.

They were wrong.

She eased from her hiding place, making sure the silencer
was attached to her gun properly and that the knife Brumley
had used on her was in her grip.

Over the past months, she'd spent a frustrating amount
of time frequenting places that Brumley was rumored to
enjoy. She'd gone through every penny of her savings to
support her search for the men who'd raped her.

And it was worth being dirt-poor for the rest of her life
if she accomplished her mission.

She pulled out a handheld PC and quickly typed in a
series of commands. Donovan wasn't the only one handy
with computers. They just bored her to tears.

In the first hour of her surveillance she'd hacked into the
estate's security monitoring system. It had been a piece of
cake. It baffled her that with as much money as Brumley
threw around, he'd actually have such a pussy surveillance
system.

She programmed the system to replay the tapes of the
last four hours, ending before the procession of cars arrived.
She'd only have two hours before they'd know something
was up, because the sun would start to sink and dusk would
be upon her.

Two hours to get in and kill the men responsible for the scars on her body and the damage to her soul.

She'd had less time to perform a mission before. This one wasn't any different. Objective must be achieved. She told herself that over and over.

She darted toward the house, keeping behind cover so she wouldn't be spotted through one of the windows. Nelson was still out front smoking his damn cigarette, and that wasn't where she'd wanted to confront him. But he didn't show signs of moving elsewhere, so she'd have to do the job there and make it fast instead of making him suffer the long, drawn-out death she wanted.

When she reached the house, she put her back to the stone exterior and inched her way toward the front where Nelson stood.

"What the h—"

P.J. whirled around at the voice and squeezed off a round before the man could shout a warning. He fell to the ground with a loud thump.

Shit! The bastard had lucked onto her and had come in from behind. What the hell was he even doing there? Had Brumley ordered his men to patrol the exterior of the house? Did Brumley realize by now that she was hunting him?

She hoped to hell she was keeping him up at night. That he lived in fear of when she would get to him. It wasn't a matter of if. It was when.

Her heart was pounding as she peeked around the corner again. Nelson was still there, but he'd just taken a last drag, tossing aside the butt as he blew out a cloud of smoke.

She shuddered, remembering the stench of tobacco on him while he'd pushed his body onto hers. Before she lost her courage, she rounded the corner, gun in one hand and knife in the other.

As much as it pained her to make his death quick, she was going to have to cut her losses and take Nelson out so she could get to her prime objective. Brumley.

"Nelson," she called out, wanting the bastard to face her and at least know who would claim his death.

He swiveled, his expression a mixture of what-the-fuck and fear.

The sound of the front door opening jerked P.J.'s attention from Nelson long enough to see that she'd been made.

A gunshot sounded and pain lashed through P.J.'s leg. Stupid motherfucker couldn't aim for shit.

She squeezed off a shot, downing the guy who came out the door. Then she turned rapidly to Nelson, who was attempting to flee. She shot him in the back of the leg, just to slow him down, and then she turned her attention back to the front entrance.

When two more men appeared, she dove behind one of the armored cars, ignoring the screaming agony in her leg and the smell of blood.

In the distance, Nelson lay on the ground writhing in pain, shouting curses and orders for someone to give him cover.

Hoping they were temporarily distracted by Nelson's rantings, she pushed herself upward, leaning on the car, and got three shots off. She ducked back down and then peered underneath the car toward the steps. One of the men was lying motionless, half down the steps, his leg dangling in the shrubbery.

She couldn't see the other, which meant he was either on top of her or he'd run back inside.

She glanced down at her leg and swore as she saw all the blood soaking her pants. It was just a flesh wound. A clean through and through. Thank God the bullet hadn't hit bone or she wouldn't be walking.

Pain she could handle.

She picked herself up again, took a clip out and shoved another in.

"Come get me, fuckers," she bit out.

There were six unaccounted for. A total of ten men had arrived, including Nelson and Brumley. Three were dead and Nelson was on the ground whimpering like a baby.

A loud roar sounded. P.J.'s brow wrinkled and then she realized it was a chopper starting up. Son of a bitch. Brumley was escaping.

Throwing caution straight down the toilet, she bolted from behind the car and ran for the front entrance. She passed the one dead guy on the steps and nearly tripped over the second guy who'd shot at her.

He was lying just inside the foyer, eyes wide open in death. Now there were only five unaccounted for. She was relieved to know she still had good aim.

Teeth clenched to ward off the pain, she shuffled as fast as her injured leg would allow through the house, gun up, clearing each room she hurried through.

When she got to the back enclosure, she saw the helicopter lift into the air.

"No!"

Goddamn it. She couldn't lose him. Not when she'd been this close.

She dashed through the doorway and raised her gun, squeezing off shot after shot at the departing helicopter. Through the glass, she saw Brumley. Made eye contact with him. The bastard actually looked at her and gave her a cocky two-finger salute.

She took another shot, even knowing it was pointless. She fired until she was out of ammo and then let her arms fall to her sides. She closed her eyes in bitter disappointment.

Failed.

She turned, having to drag her leg. It was growing more numb all the time, and as the adrenaline wore off, the pain became more unbearable.

There was still Nelson to contend with.

She popped in another clip and limped through the house, delighting in the fact that she'd tracked blood all over the posh furnishings. When she walked back out the front, she saw Nelson trying to drag himself to one of the cars.

Stupid fuck.

Unlike the idiot who shot her, she'd placed her bullet so it shattered his leg. He didn't have a prayer of walking anywhere.

She holstered her pistol and then opened the knife. The blood of the two other men she'd killed had dried on it and she hadn't bothered to clean it. It would only get dirty again.

She came to a stop just over Nelson, and he turned his head upward, his eyes full of fear as he stared into hers.

"D-don't k-kill me," he stammered. "Please, I'll do whatever you want."

She shook her head. "You're a pathetic piece of shit, Nelson. You're quite the badass when you're up against a drugged, helpless woman. Not so badass when she's armed."

She kicked him so he rolled to his back, and he let out another groan when it jarred his leg. Then she knelt awkwardly, grimacing as her own bullet wound protested the motion.

It should feel empowering to tower over the man who'd brutalized her and know that his fate was entirely up to her. That he was begging her for the mercy he'd been unwilling to give her.

But all she felt was paralyzing fear. Panic rose, making her shaky where she'd been rock steady just before. She stared into his eyes and remembered staring into them when he'd raped her. They were as soulless now as they'd been then, only then they'd glowed with power. A savagery that he'd enjoyed despite his grumbling that he preferred a fight.

The knife shook, and she tightened her grip, fully intending to mark him as he'd done her.

"Where can I find your boss?" she demanded.

He spit at her, and she backhanded him with the butt of the pistol. Blood streamed from his lips and nose as he turned back to glare his hatred.

"Tell me what I want to know or I'll gut you like a pig and leave you here to die a very slow, painful death. The buzzards might not even wait for you to die before they start feasting."

He paled and licked his lips, but he hesitated.

She flicked the blade at the fly of his pants and deftly

sliced the material so it gaped open. Then she pressed the blade under his navel and carved a line from one side to the other, drawing blood.

He screamed in pain and sucked air through his nostrils. He was gasping like a fish sucking his last breath on land.

She put the tip of the blade lower until it rested right over his dick. He went completely still, his eyes so wide with fright that they bulged and looked as though they'd pop right out of their sockets.

"Okay, okay! Just take it easy. I'll tell you what you want to know. Just put the knife down for God's sake."

"Tell me where to find Brumley," she said coldly.

"He'll be in Jakarta," he choked out. "Three weeks. You won't find him until then. I don't even know where he plans to be. But there's a big deal going down there. One of his contacts has promised him the best of the best girls. If his contact is telling the truth, this will make Brumley millions. He's already lining up buyers based on information he's received about the girls. Guy's name is Dimas. He's a big shot in Jakarta. Local businessman who's delving into human trafficking for the first time. Word is, he's delivering virgins and Brumley's clientele is going nuts. He's planning to auction them individually in an exclusive, high-security, extremely private venue on the island he owns."

P.J.'s lips curled into a snarl and a sound of rage burned deep in her chest and bubbled outward, vibrating her throat. Red clouded her vision. She raised the knife, prepared to end it now.

"Hands up!"

She froze, fear scuttling through her stomach. She turned her head to see two armed men at the corner of the house. They carried assault rifles and they were both pointed at her.

One man jerked the barrel of the rifle in an upward motion to indicate she was to raise her hands.

Fuck. She'd acted like a goddamn rookie seeing her first live action. She'd holstered the gun instead of keeping it out because she'd assumed that the house had been vacated and that all of Brumley's men had escaped with him. As Steele always said, people who assume are usually the ones who end up dead.

She'd forgotten her training, so eager had she been to exact justice. And now she was going to pay dearly for that mistake.

The two men started forward, their guns never lowering. P.J. kept her hands in the air, the knife still gripped in one of them.

She could probably take one of them out by throwing the blade when they got close enough, but she'd have to rely on the other guy either being distracted or missing if he shot so she'd have enough time to draw her own gun.

As if reading her thoughts, the two spread out, circling in a wide berth around her. Then one motioned for her to get down on her knees.

Her mind buzzed with possibilities. She had to think of a way out of this.

She started downward, taking her time, playing up the injury to her leg as if she were close to dying. She groaned and grunted before settling to her knees. The entire way down, she slowly lowered her empty hand, hoping the men were more fixated on the one holding the knife.

Just a little more . . .

"She's going for her gun!" Nelson cried out.

P.J. cringed and waited for the bullet to hit her.

To her utter shock, one of the men went rigid. A hole bloomed on his forehead and blood streamed down his face as he slowly crumpled to the ground like a deflated balloon.

She went for her gun and rolled, just as the other man went down, blood splattering everywhere.

A hand grabbed her ankle and jerked. She tried to kick with her injured leg and couldn't hold back the scream of pain. She came up with a vengeance, launching herself at Nelson. He was desperate to save his ass and she was just as determined to kill him.

She didn't have time to wonder what the hell had just happened to the other two. If she didn't take Nelson out, he would take her out.

She doubled her fist and punched him in the jaw. When he reeled back, she jumped on him, knife in hand. He grasped her wrist and squeezed, but she refused to let go of her weapon. She punched him with her free hand, but his grasp didn't loosen.

Son of a bitch. She wasn't going down to this bastard and she wasn't going to let him break her arm.

She lunged forward, head-butting him right in the nose. She saw stars, but he got the worse end of the deal. More blood spurted from his nose and his hand fell away from hers.

Using his moment of distraction, she drew up her knee and then rammed it into his crotch. He yelped and rolled, throwing her off him as he curled into a ball, one hand on his nose and the other cupping his dick.

"You're a worthless piece of shit!" she raged at him.

She kicked him in the ribs, and then remembering that someone had shot the other two, she dropped down, knife high overhead, and she struck quickly, slashing a line down his chest.

As much as she wanted to make this as ritualistic as the two earlier killings, she knew she didn't have the time and this had already been a cluster fuck from the very start.

She leaned down close, so he would hear every word.

"This is for every girl you ever tormented, tortured and raped. This is for all those babies you sold into slavery. And this is for me, a woman you had to drug in order to rape. I'm not so helpless this time, asshole."

The knowledge of his death was in his eyes and she savored it a moment before slicing his throat.

Blood gurgled out and then she heard the hissing sound as air escaped from his lungs. His eyes went glassy and his head lolled to the side.

She closed the knife, stuffed it into her pocket and started to drag herself upward. She hoped to hell one of these damn cars could be hot-wired or she was fucked for transportation. No way could she get back to where she'd parked her vehicle nearly two miles away.

She managed to gain her footing, but she swayed like a sapling in the wind. And then she heard her name. Loud and growing louder with every second.

She turned in bewilderment and then sank to her knees when she saw her entire team burst onto the scene. Cole was in front, his features carved in stone. He was focused on her. His gaze never left her as he ran toward her.

"You were the one who took them out," she said when he dropped on his knees in front of her.

"Dolphin got one," he said. "He's not a bad shot. Not as good as you, but he'll do in a pinch."

She couldn't wrap her mind around the fact that her team was here. That they'd come through right when she needed them most. She would be dead if they hadn't arrived when they had. But why were they here? How?

The question bubbled out. "What are you doing here?"

Suddenly she was shaking so bad that her teeth were clinking together with enough force to chip them.

She stared down at her hands. Hands that were covered in blood. Some hers, but mostly Nelson's. And they shook uncontrollably. Nothing she could do could stop it.

She should be jubilant. Triumphant. And instead her insides were so cold that she didn't feel anything at all.

"Did you honest to God think we wouldn't be here?" Cole demanded.

He sounded furious. The heat in his words scalded her, and yet it was so welcome she wanted to hug him. But there was also worry.

"Where are you hurt?" Cole asked with only a little less edge in his voice.

She looked at him in bewilderment.

Now he sounded impatient. "You're bleeding, P.J. You've got blood all over you."

"My leg," she finally managed to get out. "I took a bullet."

Cole cursed.

As her team gathered, something popped inside her. It was like cutting a taut rope and having it recoil like a viper.

She closed her eyes, the stench of blood and death overwhelming her.

Strong arms surrounded her, pulled her in close and then rocked her gently back and forth.

"It's all right now, P.J.," Cole soothed.

He stroked her hair and held her close.

"We're here to take you home."

CHAPTER 20

COLE gathered P.J. in his arms and carefully lifted her. Dolphin and Renshaw immediately flanked him to provide cover while he hurried in the direction of their SUVs.

"Open the back," Cole barked. "I need to be able to stretch her out so we can see how bad the gunshot wound is."

Dolphin moved ahead when they reached the wooded area where they'd parked the vehicles. He opened the hatch and Cole set her gently down in the cargo area.

He had to pry away her fingers that still clutched the knife, and he was careful that she didn't panic and react blindly. He still wasn't that sure she was completely aware of her surroundings. When the knife came free, he rapidly cut away her pants leg so he could assess the wound.

"Jesus, there's blood everywhere," Dolphin said grimly.

"Not all of it is hers," Cole said as he ran his fingers over the hole in her thigh. She flinched when he touched too close to the wound, and he cast her an apologetic look. But she didn't seem to notice.

His fingers came away bright red with blood, and he stared at it for a long moment. This was her blood, and it made him weak in the knees to imagine what would have happened if they'd arrived even thirty seconds later than they had.

P.J. was pale and shaking violently. The bullet wound was just a flesh wound from all he could ascertain. Clean entry and exit. She'd lost blood, but not so much that she would be in shock. It was her emotional state that concerned him the most.

She kept wiping her hands over her shirt, the red blood nearly disappearing in the black material. Then she'd look down, visibly upset that there was still blood staining her palms.

When she started to scrub at her clothing again, Cole took her hands and gently pulled them to him.

"It's all right, P.J.," he said in a soothing voice. "I've got you. I'll clean it off. Just give me a minute. I want to make sure you're okay."

Donovan, Steele and Baker strode up, sweat glistening on their foreheads. Cole lowered her hands, and she drew them back, wrapping her arms around her legs in a protective gesture.

Cole glanced Steele's way as Steele gave a terse accounting.

"We cleared the area. P.J. took out several of the guards, but Brumley is unaccounted for. The chopper we saw take off on our way in had to have had him in it."

"It did."

They all swung around at the sound of P.J.'s voice to see her sitting up, hunched over her knees, her eyes wild and distant.

"He got away," she said, and Cole was struck by the devastation in her voice.

Then she put her head down, so her forehead touched her knees.

Cole would have given her his complete attention, but Steele motioned for Cole to follow him. Dolphin motioned Cole away and then took Cole's place in front of P.J., talking nonsense and bullshit like it was any other day in the field.

"We've got a hell of a mess to clean up here," Steele said in a grim tone. "P.J. will take the fall, no matter what kind of worthless assholes these bastards are. I'm not willing to let that happen. Brumley has clout in Slovakia. He basically owns this area and the village. He *is* the government here and he has everyone in his pocket. I think initially he would have wanted P.J. alive just so he could make her suffer. But now that she's shown the very real threat she is, he'll sanction her death however it has to happen."

Donovan nodded his agreement. "I'm with you on this. She has to be protected at all times. The threat could come from anywhere. A sniper is a very real possibility."

Their words had a chilling effect on Cole. His mouth went dry and his pulse pounded painfully at his temples. "I'm not leaving her."

Steele gave him an impatient look. "I wasn't going to suggest you do. You and Donovan need to get her the hell out of here. I'll stay behind with the others to do cleanup and make sure nothing implicates her."

Donovan looked as though he'd argue, but Steele shut him down cold.

"You're our medic, and P.J. needs immediate medical care. We can't take P.J. to a hospital here. We've got to get the hell out of this country before Brumley has time to put a bounty on P.J.'s head. Her life won't be worth a shit now that Brumley knows for certain she's after him."

"It's a through and through," Cole said to Donovan. "Not too bad, but she's lost blood and she'll need antibiotics and stitches."

Donovan ran a hand through his hair and grimaced in Steele's direction. "All right. You guys take the scene. Make damn sure *none* of us can be implicated. KGI doesn't need this kind of notoriety. I'll go with Cole and P.J. and cross the border into the Czech Republic. When you guys are done, get your asses out of Slovakia and we'll hook up after I've evaluated P.J.'s condition so we can get the hell home."

Cole turned away, not waiting to see if there was anything further to be discussed. He wanted to get P.J. out of here. Away from death and blood and painful memories. She was hanging on by a thread. Who even knew what kind of private hell she'd been through over the last several months?

Dolphin stepped away as Cole got to the back of the SUV. P.J. was still sitting, hunched into a ball. She seemed to be trying to make herself as small as possible.

"P.J., you're going with me and Van and we're leaving now. You need medical attention, and before you protest, we're not giving you a choice. You'll cooperate or . . ."

He sucked in his breath over the mistake he'd nearly made. He was going to threaten to drug her. What an insensitive asshole it made him to even think it.

"Let's go," he barked back to Donovan.

Before he put his foot even further into his mouth.

"You drive," Donovan said. "Dolphin, you and Baker push the back seats forward so she can stretch out. I'll need to start an IV on the go and I need space to maneuver."

Then he turned to Cole. It was the first time Cole resented not having the medical training that Donovan had. He wanted to be the one taking care of P.J. and be at her side. He damn sure didn't want to get stuck driving.

"Get us into the Czech Republic. I don't care if you have to make a road. Find a way that doesn't put us in a position of having to identify ourselves or suffer any scrutiny. Leave all the gear with Steele except the bare essentials. We can't afford to be stopped with a woman with a bullet hole in her leg and an arsenal in the back of our truck."

Cole leaned into the back and slid his hand over her hair and to her nape, pulling her gently forward. It never occurred to him to be reserved in front of his team. He wasn't thinking about the team, and he didn't give a damn what they thought. All he cared about was P.J. and he wanted her to know that she was safe and, more importantly, no longer alone.

She stirred against his touch and looked up, their gazes connecting for a long moment. There was so much in her eyes that hurt him.

"I'm getting you out of here, P.J.," he said in a low voice. "Van's going to take care of you, but once we're safe, you and I are going to have a long talk."

He pressed his lips to her forehead and then broke away to hurry to the driver's seat.

CHAPTER 21

P.J. was grateful that Cole was driving as Donovan quietly attended her wound. It gave her time to collect her thoughts and regain her composure.

She'd broken down like some fucking weak-ass ninny who'd never made a kill, who'd never seen blood. She closed her eyes, horrified by the way she'd allowed her team to see her at her most vulnerable. What the fuck were they doing here anyway?

"You okay, P.J.?"

She opened her eyes to see Donovan look worriedly at her. She tried to nod but ended up bumping her head as the SUV hit a series of potholes on the crappy-ass road Cole was driving.

"Yes," she said, trying to infuse strength into her words. But she still sounded faint even to herself.

Donovan lifted the bag of fluid and secured it to the window with several strips of heavy-duty duct tape. Donovan was nothing if not a master of improvisation.

"I've started antibiotics and I'm also going to give you something for pain," he said. "It'll make cleaning out and bandaging this wound a hell of a lot easier. I'll have to stitch you up later. No way I'm going to try to use a suture kit when we're bouncing off our asses every other quarter mile."

She smiled faintly but didn't respond.

Soon she felt the burn of the medication when it hit her veins. A moment later, she relaxed and the pain started to fade into a mellow memory.

Some of her newfound zen was interrupted when Donovan began cleaning away the blood over her wound. She clenched her teeth, stared up at the roof of the vehicle and replayed Nelson's death in her mind.

She'd never considered herself a bad person. Flawed. Definitely flawed. But even at her lowest points, she'd had enough esteem and honesty to recognize her faults and strengths.

Now she'd entered the gray world where nothing is or was. Had she become the monster that she'd accused Brumley and his entourage of being? Was she no better than he, and was her soul irrevocably tarnished?

She'd hunted down and killed three people in cold blood. Never mind the others she'd taken out who'd gotten in the way of her objective. It wasn't self-defense. It wasn't to prevent her teammates from being killed. It wasn't to save someone in peril. She'd gone after the assholes who'd been in that room that night with nothing more than revenge on her mind. She'd murdered them viciously with no remorse or pity.

Maybe she was the coldhearted bitch that members of her S.W.A.T. team had accused her of being.

Fuck them. No, she wasn't going to let them back into her consciousness. That was a lifetime ago. She'd moved on. They weren't worth the dirt on her boots, and she'd be damned if she let them make her doubt herself now.

She searched her consciousness for some sign of regret. Something that told her she had a soul worth salvaging.

But she didn't regret their deaths. She didn't regret making sure they'd never hurt another human being. If that consigned her to hell, then she'd just have to plan a date with the devil.

She wanted to ask Donovan questions, but she bit her lip and remained silent. She didn't want to open the door, because if she started demanding answers from him, then he'd want the same from her.

"How is she doing?" Cole asked from the front.

The edge in his voice rattled her. It wasn't like Cole to sound so unhinged. Cole was either utterly focused on the task at hand or he was cracking jokes or hurling insults at his teammates, herself included.

It was a Cole she was familiar with and comfortable with.

But ever since the night they'd slept together, he'd become a different person. Or maybe it wasn't that he'd become someone different. He was just someone she hadn't recognized before now.

There was something possessive in his tone that nipped at her. She couldn't decide whether to be annoyed or . . . Or what? Triumphant? She shook her head, which made her surroundings spin a bit as a result of the meds Donovan had administered.

She needed to stop all this because important conclusions couldn't be reached when she was high as a kite.

"She's going to be fine," Donovan called back. "She kicked some ass and only has one measly bullet wound to show for it. It's going to hurt like hell for a while and she's going to be laid up until it heals, but she's good."

"Of course she kicked ass," Cole said, a hint of impatience in his voice.

For some reason that confidence in his words—just the way he said it—warmed her in places that had been encased in ice for the last months.

Cole believed in her. He always had. He might give her the most shit of anyone else on her team, but he was also the first one to boast of her abilities. They had a long-running rivalry over who was the better shot, but P.J. knew it was all in fun. Cole respected her. He respected her position on the team. For that matter all her teammates did. Which was more than she could say for her S.W.A.T. team.

And yet, Cole and Steele . . . Dolphin, Baker, Renshaw . . . They weren't her team anymore. She'd quit. She'd walked away. But here they were, risking their lives to save her ass.

Tears swam in her vision and she blinked rapidly, unwilling to give in to another emotional meltdown. She'd managed to remain detached for the last months. She'd switched off everything. No feelings. No memories. No fear and no pain. She couldn't lose control now. Not when she was so close to achieving her objective.

Somehow she had to find a way to break away from her—no, not her—*the* team. Break away from the team and get to Jakarta in three weeks' time.

Until she brought Carter Brumley down for good. Until that day, she couldn't sleep. She couldn't rest. She couldn't relax even for a moment.

The thought of all those innocent little girls plus the countless other women they'd victimized haunted her. She knew what it was like to be one of them. For a very short time, she'd been a victim as well, and it was enough to convince her that she'd rather die than ever become one again.

CHAPTER 22

ODDLY enough, P.J. dreaded facing Cole more than she dreaded facing Steele. Steele would be pissed, yeah. He'd already gone on record saying what he thought of her quitting the team. And yes, she'd been a total coward for only going to Steele and not facing her entire team—and Cole.

She'd been barely aware when Cole stopped the vehicle several hours after they'd fled the scene of her crime. She'd slipped in and out of consciousness when Cole had carried her inside a musty-smelling house and settled her on a couch.

When he'd arranged cushions around her for comfort, he'd bumped her leg, causing a low moan to escape her mouth.

He'd pressed his lips to her brow and murmured soft words of apology and a firm command for her to rest. She'd retreated beyond the veil of the medication, embracing the opportunity to delay the talk she knew was inevitable.

Anyone with eyes and a brain could see that things were . . . tense . . . between her and Cole. They had only to look at the way he'd been around her and they'd instantly know that their relationship wasn't as simple as teammate to teammate.

Former teammates.

It was a point she had to keep reminding herself of. She was no longer a part of KGI. No longer part of something that made her feel like she belonged.

She stared up at the ceiling, achy and wrung out from the medication. Her leg was throbbing and her skin felt clammy. When she turned her head to the side, she saw that the other members of her team had arrived.

Dolphin was propped in one of the small armchairs, his head tilted sideways, eyes closed. Across from him, Renshaw occupied the other chair and had his head straight back so he was staring upward. He was asleep too.

Guilt nagged at her. How many days or weeks had they gone without sleep because they were tracking her down? Or had they even been looking for her? If they were after Brumley, it stood to reason they'd have the same intel she'd gathered. Maybe she was alive thanks to nothing more than shit-ass luck.

She pushed herself upward and rotated so her legs fell over the side of the couch. Pain shot through her thigh. Spots dotted her vision and she nearly passed out. For several long seconds she sat there, sucking in huge mouthfuls of air. Her pulse hammered and the clammy feeling grew stronger.

She wiped at her brow, holding her palm over her forehead. It was then she realized she still had an IV attached to her arm and the bag was hanging above the couch on a hat rack.

She started to pry the tape away from her arm so she could remove the IV when her nape prickled.

"What the fuck, P.J.?"

She looked up to see Cole suddenly looming over her, a dark scowl on his face. Where had he come from? Her mouth went dry and her hand fell away from the tape. Cole immediately dropped down to one knee and refastened the tape over the port site.

"Where do you think you're going?" he demanded.

P.J. sighed wearily. The last thing she wanted was a confrontation.

"P.J., look at me."

She forced her gaze upward in response to his fierce command.

"Where the hell have you been all this time?"

She could tell he was visibly trying to keep his temper in check. If she weren't hurt, he'd probably be letting her have it with both barrels, and that pissed her off because she just wanted things to be normal and they never would be again.

"Hunting Brumley and his minions," she said bluntly.

"Yeah, I saw your handiwork on the two guys who were with Brumley that night."

She refused to let shame crawl into her soul. Nor would she try to determine if there was condemnation in his tone.

"Look, Cole, I quit the team. You shouldn't be here. None of you. I walked away."

She saw Renshaw stir and she quickly glanced in Dolphin's direction to see that he was already awake. He was sitting quietly, his mouth drawn into a pinch, his focus on the conversation between her and Cole.

"I have a mission to complete," she said. "And I can't accomplish it by sitting on my ass while I'm being babied by my former teammates."

Cole's lips curled and fire blazed in his eyes. "Former, my ass. Over my dead body will you go off on your own. You're lucky you weren't killed or that they didn't get their hands on you again."

Forgetting the others, she pushed herself forward on the edge of the couch and farther into Cole's space, bristling with as much anger as she saw in his own expression.

"This isn't a righteous mission, Cole. It's personal."

"Do you think it isn't goddamn personal for me too?" he all but roared at her.

"I can't involve you—any of you—in my mission," she yelled back. "It's not who KGI is. Never has been. I won't drag this organization through the mud. This is bloody. It's revenge, Cole."

"I damn well know it," he snarled. "And I want in. We all want in. If you think we're just going to leave you hanging in the wind, you're out of your goddamn mind."

She covered her face with her hands and propped her elbows on her knees. She was exhausted and heartsick. This wasn't what she wanted to happen.

Firm hands gripped her wrists and carefully pried her hands from her face. This time when she glanced back up at Cole, she could see Donovan and Steele in the background. Baker was standing behind Renshaw's chair. All eyes were on her. Their expressions were grim and ... determined.

"We—*I*—don't give a fuck if the mission is righteous or whether the motivation behind us taking Brumley out is revenge or to prevent more women and children from being brutalized. We stand with you, P.J. We're family. You aren't doing this alone so get over it."

"I'm going after Brumley," she said. "He's doing a deal in Jakarta in three weeks and I'm going to be there. I'm taking him out."

"Not without us," Cole bit out. "It's time for you to suck it up and learn to lean on someone."

"I couldn't agree more," Steele interjected.

Surprised, she lifted her gaze to her team leader and then glanced at Donovan. It was one thing for her team to pledge such a thing, but Donovan represented the organization. Surely he couldn't be in agreement with the others.

Donovan crossed his arms over his chest and stared challengingly back at her.

"If you think I'm going to toe the company line and lecture everyone on vigilante justice, you've got the wrong guy. That's Sam's job. I'm of the mind that taking Brumley out—*however* we take him out—will mean one less asshole in the world."

"Hooyah," Dolphin said emphatically. "That's what I'm talking about."

"Oh, and P.J.?"

She looked up at Steele when he said her name.

"You can take your resignation and stick it up your ass."

Baker and Renshaw chuckled. Dolphin grinned and snickered and Donovan nodded his agreement.

"Looks like you're stuck with us," Cole said with clear satisfaction.

She blew out her breath, shaking her head the entire time. It had to be the medication that had her tripping like this.

"I don't even know what to say."

"How about yes sir, when I tell you that you're going to take it easy and recover as much as possible over the next three weeks," Cole said.

Her brow wrinkled in disgust even as her chest tightened with unexpected emotion. God, it felt good to be back with her team. All the ribbing. The smart-ass remarks. Cutting jokes and insults left and right.

"For God's sake, don't cry," Cole said in disgust.

The others laughed and P.J. smiled through the pain, her eyes stinging with those unshed tears.

"Thank you," she said sincerely.

"Now you're just pissing me off," Steele said. "You don't thank us for doing our job. We live as a team and we die as a team, and you thinking you walked away is bullshit. You don't take a piss without my say-so, you got that, Rutherford?"

She smiled, and it felt like the first time she'd truly smiled in a lifetime. God it felt good to be surrounded by the people she considered family. She'd never been as alone as she had in the last months when she didn't have her team around her.

Her team.

"Yes sir," she said briskly.

CHAPTER 23

IT was two in the morning and P.J. was wide awake, her leg throbbing. She'd refused another dose of painkiller because she'd wanted to evaluate exactly what she was dealing with.

Though just a flesh wound, her leg still protested if she put any weight on it. She had a limited amount of time in which to heal because she wasn't staying behind while her team went to Jakarta. The truth was, she didn't want them involved even if they were determined to be. She didn't want her sins to be their own.

She pushed herself awkwardly from the bed and eased her feet to the floor. She had no hope of sleeping. She'd been out most of the day, aided by the pain medication Donovan had administered. She imagined the rest of the crew was sleeping soundly.

Donovan had arranged for the jet to take off early the next morning. After a quick glance at the clock, she knew it was pointless to even try to go back to sleep. She only had three hours before they moved out again.

The little cottage that Donovan and Cole had finagled

was barely big enough to fit two people, much less her entire team plus Donovan. They'd insisted she take the bedroom, and Cole had carried her from the front sitting room where she'd spent some of the afternoon on the couch and put her on the double bed.

If she'd had more courage, she would have invited Cole to share the comfort of the bed with her. He looked haggard and worn down. But she couldn't make the words come out.

Tentatively she took a step, bracing herself for the pain that shot up her leg and into her belly. She waited several long seconds as she sucked in breath after breath in an attempt to steady herself.

She needed the bathroom in the worst way, and she wasn't about to call for one of the guys to help her with that particular necessity.

The few feet to the bathroom took an eternity. At the door, she paused and glanced into the living room to see the guys draped all over the furniture. They looked horribly uncomfortable. Steele and Cole were lying on the floor with their backpacks shoved under their necks to cushion their heads.

Feeling about a hundred years old, she shuffled into the bathroom to do her business.

It took longer than she'd have liked. She examined the bulky bandages on her right thigh. She'd been lucky. The bullet could have shattered her femur or worse, hit her femoral artery and she could have bled out in minutes. As it was, it passed through a chunk of flesh less than half an inch from her bone.

Push past the pain.

It was a mantra that had been effective for the last six months. At times it was the only thing that kept her going.

Clad in her underwear and a clean T-shirt, she pulled the shirt farther down her legs before she opened the bathroom door. As she stepped into the hall, she came face-to-face with Cole.

He was leaning against the opposite wall, arms crossed,

one leg pulled up so that his foot rested flat against the wall.

"You should have called for me," he said tersely. "You don't need to be up walking around. You'll tear the stitches."

"I'm fine," she said, even as she gingerly took another step.

"The hell you are. Every step you take, you go even paler, and your forehead is so clammy I can see it from here."

Without saying anything further, he pushed off the wall and wrapped a supporting arm around her.

"Wrap your arm around me and hold on. Put most of your weight on me."

Relieved he hadn't picked her up and carried her, she did as he instructed and limped forward into the bedroom. At least he seemed open to her trying to get around on her own. Or mostly on her own anyway.

When they got to the bed, he helped her sit on the edge and then he plumped all the pillows so she could scoot back and sit up in bed in comfort.

After she got situated, he sat on the edge of the bed facing her. He pulled one knee up and rested his forearm across his leg as he studied her.

"How are you feeling?"

The way he said it told her he wasn't asking about her leg. She expelled a long sigh.

"I don't know," she said honestly. "I haven't allowed myself to feel anything for the last six months. But when I knelt there in the dirt with Nelson's blood on my hands, I thought to myself *you should be jubilant*. You should feel *vindicated*. Justice has been served and he'll never hurt another woman or child again."

Cole slid his hand gently over hers, lacing their fingers together. Just that simple gesture chased some of the lingering sickness from the pit of her stomach.

"Instead I just felt . . . sick. It all came rushing back at me, and I've tried so hard not to remember. I swear it was like he'd raped me all over again. Isn't that stupid?"

She tried to laugh but it came out more as a sob.

"God, I had him at *my* mercy and all I could think was that it was like being raped all over again because that's all I could remember. Him on top of me. Him overpowering me and all the hatred and revulsion I experienced."

Cole squeezed her hand, but his hand shook against hers, giving her a hint of the emotion running through him.

"It's not stupid, baby. Nothing you feel is stupid. It's how you feel, so that makes it legitimate. Do you understand what I'm saying? I won't let you beat yourself up for being human. What happened to you wasn't just a simple injury in the course of a mission. It was something no person should ever have to endure. You can't just shrug that off and pretend it didn't happen. Sometime, someway, you have to deal with it, and I don't think you have yet. I know you haven't," he added softly.

"I hate it," she whispered. "Oh God, Cole, I hated feeling that helpless. Not even when all the shit went down with my S.W.A.T. team did I feel helpless. I felt angry. I was pissed. I was disappointed. But what I did was my choice. I didn't have my choices taken away from me."

Cole leaned forward, pressed his lips to her forehead and left them there. She leaned into him, closing her eyes as they sat in silence for a long moment. Just him being there was enough. He didn't have to offer her platitudes.

When he pulled away, there was a hardness in his eyes that told her the gloves were about to come off. She nearly breathed a sigh of relief, because it was getting too heavy. She much preferred his anger to the overwhelming worry in his gaze.

"Why did you run, P.J.? Do you have any idea what that did to me? To us? The team? When Steele told me what you'd done, I felt like someone had sucker punched me. The other guys were just as bewildered. We aren't your goddamn S.W.A.T. team. We aren't dumping you when things get sticky."

The very real anger and frustration in his voice made her feel shame. There was nowhere for her to go to hide from the look in his eyes or the way he stared so intently at her.

"I didn't know what else to do," she said. And at the time it had been true. "I wasn't thinking straight. I was sick to my soul and all I could think about was revenge. I was *consumed* with hatred and shame. God, do you have any idea how it feels to be totally helpless while someone holds you down and degrades you? I felt like those bastards had taken my very *soul.*"

Cole's jaw tightened. "Yeah, I do know. Maybe not on the same level, but goddamn it, I know what it feels like to be helpless. I had to sit there and listen to the whole goddamn thing, P.J. I've never felt so helpless in my life. To have to sit there while someone I care about was savaged? It makes me sick to even *think* about."

She paused and looked up, her jaw going slack as she processed his words. Some of her shock must have shown on her face.

"Yeah, that's right, P.J. I care. I care a whole hell of a lot."

She didn't know what to say or how to react, because they both knew he wasn't talking about caring on a more casual level. Like the way Dolphin or Baker or Renshaw cared about her. This was something much deeper, and it scared the hell out of her.

Unable to do anything else, she gripped the hand holding hers and squeezed, hoping the gesture conveyed what she wasn't able to put to words.

He leaned forward, tense and hesitant. His free hand went to her face, brushing aside her hair, and then he simply kissed her.

It wasn't the burning, scorching-the-sheets kind of kiss that they'd shared that night so many months earlier. There was no impatience and no demand. It wasn't even sexual. The touch was so exquisitely gentle that it made her want to cry.

He had a way of getting to her. Past her barriers. And

there he was, at the very heart of her before she even realized he'd slipped past.

When he drew away, he rotated so that he could climb
onto the bed beside her. Then he simply pulled her against
his chest, holding her with both arms.

"Rest and let me hold you," he said in a quiet voice. "Just
you and me, P.J. Don't think about the past or the future.
Just focus on right now, you getting better, and let yourself
lean on me."

She rested her head on his chest and stretched her
injured leg down the length of his. He was warm and solid
and it felt so very good to give in and allow him to shoulder
her fears just for a little while.

It took some time to muster the courage to ask the question burning her tongue. She opened her mouth several
times and ended up closing it when her nerve fled.

"You care about me . . . even after what happened?"

At first she wasn't sure he heard her muffled whisper.
Then she realized he was merely collecting himself before
answering. His voice was chock-full of emotion. He sounded
angry, but not at her. The words came as though he struggled to get them out there without losing his composure.

"I don't give a damn about what happened other than
the fact that those sons of bitches hurt you. They put their
hands on you. What happened changes nothing about my
feelings for you. If anything the fact that you're coming out
of this so strong makes me respect your strength even
more, and I already had a healthy dose of admiration for
your ability to kick some serious ass."

She pushed upward, placing her hand in the hollow of
his chest as she looked him in the eye. "I have scars, Cole.
They aren't pretty. You saw where he cut me. There are
scars in each of those places. And they're not going away."

He touched her chin with the tip of his finger and then
kissed her almost as if he couldn't resist. Then he let his
hand slide down until his palm rested over her heart.

"I'm more concerned about the scars here," he said,

pressing inward on her chest. Then he lifted his hand to her temple and tapped gently. "And in here."

He kissed her again, this time on the forehead.

"The physical scars don't change who you are, P.J. The emotional ones do. Those are the ones I want to help you with. I don't give a damn that your body has a few more scars. Hell, I'm riddled with them and you didn't seem to mind."

Her cheeks tightened and heat rose up her neck.

He picked up her hand, the one resting on his chest, and he laced their fingers together, holding their hands between them.

"I'll wait as long as it takes, P.J. I'll do whatever I can to help you. Whatever it takes for you to heal physically and emotionally. Just know that I'm not going anywhere, and it's time for you to stop running."

She snuggled back into his embrace, nuzzling her cheek against his chest as she processed the words that still floated around her mind. Such beautiful words, and she knew he meant them. Cole wasn't the type to bullshit. He was light-hearted and fun when the occasion called for it, but at the end of the day, he was a straight shooter. He was blunt and spoke his mind.

And now that he had spoken precisely what was on his mind, she was blown away by the implications.

Here was a man who admitted he had feelings for her. Not only that, but he was also willing to wait for as long as it took her to get her head on straight and heal from the trauma she'd endured.

Hell, even more than that, he was risking his life, his reputation and his career in order to help her seek justice.

He was helping her find a way to murder another individual.

She winced at the thought of taking him down with her. She couldn't bear it. Couldn't bear it if the team was dragged through the mud with her.

She closed her eyes, secure in the knowledge that she

was safe. Cole was here, surrounding her. Offering her unconditional support.

He'd been up front with her. Had told her what was in his heart. Now she had to figure out what was in her own heart and sort out her muddled feelings for a man who infuriated and enticed her in equal measure.

The future was a very scary prospect when she didn't even know if she had a present. What scared her the most, though, was the very real possibility of screwing up a relationship with someone she genuinely cared about before it even got off the ground.

Cole deserved someone who could give him one hundred percent. Someone who could give herself without any reservations. He was a good man. Loyal. Fiercely protective. A man any woman would be lucky to have.

She could see herself as that woman, and maybe that was what scared her most of all.

And it wasn't as simple as deciding they fit and then living happily ever after. They had their team to consider. They had dozens of young girls depending on them. They couldn't afford to fuck it all up because their emotions got in the way.

As much as she wanted to be selfish and let tomorrow take care of itself, she knew she had to remain objective and make the mission her priority. For her own sanity as much as for the protection of those precious little girls.

CHAPTER 24

COLE carried P.J. onto the plane. It was almost as if he'd reached the end of his patience or just blown his resolve to let her do as much on her own as possible.

She'd limped out of the cottage with Cole's help, and admittedly he'd pretty much carried her then too, but he'd allowed her the illusion of making it on her own. He'd even allowed her to get out of the vehicle at the airfield, but after three painful steps, he muttered a curse and simply swept her into his arms.

She hadn't argued, because to be perfectly honest, each of those three steps had been agonizing and she was too exhausted to care if she looked weak to the rest of the team.

It was stupid of her to care anyway. Her team members had each gone down before and they hadn't shown their ass or insisted on making it on their own. All the pressure was of her own making. She didn't want to seem like she needed help, because she felt like she had more to prove.

Ridiculous, but there you had it. She was a woman, and her team didn't even care. It was her with the chip on her shoulder and for no reason.

Cole settled her on the back couch and made sure she was comfortable while the others took their seats and belted themselves in.

"I'm okay, Cole," she said, after he'd placed a pillow underneath her leg. "Go sit down and buckle up."

He scowled and ignored her, taking position at the end of the couch. He placed a hand over her knee to steady her so her leg wouldn't be jostled in takeoff.

She sighed, knowing it was fruitless to argue with him. He was one hardheaded male.

As soon as they were airborne, the others filtered back. There were only two armchairs making up the small sitting area along with the couch, and Dolphin and Renshaw took those while Baker slouched on the floor. Steele stood in the doorway, and it was evident he had something on his mind.

Donovan was conspicuously absent, and she didn't know if it was because he wanted to give the team privacy to hash out their issues or if Steele had told him to hang back.

"I'm going to be straight with you, P.J.," Steele said. "You're going to take it easy for the next few weeks. You aren't going back to your apartment. It's too risky. Brumley's likely got a hit out on you. And if I don't think you're ready for action by the time we make our move on him, you're grounded."

She started to protest but he shut her down before she could say the first word.

"I'll tie you up and have Sam sit on you if I have to," Steele said in a terse voice. "You'll be a liability to the team, not to mention the personal danger you'd place yourself in."

She bit her lip and didn't offer argument. It would do no good. And if she told him that there was no way in hell she was staying behind while they went after Brumley, he'd do just as he threatened and have Sam or Garrett play nanny.

So instead, she nodded stiffly and kept her mouth shut.

"The other thing is, you're not staying alone while you're recovering."

Again she opened her mouth and he damn near sliced her in two with his stare.

"This isn't up for negotiation. You aren't going back to your apartment and you aren't staying alone. You'd be a sitting duck if Brumley tried anything. So here are your choices. You stay with me or you stay with one of the team. Doesn't matter to me. But you aren't flying solo."

"You can stay with me," Dolphin offered.

"Or me," Renshaw broke in.

Baker also offered his place.

Cole was the only one who remained silent. She cut her glance sideways at him to see him sitting expressionless, his hand still cupped over her knee.

It was almost as if he were issuing her a challenge. He'd laid his cards on the table. Now it was her turn to meet him halfway. He wasn't going to offer. He wanted her to make the next move.

Damn it.

She blew out her breath while her heart was about to beat out of her chest. It was such a silly thing, but making that move scared the hell out of her. It was like jumping out of a plane and hoping like hell the parachute opened.

"P.J.?" Steele prompted.

There was another long pause while she gathered her courage.

"I'll stay with Cole, if he doesn't mind," she choked out.

His hand tightened on her knee. She could feel the imprint of his fingers on her flesh.

Dolphin cast a glance over at Cole, his brows gathering as if he didn't quite understand the strong undercurrent flowing in the room.

"Seriously, I don't mind, P.J.," Dolphin said.

Cole's voice was almost menacing. "She's staying with me."

"Alrighty then," Dolphin said, expelling his breath.

Cole's grip on her knee loosened, but he still kept his hand there, and this time when she peeked back at him, he was staring at her, his eyes full of satisfaction.

She was glad now she'd made that move. Something told her that he would have been hurt if she had wimped out of the challenge he'd thrown.

"First thing you're doing is checking into the hospital," Steele said.

"Aw fuck," she muttered.

"Save it," Cole said. "You don't have to stay, but you need to get checked out, get some meds, stitches, whatever it takes. Then I'll take you home and make you feel all better."

Heat prickled up her nape and warm pleasure flooded her heart. She had a feeling he wasn't simply talking about a little pampering and some good food. And if she was right, she knew he certainly would go a long way in making her feel very, *very* good.

CHAPTER 25

P.J. tried to get off the plane by herself, but even she had to admit defeat. Her leg was like one giant exposed nerve. Perspiration beaded her forehead and upper lip and she was clammy. Her breathing was shallow and rapid, and she wasn't sure if she needed to puke or pass out.

After trying to take two steps, her knee buckled and she nearly went down. Cole was there to catch her, and without saying a word or bitching at her for attempting to walk, he simply swept her up and marched off the plane.

She nearly groaned aloud when she realized they'd flown into Henry County, which was the Kellys' home air-field where they kept their jets hangared.

She was pleasantly surprised, however, when Cole whisked her into a waiting SUV. None of the Kellys were present. No one from KGI had met them, which meant there was no lecture to endure. Maybe her team would escape unscathed from all the trouble she'd caused.

Steele stuck his head in the door after Cole had laid her in the backseat.

"If you need anything, holler, Cole. I'll be checking in

periodically. Keep your ear to the ground and trust your instincts."

"You heading home?" Cole asked their team leader.

Steele shook his head. "I have to give report to Sam."

P.J. cringed. So much for her team not having any fallout. "I'm sorry. You shouldn't have to answer for me."

Steele eyed her coolly. "Who says I'm answering to anyone? And moreover, who says it's about you? I make the decisions on this team and I stand behind every one. If there's anything to be said, it will be said to me. Not my team."

As he shut the door, Cole glanced in the rearview mirror. "And that's the law according to Steele."

P.J. smiled. "He's a total badass. I love that about him."

Cole snorted. "You would."

"You're a pretty big badass yourself, Coletrane. I like it."

"Glad you approve," he said dryly. "Now, what do you say we get the fuck home and eat some decent food. I wouldn't feed my dog the shit we've eaten the last few days."

"You have a dog?"

"Nope, but if I did, I'd feed him better than we've been eating."

She laughed. "Can't argue with that. What's for supper?"

He glanced in the mirror again as he pulled onto the county road leading away from the airfield. "It's a perfect evening. I was thinking about grilling some steaks on the back patio and counting fireflies over the pond."

She closed her eyes and grabbed the image he described. It was so perfect it made her ache. "I'd like that," she said softly. "I'd like it a lot."

"Don't think we've forgotten about the hospital bit. Just in case you got your hopes up."

She scowled and he chuckled back at her.

"I convinced Steele that dragging you now wouldn't accomplish anything other than making you more cranky than you already are. I promised him I'd get you to Fort

Campbell tomorrow morning first thing but that tonight I was going to get you to relax and enjoy a good meal."

She was besieged by the awkward funny feeling in the pit of her stomach, the one that squeezed her heart and caused butterflies to flutter her insides. She hadn't felt this silly since her first crush in junior high.

"Thanks, Cole. I appreciate it. I'll feel much better about taking on Cathy tomorrow."

His eyebrow rose in question. "Who's Cathy?"

"My partner in crime," P.J. hedged. "She's the one who helped me fly the coop last time. I met her a couple years back. As much as we're in and out of Fort Campbell, we ran into each other, started talking. She's probably the closest thing I have to a friend."

Cole frowned at that. "You have friends."

P.J. smiled. "I meant girl friends. I don't have any girl friends. Cathy's older than I am, but she's great. She even gives me shit about not respecting you navy guys enough. She's former navy herself."

"She gets a hooyah from me then. Although I'm going to have serious words with the woman about busting you out of the hospital. That was a stupid move."

She didn't respond to that one. Maybe it was. Maybe it wasn't. But at the time it was what she had to do. She couldn't very well try to analyze her state of mind at the time because she was honest enough to know she had been a head case. Cathy knew it too, but she hadn't tried to tell P.J. she was wrong, and for that she was appreciative.

No one had broached the subject of seeing a shrink yet. She was just waiting for it. She knew the wives of the Kelly men, and even Rio's wife, Grace, had been through some heavy shit. She respected them for it. They weren't shrinking violets for women. They knew how to kick ass in their own way.

Shea especially had P.J.'s deep respect, and P.J. suspected that she and Nathan's wife could be friends if they ever hung around each other long enough. Shea had taken a lot of pain and torture on Nathan's behalf. She'd helped him survive hell and was the sole reason that he was home with his brothers after spending months imprisoned in the Middle East.

She doubted she'd ever fit into the Kelly inner circle. That was reserved for their wives, and the Kellys were fiercely protective of them. But did she want to? Had she reached a point in her life where she wanted to fit in some- where and have a network of friends to lean on for support?

Months before she would have said emphatically no. She liked her life the way it was. She did her job, she went home, no one bothered her.

But how much of that was a product of what had hap- pened on her S.W.A.T. team? She had to admit, she'd been pretty young and idealistic when she'd landed a spot on the team. Not only had she been the first woman, but she'd also been the youngest recruit ever for her particular team.

She'd had to work twice as hard to earn the same respect as the men, and she thought she'd gotten there. She thought she had their loyalty. She'd been more crushed than she wanted to admit at the time. When she'd realized how naïve and just how wrong she'd been, it had been humiliating.

When she'd hired on for Steele's team, she'd gone in expecting the worst and she trained accordingly. Gradually she'd relaxed, but she'd never let her guard completely down. Not like she'd done with her S.W.A.T. team. She'd assumed way too much with them, and she was determined not to make the same mistake again.

But Cole and her teammates were slowly proving her wrong. They'd stood behind her. Her team leader had stood behind her even at the risk of his own reputation and posi- tion within KGI.

That meant something, didn't it?

Yeah, it meant a damn lot.

"You asleep back there, P.J.?" Cole called back. "We're almost there."

She sat up, gingerly pulling herself upward so she could

see out the window. She hadn't been asleep but she'd sure been in another world contemplating her circumstances.

The SUV slowed and Cole turned onto a dirt road that was marked only by a county road number. There were no residences on the road. Only a thick stand of pine and hardwood.

At the end it opened up into a cleared area where a small house stood. In the back, a huge pond spread out for several acres. It was practically a small lake.

The house wasn't entirely what she would have expected. Maybe she'd thought he'd have gone for a more rustic look, but the home was modern looking with brick and wood and large picture windows. It looked cozy and inviting, and it fit in well with the landscaping.

Neat hedges that looked newly trimmed. A lawn that looked as though it was freshly cut. Several smaller trees dotted the open ground, and several azalea bushes and other flowering varieties lined the edges of the house.

"You own all of this?" she asked.

He pulled the SUV to a stop in front of the house, not bothering to park in the garage.

"Yep. Bought a hundred acres from a paper company who was selling off land in the area. Same company Sam got all the KGI property from. They pulled out of Tennessee. Got a pretty good deal on it. I cut enough timber to pay for the land and then built the house and had the pond dug."

"So who keeps this up for you? You're not home enough to take care of all this."

He laughed. "I have a guy who comes by when I'm away."

"Nice bachelor pad. Do you have the prerequisite man cave going on in there?"

He went quiet and then didn't respond. He got out and then opened the passenger door behind her.

"I don't want you to move, okay? I'm going to put my hands under your arms and pull you my way. It'll be easier than you trying to maneuver your body around and banging that leg up."

She didn't argue.

His arms slid under hers and his hands splayed over her chest and belly. Then he started easing her backward until her ass hung off the seat. He rotated around so he could put one arm underneath her knees and then he lifted her effortlessly from the backseat and elbowed the door shut.

"I'll get our gear later. Right now I want to make sure you're comfortable and get some pain medicine in you."

She frowned. "I don't want to sleep through the steaks and fireflies."

He laughed as he carried her toward the door. "Don't worry. I'll give you just enough to take the edge off. I don't want you snoring through dinner either."

He set her down on the front porch, careful not to let her put any weight on her leg. Then he unlocked the house and shoved the door open.

"Can you make it inside or you want me to carry you?"

She very nearly blurted that she wanted him to carry her, but how wussy would that sound?

She only had a few weeks to get her shit together, and she wouldn't accomplish that by having Cole treat her like an invalid.

Bracing herself for the inevitable flash of discomfort, she took a step, holding on to the doorframe so she didn't humiliate herself by going down.

She clenched her jaw and took another step, finding it easier if she just kept moving rather than pausing after each step. Cole hovered at her side, no doubt waiting to see if she face-planted.

Gratified that she was still on her feet and not kissing the floor, she grew a little bolder and limped into the living room.

The leather couch looked inviting, and she made it her sole purpose to get to it as soon as possible so she could sink into the waiting softness. She was already imagining a long nap with that sumptuous-looking leather hugging her body.

A few muttered curses later and she was there. Knowing

there was no graceful way to settle in, she let herself fall awkwardly onto the cushions. She grimaced when the impact jostled her leg, but then she pulled it up so she could lie on her side comfortably.

She let out a huge sigh of relief and closed her eyes for a moment. This was good. Perfect, even. She could totally stay here the rest of the day. Except they were supposed to grill steaks and watch fireflies.

"Give me an hour," she said to Cole. "Just want to rest here for a little while. Then we'll go out and watch the sun go down."

He smiled and reached down with his hand to touch her cheek. It was such a simple gesture, but it was sweeter than any kiss or more overt sign of intimacy.

"Take all the time you need. I'll go take stock of what's in my freezer."

CHAPTER 26

COLE watched P.J. sleep from the chair across the room. It's where he'd found himself for the last hour, studying her as she rested.

Such a complex individual in a small package. She had layers that would take him forever to completely unravel, and yet he looked forward to the challenge. Life definitely wasn't boring with P.J. around.

Looking back, he wasn't even certain when she'd become such an integral part of his life. He'd admit he'd been somewhat of an asshole when she'd first been brought on board. He'd been skeptical of her skills because she was a woman. It had been hard for him to look at her and imagine a kick-ass warrior that the team needed.

She'd very quickly proved him wrong, and he was man enough to admit he'd totally fucked up and had been a complete dickhead chauvinist.

P.J. had taught him a lot, though. She'd changed his outlook on most women. By watching her, he'd learned not to assume that women were weaker just because they were female.

She carried her weight and that of the team sometime. He admired the hell out of her and would have told her on multiple occasions if he hadn't known he'd have gotten his ass kicked for it.

In essence she was absolutely perfect for him. He wanted her. More than he'd ever wanted another woman, and she was certainly the first woman he'd actually considered that he'd like a long-term relationship with.

Marriage?

He'd resolved early on that he wasn't the kind of guy that was cut out for a wife, kids and the whole nine yards of domesticity. He liked action. Liked the thrill his job provided. He'd never be happy settling into a nine-to-five job, coming home to check things off the honey-do list. And he knew there weren't many women who would put up with his schedule. Never knowing when he'd come home or when he'd get called up on another mission. He couldn't blame them either.

But what if the woman he fell for lived for the same things he did? Could it work? Would they be able to stay on a team together if they were romantically involved?

The bad thing was, he figured P.J. would handle it just fine. But would he? Could he stand to go out on a mission with the woman he loved at his side, knowing it was possible she wouldn't make it back or that she could get seriously injured?

Hell, it had already happened.

After their one-night stand, he'd gone batshit crazy at the idea of her being used as bait to lure Nelson into a trap. He'd been right, but if it had been any other woman, would he have been so adamant about her performing her job?

Probably not.

Which meant that he wouldn't take it any better in the future when P.J. put herself on the line, and he knew P.J. This incident wouldn't slow her down. It would likely make her that much more determined not to let what happened to her interfere in future missions.

His first instinct had been to protect her. He hadn't

considered what was best for the mission. Or the people they were trying to protect by bringing Brumley down. He'd only cared that P.J. was risking herself, and he'd wanted her in a role that assumed less risk.

It was a hell of a dilemma for him, because he wasn't sure if he could give the team one hundred percent as long as P.J. was involved. And she'd never allow him to shield her from the reality of their jobs. He'd have less respect for her if she did. But it didn't change the fact that he was a basket case at the idea of her incurring huge personal risk.

He rubbed his hand over his face, weary from the sheer weight of his worry and indecision.

He wanted P.J. He thought he might even love her. But could he commit to her knowing the kind of baggage they'd both bring to the table? Would it be fair to her and her position on the team to have a crazy-ass lover and teammate whose sole objective was to keep *her* safe and fuck the rest of the world?

And even if it wasn't fair, it was far too late, because he'd already laid out his cards. He'd told her he was here. That he'd wait as long as it took for her to get her head on straight again.

Even as he thought the last, he winced at how it sounded. Get her head on straight? You used language like that for someone who'd fucked up. For someone whose head wasn't in the game.

That wasn't the case with P.J. She hadn't fucked up. She'd done everything right and had paid a steep price for that. He couldn't fathom how she'd been able to keep it together this long.

As he stared at her features, softened by the veil of sleep, something inside him twisted and knotted. The problem was, she'd kept it together *too* well. Which meant at some point, she had to break. No one could completely turn it off forever, and what had sustained her all these months was hunting for the men who'd hurt her. Once she no longer had that objective holding her together, what would happen?

She'd need him—someone—then more than ever. The

question was, would she accept his help? Or would she push him away, determined to shoulder everything on her own?

He shook his head. "I won't let you do that, P.J.," he whispered. "I don't know what exactly it is that we have, but I'm not willing to let it go no matter how hard it is."

Relationships took work. He'd seen the evidence of that enough times just by observing the Kellys. Ethan's wife, Rachel, had been through hell, and her road to recovery had been a bumpy one.

But P.J. was worth it. She deserved happiness. She deserved a man who stood by her and with her. Someone who allowed her to be herself. Even if it killed him, he was going to be that man. Encouraging her to be the kick-ass woman he knew her to be and not holding her back no matter how hard his gut screamed at him to shield her from anything that could ever hurt her.

Love sucked.

Love required sacrifices that were hard to make. It required him to go against every instinct so he didn't crush what made P.J. so special to begin with.

If this was what falling in love was about, he wasn't sure whether he wanted in or not.

And yet, the idea of P.J. not being in his future as more than just a team member he hung out with sucked. It didn't really matter what he wanted or what was easy at this point, because the decision had been made for him.

P.J. was his. And yeah, it wouldn't be easy, but nothing worthwhile ever was.

He liked her just the way she was. All hard-ass, stubborn, independent and capable of kicking anyone's ass. Even his.

He wouldn't change a goddamn thing about her.

The sudden surge of emotion caught him off guard. It was as if admitting to himself the depth of his feelings for P.J. made him want to act on them now. He wanted her to know, for her to feel, what she meant to him. How long had he carried a torch for her?

He couldn't pinpoint an exact time or place. Rather, she'd gradually grown on him as he'd grown to respect and admire her. Over time his feelings had changed to something intensely more personal, and now here he was watching as she slept on his couch in his home.

He had her exactly where he most wanted her, and his hands were tied and he was unable to act on the attraction between them.

Still, he found himself getting up so he could be closer to her. He knelt in front of the couch, his fingers going to trace the baby-soft skin on her cheek.

Her hair was pulled into a ponytail, as it always was, but tendrils escaped and floated down her face, giving her an air of vulnerability that made his chest tighten.

He'd seen her at her most vulnerable. At her lowest point. It was an image he wished he could wash from his memory. Her broken and bloody, her eyes awash with shame.

Even now it was like a punch to the stomach. He couldn't even think about it without wanting to put his fist through a wall.

He lowered his lips to brush across her brow, and then, because it wasn't enough, he let his mouth linger, simply absorbing the sensation of having her so close.

He inhaled deeply, taking in the fragrance of her shampoo and the smell of her soap, a scent he now identified as uniquely hers.

She stirred beneath him, and then her eyelids fluttered open. He pulled away because he didn't want to panic her if she was still half asleep. But she smiled at him, her eyes flashing with instant recognition.

"Did I sleep too long?" she whispered.

He smiled and shook his head. "Not at all. You've been out for a couple of hours. I figured you needed to catch up."

"Oh good, so I didn't miss the steaks?"

"Nope. They're marinating now, and as soon as I get the grill fired up, I'll throw them on and we can hang out on the patio if you feel up to it."

She let out a soft sigh that sent a streak of pleasure

through his senses. She'd made sounds like that the night they'd spent together. Sounds of satisfaction, like she was happy in the world.

He'd do anything he could to give her those small moments. Anything at all to remove the shadows in her mind. He wanted to give her new memories to replace the painful ones.

"Know what I'd really like?" she asked, a wistful note to her voice.

He almost laughed, because at present, she could ask for anything at all and he'd damn near kill himself making sure she got it.

"What's that?"

"A really long, hot shower."

He frowned a moment, contemplating the possible ramifications.

"I'm not sure you should be standing that long on your own."

Her face bloomed with color—one of the few times he could ever remember her blushing.

"I can make it," she said. "As long as I can brace my hand on the shower wall, I'll be fine. If I have any trouble, I promise I'll holler for you."

"Works for me," he said, giving in. Not like he'd have denied her anyway. "I'll help you into the bathroom, make sure you have all the stuff you need, and then I'll wait in the kitchen."

"That sounds heavenly. Help me up?"

She reached out her hand and he stood, letting his fingers twine with hers. She pulled herself into a sitting position, gingerly letting her legs slide over the side of the couch.

He should have taken her straight to Fort Campbell. It's what Steele had wanted, but Cole had wanted her here. He wanted to give her some downtime and not take her to a place where she'd be constantly reminded of her injury and how she'd gotten it.

Besides, P.J. was tough. She wasn't going to wimp out over a simple flesh wound.

"How about you let me give you some pain medication so you can enjoy the evening," he said.

For a moment he thought she would refuse, but then she sighed. "Okay."

"I'll have it for you when you get out of the shower. I put your bag in the spare bedroom. Holler if you need anything."

She nodded and then started in the direction of the bathroom. Though she'd never been here before, she found her way around well enough. It wasn't like the house was so huge she'd get lost.

After reassuring himself she wasn't going to fall, he hurried out to light the grill, not wanting to be outside for long in case she needed him.

When he returned inside, he went to the bathroom and put his ear to the door. Hearing the water running, he relaxed and went back to the kitchen so he could start on dinner preparations.

If he had his way, he and P.J. were going to enjoy a peaceful evening together. Just the two of them. No team. No job. No outside world.

CHAPTER 27

P.J. felt about two hundred percent better after boiling herself in the hot shower. She'd even removed the bandages from her wound and cleaned it too. She'd get Cole to help her reapply the dressing until she got it looked at the next day at the hospital.

She put on a pair of gym shorts so the wound was easily accessible and then pulled on a T-shirt, not bothering with a bra. One, she didn't have that much up top to worry over, and two, Cole had already seen everything she had. They should be well past the coy and modest stage by now.

After putting on socks to keep her feet warm, she carefully made her way back toward the living room. Cole wasn't there, but she heard noise from the kitchen, so she went in search of him.

He was just placing the steaks on a platter to take them outside when he looked up and saw her.

"Hey," he said softly. "Feel better?"

"You have no idea," she breathed. "Almost human again."

He set down the plate with the steaks and wiped his

hands on a towel. Then he picked up a medicine bottle, shook out a pill and handed it to her.

"Just a sec, I'll get you some milk to take it with. Not a good idea to take these on an empty stomach."

She took the pill and waited while he poured a glass of milk and pushed it toward her on the counter. She sipped at the milk, grimacing before finally popping the pill into her mouth and drinking more to down it.

"Not a milk fan?"

She shook her head. "I don't even like the smell of it. I get my calcium by eating cheese. Lots of it."

"What would you like to drink with dinner? I'd offer you a beer but it wouldn't go too well with that painkiller you just took."

"Tea or water is fine. I'm more focused on the steak anyway. I'm already drooling over it and it's still raw."

He grinned. "Girl after my own heart. I'm a big fan of cow."

"Oh, I'm not particular. I'll eat a chicken or a pig with as much enthusiasm."

He glanced down at her bare leg and frowned. "That wound looks pretty nasty. We should get another bandage on it."

"Yeah, I thought you could help once you got the steaks on. I wanted to clean it in the shower. Plus the hot water felt good on it."

"Can you make it outside or you want me to go put the steaks on then come back for you?"

She took a hesitant step forward, gripping the countertop. "You lead and I'll follow. I'll do my very best not to take a header."

He smiled and picked up the platter, placing the tongs on top. As he walked out of the kitchen to the French doors overlooking the patio, she followed slowly behind him. By the time she made it to the door, he was already putting the steaks on the fire.

She stepped outside and breathed in the honeysuckle-scented air. Crickets chirped in the distance and the low hum of tree locusts rose in the evening air. The sky was covered with the pale shade of dusk and the sun was barely clinging to the horizon as it slipped lower and lower.

It was a perfect evening for a cookout.

She took a seat at the table and stretched her leg out to its full length underneath. The pain medication was already dulling the vicious ache, turning it to a more tolerable hum.

"It's beautiful here," she said as Cole lowered the lid to the grill.

"I like it. It's close to work but it's still private. I don't have to worry about tripping over anyone when I'm here. It's kind of nice after coming off a mission to hole up away from the world for a few days."

"Steele had been bugging me to move out this way. You know, before that last mission and all."

Cole studied her intently. "And? Were you considering it?"

"I don't know," she said honestly. "Before, I would have likely given it thought but probably would have put it off or made an excuse. I was comfortable in my routine and I liked that work was a world away from where I lived."

"And now? You said *before* like things have changed, or at least your thinking has."

She gazed over the pond, watching as the first firefly popped and glowed a line over the water before blinking off again.

There was something mesmerizing about fireflies. Something that took her back to her childhood when things were simple and summer days were spent chasing dreams.

It was a wake-up call that so much of her adulthood had been spent being unsatisfied with herself, her relationships and her jobs.

When had she changed from a laughing little girl dreaming of changing the world to a cynical adult who believed the world wasn't savable?

"P.J.?"

Cole broke softly into her thoughts, and she realized he was waiting for a response to his question.

"Now I'm not so sure. It was actually the night you came into the bar when I had this moment of realization that I was still living in the past by hanging around in Denver. There's nothing for me there. No reason to stay. No ties. Nothing. At least here I'd be closer to work if nothing else."

"You'd have me," he said.

She lifted her gaze to his and their eyes locked. He didn't flinch away. Didn't try to hide anything from her.

"I don't want to screw up our friendship. I can't lose that, Cole. It's too important to me. It's why I reacted the way I did the morning after, because all I could think was how stupid I'd been to risk something that means so very much to me."

"You aren't going to lose me, P.J. Don't doom us before we even give it a shot."

She dropped her gaze and returned it to the pond again, counting the fireflies as they danced through the air. More and more were popping into view, and the sounds of night grew louder. In the distance, an owl hooted, sending an eerie shiver down her spine.

Was he right? Was she guilty of not even giving them a shot? Of shooting them down before they even gave it a chance?

She was being a total chickenshit and offering up lame excuses when at the heart of the matter she was just . . . afraid.

"What if it doesn't work out?" she asked, voicing one of those fears. "What if things end badly between us? We still have to work as a team, and if we fuck things up, it creates tension for the entire team yet we have to work together. Our camaraderie is what makes us so damn good. We could fuck up not only ourselves, but the entire team. Worse, we could end up getting one of the others killed. I don't think I could live with that."

"If it ever comes down to that, I'd be the one to leave," he said quietly. "I'd never force you out, P.J."

"It would still devastate me," she whispered.

"Don't you believe in forever?" he asked. "What about

all those romance novels you read? Don't they preach the happily-ever-after message?"

His words put an ache in her heart. She wanted happily ever after more than he could possibly know. She wanted forever. Problem was, she just wasn't sure she believed in it anymore. It was why she clung to her fiction so much. She immersed herself in books because there she could be anyone and it was easy to believe in love and happily ever after.

"You'd make an awesome romance heroine. I'm just saying."

She smiled. "You'd make a pretty badass romance hero too."

"See? It's fate. Or destiny. Whatever you want to call it. We're meant to be together. Wow, I'm starting to sound like a total pussy!"

She laughed, but the problem was, she was beginning to feel the same way. Cole just . . . fit. There wasn't anything she didn't like about him, even when he was annoying the shit out of her.

It was fun to bicker and snipe with him. He gave as good as he got but he never carried a grudge. Never took it too seriously. And he didn't let his ego get in the way of things. She'd saved his ass plenty of times and he never resented her for it.

Her KGI team was everything her first team wasn't. Loyal. They respected her. They stood by her even when it meant putting their jobs on the line.

The sudden thought occurred to her that she was a flaming hypocrite. It was like being blindsided by a right hook. Her thoughts must have been reflected on her face, because Cole's brow wrinkled in concern and he sat forward.

"What's up, P.J.? You okay?"

She let out a disgusted sigh and rubbed her forehead in agitation. "I was sitting here comparing S.W.A.T. with KGI and I was being all smug and self-righteous thinking that my team here is everything my old team wasn't. I've been so pissed at them for so long, but it occurred to me that I'm a huge fucking hypocrite."

He reared back in surprise. "Why the hell would you think something like that?"

"I turned my lover in for being dirty. I was so self-righteous and so 'must do the right thing' and I was so black-and-white back then. There were no reasons, no explanations. No excuses. You were either right or wrong. No in between. And yet here I am, having murdered three men in cold blood and casually plotting the death of a fourth. My hands are so stained with blood that I'll never wash them clean. At least Derek wasn't hurting anyone. He didn't kill anyone. He stole money from losers and drug dealers."

Cole scowled, his face darkening as he stared back at her. "You aren't comparing yourself to that asshole."

She made a sound of impatience. "Look at it objectively, Cole. I turn him in for being on the take. I get hung out to dry and I'm bitter because everyone turned on me. Shit happens here, I go off on my own and kill three men. Who's the bigger criminal? You guys have every reason to wash your hands of me."

"Now you're just pissing me off. It's not like you to be all martyr-like. Shut the fuck up and give yourself a break. You can't compare your situation to the dumb fuck you used to sleep with."

She blinked for a minute and then burst out laughing. Oh God. This was what she loved so much about Cole. He didn't let her get away with stupid shit and he always gave it to her straight.

Cole still looked disgruntled. "Those bastards needed killing. Even if they hadn't done what they did to you. What they've done to countless women and children is enough to take them out. You did the world a favor, and I'm not going to let you get down on yourself because you don't regret killing them. Does it make it better if you lament and feel guilty over killing them? If you're looking to me for judgment, you're shit out of luck. I'm not much of a black-and-white kind of guy. I spend too much time in those gray areas."

He got up and busied himself flipping the steaks. The sizzle was loud and the wind carried the scent of charcoal and cooking meat to her nostrils. She sniffed appreciatively and her stomach rumbled in response.

When he finished, he walked past her. "I'm going to turn the outside light on and get some bug spray so the mosquitoes don't carry you off. I'll be right back."

The door opened and closed and she was left alone counting the fireflies and reflecting on the conversation they were having.

Was she nothing more than a hypocritical, self-righteous prig? She'd always felt holier than thou about the fact that Derek was involved in shady dealings while on the job. It had affronted her and pricked her sense of honor. She'd been utterly disappointed that he hadn't upheld her lofty ideals. In her mind he'd failed not only himself and his team, but he'd failed her, and maybe that was why she'd never been able to forgive him.

But no matter what Cole said, she was no better than Derek. Her reasons may have been different for crossing that line, but the end result was the same. She'd crossed a line, and she could never go back.

Worse, she had no desire to go back. She felt no guilt, only savage satisfaction that she'd taken out three of the four men that she'd vowed revenge on.

It wasn't pretty. It certainly wasn't righteous. But she wasn't ducking the issue. She knew what she was. A cold-blooded killer.

What was Derek's sin when compared to hers?

She felt some of that old animosity ease and was able to let go of some of the resentment she'd harbored for so long. She'd sold Derek out, whether it was the right thing to do or not. For so long, she'd felt betrayed by him, but in essence it could be said that she was the one who betrayed him.

Hell of a time to have an epiphany and discover shit about yourself.

The light flashed on and then the door opened. Cole came back out carrying a glass of tea in each hand and a can of bug spray under his arm. He set one of the glasses in front of her and then leaned down to spray the insect repellent over her legs. She reached to cover her tea so he could spray her arms. When he was finished, he returned to his seat.

He leaned back in his chair and eyed her curiously. "So tell me what P.J. stands for."

She blinked and then stared at him, perplexed for a moment by the shift in conversation. She hadn't considered that the rest of the team didn't know what the initials stood for. Steele certainly knew because he'd barged through her background, leaving no stone unturned before he hired her on. She was sure Sam, Garrett and Donovan had done the same.

No one called her by her real name. Never had. A fact she was grateful for. She'd always wondered what she'd done to piss her mother off that she'd stick P.J. with such a hokey name.

"Come on, P.J. Give. I've never slept with a woman whose name I didn't know. Until you. It's kind of making me feel like a man whore."

She burst out laughing. "I ought to not tell you now so you can wallow in your man-whore-ness a little longer."

"You mock my pain. I have standards, you know."

She snickered again and then pinned him with a glare. "I'll only tell you if you swear to, first, never tell another soul, and second, never ever call me by my full name in public."

He held up his hand. "I swear."

"Penelope Jane," she mumbled.

"What's that? I couldn't hear you."

"Penelope Jane!" she said louder.

His nose wrinkled up. "Seriously?"

She sighed. "Yeah, seriously. Now maybe you see why I just go by my initials."

"You don't look like a Penelope Jane."

He looked genuinely baffled and was studying her like she was some weird, undiscovered species of bug.

"So what do I look like then?" she demanded.

"You look like a P.J."

She laughed again. "Well that's good, I suppose. I'm okay with looking like a P.J."

"Penelope Jane Rutherford," he said, as if he was testing the sound of it on his tongue. "I don't know, it's kind of growing on me. It's kind of pretty sounding."

"Don't get any ideas, Coletrane," she growled.

"There aren't enough Penelopes in the world. I don't know anyone named that."

She rolled her eyes. "Aren't those steaks done yet? I'm starving over here."

He shoved back his chair and flipped up the lid to the grill. He poked at one then flipped and flipped again.

"Nope. Need about five more minutes. I didn't even ask you how you like your meat."

She choked and covered it with a cough. When she looked back up, he was giving her a glare of impatience.

"For God's sake, you dirty-minded heifer."

She laughed and kept on laughing. "Oh come on, Cole. You have to admit, it sounded kinky. I mean, I could have said I like my meat hard."

He sighed and shook his head.

"Medium is fine," she said with a grin. "I like a little pink but not bloody."

"I'm heading in to get the potatoes out of the oven and all the fixings for them. As soon as I get back, I'll take the steaks off the grill and we can dig in."

"Awesome. I can't wait. The smell is killing me!"

Alone again for a few moments, P.J. marveled at how light she felt. It was almost as if the last six months hadn't happened. Like she and Cole were carrying on like always. Only this time it was more intimate. More personal.

The one thing she gave thanks for is that their one-night stand hadn't made things awkward between them. And who knows, maybe it would have under normal circumstances.

Their fling had been the start of a series of events that

even now she had a hard time believing. From that night forward, things had been insane, and she would never have believed she'd be looking back at the past six months remembering just how much her world had been altered.

"How's the leg?" Cole asked when he returned with potatoes.

He plopped one onto her plate and then set down the tray with the butter, sour cream and cheese so they were in easy reach.

Leg? She hadn't even thought about her leg the entire time they'd been talking. She had to concentrate hard to even feel the low hum of pain that was ever present in the background, muffled by the medication he'd given her.

"I'm good," she said, and meant it. She was better than she'd been in a very long time.

He bent and kissed her forehead, surprising her with the sweet gesture. She closed her eyes and savored the feel of his mouth on her skin. The kiss was full of warmth and comfort. Two things she was badly in need of.

He broke away and went to the grill. A moment later, he dished up the steaks and returned to the table. He forked a huge rib eye onto her plate and then served his own.

The smell was absolutely divine. Her mouth watered and she was already making a grab for her fork and knife, not even bothering with the potato right away.

The first bite made her moan with pleasure. It also made her realize how hungry she was.

She attacked her meal. There was no other word for it. She cut into it like she was afraid it was going to sprout legs and run away.

For several long minutes, they ate in silence and she focused solely on the wonderful experience of eating a delectable piece of prime steak. It was as close to a religious experience as she was going to come.

"I'd ask how the steak is, but your expression says it all," Cole said in amusement.

"Mmmm" was all she could get out.

They continued to eat, and she eventually slowed down

as she began getting that overstuffed feeling. It was nice, though. She knew she hadn't taken the best care of herself over the last months. Some days she hadn't eaten at all. Her entire focus had been revenge. She'd been consumed, and to a degree she still was.

"You want to head back in and go to bed or you want to hang out here and shoot the shit some more?" he asked as he pushed his plate away.

She was bone tired, even after her nap, but she didn't want the evening to end. She was more relaxed than she'd been in longer than she could remember. Sure, the pain medication helped, but being here with Cole was a balm to her soul.

"I like it out here," she said. "It's a gorgeous evening. Cool but not too cold. And the fireflies are giving us quite the show. You can see the reflection off the water. I could sit here forever and just watch the glow."

"I could watch you watching them forever," he said.

She felt his gaze on her and turned just so she could see him in her periphery. His eyes never left her. He seemed content to just watch her.

"So tell me about your family," she said. "You don't ever mention parents or siblings. I know Dolphin has a sister. He visits her a couple times a year. He hates his dad. Takes care of his mom quite a bit. Baker's parents are divorced and he doesn't see much of either of them. Renshaw mostly stays with his folks between missions because he figures there's no point in buying a home when he's never there. But you and Steele never say anything, not that Steele being closed mouthed is a huge surprise," she said wryly.

"Look who's talking," he pointed out. "I know nothing about your family. Or your past, other than what I've recently learned about S.W.A.T."

"Okay so you give and I'll give," she said, raising one brow in challenge.

"Seriously? You're going to tell me all your secrets?"

"Oh good grief," she muttered. "I'm the most boring person on the planet. I'm boring in self-defense because my upbringing was on the weird side."

Cole's brows went up. "Okay, now you have me curious."

She smiled sweetly. "Oh no, you first."

He shook his head. "Not much to tell, really. My folks were killed in a car accident my senior year of high school. I'm an only child, so no siblings in the picture."

"Oh damn," she said softly. "That had to suck."

For a moment she could see lingering sadness in his eyes. "Yeah, it did. I still miss them. I had a college scholarship to play baseball. I was a star player in high school. Took our team to the playoffs and we won the state championship my senior year. A week before my parents were killed."

"I had no idea you played baseball," she said in surprise.

He shrugged. "After they died, I was at loose ends. I mean I just kind of fell apart. Didn't go to school. Gave up my scholarship. Had people telling me I was fucking up life and my chance at the pros and it wasn't what my parents would have wanted. All I knew was that the two people I loved most in the world were gone and I didn't really give a fuck if I didn't play for a pro team. Why would I when they'd never be there to see me?"

"Yeah, I get it," P.J. said.

"So I grieved for a while. Felt sorry for myself. Wondered what the fuck to do with my life. I woke up in the middle of the night one night and thought, why not join the navy? I have no idea why I picked that branch. It was a total impulse decision and I went the next day to the recruiter so I couldn't change my mind. Turned out to be the best decision I ever made. It's made me who and what I am today. I was scared shitless going in, but once I got through boot camp everything just clicked into place."

"So why'd you leave then?"

"Good question. Honestly I think it's because I'd reached a goal and I kept thinking what next? I was a SEAL. I achieved something very few others do but I still felt restless. I heard about KGI through one of my buddies and it sounded right up my alley. I met with Sam and Garrett and then I resigned my commission. The rest, as they say, is history."

"I bet you just had issues with authority and having such a rigid set of rules to live by," she teased.

He smiled ruefully. "I admit, I like working for KGI and for Steele. I already told you I'm a gray-area guy. Not that there aren't plenty of gray areas in the military, but KGI kind of makes their own rules. They choose their missions. When you belong to Uncle Sam, you do what you're told whether you agree with it or not."

She nodded her understanding.

"So what about you? You never mention family."

She grimaced. "I grew up in a very religious environment."

He reared back in mock surprise. "You? Religious? With that mouth? You must have been the bane of your mother's existence."

"Ha-ha. You're so funny. I was a very sweet, nonviolent child, I'll have you know."

He had just taken a drink and he snorted and then choked as he tried to swallow it down without spewing.

"I bet you used to give the boys hell and I bet no one messed with you on the playground."

She sighed. "I was painfully shy. I was different from the other kids. No television. Just books. I wore dresses until I was a teenager. Wearing jeans to school my junior year was my big act of rebellion."

He looked at her in utter confusion. "You're serious, aren't you?"

She nodded. "Yup. I had a charismatic upbringing. Very holy-roller type of environment. Never cut my hair. Didn't wear pants. Very patriarchal church and home life."

Cole shook his head. "You've blown my mind. How in the hell did you go from that to where you are now?"

"My uncle was a big hunter and he used to take me. He'd let me dress up in camo and I felt like such a badass. We'd spend time sighting in our rifles and I was a natural. He encouraged my marksmanship. My mom had a fit when she realized just how much time I was spending 'playing with the devil's instruments,' as she put it."

"Wow," Cole said. "I'm at a loss for words. It boggles the mind. I wouldn't have guessed your background in a million years."

P.J. chuckled. "Yeah, most people wouldn't."

"So what happened? I mean, what did they think when you joined S.W.A.T., and do they know what you do for KGI?"

Her lips turned down, and for a moment she was silent as she relived the last time she'd seen her mother.

"We uh . . . don't speak."

Cole frowned. "Ever?"

"Not since I left high school. She washed her hands of me. Said I'd never amount to anything. I was too bent on a life of sin. My older brother was already a pastor of his own church, and I guess they thought I should be more like him. The way I figure it, they pray for the world, and I save it."

"So you seriously don't talk to them? It was over? Just like that?"

The incredulity in his voice bordered on condemnation and it rubbed her the wrong way.

"I couldn't be who they wanted me to be," she said quietly. "And they weren't willing to accept anything else. It wasn't my choice."

Cole grimaced. "I'm sorry. I probably sound all judgy. It's just that I'd give anything to have my parents back. I can't imagine not speaking to them or seeing them."

"No, it's okay. I'm being too touchy. I guess they're still a sore subject for me. I hadn't realized how much of one."

"What about your dad? I mean, all you've mentioned is your mother and how she felt."

P.J. curled her lip in disgust. "For such a patriarchal system in the church and supposedly the home, my mother wore the pants and my father was a spineless coward who shied away from any conflict. He wouldn't have stood up for me or anyone else against my mother. She ruled the roost and it was her way or the highway."

Cole shook his head. "That sucks. I guess I get why you

have such a take-it-or-leave-it attitude. Can't say I blame you."

"I just stopped trying to be someone I wasn't for people who'd never be satisfied with the end result anyway. Trying to please my mother was like trying to push a rope through the eye of a needle. I think my biggest sin was being born a girl who preferred to do boy things. She just wanted me to look pretty and marry young."

"Lucky for me you're such a rebel," Cole said with a grin. "It would suck if you were married with half a dozen hellions attached to your apron strings."

She shuddered. "Thanks for that image."

He laughed. But then his expression grew serious. "I like you just the way you are, P.J. Don't ever change. You're a very special woman. Don't ever think you aren't."

Warmth traveled to the very heart of her. Into her soul, chasing away long-held shadows and allowing the sun in after an endless winter.

She stared into his eyes, soaking up all the warmth she could. "I just want to say thank you, Cole."

He cocked his head. "What for?"

"Everything. For being you. For being so patient with me. For having my back."

His eyes softened. "I'll always have your back, P.J. You'll never have to look far to find me."

CHAPTER 28

P.J. was awake early the next morning. Her leg was stiff and she could barely move it to get out of bed without screeching pain shooting up her thigh.

She flexed and stretched her leg, grimacing as she tried to loosen the muscles.

Knowing she'd have to strip down when she got to the hospital, she opted to wear sweats and a T-shirt, this time pulling on a sports bra.

When she limped into the kitchen, she saw Cole at the table drinking a cup of coffee and reading the paper. It struck her how domestic the entire scene was. All that was missing was for her to walk over, kiss him and say good morning.

Was this what it was like for married couples? That comfortable existence that bordered on boring?

Cole looked up from the newspaper and his eyes warmed when he saw her. "Morning, P.J. How's the leg?"

Yeah, she could totally see them falling into this kind of routine. She loved that he seemed happy to see her. Would that ever lessen? Would they end up taking each other for granted? Would they lose the easy friendship between them and start sniping like an old married couple?

She shuddered at the thought. She was getting way ahead of herself anyway. They had far too many issues to work out before she could start thinking about long-term commitment.

"It was pretty stiff when I got up," she admitted. "Hurt like hell but I worked out some of the kinks, and if I keep moving, it stays loose."

He frowned. "Sit down. Let me get you something to eat and then I'll give you a pain pill. We'll leave as soon as you're done eating. I figure the quicker we get over there, the sooner we can get out and you aren't stuck the entire day at the hospital."

"You know me so well," she said with a grin.

She settled into a chair and watched as he fussed over her. It was such an odd sensation. She and Derek had been together two full years and had never developed the easy rapport she and Cole had. And she certainly couldn't ever imagine Derek actually doing the little things for her that Cole did.

The sex had been good. She'd give that to Derek, but in the end, that's all there'd been to their relationship. Sex. No emotional connection. No loyalty. Nothing she couldn't have gotten with any other man.

She'd always known that Derek felt threatened by her, but she'd ignored the simmering resentment, chalking it up to being the only woman on a male-dominated team. He never missed an opportunity to take her down a few notches and fuck with her confidence.

With Cole—and the other men on her team—there had been only acceptance and appreciation of her skills with a rifle. She hadn't known how truly difficult things had been for her on her old team until she'd joined KGI. Comparing the two now made her feel stupid for sticking with her old team as long as she had.

She had a good thing here, and she'd very nearly thrown it all away. Thank God they hadn't let her.

Her heart squeezed and emotion knotted her throat. They'd fought for her and hadn't let her walk away. Maybe they'd never know how much that meant, especially at a time when she most needed support and someone to anchor her.

A few minutes later, Cole served up scrambled eggs, bacon and toast along with orange juice. He set a pill beside her glass with instructions to take it after she'd eaten. Then he settled back into his chair and watched as she dug in.

"Not going to eat?" she asked around a bite.

"I already ate. Was just keeping the food warm for you."

"Thanks," she said softly, realizing she'd said that a lot lately. But could she ever really fully verbalize the scope of her gratitude?

"Eat up and we'll hit the road. I know you're probably still in a lot of pain, but I was thinking if we get you all checked out and premedicate you for the evening I could take you out on a date."

He hesitated and sounded a little nervous.

"You mean like on a real date?" she blurted.

"Yeah, you know. I take you someplace nice to eat, or as nice as we have in this neck of the woods. We relax. Have some good conversation and then maybe I get a kiss good night. One of *those* dates."

She smiled and then felt her smile grow even bigger until her teeth were flashing. "I'd like that. It sounds fun."

He visibly relaxed. His relief was so endearing that she wished they were closer so she could reach out and touch him. She'd never considered herself a needy person, but she needed . . . him. Needed the comfort of his friendship and the promise of something more.

"Then let's get moving so we can get this over with. Maybe after dinner we can rent some B movies and I'll make us popcorn."

"Cheesy disaster movies!" she exclaimed.

He grinned. "I knew you were my kind of girl."

"WELL I'm glad to see someone on your team has some sense and dragged you back kicking and screaming," Cathy said, sharp disapproval in her eyes.

P.J. sat dutifully and endured a stern lecture from her friend while she clipped out the stitches Donovan had set and then cleaned the wound.

"I was pretty pissed when I heard you went AWOL and nobody heard from you for six months," Cathy continued. "If I'd known you were going to do something that dumb-ass, I'd never have helped you get out of here that first time."

"You shouldn't have anyway," Cole said, a low growl in his voice.

Cathy sent him a glare over her shoulder and sniffed disdainfully. "Women have to stick together. You couldn't possibly understand the girlfriends' code. A good friend will bail you out when you land in jail, but a *very* good friend will be sitting beside you in that jail cell."

"How does that make any sense?" Cole asked, clearly baffled.

P.J. laughed. "What she means is that helping out a friend may not always make sense, but we do it anyway because that's what friends do."

"Is it any wonder men have no clue what goes on in a woman's mind?" he grumbled.

Cathy rolled her eyes. "Clueless is about the right description for men in general. Besides, as much as I didn't like it, P.J. did what she had to do at the time."

She glanced up and met P.J.'s gaze. "That doesn't mean that you need to go off like that again."

"Yes, ma'am," P.J. said meekly. "My team has made me see the error in my ways."

"Good men. Always did like them."

"What? You just said we're all a bunch of clueless idiots," Cole sputtered.

Cathy grinned. "Can't have you getting the big head."

Cole shook his head as Cathy set the last suture. Then he moved forward, looking at P.J.'s leg over Cathy's shoulder. "How's it look?"

"Donovan did a good job," Cathy said. "The wound is clean and free of infection. I'd still like to send her home with a prescription for antibiotics just in case. If she notices any redness or swelling around the wound, she needs to start on them immediately. If she starts running a fever, feels bad or just feels off in any way, you'll need to bring her back in so we can have a look-see. Donovan did an adequate job of stitching but I wanted to get in there and see for myself what we were dealing with."

"What kind of recovery time are we looking at?" Cole asked.

Cathy turned to face Cole. "Well, if she takes it easy and stays off her feet and doesn't try to do too much too soon, I'd say a couple weeks. But good luck getting her to do just that."

Cole snorted. "Tell me about it."

"Hey, guys?" P.J. broke in. "Hello? I'm sitting right here. Stop talking about me like I'm not present."

Cathy gave her a dismissive look. "I know better than to tell you all this with no witnesses. You only hear what you want to hear and disregard the rest. At least now Cole will know what you're supposed to do and make sure you do it."

"Sometimes friends can be a pain in the ass," P.J. grouched.

Cathy grinned. "That's what friends do, sugar."

P.J. smiled back at her. "Thanks, Cathy. I appreciate everything."

"Just focus on getting better. That's the best thanks you can give me." Her expression sobered and she put her hand on P.J.'s arm, squeezing lightly. "I worry about you, P.J."

"You don't have to worry about her anymore," Cole said firmly. "I fully intend to make sure she takes it easy and does what she's supposed to."

Cathy's eyes widened and then a broad smile split her lips. "Well, okay then. It would seem P.J. has met her match."

Cole cut a glance in her direction, those blue eyes gleaming with promise. "Oh yeah, most definitely."

Cathy took a step back, surveying P.J. with apparent satisfaction. Then she pursed her lips and said, "I'd give you a pair of crutches, but something tells me you wouldn't use them."

P.J. wrinkled her nose in distaste. "No. You're right. I wouldn't. I limp along just fine. A little pain isn't going to kill me."

Cathy shrugged. "Hardheaded woman. Okay, well I'm done with you. I'll give you back to Cole so you can be a pain in his ass instead of a pain in mine."

P.J. laughed and then slid gingerly off the bed. She held on to the edge for a long moment before pushing off to stand on her own.

Cole hovered at her elbow, his brow creased with concern. But he didn't make a fuss or a scene in front of Cathy, which she totally appreciated.

He did remain solidly at her side as she maneuvered her way out of the exam room and into the hall.

"You okay?" he asked quietly when they got outside the hospital.

She nodded. "Yeah. Hurts like a mofo, but I can deal."

He helped her into the passenger seat of his truck and then reached over her to snag a bottle of water in the center console. Still standing there, he opened the glove compartment and retrieved the container holding the pain medication.

"Here, go ahead and take another pill so you stay ahead of the pain. And if you want to take a rain check on tonight, we can go back to the house so you can take a nap on the couch."

She laid her hand over his and he went completely still. She could feel the hitch in his breath as it stuttered over his lips.

"I want to go, Cole. I'll take the pill and I'll be fine. I'm looking forward to our . . . date."

He touched his knuckle to her face and brushed it down the curve of her cheekbone. Then he simply leaned in and kissed her forehead. "So am I."

CHAPTER 29

"OH my God, I'm stuffed," P.J. groaned as she pushed her plate away. "That was so freaking good."

Cole had taken her to this little hole-in-the-wall restaurant that resembled a shack twenty minutes from his house. They served a variety of country-style food, but the seafood was out of this world.

She'd ordered the seafood platter and damn near ate the entire thing.

"I practically live here when I'm home," Cole said. "Not that I can't cook, but the food is great and the prices are reasonable. No sense cooking for one when I can come here."

"If I had a place like this to eat, I'd never cook either," she said.

"Glad you enjoyed it. You need a few more meals like this one." His tone grew serious. "You lost a lot of weight over the last six months, P.J. Weight you couldn't afford to lose. You could stand to pack on a few more pounds."

If he didn't sound so genuinely concerned, his comment

would irk her. But it was obvious he was worried, and she couldn't fault him for that. She'd had plenty to say to him when he was convalescing after taking a bullet. It was her turn to shut up and take it.

The waitress walked up and P.J. sat back with a satisfied sigh while Cole settled the bill. So far this dating thing had been . . . nice. They'd had a great meal and casual conversation. It had been fun, and when was the last time she could say she had a good time?

The last months had been anything but fun.

For that matter the only fun times she could recall were the times she spent with Cole and her team. They were who she felt at-home with.

"You ready?" Cole asked, shaking her from her thoughts.

She pushed back her chair and then braced her palms on the table, keeping most of her weight on her hands until she had her feet under her.

As she turned toward the doorway, Cole slid his arm around her waist, pulling her into the shelter of his body. She fit perfectly underneath his arm, her head just on level with his shoulder.

Without giving it a second thought, she wrapped her arm around him in return as she limped toward the exit.

There was a chill to the air tonight that had been absent the night before. Spring was still deciding if it was here to stay and winter was fighting a losing battle.

She shivered lightly as the wind picked up, and Cole rubbed his hand up and down her arm to warm her.

"I'll build us a fire when we get back to the house if you like. We can kick off our shoes, get in some comfy clothes and park it on the couch to watch our movies."

"Mmm, that sounds nice."

It sounded . . . romantic. A cozy evening on the couch at home watching movies. It was something she'd have done as a teenager, and now, knocking on the door to thirty, she was just as giddy as her teenage self used to be.

"Hey, how old are you, Coletrane?" she blurted.

He stopped in the process of opening his truck door for her and looked at her with a raised brow. "Thirty-two. Why?"

She shrugged. "No reason. I just realized I never knew how old you were."

"And it occurred to you that you just had to know right this moment?" he asked with a chuckle.

He opened the door and waited as she slid into the seat. Then he walked around to get in on his side.

"Well, yeah," she said as he pulled out of the parking lot. "It would be kind of weird if you were younger than me."

He glanced sideways at her. "Why the hell would it be weird? And *am* I younger than you?"

"No. I'll be thirty this year. And I don't know why. I've just always assumed you were older."

He shook his head. "You get some strange ideas, P.J. Age is irrelevant. Whether you were older or younger than me wouldn't change how I feel about you. I hope to hell it wouldn't affect how you felt about me."

The last thing she wanted was to cause dissension between them.

"Honestly, I was just curious. It's no big deal."

She had her elbow propped on the console, and he reached over, sliding his fingers down her arm until he got to her hand. Then he simply picked it up, curled his fingers around hers and rested their joined hands between them.

For a long moment she simply stared at his hand cupped over hers. Warmth spread up her arm and into her chest. It was the simplest thing in the world. At her age, it shouldn't send an odd flutter through her chest or make her feel like a breathless teenager on her first date.

But he had that effect on her. She felt like she was being courted. God, what a silly, outdated word, but it was so appropriate. Cole seemed to have an old soul when it came to relationships, and she thought it was kind of cute.

The men she was used to going out with forwent the courting phase and went straight for the fly of her jeans.

There was nothing slow or patient about their methods. It was usually a question of "do you want to fuck or not?"

Clearly she'd been hanging out with the wrong guys.

"You're quiet," he said.

She laughed. "I was just thinking that I've been hanging with the wrong guys."

"Oh? Do tell. What prompted that epiphany?"

"The guys I was with in the past were douche bags. I can't think of a single one who ever held my hand, offered me pain medication, cooked me breakfast or wanted to watch cheesy disaster movies on the couch."

"Appalling," he said in mock shock.

"I know, isn't it?"

He picked up her hand and kissed it. "I'm glad you've seen the error of your ways."

She smiled and leaned back against the headrest. Damn but she could really fall hard for this guy. Her teammate. Someone she had no business entering a relationship with. It could fuck up all sorts of things. Or it could end up being the start of something truly wonderful.

Oh, to have a crystal ball.

It was completely dark by the time he pulled into his driveway. The porch light glowed warmly, illuminating the homey feel of his house.

Welcome home, it seemed to say.

Cole cut the engine and hopped out, hurrying around to her side as she opened her own door. He reached in to take her hand and helped her out.

Still holding her hand, he shut her door and then headed toward the porch, matching his step to her awkward, slower one. She leaned on him a little harder when she navigated the steps but was pleased with the progress she was making.

He flipped on the lights as they entered the house, and he took her to the couch first, insisting she sit back. He lifted each foot in turn and slid her tennis shoes off, tossing them to the side. Then he dragged the ottoman from its position in front of the armchair over to the couch so she could prop her leg up.

"All comfy?" he asked.

"I couldn't be any more comfortable," she replied.

"I'll just go get us something to drink and throw a bag of popcorn in the microwave and then we'll crank up the end-of-the-world movies."

"Awesome!"

She watched as he walked away and continued staring when he disappeared from sight. She was falling so hard for him and she was awash in the giddy sensations of a new relationship. When everything was new and fresh and every little thing was exciting. When each touch was a thrill and you savored even the briefest contact.

They'd already had sex, for God's sake, but this was completely different. It was as if that one night they'd shared together was a lifetime ago and erased from the equation. They were starting brand-new, as if they'd just met, only the ease in which they got along hinted at a long-standing friendship that was charting new territory.

He returned five minutes later with a bowl of popcorn and two cans of cola. He handed her a drink and the popcorn and then went to the television to retrieve the remote.

As he settled onto the couch beside her, he turned on the TV and started flipping through the menu of movies they could watch.

"So what'll it be? The world taken over by aliens or the world engulfed by a giant tsunami?"

"Definitely the aliens. Can't kill a tsunami. The alien movie will have lots of gratuitous violence."

"Excellent choice. Aliens it is."

He leaned back, putting his arm over her head and then down around her shoulders. He pulled her close, and she was happy to snuggle into his side. The popcorn was sitting on his lap within easy reach, and she munched idly as the movie began.

"You realize how unrealistic this is," P.J. said, an hour into the movie.

"I would have never guessed," Cole said dryly.

"Well come on. Put KGI up against the aliens. We'd

take them out in two seconds flat. These aren't even scary aliens. Why do they keep fighting them hand to hand? Just throw a fucking grenade and take out the lot of them."

Cole laughed. "You have a point, but then there'd be no action and no conflict, thus no movie."

"Speaking of like dudsville for an alien movie, remember that Mel Gibson movie with the aliens and there's all this tension and hoopla over the alien invasion and he and his kids survive the night and then they hear on the radio the next day that some tribe in Africa discovered a way to kill them all and boom it was over? Talk about total letdown."

"Well, if I remember right, the aliens weren't really the point of that movie," Cole said.

"Yeah, well, they should have been. It was more interesting than the hokey come-to-Jesus moment the guy supposedly had."

Cole laughed and shook his head.

"I don't want to have to think during a movie," P.J. said. "I just want brainless violence and lots of cheesy action."

"Are you trying to tell me your IQ isn't setting the world on fire?"

She elbowed him in the gut and he let out a yelp. He wrapped both arms around her, trapping hers against her body, and then he grinned triumphantly at her.

"If I didn't have an injury, I'd totally kick your ass right now, Coletrane."

"Yeah, yeah, all bark and no bite."

His mouth hovered precariously close to hers, so close she could feel the warmth of his breath over her lips. She glanced up, meeting his gaze, wondering if he was thinking the same thing she was thinking.

"I'm going to kiss you, P.J."

Evidently he was.

"I was hoping you would," she whispered.

His mouth covered hers, warm and sweet. He relaxed his grip on her arms and slid one hand up to her face to cup her cheek as he deepened his kiss.

His tongue delved over hers, salty from the popcorn, with a hint of butter and the sweetness of the cola. His fingers dug into her hair, around to the back of her head and then down to her nape.

"Make love to me, Cole."

He pulled back in surprise, his eyes narrowing with concern.

"I don't want to push you into anything, P.J. It's probably better if we wait until you're ready."

"I'm ready," she said, plunging ahead recklessly. "I want this. I want *you*."

He stared at her a long moment as if he couldn't make up his mind. She pulled him down into another long kiss, this time making sure she was the aggressor.

When he broke away this time, his breaths came in ragged bursts. His chest heaved and it was clear he was battling his urge to give in.

"I distinctly remember you saying you were going to take me home and make me feel all better," she said.

"Christ, P.J. Are you sure? This is too important. I don't want to fuck this up."

She stroked her hand over his jaw. "Please."

It was the *please* that seemed to do it. He pushed himself up from the couch and then reached down, sliding his arms underneath her, and plucked her from the cushions.

He strode toward his bedroom and shouldered the door open.

"Get the light," he directed.

She swiped her hand along the wall until she found the switch and then flipped it up, flooding the room with light. He carried her to the bed and gently set her down.

"We have to be careful," he said. "I don't want to hurt your leg. Let me take off your pants first."

Her leg was the last thing she was thinking of. She wanted him close. Wanted to replace the memory of Nelson and Brumley with Cole. Just Cole. He'd chase away her demons. She was sure of that.

He carefully slid her sweats down over her hips and

down her legs, taking care not to bump her wound. His fingers grazed her skin, setting fire to her senses. A thousand chill bumps danced across her thighs and midriff when he let his hands glide back up her bare legs and then under her T-shirt.

He pulled upward, baring more of her, and she lifted her arms over her head, a signal that it was okay for him to take the shirt too.

Now left in only her bra and panties, she trembled as shadows lurked in her mind. She forced her attention to Cole, refusing to allow anything to ruin this moment. But even so, a chill settled over her.

Her scars were there for him to see, and they were still raw looking. Ugly. Marks put there by other men.

"Tell me what you want, P.J. You're calling the shots here. Tell me how to please you."

"I'm cold," she whispered. "Make me warm, Cole. Please take away the cold."

He stripped out of his clothing and carefully lowered his body to hers. He stroked her hair away from her face and kissed her, long and leisurely.

He broke from her mouth and pressed a tender line from her lips down her jawline and to the sensitive flesh beneath her ear. More goose bumps broke out, but this time she didn't feel the same chill she had before.

His warmth bled into her, soothing away her fears and giving her soul deep comfort.

Holding her tightly to him, he rolled so they were resting on their sides. His hand smoothed down her arm all the way to her fingertips and then on to her hip before slowly gliding upward again, this time going underneath her arm, over the curve of her waist and to her breast.

His pace was slow and lazy, as if he had all the time in the world. He seemed determined not to rush her, and she realized for the first time how hard her rape had to have been for him as well.

Even now, despite the slow pace he'd set, his jaw was tight, and she could tell it was difficult for him to go this

slow and be this patient. In that moment, she fell even
harder for a man she was already well on her way to completely falling for.

"Kiss me," she whispered. "Make love to me."

He groaned softly as his lips melted over hers. Their
tongues met and tangled. Hot and wet. Breathless and needy.

His hand moved downward, between her legs, sliding
through her wetness, teasing and caressing in gentle strokes.

"We have all night, baby," he murmured. "Let's not
rush. I want to make sure you're with me every step of
the way."

She sighed and snuggled closer to him, wanting and
needing that flesh-to-flesh contact. Her leg protested
fiercely when she slid it over his, but she didn't care. Nothing was going to ruin this moment for her.

He made his goal to touch every inch of her skin. No
part of her body went untouched. He licked and kissed his
way from her toes all the way to her eyelids. He gave extra
attention to her breasts, teasing and toying with the nipples
until they were straining upward, begging for more.

But it was when he traced the lines of each one of her
scars and then followed his fingers with his mouth, sweetly
kissing every puckered inch of the wounds, that her heart
squeezed and she found it hard to breathe.

He was telling her without words that her scars meant
nothing to him. He didn't shy away from them. Didn't
recoil over their ugliness. He made certain there was no
doubt in her mind that he accepted every single part of her.

God, but she wanted to cry. She wanted to let go of the
grief that had plagued her for so long. She felt safe with
Cole. Her harbor. Her shelter. The one person she could
turn to and he'd never think her weak.

His palms glided warmly over her body. His fingers
stroked and his mouth made love to her all on its own.

She was senseless with need, and pleasure was molten
lava in her veins. More potent than the strongest drug.

She was in a haze, her surroundings blurred. She felt her
legs being parted, felt the twinge of pain as her injured leg

protested the movement. Then a hard body covered hers and panic splintered through her consciousness, bringing an abrupt halt to every pleasurable sensation she'd been fully immersed in.

She reacted blindly, desperate to defend herself. She'd never allow anyone to hurt her that way again. A sob escaped, loud, like thunder in her ears. She fought desperately, pain lancing up her leg until she cried out.

She rolled, trying to get away, and she fell onto the floor, the blanket from the bed tangled around her feet. She nearly blacked out from the pain after landing on her injured leg. Or maybe she had.

It was as if she were two completely different people. One who embraced the idea of making love to Cole as if nothing had ever happened to her—one rooted solidly in denial—and the other? Still trapped on that couch in Vienna, powerless against the effects of the drug while two men raped her body and mind.

And the one currently winning the battle for self-preservation was that terrified, brutalized victim that she'd tried so hard to forget existed for the last six months.

When some of the overwhelming panic dissipated and she became aware of her surroundings once more, she was sitting on the floor, her arms wrapped protectively around her body as she rocked back and forth. Tears were streaming down her face and she was helpless to stop them.

Oh God. What had she done?

A blanket fell over her shoulders and was pulled tightly around her until she was covered. Eventually some of the awful shaking ceased and warmth began to bleed back into her body.

She was lifted, cradled against a hard chest and then set on the edge of the bed, that blanket still securely wrapped around her.

"P.J. P.J., baby, it's all right. You're safe. Nobody can hurt you here. It's me, Cole. Okay? Open your eyes. Look at me, honey. Look at me so I know you're all right."

She blinked and then tried to focus on his face. He was

kneeling in front of her, and she could barely make out his features for the tears clouding her vision.

"I'm sorry," she croaked out.

"Oh God. Don't apologize, baby. Never that."

He moved to sit beside her on the bed and pulled her into his arms. She burrowed tightly against him, seeking more of his warmth. She pressed her face into his neck and closed her eyes. She wanted to die. She was horrified by what had happened. She wasn't even sure *what* had happened. One minute she'd been wrapped up in the beauty of their lovemaking and the next she'd been so filled with panic that she'd completely freaked out.

She clung to him, humiliated by the tears that wouldn't end. She was shaking from head to toe, and the memory of that night was so vibrant in her mind that no amount of wishing would make it go away. She could still smell her own blood, remembered how it felt, slick and sticky against her. She started to gag, and Cole gripped her tighter.

"Deep breaths, P.J. In and out. Real slow. Come on. Breathe with me."

He pulled her away so she was forced to look at him, and he stared intently, mimicking the inhaling and exhaling he wanted her to do.

"Tell me if you're going to be sick. I'll take you into the bathroom."

She shook her head blindly, determined not to let herself lose more control than she already had.

Gradually her pulse slowed and her breathing steadied. The shaking stopped and the panic eased. The images faded into the shadows and the smell of blood left her.

But the tears kept coming, slipping over her cheeks as she stared numbly at Cole.

"I'm sorry," she said again. Because what else was there for her to say? What guy wanted to have sex interrupted by a major meltdown and then have to ask the woman if she needed to be sick?

And God, she'd been the one who'd pushed! He'd wanted to wait. He hadn't thought she was ready. He'd wanted to take things slow. She'd been so sure. But it was just more of her refusal to accept what had been done to her. If she didn't think about it, then it didn't exist. Only now, the past had come back to bite her on the ass in a major way.

"I'm sorry," she whispered. "I'm so sorry for ruining everything."

He looked furious, and he shook his head emphatically. "You aren't apologizing for this. It's me who should be apologizing. I *knew* you weren't ready for this and I should have put a stop to it. I'm a complete asshole for even contemplating making love to you so soon after what happened."

She shook her head just as emphatically. "No. I thought I was ready. I mean, I was. I don't know what happened. I wanted it, Cole. I wasn't scared. I was right there with you and then bam, out of nowhere, panic. Oh my God, the panic was paralyzing and all I could see was *them* and I even smelled my blood. I *felt* it. Sticky and wet on my skin. How it felt when he smeared it over me with his own body."

She shuddered and physically recoiled from the images she described.

Cole's eyes were murderous and his jaw was so tight it bulged.

Her first instinct was to flee, and she fought it with everything she had. She made herself sit there and face Cole. She had to do this. She had to face it. It wasn't going away no matter how hard she wished it.

"Don't let me run from this," she blurted. "It's what I do. I run when things get tough. I ran from my old team and the situation there. I ran from the reality of what happened to me in Vienna. I ran from you and my team because I couldn't deal with what happened. Don't let me run from this," she begged.

He stroked her hair with his hand and gently kissed the top of her head. "If you run, I'll just go after you and haul you right back to me."

She let out another quiet sob, nearly choking on it in an effort to prevent it escaping.

"Why do you even want to be involved with me?" she

asked. "I'm a complete mess. I don't have my head on straight. I'm a master at fucking up everything that's good in my life."

"But you're my mess," Cole said quietly. "I don't need you to be perfect. I just need you to be you because that's who I care about."

She reached for him, hugging him tightly to her. He hugged her just as tightly, his arms like steel around her body.

"It's going to be okay, P.J.," he whispered next to her ear. "I'm not going anywhere and we'll get through this. Together."

She closed her eyes, savoring the promise. It was the only tangible thing to hold on to when so much else was steeped in murkiness. She couldn't trust herself. Couldn't trust her state of mind. But she could trust Cole. He wouldn't let her go.

CHAPTER 30

COLE paced the kitchen floor, wondering for the hundredth time if he'd made a huge mistake. He wasn't sure how P.J. would take it. It had been presumptuous of him to barge ahead and follow through with his idea, and now he was having serious doubts. The last thing he wanted was to piss P.J. off and have her cut and run like she said she often did.

He blew out a huge breath and ran a hand through his short-cut hair. Damn it but he'd blown it big last night. He damn well knew that he shouldn't be making a move that soon after her rape.

And the very fact that she seemed to be handling it so well should have been a big-ass warning sign. She'd been in denial ever since the night those bastards had hurt her. She'd shoved everything back, refusing to face it because that's what she had to do in order to cope. She'd focused all her energy on revenge.

He felt like a total bastard. She'd fallen completely apart. He'd ended up holding her until she'd drifted off to sleep, and he'd made damn sure he got up before her so she wouldn't feel any awkwardness when she woke up.

It pissed him off that she'd actually thought she had to apologize to him. *Apologize*, for Christ's sake. He was so disgusted with himself.

To take his mind off the phone call he'd placed just moments earlier, he busied himself making breakfast. He was going to bring her breakfast in bed and make damn sure that there was no awkwardness between them or that, God forbid, she'd try to apologize again.

He plated the pancakes, took the pan of bacon off the burner and then put the pieces on a saucer. After grabbing the bottle of syrup from the pantry, he arranged everything on a breakfast tray and started for the bedroom.

She was still fast asleep when he entered the room. The satisfaction of seeing her asleep in his bed, her head on his pillow, was overwhelming.

She looked like she belonged there. Belonged to him.

There were deep shadows under her eyes as if she hadn't rested well the night before. They made her look much more fragile than he knew her to be. Or maybe he'd made a mistake by assuming she was a lot stronger than she was.

He lowered himself to the edge of the bed, tray across his lap, and he quietly called her name. "P.J. Wake up, baby. I have breakfast for you."

She stirred and mumbled something in her sleep.

"P.J., wake up," he said again.

Her eyelids fluttered, revealing cloudy green eyes. She looked confused, as if she were trying to gather her thoughts. He knew the moment she remembered everything that had happened. Her lips turned down into a frown and shame darkened her eyes.

"Hey, I brought you breakfast," he said, determined not to allow her to feel even a moment's awkwardness.

She carefully pushed herself upward, grimacing when she flexed her leg. She grabbed one of the pillows and put it behind her back so she was propped up, and then he placed the tray over her lap, pulling out the legs so it was steady.

"It smells wonderful," she said with a wan smile.

"Dig in. I already ate, but I'm happy to keep you company while you enjoy."

She glanced nervously at him then retreated, focusing on the food in front of her.

He cursed under his breath and wondered again if he'd made a huge mistake. He may as well lay it all out, and if she got mad, deal with it then. He could always call Sam back and cancel the whole thing.

"I made a phone call this morning," he began. "This may not be something you want to do, and I'll understand if it pisses you off. I just thought that it might help."

She cocked her head and stared back at him, her brow furrowed in puzzlement. "Why would I be pissed?"

He grimaced. "I arranged for you to hook up with the Kelly women today. I told Sam I'd drive you over after breakfast so you could spend some time with Rachel, Sophie, Sarah and Shea."

She blinked in surprise. "Oookay."

He could tell she was confused and he rushed to provide an explanation. Hell, it had sounded good at the time. Now it just seemed silly.

He rubbed his hand over his nape in agitation. "Look, I just thought . . . I thought that since they'd gone through some of the stuff you're going through, they could help. I don't know, maybe you could talk to them about it. I thought it might help to know you aren't alone. They've endured some pretty heavy shit. Especially Sarah. She was raped too."

For a long moment P.J. just stared at him. He swallowed nervously, anxiety nipping at his gut. The last thing he wanted was to fuck things up between him and P.J. And this may very well be the thing to do it.

P.J. was intensely private, if nothing else. She wasn't the kind to spread her business far and wide. He was only now learning shit about her that he never knew, and he'd worked with her for four years.

But then her expression softened and her eyes glowed with a warm light.

"Thank you," she said. "It was very sweet of you to think of doing that for me."

Relief was crushing. He damn near wilted on the spot.

"So you aren't mad?"

Her brow furrowed even deeper. "Mad because you care about me? Enough that you'd drive me all the way out to the KGI compound because you think meeting up with the Kelly wives would help me? You're a very special man, David Coletrane. I don't know why the hell you bother with me, but I'm so very glad you do."

It was all he could do not to haul her into his arms and never let her go.

"Okay then," he said gruffly. "If you want, finish up and get dressed and we'll set out as soon as possible so it's not too late when we get back."

She smiled and forked another bite of pancake into her mouth. "You know, I could get used to this kind of five-star service."

He relaxed, warmth spreading through his chest. If this was what it felt like to be in love, he figured he didn't mind it so much after all.

CHAPTER 31

THE ride to the Kelly compound was tense and silent. Cole attempted to make small talk several times, but P.J.'s mind was preoccupied with the upcoming meeting with all the Kelly women.

The truth was, they made her uncomfortable. She had no idea what to say around them. Had nothing in common with them. She had no idea what to say about babies and girly stuff, and the very last thing she wanted was some come-to-Jesus moment where they got touchy-feely and bared their souls.

The mere idea had her in hives.

But Cole had arranged it because he truly cared about her, and she knew he had her best interests at heart. So how could she possibly refuse without being an ungrateful bitch?

She couldn't.

Cole had been so nervous and so worried that he'd stepped over the line that she would have done anything at all to reassure him.

So what if she'd rather face an entire squad of crazy-ass terrorists than four other women?

After what she'd put him through last night, she owed him a lot, and if it made him feel better, she'd endure damn near anything.

When they pulled into the compound, P.J.'s eyes widened at the progress that had been made. It looked very much near to completion. There was a helipad, training facilities and a firing range. The only thing that looked as though it wasn't finished was the single airstrip where the Kelly jets could land and be hangared.

A lot had happened in six months. She suddenly felt out of the loop. A stranger among people she'd worked with for four years.

Her eyes widened when she saw a group at the firing range. She recognized Nathan, Joe and Swanny but not the other two with them. And one of them was a woman. Her blond hair was gathered into a ponytail and she wore a baseball cap, but it was obvious she was female.

She was much smaller in stature than the man she stood beside. He dwarfed her, but then he was bigger than Nathan, Joe and Swanny. Even from a distance she could tell he was a big, muscled man.

"New recruits?" she asked lightly.

"She's not replacing you, P.J."

P.J. blinked. Okay, so maybe the thought *had* crossed her mind. Not that she was being replaced, exactly, but that maybe before they'd found P.J. again they'd brought this woman on board to fill the vacant spot on Steele's team.

"She's on Nathan and Joe's team. Donovan has wanted to add a third team for a while. Nathan and Joe are taking it. Swanny's on it and they recruited Skylar and Zane."

"Oh," P.J. said, trying to ignore the surge of relief that flooded her.

He continued driving past the range and to the houses that were nestled at the back of the massive expanse of land that KGI owned.

"Ethan and Rachel's house is done," P.J. said.

"Yep. Everyone's is finished. Well, except for Van and Joe's. Van's the holdout. He's still living in the log cabin on the lake and Joe's been bunking with him. But everyone who is married is living inside the compound."

"Even Marlene and Frank?"

Cole smiled. "They don't want to move from their house. They say there are way too many memories wrapped up in the house they raised their family in. Sam's pissed about it, and last I heard, he and Garrett were trying to have an exact replica of their house built here."

P.J. nodded. "After what happened to Marlene, I can imagine her sons' worry. She needs to be safe. KGI is only going to gain more enemies as time goes by. They certainly aren't going to be making any friends."

"That's true. It's why Steele and I didn't want you to stay alone in Denver. You'd be a much easier target. I'm sure Brumley isn't just sitting around twiddling his thumbs and waiting for you to flush him out of whatever dark hole he's crawled into."

P.J.'s face darkened into a scowl. "I wish the son of a bitch *would* find me. Would save me the trouble of going after his ass."

Cole reached for her hand and squeezed. "We'll get him, P.J."

As they rolled to a stop in front of one of the houses, P.J. suffered another bout of nervousness. Which was pretty stupid considering she'd faced gun-wielding maniacs and dodged grenades and countless other explosives plus an entire army of crazy-ass terrorists with machine guns all shooting at her.

She didn't wait for Cole to come around to help her. It suddenly seemed important that she could make it on her own and that she wouldn't show any weakness.

It nearly killed her to put her injured leg down and put weight on it, but she gritted her teeth and used the door for leverage as she got out.

Before she and Cole made it to the front of the vehicle, Sam met them at the steps to his house.

He gave P.J. a long, assessing look. "How are you?" he asked quietly.

She swallowed. Okay, this was definitely awkward. She really didn't want to get into any particulars with Sam. She cleared her throat of the knot forming. "I'm fine. Cole's taking good care of me."

"Sophie and the others are around back on the patio playing with Charlotte. Can you make it or do you need help?"

"I'm fine," P.J. muttered again.

Her damnable pride was rearing its ugly head again, but she was not going to ask her boss for help. He was likely pissed off enough at her as it was. She'd probably caused him enough grief for an entire year.

She limped toward the gate that would take her around to the back of the house. It made her a total chickenshit that she wanted Cole with her, and she knew he'd come if only she asked. But this was supposed to be for her. Cole had gone to a lot of trouble, and she didn't want to let him down. She didn't want to let *herself* down.

She hesitated when she heard a child's shriek of laughter and the accompanying laughter from the adults. She stood at the corner, watching the blond-haired little imp run after a golden retriever puppy while the women sat on the steps of the deck watching with big smiles on their faces.

They didn't look like women who'd undergone the same kind of shit P.J. had been through, even though she knew differently. P.J. had been a part of each mission that had brought these women back home where they belonged. And they'd all endured their own version of hell. They were survivors. They were fierce. And shit, it killed her to admit it, but they intimidated her because she didn't feel like she measured up. Especially after her freak-out last night.

She continued to watch from a distance, her gut tightening more with each passing moment. Of the four women, P.J. knew the least about Sarah. She was quieter and more withdrawn than the others. It always made P.J. grin that Garrett stayed in trouble with her over his potty mouth and was forever slipping up when she wasn't around.

Cole had told her that she'd been raped before she and

Garrett had met and that Sarah's brother had killed the man responsible. P.J. had silently cheered him on, even back then before her own attack had happened.

A man couldn't be all bad if he was willing to take out the monster responsible for hurting his sister.

P.J. most identified with Sophie, Sam's wife. She was a fighter. Even five months pregnant and running for her life, she'd kicked some pretty serious ass. Hell, she'd even shot her own father. That took some balls.

But Rachel was also a resilient, kick-ass survivor in her own quiet way. Of all of them, she'd endured the most for the longest. A year in hell. One P.J. couldn't even begin to imagine or fathom. What Rachel had suffered made what P.J. had experienced seem insignificant in comparison. P.J. had worried that Rachel may not ever fully recover. P.J. had been there when Ethan had carried her out of the jungle. She'd seen Rachel at her lowest point. But she'd come a long way from that frightened, powerless victim she'd been, and she'd made great strides thanks to the support network around her.

P.J. was envious of that if she was honest with herself. Every single Kelly would lay down his life for her or any of the other Kelly women. No hesitation. No regrets.

She was so absorbed in her analysis of the women that she failed to notice Sophie walking her way until the other woman was directly in front of her.

"Hi, P.J.," Sophie said with a smile. "Cole said you were coming over. I'm very happy you did."

P.J.'s palms were damp but she resisted the urge to wipe them down her pants. She managed a convincing smile back.

"Er, thanks for having me. I mean, it was nice of you guys to put your day on hold."

Sophie waved her hand. "Come on over. The only part of the day we put on hold was the opening of the wine. Now that you're here, we're going to remedy that." She finished with a genuine, warm smile that made P.J. relax and lose some of the awful tension in her gut.

She limped behind Sophie and found herself the object of scrutiny of the other three women as they watched her approach. Sure enough, as Sophie had said, there was a wine bottle and glasses on the patio table.

It reeked of a girly social. All that was missing was a teapot, some cute little mini sandwiches with the crusts cut off and some funky dip that looked like a cat puked in the bowl.

P.J. was more used to beer, bad music and even worse company. It surprised the hell out of her that she was actually starting to think this wasn't going to be such a bad afternoon. It might even be . . . fun.

"Here's P.J., finally home," Sophie said. "She's going to hang out with us today while she's recovering. I figure she needs a break from Cole by now." She turned back to P.J. "We've all been so worried about you."

P.J. started to defend Cole, but she realized the other woman was simply teasing her. She shrugged off any remaining reluctance and offered a hesitant but genuine smile in the other women's directions. They'd worried about her? They'd actually known she was gone? P.J. couldn't imagine the overprotective Kellys allowing their women to know a whole lot about what went on with KGI. She wouldn't have imagined that they would have known she'd left, much less worried over that fact.

"Hi, P.J.," Shea offered, a broad smile widening her pretty features.

"How's your leg?" Rachel asked in a soft voice. "Ethan said you were shot."

P.J. looked down with a rueful smile. "It's not too bad. A clean through and through. Could have been much worse. I'll be back in action soon."

Sarah shuddered. "I don't see how you can live with the constant danger. And you're so casual about being shot!"

"Just part of the job," P.J. said easily. "It's something you get used to."

"Well, come and sit," Sophie insisted. "Get off that leg. You need to have your feet up. Let me get you a glass of wine. I've told Sam to go find something to do and for the men not to bother us today. They're probably somewhere cowering in fear of what evil plan we're hatching."

P.J. allowed herself to be ushered into one of the chairs, and then Shea dragged another over so she could put her leg up.

A sudden thought occurred to P.J., one that alarmed her, and she glanced up at Shea, her brow furrowed. "You aren't going to do any of that mind-meld stuff to help my leg, are you? I know how much that hurts you, so don't even think about it."

Shea blinked for a moment and then burst out laughing. "Mind meld. That's a new word for it. And to answer your question, no. I'm afraid my gift is random. I can't connect to people at will. My sister can, but I can't."

P.J. felt embarrassed at just blurting it out like that, but the last thing she wanted was for Shea to take on her pain. It would piss Nathan off and cause a big fuss. Not to mention, P.J. had witnessed firsthand just how much suffering it caused Shea when she helped others with her extraordinary gift. It was her injury and she could deal with it.

Shea and her sister, Grace, who was with Rio, the other team leader, had unique abilities that defied scientific explanation. There was a whole bizarre story behind it, involving experiments and pairing certain couples with supernatural abilities together to see what offspring they produced. Shea and Grace had been two such experiments that had managed to escape and break free from the people who wanted to harness and use their abilities for their own purposes.

The whole thing was beyond P.J.'s scope of understanding. She wouldn't have believed any of it if she hadn't seen for herself the results of one of those mind-melding sessions.

It reminded her of her charismatic religious upbringing and the whole idea of faith healing. None of it made any sense to her.

"How is Grace?" P.J. asked, directing her question at Shea. "And Elizabeth? How is she adjusting? Do you get to see them often?"

Shea smiled ruefully. "Not as much as I'd like, but that mind-meld thing is better than a cell phone. I can talk to her whenever I want, so it makes the times I can't see her not seem so bad. And Elizabeth is such a darling. Way too old for her age. She's had to grow up so fast, but Grace and Rio both love her so much already."

"I'll admit, it was hard to picture Rio as a daddy," P.J. said, a crook in her lip. "He's so intense and broody. But he also has a soft spot a mile wide, so I guess it's not so out of the realm of believability. I'm glad they're doing well, though. The last time I saw either of them was at your wedding."

Shea's entire face lit up, her smile dazzling. She exchanged smiles with Sarah, with whom she'd shared a wedding. It had been the Kelly lovefest that had sent P.J. to her seedy bar in Denver in a funk. Now she realized she'd just been jealous and lonely.

It made her wince to admit that she'd actually been jealous of all the love and support of the huge Kelly family, but she was brutally honest with herself. Well, when she wasn't in denial . . .

Sarah poured her a glass of wine and handed it across the table to P.J. but then drew up short just as P.J. reached for it.

"You haven't taken any pain medication, have you? We didn't even think about that. You have to be in a lot of pain and we should have had the sense not to plan wine."

P.J. smiled at Sarah's genuine worry. "I'm drug free. No need to worry that I'll be stoned after a glass of wine. My last dose was yesterday evening. I'm trying not to take it unless I have to or Cole makes me."

The others laughed.

"If Cole's anything like our husbands, and I'm sure he's just as much an alpha, hardheaded male, then you have your hands full," Rachel said with a rueful smile.

"He's been great," P.J. said softly.

She lowered her gaze when the other women shared a smug smile, and she sipped idly at her wine, wondering when one of them was going to bring up the delicate situation that was essentially the elephant in the room. And her reason for being here in the first place.

She watched as Sophie scooped three-year-old Charlotte into a hug and then tickled the toddler's tummy until she shrieked with laughter.

P.J. had to admit that Charlotte was a complete cutie-pie. She almost made P.J. long for sweet-smelling babies and sweet little belly laughs. Almost.

There had been a time when P.J. had considered that she was ready to settle down, have a baby or two and do the whole American pie-and-picket-fence thing. Derek had quickly dissuaded her of that notion.

He hadn't wanted children, and moreover, he didn't want marriage. He thought it was an outdated, old-fashioned concept and that in the modern world, it made no sense for a man to commit to one woman.

Okay, so he was a complete dickhead. She knew that then even if she hadn't immediately given him his walking papers.

Oddly enough she'd been less tolerant of him being a dirty cop than she had been of his views on love, marriage and family.

Since then she hadn't given any thought to anything except her job and making sure she was the best damn sniper and soldier she could be.

All plans of marriage and family had been thrown out the window. And since then, she'd decided she just wasn't mother material. What kind of parent could she be with the job she held? She loved her job and knew she'd never be happy giving it all up for home and hearth.

She wondered what Cole's opinions were on the subject.

She shook her head, determined not to travel that path. It was a good way to set herself up for disappointment. Besides, what the hell was she doing debating children and marriage when she was a cold-blooded murderer plotting to make her next kill?

Fat lot of good it would do her to be dreaming in a jail cell. For that matter, if she was caught in some shit-hole country, it wasn't the U.S. justice system she'd have to worry about. She'd be in some deep, dark place subject to treatment that would make what Nelson and Brumley had done to her a total cakewalk.

Was it worth it? Was it truly worth her life to take Brumley out?

She needed no time to answer that question.

Hell yes. She didn't even hesitate. It wasn't just her who'd suffered at that monster's hands. So many babies. Young women. She couldn't even begin to think of the atrocities so many girls had suffered before. And how many would suffer in the future if she didn't shut this asshole down.

Her life certainly was worth it when she compared it to the hundreds—thousands—of girls she could save by taking his miserable ass out.

"I have no idea what you're thinking, but it must be pretty awful," Sarah said.

P.J. blinked and looked at Garrett's wife, who was sitting across from her in a lawn chair. For that matter, all the women were staring intently at her.

P.J. offered a grimace. "Nothing worth talking about. Just an asshole who needs killing."

Sophie lifted her brow. "Several come to mind when you say that."

Rachel gave a wave. "Don't listen to her. She's pretty bloodthirsty."

P.J. cracked a grin. "She sounds like my kind of woman."

It was then that P.J. realized Rachel wasn't drinking any wine, and for that matter, only four glasses had been placed on the table. She frowned and held her glass in Rachel's direction. "Do you want some wine?"

Rachel's cheeks tinged a soft pink and her eyes lit up like twin sunbeams. Then she patted her softly rounded belly that P.J. hadn't noticed before. P.J.'s mouth fell open.

"You're pregnant?" P.J. asked.

"With twins!" Rachel exclaimed, her smile getting bigger all the time.

"Holy shit!"

The women all laughed at P.J.'s reaction. P.J. shook her head. "I had no idea. Looks like I've missed a lot in the last six months."

"If you only knew," Sarah muttered.

P.J. lifted her eyebrows. "What?"

Rachel sighed. "While you were AWOL, we sort of had an incident at the school where I'm teaching again. The mom and dad of one of my students split up, and the dad went bonkers and came to the school with a gun and held my class hostage. This was just a few days after I'd found out I was having twins. You can imagine that Ethan didn't take any of this well."

"Did they go in and take the fucker out?" P.J. demanded. Then she bit her lip, glancing in Charlotte's direction. "Sorry."

The others laughed.

"Yep, they did," Sophie said with a grin. "They pissed off a whole host of people in the process, but the real heroine was Rachel."

Rachel blushed and shook her head. "I was terrified."

"I'm sorry I wasn't here," P.J. said quietly. She felt protective of these women. Like they were hers. She'd had a hand in every mission that dealt with them, and it bugged her that while she'd been out seeking revenge, Rachel could have been killed.

"You're here now," Rachel said. "And that's all that matters. KGI isn't the same without you, P.J."

Shea leaned back in her chair and pried a leaf from Charlotte's hand before it made it to her mouth. Then she turned to look directly at P.J.

"Look, P.J., I know Cole called and talked to Sophie, and yeah, he told us about what happened to you, but we already knew. KGI is family, and even though you don't hang around us that much, we all care about you a lot. You've been there for each of us when we needed someone the most. You've risked your life for all of us. You risk your life to keep the men we love safe. That makes you very special to us whether you know it or not. It also makes us very invested in what goes on with you. When we heard what happened, we wanted to go kick that fucker's ass every bit as much as the guys did."

P.J. bit the inside of her mouth to keep it from flapping open. She didn't really know how to respond to Shea's impassioned statement. She hadn't ever considered that she meant crap to these women. It baffled her that they thought about her at all. She was just a member of a team that worked for or with their husbands. No one special. Certainly not *family*. Right?

And yet the mere word had sent a warm flush straight into her heart.

"And I said all of that to let you know that we aren't here to psychoanalyze you. We aren't going to pry into your thoughts. What we do want you to know is that we're here for you. Anytime. Whatever you need. If it's someone to talk to. If you just want a shoulder to cry on. If you just want to bitch and scream. We're here. Never hesitate to call us or come over. You may not be a Kelly in name, but you belong to us and we take family very seriously."

Sophie clapped, a broad smile on her face. "Very well said, Shea. Wow, you're coming along just fine." She turned a teasing smile toward P.J. "It wasn't so long ago that we were having to convince her she was part of the family and that it was okay to lean on us."

Sarah leaned forward, her expression serious, her eyes full of understanding. "I was raped too, P.J. I know what it feels like. I dealt with it by ignoring it. I shut everyone out. I just wanted to be left alone."

"Yes," P.J. said fiercely, finally latching on fully to part of the conversation.

Sarah's admission was everything that P.J. had done herself, and as silly as it sounded, it made her feel not quite so alone that she wasn't the only one who'd reacted to what had happened to her the way she had.

"I just didn't—don't—want to think about it," she finished painfully.

Sarah nodded. "I get it. I do. But when you let it go like that for so long, you eventually reach a breaking point."

P.J.'s heart thumped, making her feel a little light-headed. She wanted to confide in her so badly about what happened the night before. The words were burning her lips, but she was so ashamed, and it simply wasn't in her nature to confide in others.

She'd always been a loner. It was something drilled into her from the time she was a child. That wasn't going to change in the course of a single day, the first time other females extended their hand in friendship.

When a child couldn't even count on her parents, how the hell was she supposed to be able to count on anyone else?

But who said there were rules she had to follow? Just because she was one way her entire life didn't mean she couldn't take steps to change, even if they were baby steps. She was tired of feeling so alone all the damn time. If that made her weak, then fine. She was weak.

She rubbed her face tiredly and sat there a long moment before she finally worked up the courage to say what she'd nearly blurted out just moments before.

"I freaked out last night," she admitted. "I thought I was ready. I never really thought about it. I mean, I'm a logical person and I have no trouble separating out what those bastards did to me with the reality of having someone you care about touch you. I know Cole would never hurt me. I *know* that! And yet one minute I was in the most fantastic place in the world and the next I was in full-scale panic and hyperventilating all over the place. I no longer knew where I was or who I was with. I was so scared that I couldn't even function. How stupid is that?"

"It's not stupid," Rachel said in a tone that told P.J. she knew exactly what she was talking about. "I still have episodes of panic and utter despair. Despair doesn't even begin to describe the absolute desolation or the feeling that you're lost in hell and no one will ever find you. I wake up in the middle of the night thinking I'm back in that horrible hot-box, in the dark, alone, knowing I have no way out."

"I have a pretty awful confession to make," Sarah said with a grimace. "On our wedding night, I had a panic attack when Garrett tried to make love to me. Talk about stupid. We'd made love so many times before and I was fine. Maybe it was the stress of the wedding. I have no idea. But I freaked out when he touched me, and he spent the rest of our wedding night holding and comforting me. I've never felt so awful in my life. I ruined what should have been the most special night of our lives."

P.J. felt a twinge of sympathy for the other woman. She knew *exactly* how that felt. It was the way she'd felt the night before when she'd all but begged Cole to make love to her.

"Ahh honey, I'm sorry," Sophie said, reaching over to squeeze Sarah's hand. "I'm sure Garrett was fine with it. He loves you so much."

"Oh, he was. It was me who wasn't fine with it. I'm so tired of allowing that bastard who raped me to control my life. I don't want him in my life or my marriage and I damn sure don't want him in bed with me and my husband."

The others giggled. Then Sarah stifled her own laughter and everyone joined in, laughing at the image of another man in bed with Sarah and Garrett.

It lightened the mood and injected some much-needed levity into the conversation.

"I'll tell you like we told Shea," Rachel began. "It may sound stupid, and the initial reaction is denial, but sometimes you just need someone to talk it out with. I avoided therapy for the longest time because it frustrated me that I needed to go see a complete stranger so that I could deal with the things that had happened to me. But once I got over that feeling of ridiculousness, it really did help."

"Same for me," Sarah interjected. "And I tell you something else that really, really helped. Talking to Garrett and being honest with my feelings. He's been so understanding, and I can't imagine Cole would be any less so."

P.J. felt heat rise into her cheeks. "You guys are kind of assuming that Cole and I are a slam dunk."

Sophie snorted. "Oh please. The man was a walking corpse after you pulled your disappearing act. You have that man so tied up in knots it isn't even funny."

The others nodded their agreement.

"Well hell," P.J. grumbled. "It's apparent nothing stays secret around here."

They hooted in laughter.

"I'm afraid that's the drawback of being part of a noisy, very close, very intrusive family. There isn't much everyone else doesn't know," Shea said.

"But it's the very best kind of family to be a part of," Rachel said softly. "I wouldn't trade them for the world."

"As long as we're making confessions, I'll make one more," P.J. said with a grimace. "I was dreading this. And to be honest the only reason I agreed to come was because Cole was in agony after he made the call to Sam, thinking I'd be pissed that he arranged it without talking to me first."

The others smiled but waited for her to continue.

"But I really am enjoying myself and I want to thank you for going to all of this trouble for someone you don't even really know."

"You've done so much for all of us," Shea said. "You say you're just doing your job. But to us, you've not only put your life on the line for us individually, but you go out every time our husbands go out and you're a big part of the reason they come home to us again. There is nothing we can ever do to repay you for that, so if there is ever anything any of us can do, we don't just want you to ask, we *expect* you to ask."

P.J. smiled, warmed through by the genuine regard and acceptance the other women had bestowed on her.

The world might well be coming to an end, because P.J. Rutherford was actually making *friends*.

CHAPTER 32

"SO how did it go?" Cole asked on the drive back to Camden.

"It actually went well," she said.

She reached over to slide her fingers around his hand, surprising him with her overture. He picked up her hand and put it on his leg, his grip firm.

"You were sweet to do that for me, Cole. I really appreciate your caring," she said in a quiet voice. "They didn't pry. And they didn't push too hard. They just let me know I wasn't alone and that they were there anytime I needed a shoulder. It was kind of . . . nice."

He squeezed her hand. "I'm glad. I hate that you seem so alone, like you're isolated from the rest of the world. There are so many of us who care about you, P.J. I just wanted to show you that."

Her heart did a complete somersault in her chest. This man was so damn perfect and he actually wanted her. It defied all logic, but she wasn't going to argue.

"Thank you. I do feel better. It was nice to get out for an afternoon. The Kelly women are nice."

"Yeah, they're pretty special, but not as special as you."

She blushed hotly but smiled her happiness over his assessment.

"Hey, when we get to your place, do you have wireless Internet? I need to get on my laptop. It's been forever since I checked email and messages."

"Sure. I'll get you hooked up, no problem."

"What sort of divine delicacies can I look forward to tonight?" she teased.

"Was thinking of cranking up the grill and doing something quick, like hamburgers."

"Yum. That sounds perfect!"

He smiled. "You're awfully easy to please."

Impulsively, she leaned across the truck and kissed him on the cheek. He glanced over in surprise when she pulled away, but pleasure glowed in his eyes.

"What was that for?"

"Just seemed like the thing to do," she said.

"Well feel free to do it more often," he encouraged. "I assure you I won't mind."

When they arrived at his house, she again got out without any help from him. She limped toward the house, and whether it was her mood or the wound wasn't bothering her as much, her step was quicker and more confident.

Her assessment was verified when Cole commented that she seemed to be getting around better.

She went to her bedroom and pulled her laptop out of her bag. The battery was likely dead, so she retrieved the cord and went in search of a place to plug it in.

Cole was in the kitchen pulling stuff out of the fridge, so she opted to set up her computer on the bar and settled on one of the stools.

After plugging in to begin the charge, she opened it and searched for his wireless connection.

"Hey, do you have a password to get on?" she asked.

To her surprise, his cheeks darkened with color, and instead of telling her the password, he walked around to her laptop and swiftly typed it in.

She stared at him in curiosity. "Don't trust me?"

"Nah, just figured it was easier if I typed it," he hedged.

"So how am I supposed to connect if you aren't just right here?" she asked innocently.

"Since I don't plan not to be right here with you, it isn't an issue."

"Oh come on, Cole. You've got me curious. I could swear you blushed when I asked for the password. What is it, some kind of X-rated guy thing? Like *bigboobs* or something like that?"

Cole sighed. "The password is *Pjshot*, okay? Happy?"

Her eyes widened and she stifled her laughter. "P.J.'s hot? That's the password? How long have you had this network?"

"Three years, okay? Now can we change the subject?"

He was so cute in his embarrassment and it made her want to squeeze him.

"So you were checking me out that long ago, huh?"

He sighed. "I was checking you out from the day you joined our team."

"That's so cute," she said with a grin.

"Cute?" he grumbled. "God, I feel like some kind of horny teenager who just got busted making out on the couch by his mother."

Still grinning, she logged on to her email and began scanning the subject headers.

When she got to one buried below a dozen others, she froze and her heart sped up, beating painfully against her chest. With shaking fingers she clicked on the message.

She had to read it several times because adrenaline was making her jumpy and she had a hard time processing the message.

> B in town. Something big going down. Several of the girls were hired. Can't say more in email. I'll talk in person if it's just you.

The email was from one of the call girls P.J. had befriended in her quest to track down the four men who'd been present when she was raped. Katia—P.J. didn't know her real name—had been an invaluable source of information, but she was also extremely paranoid and spooky. With good reason. Brumley wouldn't hesitate to shut anyone down he perceived as a threat.

She quickly checked the date the email had been sent and breathed her relief when she saw it was sent the previous evening. So it hadn't languished for days while P.J. had been out of touch.

With shaking hands, she shut the laptop, her mind in vicious turmoil.

It had been so easy to forget her objective when she was a world away with people who cared about her. The last days with Cole had enabled her to shove Brumley into the back of her mind. She'd relaxed her guard, had been able to pretend she was flirting and forging a relationship.

Last night should have told her that there was no way she could move forward with her life until she'd taken care of her past. But even after her panic attack, she'd still refused to focus on the task at hand.

She had to get to Vienna and talk to Katia. What if Nelson had been wrong about Jakarta? What if he'd outright lied, purposely sending P.J. on a wild-goose chase? He could have been protecting his boss with his last breath.

What if they could take Brumley down before the deal in Jakarta?

Her mind was filled with a thousand what-ifs.

"Hey, what's wrong? You're pale," Cole said, concern an edge in his voice.

"We need to talk," she said more sharply than she intended.

Cole dropped what he was doing and walked around to take the bar stool beside her, turning so he faced her.

"What's up?"

He was all business now, his expression serious, and he was focused solely on her.

She let out her breath, hoping like hell she wasn't making a mistake confiding in Cole. But she trusted him. It was time to see just how their relationship was going to work.

"Okay, you know I was gone for six months and I managed to take out three of Brumley's men. You were there when I took out Nelson."

Cole nodded.

"What I never told you was how I was able to get so close. How I got my intel and knew where to find them each time."

Cole nodded. "Yeah, I wondered since you weren't using the team for support."

"The night of the party, when Donovan and I went in, I saw several very high-class girls hooking up outside the gate with single men going into the party. Donovan explained that they were very expensive working girls. A date for the night plus whatever went on behind closed doors when it was all said and done."

Cole nodded again.

"Well it occurred to me that these girls were probably in the know. They know when the parties go down. They know who the players are. And that if I got close to one of them, I could tap a valuable source of information."

Cole frowned. "Okay."

"I could only find one willing to talk to me. She calls herself Katia. The rest were obviously afraid and unwilling to risk talking to me. I can't say I blame them. They're pretty much nameless, faceless women no one cares about. No family to be concerned if they disappear. They'd probably not even cause a ripple if they suddenly went missing.

"Anyway, Katia was willing to talk to me, but she was extremely cautious. Always met in secret. She was adamant that I was the only person she would talk to, and if I didn't show alone, she wouldn't open her mouth. So I paid her for info. She'd tell me when a party was planned or even when she'd heard about a deal going down. Apparently a lot of the guys these girls pick up have loose lips after sex and they like to brag about how powerful they are."

"So she told you how to get to the first three men," Cole said grimly.

"Yeah. She never gave me a bad lead, so I figure she's entertaining some people pretty high up in Brumley's organization, if not Brumley himself."

"Okay, so what does that have to do with now?" Cole asked impatiently.

"I got an email from her," P.J. said, her fingers still shaking despite her best effort not to let the email rattle her. "She says something big's going down in Vienna with Brumley. She wouldn't say more. She wants to talk to me in person."

Cole reared back, automatically shaking his head. "Oh hell no. Fuck no, P.J. Not going to happen."

P.J. put her hand up, pissed because it was still shaking. The last thing she needed was for Cole to think she was afraid, because she'd never get him on board then.

"Think about it, Cole. I'm not going after Brumley alone. I just need to see Katia and find out what she knows. It's possible Nelson completely misled me when he told me about the deal going down in Jakarta. Think about it. His dying breath and he sends me in the opposite direction to where Brumley will really be. The ultimate fuck-you. I need to get to Vienna and talk to Katia so we know where this deal is going down. If we're off in bumfuck Jakarta while he's doing a deal in Vienna, he's home free. We may never find the fucker again."

"If you think I'm letting you go off to Vienna by yourself, you're out of your goddamn mind."

He looked angry now. His entire body was tense and his eyes blazed with purpose.

She put a hand on his arm and gently squeezed. "I wasn't planning to go alone, Cole. I was hoping you'd go with me."

CHAPTER 33

COLE'S agitation level was off the charts. He stared back at P.J. realizing she was utterly serious. His gut was screaming because all he wanted to do was keep her safe under wraps, in his sights, at his home, where he knew damn well she was safe.

The last few days had been . . . idyllic. They hadn't even touched on the subject of Brumley or Jakarta or any of it. He'd secretly hoped that with enough time, he'd be able to convince her to let KGI go after Brumley and leave her out of it entirely.

It was an unrealistic hope at best, but he'd fooled himself into thinking it was a possibility.

"P.J., this is stupid. You honestly want to go off without the team on a fact-finding mission? You're hurt. Or do you not remember taking a bullet to your leg? You can barely walk. The last thing you need is to be running all over Vienna."

P.J.'s lips thinned and she had that stubborn pit bull look that she got when she was pissed—and determined.

"I won't be running all over Vienna," she said tightly.

"And there's no point getting the entire team involved when this may amount to nothing. There is also the fact that if we go in as a team, we aren't going to go unnoticed. And thirdly, there is no way Katia is going to talk if I show up with a bunch of testosterone hanging over my shoulder."

Cole frowned, but she continued on.

"You're making more of this than needs to be made. It's a simple trip to Vienna. In and out. We could be back in three days. I go see Katia. Find out what information she can give us. If something's going down soon, we call up Steele and get the team in place. If nothing's going down, we simply return and wait for Jakarta. I can't afford not to jump on this lead, Cole. You knew from the start that I wasn't going to rest until I nailed that bastard, not only for what he did to me, but for what he's done to all those babies," she said fiercely. "If you won't go, then I'll damn well go myself."

Fuck a duck.

He knew he was overreacting and he knew he just wanted to keep her wrapped in bubble wrap so nothing could ever touch her again. He also knew that it was a stupid idea because she'd never allow it. Just like he knew in the back of his mind, no matter how much he'd like her not to go to Jakarta, that she'd be there with or without her team's approval, and she wasn't going to sit back and let her team take on a mission she'd sworn to carry out.

It drove him insane, but at the same time he admired her for her resolve and her commitment to her purpose. He wouldn't respect her half as much if she rolled over and allowed others to take up the fight for her.

"Damn it, P.J."

Her expression eased because she knew she'd won.

"I'll get online and book us the next flight out of Nashville," she said. "We'll have to connect in New York, and it sucks, but we'll be going without any sort of equipment. But I know a supplier where we can get what we need in Vienna."

"Made quite a few friends over there," Cole bit out.

Her expression sobered. "I did what I had to do to bring those bastards down."

He reached forward, framing her face with both hands. "I want you to be careful, P.J. You mean a whole hell of a lot to me. I'm not going to just stand by while you put yourself on the line. I'm going to be with you every step of the way. This is no longer just your fight. It's *our* fight. Those bastards hurt someone I care about. That makes it my fight too."

She leaned in, resting her forehead against his. In that moment she seemed utterly fragile and vulnerable, and it only intensified his resolve that she wasn't going to do this alone.

He moved his lips, just enough that they met hers. He kissed her once, retreated, then kissed her again just as softly.

"You make those reservations. I'm on board until I see that we're getting into a dangerous situation. If that happens, I'm pulling you back, and if I have to sit on you until our team arrives, then that's damn well what I'm going to do. Got it?"

She smiled. "Got it."

TO reserve a flight, P.J. ended up having to call the airline, and then they had to literally pack a bag and get out the door within an hour. Making any decision that quickly didn't sit well with Cole. He was more of a measured, sit back and think out all the potential issues kind of guy. P.J. was more of a take the bull by the horns and let all hell break loose girl.

If this was any indication of how their relationship was going to go, he was royally fucked.

All the way to Nashville, he second-guessed his decision to go along with P.J.'s plan. There were a hundred different reasons why it was a bad idea, but there were also reasons why it made sense.

If it went down just as she'd explained and they were merely going to Vienna to meet her contact and then make plans accordingly, he didn't see the harm.

But there were so many things that could go wrong that it made his head spin.

Even if it pissed her off and she never spoke to him again, he was going to make damn sure she didn't put herself in any danger. A quick visit to the call girl and then they'd put their heads together and call in the team.

It sounded simple on paper, but his gut was full of dread, because nothing was ever that simple. And he—and P.J.—had already paid the price for him ignoring his gut once.

They made it to Nashville with only minutes to spare before they would have missed the check-in for their flight. The seats were economy, which sucked. Cole was a bit spoiled, making most of his trips on the Kelly jet where he wasn't subjected to crying babies, kids throwing tantrums and assholes trying to take his seat before he'd even boarded.

Worse, the transatlantic flight had a connection in London and then a flight to Vienna. All in coach.

P.J. was tense and wired for sound the entire way to New York. They didn't speak during the flight, but he could see the wheels turning in her head.

She'd switched from the easygoing, relaxed P.J. who he'd been able to draw out the few days they'd spent together, to the P.J. who was ready to shed some serious blood.

Not that he didn't get seriously turned on when P.J. got all kick-ass. Something about that woman when she got all badass just flipped all his switches, and some he didn't even know he had.

But this time he was worried. This was too personal. She'd lost all objectivity. It wasn't a mission where they could disengage their emotions and do the job expected.

This was revenge, and while he couldn't blame her for wanting to nail the bastard who'd not only hurt her but had deeply shaken her confidence, a big part of him wished that she could just walk away and heal.

When they arrived in New York, they only had forty-seven minutes to make the next leg of the flight, and it took extra time boarding because they had to present their passports. They were one of the last to be seated, and sure enough, some dickhead had plopped down in Cole's seat, and when Cole stood in the aisle, the jerk actually had the balls to ask him to trade.

Cole gave him his best snarl and told him to get his ass up, but in the end, P.J. was the one to get him moving quickly. She leaned over, whispered something in a low voice and suddenly the man couldn't get out of the seat fast enough.

He and P.J. settled into their seats and Cole glanced over in question.

"What did you say that made him change his mind so quickly?"

She grinned. "I just told him that I suffered from multiple personality disorder, was deathly afraid of flying and that I had to have you sitting next to me so I didn't have panic attacks."

Cole chuckled. "You're diabolical. I love that about you."

She shrugged. "Hey, it got the job done."

"I hate assholes who just assume you're willing to trade for their shitty-ass seat just because they like your seat better," Cole grumbled. "Shit like that is why I prefer flying first-class."

The flight to London was long, and it gave Cole too much time to ponder all the reasons this was a bad idea. His gut was gnawing on him, but he was already in, and there wasn't much he could do at this point except hope his gut was wrong.

After changing flights in London, they slept for most of the flight to Vienna. By the time they dragged their carcasses out of the airport and got into their rental car, Cole felt like he'd been rode hard and hung up wet.

"Did you email your call girl already?" he asked as they drove toward the hotel.

P.J. shook her head. "I didn't want to risk her wanting to meet immediately and then getting spooked when it took more than twenty-four hours to arrange a hookup. After we check into the hotel, we need to go see my contact and then I'll email her once we're prepared."

Cole had to admit, P.J. had her shit down. It scared the hell out of him that she had been scouring the dark holes of Vienna in search of an arms dealer by herself when he'd been half a world away going nuts worrying about her.

They checked into a hotel, and just when he would have fallen face-first onto the bed, P.J. was dragging him out the door again.

"I don't have this guy's number, but I know where he hangs out," P.J. said. "I just hope we're lucky and he can be found. We'll take a cab. I don't want to draw any attention by driving right up to this place."

"What kind of place are we talking about?" Cole asked warily.

The very last thing he wanted was to go into some shit hole unarmed.

"It's not the Ritz" was all she said as they hopped into the taxi.

She had the driver drop them off at an intersection in a part of the city that immediately raised Cole's hackles. Hell, it was broad daylight and he was still uneasy.

They walked two blocks then ducked into an alley that smelled like it was a sewer drop. The narrow cobblestone street that fed into the alley was barely wide enough for a scooter to pass through, and the potholes were big enough to be small ponds.

Carved into stone walls that had to be centuries old was a metal door that looked like it had been the victim of police battering rams. More than once. The padlock dangled precariously from the latch.

P.J. gave three sharp knocks, and a moment later a guy who was three times Cole's size opened the door and stuck his head out.

He had long, stringy hair that hadn't been washed in at least a week and a jagged scar that curved the entire side of his face.

His eyes glimmered in recognition when he saw P.J., and his stance relaxed.

"I need to see Kristoff," she said.

"I'll see if he has time for you," the bigger man rumbled.

"Tell him it's important."

Without a word the guy closed the door, leaving P.J. and Cole in the dank-smelling alley.

"This can't be a good idea," Cole muttered. "I was out of my mind for letting you do this."

"Kristoff will get us what we need," she said confidently. "Besides, he likes me."

"Well thank God for that," Cole said sarcastically.

A moment later, the hulk opened the door and gestured for them to come in.

The inside smelled little better than the alleyway. It was dark and smelled strongly of cigar smoke and alcohol.

P.J. forged confidently ahead and Cole followed close behind her, determined to stick close to her in case it all went to hell.

They went down a long hallway and the hulk stopped at a doorway and opened it, motioning P.J. and Cole inside. Cole breathed a sigh of relief when Hulk remained outside, shutting the door behind them.

Kristoff was sitting behind a desk, smoking a nasty-smelling cigar that made Cole want to gag.

When he saw them, he slid his feet off the desk and smiled in P.J.'s direction.

"So, what brings you back?"

"I need weapons," P.J. said bluntly. "At least two semi-automatic rifles and two handguns. If you have something small that can easily be concealed, I need two of those too."

Kristoff studied her intently. "I got word of the three guys you took out. Major players in Brumley's network. Impressive. He's got a contract out on you. Offering big bucks to the person who can bring you in. Alive or dead. He doesn't care."

P.J.'s gaze narrowed. "Don't fuck me over, Kristoff."

He laughed. "I have money. What do I need Brumley's for? Besides, I have a lot of money riding on you taking him down first. So don't let me down, eh?"

"About the guns," she said impatiently.

Kristoff got up from his seat, pushed a button and the far wall revolved, revealing an entire arsenal arranged on the inside wall.

"Take your pick. We'll talk price after you make your selections."

P.J. strode to the wall, examined a few of the weapons and then tossed one of the rifles in Cole's direction. He caught it and examined the M-16.

"It'll work," he said.

She then tossed him a handgun.

"I'm assuming these will fire," Cole said in Kristoff's direction.

Kristoff immediately bristled. "I sell only the finest arms. You won't find fault with any of my stock."

P.J. chose her own weapons then tossed another smaller pistol in Cole's direction.

"Give us what ammo we need and we'll be on our way," P.J. said shortly.

Kristoff lifted an eyebrow. "We haven't talked price yet."

"Ten grand for the lot," she said coolly. "Cash. American dollars."

"Fifteen. You picked six of my best pieces."

"You get ten or no deal."

Cole blinked, impressed with P.J.'s calm. The woman had balls.

Kristoff looked pained for a long moment and then he sighed. "Only because I'm planning to make twice as much when you take out Brumley. But if you fail, I'm coming after you for the other five grand."

P.J. snorted and dug into her pocket, pulling out a wad of cash Cole hadn't even know she'd had on her.

She tossed the bills onto Kristoff's desk.

Kristoff meticulously counted each hundred-dollar bill and then went to a cabinet and pulled out boxes of ammo, setting each onto the desk.

"Still providing curb service?" P.J. asked.

"Of course. Can't have you walking onto the street

carrying all that shit. A car will be waiting at the end of the alley. I'll have Franz take your purchases."

"Nice doing business with you, Kristoff. I'll do my best to make sure you win your bet."

His teeth flashed. "See that you do. I'm a very sore loser."

CHAPTER 34

P.J. sat at the small desk in the hotel room typing an email to Katia while Cole lay sprawled on the bed, eyes closed. She doubted he was asleep. She'd known Cole to go without sleep for days when the situation called for it.

She'd purposely not told him much in the way of details before they'd flown to Vienna because . . . Well, he wouldn't have gone, and worse, he would have carried out his threat to physically restrain her to keep her from going.

Brumley hadn't just become another target, a mission she had to fulfill. He'd become an obsession.

When she slept at night, she saw him in her dreams. At times, she could feel the knife in her hands, and hear the gurgle of blood as he took his last breath. It was an image that haunted her day and night, and until she made it a reality, it would continue to haunt her.

She hit send on the email but left her laptop open and her sound up so she'd know the moment a response came in.

Then she crawled into bed next to Cole and laid her head in the crook of his arm.

As she'd suspected, he wasn't sleeping. He turned in to

her immediately and wrapped his arm around her body, pulling her in even closer.

"So is this what you did for the six months you were gone?" he asked seriously. "Hid out in shitty hotels, hung out in back-alley shady businesses with men named Kristoff or befriended hookers?"

"Basically yeah. I changed hotels every few days. I was always worried Brumley would find me, especially after I made the first kill and left my signature so to speak. He's not dumb. He had to have known it was me. Especially when his right-hand man showed up the night he raped me with a knife wound to his back, reporting that I'd escaped."

Cole let out a string of curses. "I don't know what pisses me off more. That you got involved in this at all or that you didn't trust me or your team enough to let us in on what was going down."

"Would you drag the team into a personal vendetta, Cole? Really? If you were planning to murder someone, would you really ask the team to back you up? Because no matter how you color it, I'm killing these men in cold blood. It's not self-defense anymore. I hunted them down and I cut them to ribbons before killing them."

He went silent, and she knew she'd made her point.

"I hate that you're even involved now. I hate that Steele and the others got involved. It tarnishes KGI as a whole. What happens when Resnick gets wind of this shit? And you can't tell me he won't. The man knows goddamn everything. I bet the president is even afraid of pissing that man off because he knows so much."

He put a finger to her lips. "Shut up. It doesn't matter what you want or don't want at this point, because we're involved. There's no going back now. And we aren't leaving you to do this alone, so just shut the fuck up and deal with it."

She smiled and leaned in to kiss him when her laptop beeped, signaling an incoming email.

She scrambled off the bed and hurried to the desk. Her breath caught when she saw Katia's response sitting in her inbox.

Must meet with you right away. Important.
Come alone.

"This is it," she said to Cole. "She wants to meet right away. Says it's important and to come alone."

"Fuck that," Cole snarled.

P.J. held up her hand. "Of course I'm not going alone. If I was, I wouldn't have bothered to bring you along, so keep your underwear on."

He looked slightly mollified, but he rolled out of bed, stuffed the larger handgun in his shoulder holster, slid the smaller pistol in his ankle holster and then loaded a magazine into the assault rifle.

P.J. armed herself but placed her rifle into a duffel bag and then reached for Cole's so they could get out of the hotel without their weapons being seen.

"You drive," she directed as she threw the bag into the backseat. "I want you to park a block away from Katia's apartment. I'll go in, see what she has to say and then be right back out. I'll need you to watch the building."

His lips tightened but he didn't argue.

They drove across town, gradually getting into an area that had deteriorated over the years. Many of the buildings were in disrepair and most of the businesses had moved closer to the city center.

Katia's apartment was actually a nice place. On the inside. The outside was a crumbling building with graffiti on the walls and iron bars covering each of the windows.

She had told P.J. that the rent was next to nothing, and with the money she pulled in from servicing her wealthy clients, she could afford to make the inside a palace.

After instructing Cole where to park, P.J. armed herself and opened the passenger door.

"Give me half an hour. I don't know what all she has to say, but if I'm not out by then, come in after me."

"I'll give you twenty," Cole said bluntly. "She can't have *that* much to say. I don't like this place. I don't like this whole situation. My gut is screaming like a motherfucker."

"Okay, twenty," P.J. agreed.

She wouldn't admit it, but her gut was doing its own bit of bitching. She was uneasy about this whole thing.

She got out, closed the door and hurried toward the entrance to the building. She wasted five minutes waiting for the service elevator to grind to a halt on the ground floor. She rode it to the sixth floor and got off, making a beeline for the end of the hall where Katia's apartment was.

She knocked softly, and the door squeaked open an inch the minute P.J. knocked.

P.J. made a grab for her handgun and carefully pushed the door open so she could see inside.

"Katia?" she called softly. "It's P.J. You here?"

She stepped inside, gun up and pointed as she swept the living room. The television was on. Some European soap opera. She entered the kitchen and found nothing out of order so she headed for the bedroom.

The door was ajar and P.J. nudged it open with her toe, staying back before swinging around, gun aimed inside.

Katia was lying on the bed in a pool of blood.

Son of a bitch!

P.J. raced over, reaching for Katia's neck to try to find a pulse, but drew up when she saw the macabre sight before her.

The woman was naked, with slashes to the insides of her thighs, under her breasts and one down her midline.

Her throat was so horribly slashed that but for a small piece of flesh at her nape, she'd been all but beheaded.

P.J. bent over, nausea so overwhelming that she had to suck in breath after breath through her nose to keep from emptying her stomach.

On the desk, her laptop was open to P.J.'s last email.

P.J. touched a finger to Katia's arm to find it cold and stiff. She'd been dead for a lot longer than when P.J. had received that last email.

Her blood ran cold. This has been a complete setup.

It was then she noticed the note lying on the bed, blood smeared over the paper.

She picked it up and her stomach bottomed out.

If you have any interest in keeping your teammate alive,
you'll come to me tomorrow morning at ten a.m. Alone.
Unarmed. It's your choice. You or your teammate. If
you don't show, I'll assume your choice has been made.

—B

What the fuck? No way they had Cole. It was a complete
bluff. Did they think she was stupid? She turned and ran
from Katia's apartment, not bothering with the elevator.

She flew down the six flights of stairs and burst out of
the building, at full sprint as she ran down the street to
where Cole was parked.

But the car was gone.

Oh shit, oh shit, oh shit.

No way they had Cole. No fucking way.

She yanked out her cell and punched in Cole's number.

"Come on, come on," she said anxiously.

But it wasn't Cole who answered. It was a voice she'd
heard in her nightmares every night for the last six months.

"Didn't believe me?" he asked in amusement. "I have
your boyfriend here. He's pretty pissed. He'll be lucky if I
don't kill him before you get here, but a deal's a deal. You
for your teammate."

"Where?" she croaked.

"Be watching your email. I'll provide the location at
nine in the morning. Until then, sleep well, P.J. Rutherford.
And remember this. If you're so much as a minute late, your
friend here is dead. If you show up with anyone, if I even
think you have backup, he's dead. If I find a single weapon
on you, he's dead. Are you getting the picture now? I have
no use for this man. But you . . . You, I have use for. We
have unfinished business. Get here on time and follow my
directions. Do that and he goes free. Understand?"

Before she could respond, Brumley cut the connection,
leaving P.J. standing on the street corner numb to her toes.

CHAPTER 35

P.J. returned to her hotel, packed her shit and immediately checked out. She moved to a hostel across the city, provided a fake name, and paid cash—more than triple the cost of the room so she didn't have to provide her passport.

She was a wreck. A complete and utter wreck, and she was so pissed that she knew she had to get a grip or she was going to get herself and Cole killed.

She didn't believe for a minute that Brumley was going to let Cole walk away once P.J. surrendered. The dumbass must think she was a complete moron to swallow that line of bullshit.

The first thing she had to do was call Steele, and it was a call she dreaded with every fiber of her being. But for Cole, she'd do anything. Even if it meant never working for KGI again. And this would likely do the trick. She could only push her team leader so far. He wasn't exactly known for his understanding.

He expected you to obey orders without questions and do your job. You did those two things, you got along fine. If not, there was a serious problem.

She made the call with a huge knot in her stomach. He answered on the second ring.

"Steele," he said shortly.

"Steele this is P.J. We have a situation."

Steele immediately became alert. "Give me the run-down."

Never one to mince words. He wanted things short and concise and to the point. No unnecessary bullshit and no excuses.

"Cole and I came to Vienna to follow up on a lead from a contact I made while I was over here. She led me to believe that Jakarta was a false lead and that something big was going down over here. Cole and I planned to check it out because my contact will only talk to me. After we learned what there was to learn we were going to call in the team."

P.J. had to hold the phone away from the ear as blistering obscenities poured through the other end.

"What the fuck were you two doing going off without telling me a damn thing, and furthermore why the hell did you two go alone?" he demanded.

She didn't have time to answer his questions.

"My contact was dead when I went to her apartment. Brumley's calling card. Brutalized and she had her throat slashed. Just like I killed three of his men. It was a clear message to me. And he left a note saying he had Cole."

"Son of a bitch. You went in alone? Without backup? Have you lost your goddamn mind, P.J.? You're acting like a wet-behind-the-ears rookie recruit and I expected better from you."

"Look, we had our bases covered. We went in prepared. Brumley set us up. He got to my contact first, killed her and then sent me an email from her laptop. While I was inside, they nabbed Cole, who was parked a block away waiting for me to come out."

"And what now?" Steele snapped.

"He wants me to trade myself for Cole."

"Over my dead body," Steele said icily.

"Look, I don't believe for a minute he'll let Cole go free

once he has me. Which is why I'm calling you. I'm not stupid, Steele, even if you think so. I've thought this through. If you and the others get on a plane now you can make it pretty damn close to the time I'm supposed to meet Brumley. Problem is I don't know where yet. But I have a tracking device I'll wear so you'll know how to find me. I need you to get your asses here as quick as possible so we have backup. I can't wait for you before I go in because I do believe he'll kill Cole out of spite if I'm so much as a minute late. But if I get there, I can stall for time until you guys make it in. I'll do whatever I have to do, whether it's seduce his sorry ass or let him take another shot at me. As long as Cole survives, it doesn't matter what happens to me."

"You aren't trading yourself for Cole," Steele said tersely. "Do you honest to fuck think he'd ever be able to live with himself if you did that?"

"At least he'd be alive," she said softly. "No one on my team is going down for me."

Steele cursed again.

"How soon can you be here?" P.J. demanded. "I meet him at ten in the morning. I figure it'll take you guys all night and into the morning to get here. We'll be cutting it close. I need you there as close to ten as possible. I don't know what his plans are. He may just kill us as soon as I show up. I'm hoping to play with his ego a bit to buy us some time. Just be here, Steele. I'm counting on you."

"We'll be there," Steele snapped. "You just stay your asses alive until we kick some fucking ass. You got it, Rutherford? That's a goddamn order and one I expect you to follow."

It was one order she had absolutely no problem following.

CHAPTER 36

P.J. didn't sleep that night. She went through a dozen scenarios in her head, but none of them did any good, because she had no idea what she was up against.

And the bastard was toying with her. She checked her email repeatedly, hour after hour, and no information came through.

It wasn't until eight thirty the next morning that the e-mail popped into her inbox.

She pounded the table in frustration, because all it said was that a car would pick her up at nine thirty at the Stubentor subway stop.

With no information to leave for Steele, she was going to have to rely solely on the tracking devices and hope to hell they weren't discovered before Steele arrived and got a bead on her location.

She affixed one of the patches to the bottom of her foot, and the other she attached to the elastic she used to pull her hair into a ponytail.

Praying Steele and company arrived soon, she left her

room at the hostel, asking directions to the nearest subway station.

It was funny that she couldn't remember any other mission. Didn't remember how she felt, if she'd been scared, if she'd worried about dying or getting one of her teammates killed.

The old P.J. had been cocky and self-assured. The new P.J. had a much better grasp of just what could go wrong, and she was certainly more in touch with her mortality and that of her teammates.

No one was going to die if she had anything to say about it.

She rode the subway in tense silence, wondering if Steele and her team had arrived, hoping that they'd been able to pick up the signal on the tracking devices.

The bastards would probably frisk her pretty hard, but her hope was that if they found one of the tracking devices, they wouldn't even bother looking for a second. And she'd purposely worn a plain T-shirt and jeans because there wasn't a possible way to conceal anything, and she wanted Brumley to think she'd complied one hundred percent with his orders.

When her stop arrived, she got off and glanced warily around. She wasn't entirely certain what she was looking for, but she figured the assholes would find her quick enough.

And she was right.

She hadn't taken more than a few steps off the platform when she felt the barrel of a gun pressed painfully into her back.

"Keep walking and don't do anything stupid."

The accented voice was an assault to her ears. She wanted nothing more than to let loose and kick the fucker's ass, but she controlled her rage and walked meekly in the direction he pointed her.

She was shoved into a waiting car and ordered to lie down on the seat.

She did as she was instructed and waited an eternity as the car drove for what seemed like forever before stopping again. She waited for the man to open the door and tell her what he wanted. She didn't want to risk pissing him off this early in the game.

Patience was the word for the day. Stall. Whatever it took to get Steele and the team in position.

"Get up and don't try anything stupid," the man barked.

She rose slowly, making sure her hands could be seen.

As soon as she was out of the car, the man shoved her toward the entrance of what looked to be a damn fortress.

She cast a quick glance behind her, taking in the wrought iron gate and high security fence, not to mention the armed guards that patrolled the perimeter.

It wouldn't be easy, but she had every confidence that Steele would expertly handle whatever obstacles he encountered.

Her main focus now had to be Cole and making sure he was alive and okay.

She stumbled up the steps, her leg protesting the strain she was putting on it. Then she exaggerated her limp as they entered the house. The weaker they assumed she was, the better opportunity she had to catch them off guard.

She nearly groaned when he directed her to a spiral staircase that led to the next level. Noticeably grimacing, she navigated the stairwell at a snail's pace. She didn't have to fake the discomfort this time.

The man pushed at her, obviously in a hurry, and she bit back the retort that burned her lips.

When they finally reached the top, he directed her down the long hallway to a door at the end. Once there, he knocked sharply and awaited the summons.

She held her breath when the door opened, not knowing what to expect on the other side. The man shoved her inside and she stumbled, her leg not able to take the sudden push.

She went sprawling onto the hardwood floor, and when she looked up, the object of her nightmare was standing across the room, a satisfied smirk on his face.

Quickly taking stock of the rest of the room, she counted

three other armed guards plus Brumley. Then her gaze lighted on Cole and her heart stopped.

He was bound to a chair and his face was a mess. Dried blood crusted his nose and mouth and a bruise darkened one eye. Rage filled her, roaring through her veins, giving her the impetus to pick herself up and face Brumley down.

"So you came," Brumley said. "I wondered if you'd leave your teammate to save your own ass. Maybe I underestimated you."

"You've made that mistake a few times," P.J. snarled. "So what's the deal, Brumley? You said me for him. I'm here, so let him go."

Even though she knew he had no such intention, she'd play his game for as long as possible.

Brumley dismissed the man who'd escorted her up, who left, closing the door behind him.

Then Brumley turned his attention back to her, his eyes gleaming with amusement. "So we meet again at last. You know, I should have let Nelson have his way when he asked to keep you around as a pet. I think you would have been fun to play with. And it wouldn't have cost me three of my men."

P.J.'s lip curled into a snarl. "You aren't man enough, Brumley. The only time you can get it up is when the woman is drugged and helpless. You couldn't take me in a fair fight."

"Shut the fuck up, P.J.," Cole barked.

She spared him a glance, and he was seething in fury over her baiting Brumley. Every muscle in his body was straining against his bonds. He was one ball of pissed-off alpha male.

"You play a dangerous game," Brumley said softly. "What do you hope to accomplish? I win. I have you. I have your teammate here. You can't possibly hope to win."

"The deal isn't about winning," she said calmly. "You said me for him." She jabbed her thumb in Cole's direction. "So let him go and then it's just you and me. Want me to strip down? Make it easy for you? Let's see if you can get it up when I'm not out of my mind and unable to move as a result of your drug."

She cut her eyes toward Cole, telling him silently not to react. She just hoped to hell he got the message.

"I was thinking more along the lines of a long-term arrangement," Brumley countered. "I have a nice little cage that would be perfect for you. My little pet. Play with you awhile then put you back in your cage. After a while you'll be grateful for whatever attention I give you. I'll have you broken in no time flat."

She laughed. "In your dreams."

Brumley lifted an eyebrow. "So strip. If I'm satisfied with your performance, I'll let your precious teammate go."

"Going to fuck me right here in front of everyone?" she taunted. "I don't know if I'd want your men to know you're an impotent little shit."

Brumley advanced on her but she stood her ground. He wrapped his fist in her hair, pulling her up close. Then he backhanded her but held her tightly so she didn't fall away.

"Watch your mouth or I'll kill him right here in front of you and then I'll have you while you watch him dying."

P.J. held out her hands. "Okay, you win. You're the boss. Tell me what you want."

"Strip," he said again.

She blew out a breath. This is not what she wanted. For all she knew the asshole would pass her around to his little guard dogs, who were all leaning forward in interest now.

But she needed at least one of them close if she had any hope of getting a weapon.

"Want a striptease or you just want it done?" she snapped.

Every minute she could keep him talking gave her much-needed time for Steele to get here.

Brumley motioned to one of his men. "Get her out of her clothing and make it quick."

She held her breath, every sense on high alert.

The man closest to Brumley went forward eagerly.

"Put your hands up and don't make a move," the guard said to her in a terse tone.

Slowly she raised her arms while he pulled a knife and made quick work of her shirt.

Cole went crazy. The chair he was positioned in bumped and threatened to shatter, forcing one of the other guards over. He pulled a gun and held it to Cole's head.

"For God's sake, P.J., don't do this," Cole pleaded.

She didn't dare even look his way. She couldn't lose her focus.

When the man charged with undressing her got to her jeans, he yanked at the button of the fly and then slashed downward, coming perilously close to slicing through her skin.

She was standing in just her bra and panties and she'd never felt so vulnerable in her life.

Stop it!

She wouldn't go back to being that scared, helpless woman she'd been the first time Brumley had raped her. She wouldn't let that woman come in and take control. This time *she* was in control. She was in the driver's seat and he'd take nothing from her. She'd die before she allowed him to touch her again.

She kept close watch on the man divesting her of her clothing. His gun was so close, almost within reach. So very close. She held her breath, needing him to turn just a bit more.

Shit, she'd lost track of the third man. One was guarding Cole, one was stripping her down, but where was the third guy?

She couldn't pretend modesty and suddenly start acting the shy maiden when she'd boldly confronted Brumley and issued her challenge.

Fuck.

She cringed when the asshole slid the blade underneath her bra right in the hollow of her breasts. A sick feeling assailed her when the bra fell away and then he moved the blade lower to her panties.

Oh God, help me. Please, please let Steele be close.

She might not be able to get herself and Cole out of this one on her own.

The man stepped back and she lost any opportunity of grabbing his gun. She was left alone in the middle of the room, naked, with the eyes of these bastards feasting greedily on her.

Then she finally located the third guard. He'd been behind her, toward the corner, but now he stepped forward, wanting to look his fill as well.

The anticipation on the guards' faces told her it was very likely that Brumley didn't mind sharing his property.

Brumley took a step forward and she could see the bulge in his slacks. The bastard was completely turned on by the scene before him and he likely savored the idea of raping her right here in front of Cole.

"Okay, I'm naked," she said coolly. "Let him go."

Brumley cast a glance in Cole's direction. Cole's expression was murderous.

"And let him miss out on the fun?" Brumley asked. "What better satisfaction would it be than to fuck you right here while he watches?"

"That wasn't the deal," she snapped.

"So sue me."

She bared her teeth even though she'd known that was precisely what he planned to do.

He took a step toward her, and for a moment she was taken back in time to when she'd been forced to endure his suffocating weight, the smell of her blood. The horrible pain he'd inflicted and then when he'd pushed himself inside her body.

Brumley's gaze wandered down her body, staring at the scars from the wounds he'd inflicted. There was a sick satisfaction in his gaze.

"Just think. Those marks—my marks—will be on you forever. Every time you see them, look at them, you'll be reminded of me. I plan to add more. I'm not going to kill you, P.J. I'm going to keep you alive, but you're going to wish you were dead. I guarantee you that."

It took all her effort not to allow him to see the paralyzing fear and revulsion that exploded through her body. She
wouldn't give him that satisfaction. If she died today, she'd
die fearlessly and she'd take this son of a bitch down
with her.

She felt the presence of the guard behind her. He'd
moved in close until she could feel the desperate lust radi-
ating from him. Maybe Brumley planned to have him hold
her down while Brumley raped her. Whatever the case, she
couldn't wait a minute longer for Steele. She was going to
have to get out of this one herself.

She pinpointed the positions of the other men. The one
that most worried her was the one holding a gun on Cole.
However, he was far too focused on the scene playing out
before him and he'd actually lowered the gun a few precious inches. Enough that if he got a shot off, Cole had a
damn good chance of surviving.

Then she made her move.

Rotating on her good leg, she connected with a solid
right hook to the face of the guard standing behind her.
Then she yanked his gun from the holster and shot the
guard standing closest to Cole.

She dropped and rolled, firing off a series of rounds at
the guard she'd taken the gun from and then she frantically
tried to locate the last armed man.

The fucker had dived behind the desk while Brumley
reached for his own piece. Shit!

She rolled until she got a clear view in the cutout of the
desk and kneecapped the other fucker, making him howl in
pain. As soon as he leaned down to grab his knee, she put
a bullet through his head.

Another shot sounded, and for a moment she thought
she'd been hit. But she felt no pain.

Oh no. Oh God no. *No, no, no*!

She scrambled up to see Cole slumped over, blood
streaming down the right side of his body. Then blinding
pain overwhelmed her as Brumley hit her in the face with
the butt of his gun.

She went reeling, the gun flying from her hand. She landed several feet away, her face exploding with pain. Goddamn, it felt like he'd broken her damn jaw.

He loomed over her, holding the gun to her head, but she reacted quickly, lashing out with her good leg, knocking the gun from his grasp.

She struggled up, but he was on her, yanking her to her feet, landing another blow to her already injured jaw.

By sheer determination, she remained conscious and pushed aside the pain. She hung tenaciously to Brumley when he tried to throw her toward the couch. If he ever got his weight over her, she was done for. He outweighed her by two hundred pounds. She rammed her knee into his testicles, and suddenly she was free, his howl of pain echoing sharply in her ears.

Where was a damn gun?

Was Cole alive?

Brumley recovered quickly and they circled each other like wary predators. But her concentration was divided because she was heartsick over the idea that Cole had been shot. He could be dead.

She glanced Cole's way again and Brumley struck in that moment of inattention, landing a kick to her injured leg. Agony lanced up her thigh. She let out a cry of pain and crumpled to the floor, unable to catch herself before impact.

"Goddamn it, P.J., I'm okay. Now get your ass up and kick his fucking ass," Cole yelled.

Relief made her dizzy. But she was also suddenly imbued with strength and purpose. Cole was *alive*. All she had to do was take out this asshole and her objective would be achieved. Revenge would be hers. And the son of a bitch would never hurt another woman or child again.

She pushed herself up just as Brumley launched another attack. She rolled and did a round kick with her uninjured leg, connecting with his balls for a second time. If she had her way, he wouldn't have any left when she finished with him.

Where was a goddamn weapon? A gun? Knife? Anything?

She rolled again, trying to muster the strength to get to her feet, when her hand glanced off the knife that had been used to cut off her clothing.

She grabbed for it and held on for dear life. This time when Brumley came after her, she lashed out with the knife and got him right in the gut.

He howled in pain and jumped back. This time he didn't advance on her, having figured out the odds had turned in her favor.

He made a dive for one of the guns and P.J. leaped after him, rolling over his body and kicking the gun in Cole's direction.

As soon as she made contact with the floor, it knocked the breath out of her and Brumley was on her in a split second.

They rolled, his hand crushing her wrist in an effort to make her drop the knife. Oh hell no. She wasn't going down like this.

She waited until he dropped lower, trying to use his weight to his advantage, and she head-butted him right in the face. Pain lanced down her spine as he rolled away from her, but she couldn't afford to let it stop her now. Her whole body felt like it had been through a meat grinder, but she was so close. So damn close to victory, she could taste it.

"Behind you, P.J.!" Cole yelled.

She dropped and rolled again, barely missing Brumley's charge. Again they were both on their feet facing off like two bulls. Blood dripped from them both. She had no idea where she was bleeding from. There wasn't a single part of her body that didn't hurt. Her entire concentration was on making Brumley bleed *more*.

He feinted left and that's when she had him. She went low and took him down when he was off balance. She rolled atop him and punched him right in the face. And then again. She punched until she was sure she'd broken her hand again.

Then she grasped his head in both hands and slammed it down onto the floor until he was nearly unconscious.

"P.J., P.J., baby, you got him."

Cole's soothing voice filtered into the haze wrought by her rage. She glanced up, for the first time connecting with Cole. He was alive. Bleeding, but alive. Then she glanced down at Brumley, whom she was still sitting astride. Naked.

She felt no shame this time. She was the victor. She'd taken this motherfucker out. Her. Just a helpless woman he'd once raped.

She bent low, hissing so he'd be sure to hear. "How's it feel, asshole? To know I'm not so helpless now and I kicked your fucking ass."

She picked up the knife she'd dropped and casually popped the buttons on his expensive, bloodied, silk shirt. Panic entered his eyes when he figured out her intention.

The door to the room flew open and she scrambled for the gun lying close to Cole. It was slippery and she damn near dropped it, and then heard Cole's voice, soothing. Calming her from the panic that had taken hold.

"It's all right now, P.J. It's just Steele and the rest. They're here now. It's all right."

But it wasn't all right. She didn't even spare her teammates a glance. She returned her attention to the bastard she had pinned to the floor. She didn't care what her teammates were seeing. That she was naked and bloody. She'd sacrificed all pride in her pursuit of justice. And now it was hers for the taking.

She finished cutting off his shirt and Brumley started babbling and pleading for his life.

Pathetic, ball-less worm.

"Don't kill me," he begged.

She laughed, and the sound was cold in the room. Not at all like P.J. This was a different P.J. This was the cold-blooded killer she'd become.

"Give me one good reason I shouldn't cut you up like you did me and then let you die a long, painful death," she spat.

"P.J."

It was Steele. That one word cut through the haze and brought her back to reality.

She turned, expecting censure. Expecting him to tell her to stand down. What she saw were her teammates with rage in their eyes.

Steele was at the forefront, his eyes brimming with understanding.

"It's your call," he said quietly. "Resnick wants him alive, but fuck Resnick. Whatever you decide, we're behind you one hundred percent."

It was then that Brumley broke down, weeping like a distraught child. Maybe he saw the promise of death in P.J.'s eyes. And after hearing her team leader all but sanction his death, he started babbling faster than P.J. could keep up.

"I'll give you whatever you want. Money. I have money. Information."

He latched onto that greedily. "I have names and contacts. I have records of every deal I've ever made. You could take out a lot of very important people who deal in child trafficking. I'm just the middle man. I'm nothing."

P.J.'s lips curled into a snarl. "Yeah, you'd probably love to be turned over to Resnick. You'd cut some cushy deal, sing like a bird and then be free in no time. I don't trust you, Brumley. You'd say anything to save your own ass."

Dolphin and Renshaw ran to where Cole was still sitting, tied to the chair. They quickly untied him and started applying a pressure dressing to the wound.

Steele and Baker stood by the door, guns still drawn, their gazes never leaving P.J.

"I can prove it," Brumley gabbled. "In my safe. There in the wall. I'll give you the combination. You can see. I have records of everything. Recorded conversations. Details of deals. When and where. It's all there, I swear it!"

"Baker, check it out," P.J. ordered.

Baker removed the painting and then waited as Brumley stuttered out the combination. A moment later, Baker started pulling out stacks of currency and with it a ledger and several memory chips.

Baker flipped through the ledger and let out a low whistle.

"Apparently our asshole here does business with some very important people. Resnick would come in his pants to get his hands on this."

"See!" Brumley panted. "I told you!"

P.J. looked at him in disgust and then pressed the blade into his throat until a line of blood appeared.

"Wait! You said you wouldn't kill me!" Brumley said in panic.

She slashed deep, cutting his windpipe, air escaping in a long hiss.

"Sue me."

CHAPTER 37

P.J. let the knife fall from her hand, clattering to the floor. Numbness had crept in along with the realization that she'd done it. Her revenge was complete.

Her rapists were dead. Her mission was done.

A shiver took over, and she realized that she was still astride Brumley, naked and cold, shaking like a leaf.

And then her team was there, surrounding her.

Mortification gripped her and she clutched her arms to her in an attempt to cover her body.

Steele wrapped a blanket around her shivering form and pulled her up and away from the blood and the sight of Brumley's dead body.

"Are you hurt?" Steele demanded, his hands on her shoulders, holding the blanket in place.

It seemed a senseless question when she was bleeding all over and her face must look like a train wreck.

"Cole," she croaked out. "How is Cole?"

She broke away, uncaring of anything but Cole. She rushed to where he still sat on the chair he'd damn near torn apart in his desperation to get to her. There were rope burns at his wrists and a bulky pressure dressing on his shoulder. But he was alive.

As soon as she pushed her way past Dolphin and Renshaw, Cole staggered to his feet and met her halfway.

Ignoring his injuries, ignoring hers, he crushed her to him, holding on as if he'd never let go.

"My God, you scared me, P.J.," he whispered against her ear. "Don't ever do that to me again. Swear to me you'll never do that again. I almost lost you. I can't lose you again. Never again."

She clung fiercely to him, fearing what would happen if she let go. She could literally feel the threads holding her in place loosening and starting to fray. She didn't know how much longer she'd be able to keep it together.

"Baker, get everything out of that safe," Steele ordered. "We need to clear out of here double time. I don't want any sign that we were here."

Renshaw snorted. "I think the dead bodies will give it away."

Steele pinned him with a glare. "They may speculate as to who and what, but I don't want them to have irrefutable proof. I want everyone out and this place clean on the double."

"Yes sir," Baker said.

Baker gathered everything from the safe and began stuffing it into his pack.

Renshaw began a wipe down of all the surfaces that could have been touched and then started working on the doorway, the knobs and the frame.

P.J. was still holding tightly to Cole, knowing if she let go, she was a goner.

Steele walked over to them.

"Can you make it down without help?" he asked Cole.

"Yeah, I'm good. But she's not."

"I know," Steele said quietly.

He gently pried P.J. away from Cole. She went ballistic, stretching her arms out to Cole, not wanting to be separated from him for even a moment.

"Shhhh, P.J.," Steele said gently. "It's over now. You're safe. Cole is all right."

But her shattered mind couldn't process anything but her need to be close to Cole.

She was still struggling when Steele swept her into his arms. After ordering Baker, Dolphin and Renshaw to complete the cleanup, he headed out the door with Cole following closely behind.

P.J. went limp, the pain from her struggles overwhelming her. She laid her head on Steele's shoulder and closed her eyes, so many different emotions bombarding her until she was utterly overwhelmed.

Relief. Pain. Sadness. Grief. Vindication.

Justice.

She clung to the last word knowing it was the most appropriate of all. Justice had been served. Brumley would never pose a threat to another woman or child again.

Steele carried her out of the gates that had been blasted open, and she gazed at the twisted iron, the carnage that had been wrought when her team had blown their way in.

A moment later, Steele set her down into the back of an SUV and eased her into a sitting position. He carefully pulled the ends of the blanket around her, tucking the ends like she was a child incapable of doing even the simplest task for herself.

"I'm going back to round up the others so we can get the fuck out of here," Steele said. And then he strode away, leaving her and Cole alone.

She sat hunched over and Cole closed in, pulling her into his arms. She closed her eyes and simply inhaled his scent. The blood, sweat, dirt. She didn't care. He was alive. They'd made it. Brumley was dead.

"It's over, baby," he murmured. "It's finally over. You kicked the ever-loving shit out of him. You scared me to death, but I never doubted you for a moment."

She sighed and rubbed her cheek against his shoulder. Her voice trembled and shook when she spoke. She had to work to get the words past her stiff, cold lips.

"It's over, but will I still see him at night when I close my eyes? Will I still see him in my dreams and relive that moment of helplessness again and again?"

He slipped his fingers under her chin and gently nudged it upward until she met his gaze.

"I'm going to be right beside you every step of the way, and every time that asshole enters your mind, I'm going to push him right back out again. For every bad dream you have, I'm going to replace it with something wonderful."

She leaned her forehead against his chest again. "I love you, you know."

He put his mouth to the top of her head, and she could feel his smile. "Yeah, I know. And I love you just as much. What do you think we should do about that?"

She made a garbled sound that could have been panic or satisfaction. Maybe a little of both. It was so hard to get her thoughts together and this was so very important. She had to get this right.

She raised her head so she could look him in the eyes, so she could see that love—for her—shining like the warmest light in the darkest corner of hell.

"It probably means we should do something stupid like move in together. But I draw the line at popping out babies."

He laughed softly, his bloody mouth working into a semblance of a smile. "What, you don't want to raise a brood of little snipers?"

She shuddered. "No."

He hugged her fiercely. "I'm fine with that. As long as I have you. We make a good team, Penelope Jane. On and off the job."

She pulled back again and eyed him suspiciously. "No demand that I quit my job so you can shut me away and keep me safe?"

"Hell no. Who would save my ass on a mission? I'm counting on you to protect *me*!"

She laughed, despite the gut-wrenching pain it caused her, and let go of some of the horrible tension knotting her gut. "I'll do my best."

She hugged him again because she just couldn't stop touching him. "I love you," she said fiercely. "I'm sorry I couldn't say it before. But it was there. Maybe it's always been there. It'll always be there, Cole. I swear it."

He stroked her hair, raining little kisses over her brow and head. "We would have gotten there eventually. Our dating time just happened to be over bullets, grenades and hostage rescues. We'll never be normal, but screw normal, eh?"

"Yeah, screw normal," she said, her voice muffled by Cole's shirt.

"Let's go and load up."

Steele's voice penetrated the warm glow that P.J. existed in and brought her crashing back to reality all too soon.

They still had to face the music for their actions, and it could very well mean that she no longer had a future with KGI.

CHAPTER 38

FOR the first time since she'd come to work for KGI, P.J. openly defied her team leader. Technically what she'd done before hadn't been defiance, since Steele hadn't specifically told her *not* to do the things she'd done. He couldn't very well have told her since she didn't let him in on her plans.

And technically she'd resigned from the team so anything she'd done in that six months had been done solo, not as a member of the KGI organization. Never mind that Steele had told her where to stick her resignation.

But when Steele announced his plan to dump his team back home in Tennessee and go alone to meet with Sam, Garrett and Donovan to turn over the intel collected from Brumley, P.J. had drawn a hard and fast line in the sand.

She refused to allow Steele to take the rap for her actions and her decisions. Cole had stood firmly beside her on that count, stating that he and P.J. would both give an accounting to the Kellys. No way in hell they were throwing Steele under the bus.

Steele hadn't been happy about the matter, but there

wasn't a lot he could do when faced with two determined
people who would go to Sam, Garrett and Donovan with or
without him.

Since Steele had all but hijacked a Kelly jet—without
permission—P.J. figured he had enough to answer for
without taking the blame for her crimes.

After the adrenaline had worn off and Cole was sure of
P.J.'s safety, his injury hit him a lot harder than it had initially. He'd lost a lot of blood and had begun to weaken
during the flight home.

Without Donovan, they had limited medical aid they
could give him, but Steele changed the dressing often and
made sure he had pain medication to keep him calm and
still.

P.J. hovered next to Cole, never leaving him. She held
his hand, bullied him mercilessly and vowed to kick his ass
if he even thought about doing something stupid like dying.

Steele tried to get her to rest—she was in little better
shape than Cole—but she remained steadfast in her refusal
to leave Cole's side.

She was literally drooping, pain gnawing at her body,
when she felt a prick and turned, stunned, to see that Steele
had injected her in the arm.

"What the hell was that?" she demanded.

"Something for pain and something that'll help you
rest. You're about to fall over and anyone with eyes can see
you're in agony. Give it up, P.J. You aren't helping Cole by
hanging over him looking like something the cat dragged
in. He's worried sick about you, so he won't calm down and
rest."

The medication was already making her swimmy. Her
limbs grew heavy and her eyes were increasingly harder to
keep open.

"Damn it, Steele," she slurred out.

"Curse at me later," he bit out and then promptly caught
her as she fell over.

Cole picked his head up, his lips drawn into a grim line
of satisfaction. "Thanks, Steele. I was worried she was

going to fall over any second. She needs the rest. She got the hell beat out of her back there."

"You didn't fare so well yourself," Steele said dryly.

Steele laid her down, brushed the hair from her face and then carefully arranged a blanket over her. Then he returned to Cole.

"How bad is it?" he asked tersely.

"Hurts like a son of a bitch, but I'll live," Cole said. "Nothing I haven't lived with before."

Steele sat down in one of the armchairs across from the couch where P.J. and Cole were both sprawled.

"You both could have gotten yourselves killed."

Cole nodded. "Yeah, we could have. But P.J. didn't let that happen. She's a mean son of a bitch when she gets pissed."

A half smile cracked Steele's lips. "Yeah, I hear you."

Cole sobered and then stared over at his team leader. "How's this going to play out for me and P.J. being on the same team?"

Steele was silent for a moment.

"I won't sacrifice my relationship with her for a job," Cole said.

Steele snorted. "It's a good damn thing, because I have no intention of letting either one of you go. It's annoying the shit out of me that I'm going to be out of action for the next while because two of my team members are going to be laid up and then you're probably going to want time off for a goddamn honeymoon."

Cole grinned. A honeymoon sounded pretty damn good. He glanced to where P.J. was passed out on the couch. They both had some healing to do, but the future was looking pretty damn bright.

Then he looked back to Steele and sobered. "How is this going to go down with Sam? I know we fucked up. I'll take full responsibility."

"Shut the fuck up," Steele said rudely. "I'll take care of Sam."

Cole grinned and relaxed. Steele was a complete hard-ass but Cole wouldn't work for anyone else in the world. The day Steele no longer led a KGI team was the day Cole hung up his gun and became an average Joe with a nine-to-five job.

"Get some rest," Steele said. "We don't land for several more hours and you're going straight to the base hospital."

Cole groaned. "I swear, they need to just reserve a room with my name on it as many damn times as I've been in there."

"Between you and P.J., they're going to need to name an entire wing for you," Steele said dryly.

CHAPTER 39

P.J. was technically released from the hospital before Cole, but she'd insisted on staying by his bedside until the army doctor thought he was well enough to be discharged.

Steele arrived on the day Cole was being released. In terse tones, he told them that Sam wanted the team at the KGI compound. He wouldn't say anything more when pressed, and that worried P.J.

It was the day of reckoning. A day she'd known would come. She just wished Cole and the rest of her team wasn't involved.

The ride from Fort Campbell to the KGI compound was tense and silent. Cole's hand crept over P.J.'s and he squeezed as if to say it would be all right. But neither spoke, and she knew that the impending confrontation weighed heavily on Cole's mind every bit as much as it did on hers.

Even Dolphin, who typically had something to say for every occasion, was as silent as the rest of the team.

Steele drove while P.J. and Cole sat in the middle seat with Renshaw and Baker in the back. Dolphin rode shotgun, and it was the longest P.J. could ever remember no words being exchanged between the teammates.

Were they angry with her? Resentful? Pissed because she'd dragged them into her own personal vendetta?

She was torturing herself with all the possibilities.

By the time they pulled into the compound, P.J. was a wreck.

They parked outside the war room and got out, Dolphin and Steele helping P.J. and Cole. But she was determined to walk into this meeting with no vulnerability. She didn't want it said she played on anyone's sympathies, so she shook off Dolphin's supportive arm and strode toward the entrance, ignoring the protests of her leg.

Her face was a mess, bruised and still swollen from her fight with Brumley. The X-rays had shown no fracture of her jaw, though Cathy had sworn it was broken when P.J. had been brought in.

Chewing would be tough for a while, but she could deal.

She punched in the security code to gain access into the war room and she walked—or rather strode stiffly in her attempt not to limp—into the room where the Kelly brothers were gathered.

She frowned as she glanced around. It was just the Kellys; well, not even all of them. Nathan and Joe weren't present.

Hell, not even Ethan was there, which meant that this was going to be a come-to-Jesus moment between the three men who officially ran KGI and the team that was in the proverbial dog house.

"P.J.," Donovan said in greeting. "I'd say you're looking good, but even I can't pull off that kind of lie with a straight face."

She relaxed at the teasing and grinned crookedly at him. Damn, but it even hurt to smile.

The rest of her team filed in behind her, and an awkward silence fell over the room.

Cole came up behind her and put his arm around her

shoulders, pulling her in close to him. It was obvious he was sending a message to everyone. He was with her. He had her back, and whatever affected her, affected him.

Sam cleared his throat and leaned against the edge of the large planning table in the middle of the room. Donovan and Garrett flanked him, and all of their expressions were serious.

"We have a serious problem here," Sam began. "KGI as an organization can't be associated with vigilantism. The Austrian government is screaming. The U.S. government is screaming. Resnick is screaming. And I'm stuck playing dumb about it all. While the respective governments may swallow my cock-and-bull story, Resnick's not going to bite. He knows better."

"Fuck him," Cole said rudely.

Donovan coughed and covered his mouth. P.J. could swear he was holding back laughter, but then his expression reverted back to that pinched tight-ass look his brothers were wearing.

Sam held up a hand. "Resnick is mollified by the information we were able to provide him. Of course we wouldn't explain how we came by it, but he's about to cream himself because he has the leverage to bring down a lot of the big players in child trafficking, which in turn gives him more power, which in turn gives him more protection. He's skated a pretty thin line with the shit that went down with Shea and Grace, and he's spent plenty of time wondering when he was going to be taken out. This gives him plenty of insurance, so to speak. Before long, the damn president's going to fear Resnick. If he doesn't already."

"So get to the point," Steele said impatiently, speaking for the first time. "Two of my team members were only discharged from the hospital a couple of hours ago. You wanted us here, but they need to be in bed."

Garrett cleared his throat. "After much discussion between the three of us, it's been decided that as a disciplinary measure, Cole and P.J. are going to be put on

administrative leave, effective immediately for a period of
sixty days, and both will have to undergo a full medical
exam and receive clearance from the physician before they
can report back for duty."

Cole's brow furrowed. "Administrative leave? What the
fuck does that mean?"

"It means you're out of action with pay for the next two
months," Donovan said, a twinkle in his eye.

"Steele, you'll report to the KGI facilities five days from
now with Dolphin, Renshaw and Baker and you'll head
training of the newest KGI team until we're satisfied they're
capable of working on their own," Sam continued. "They're
good. But good isn't acceptable. We want the best."

P.J. stared between the brothers, her eyes narrowing
suspiciously. Two months' paid leave? Steele reporting to
train new recruits? This all sounded like talking out the
other side of their mouths. We have to sanction you, but oh,
here's your cushy punishment.

It sounded an awful lot like a way for her and Cole to
recover with full pay and not feel pressured to return to the
job too soon.

Her eyes stung and she hastily wiped at one with the back
of her hand, embarrassed as hell that she was all choked up
with emotion.

Damn but she loved working for these guys.

Even Steele wore a smirk that said he saw right through
Sam's bullshit.

Sam turned his gaze on Cole and P.J.

"I don't want to see either of you for the next two
months. I don't even want to know you exist. For the next
two months you're straight civilians and I better not have to
bail your asses out of trouble. Got it?"

P.J. and Cole both nodded at the same time, and Cole
squeezed P.J.'s shoulders. She didn't dare try to say anything, because she didn't trust herself not to do something
completely stupid like get all choked up or, God forbid,
start hugging people.

"That's all I have to say," Sam said. "You're all dismissed. Steele, I'll see you and your guys in five days. P.J. and Cole, I better not see you period."

Grinning, her team turned to walk out the door. They all knew the entire disciplinary action was bullshit. As P.J. turned to walk out with Cole, Sam called out to her.

"P.J., a word if you don't mind."

She paused and then said to Cole, "Wait for me outside?"

Cole surprised her by kissing her right there in front of God and everybody. But then he had less of a problem with public displays of affection than P.J. did. She wasn't as comfortable letting everyone in the world see into her personal life.

"I'll be right outside," he said as he walked behind Steele.

P.J. turned to Sam, feeling nervous now that it was just her and the Kelly brothers. But Garrett walked past her, evidently not hanging around for whatever Sam wanted to say to her. Donovan also left Sam's side, but he stopped in front of P.J. and then pulled her into a hug.

"I'm very proud of you, P.J.," he murmured against her ear. "And I'm damn glad you're back where you belong."

Her stomach dropped. She returned his hug fiercely, not even realizing until that moment just how much she needed to hear that.

He let her go, touched a finger to her bruised face and then followed Garrett out.

It was just her and Sam in the room and she bravely faced him, determined to take whatever it was he would say. She deserved his censure. Deserved it publicly, though she was grateful he seemed inclined to do it privately.

"How are you, really, P.J?" Sam asked quietly.

Startled, she could only stare at him. She didn't even know how to answer his question, because in truth, she didn't know how she was. She hadn't had time to evaluate her situation or how she felt about anything at all, because her entire focus had been on Cole and his recovery.

"I think I'm okay," she said truthfully. And maybe she was. She felt lighter. Not as weighed down. Not as *angry*.

"I'm glad to hear it. We've—I've—been worried about you. I don't want to lose you. You're too good. You're family."

Her mouth wobbled and she steeled herself, determined to be professional.

He blew out a long breath. "Officially I can't sanction what you did. But off the record? I'm glad you kicked the ever-loving shit out of Brumley and his cronies, and I want you to know that officially or unofficially, I and KGI have your back. One hundred percent. Always. And don't ever doubt it."

Oh goddamn, she was never going to make it through this.

Sam leveled a stare at her that was so full of understanding and concern that her chest tightened and her throat swelled.

"When we went in and rescued Rachel, I had every intention of going back myself. For revenge. For information. I had every intention of doing *whatever* it took to get the information I needed and wanted so that I would know my family was safe.

"I understand how you feel, P.J., and I want you to know that I'm not judging you, because in your shoes, I would have done the exact same thing if what happened to you had happened to any member of my family. And you *are* family. In the future you should be willing, and I will demand that you be willing, to rely more heavily on your family instead of going it alone.

"I'm not pissed because you did what you did. I'm pissed because you thought you had to do it alone and that you couldn't come to us for help. I would have used every resource available to KGI and to me personally to track that bastard down and make him pay. Never believe for one moment that you're alone. Are we understood?"

Silent tears slipped down P.J.'s cheeks. It was too much. For too long she'd carried her burden alone, and now there were multiple people only too willing to share in that load.

"Thank you," she whispered.

He walked hesitantly toward her and then wrapped his arms around her in a gentle hug.

"You just looked like you needed one," he said. "Now get your ass out of here before Cole gets impatient and worried and comes back in after you. And I want you two to take it easy for the next two months and come back completely recovered."

"Thank you," she said as she pulled away. "For everything, Sam. For understanding."

He smiled. "Just remember that you have people who care about you. And don't be afraid to ask those people for help. You could have saved yourself a whole hell of a lot of trouble if you'd just stuck around."

She nodded, not disputing his statement. Even though she didn't regret the track she'd taken. She was at peace with her decisions. She was at peace with the choices she'd made. Now she just wanted to put it all behind her and move ahead with Cole.

She walked out into the sunlight, squinting at the wash of sunshine. Then she breathed in the sweet scent of honeysuckle she so associated with the lake and the KGI compound.

She didn't have to look far to see Cole. He was waiting for her just a few feet away, and his whole face changed when he saw her.

He'd been talking with Dolphin, but as soon as he looked her way, his eyes softened with so much love that it made her weak. And a little scared.

Knowing someone cared about her that much meant she had the power to hurt them, and she'd do anything at all never to hurt Cole again.

As if sensing her inner turmoil, he broke away from Dolphin and walked slowly in her direction.

"Hey, everything okay?" he asked.

She leaned into him even though he hadn't initiated contact. She just wanted that closeness and to be near him. She wrapped her arms around his waist and laid her head on his chest, surprising him with her spontaneity.

He was likely thinking she was on the verge of melt-down because she'd just hugged him in front of everyone and didn't give a shit who was looking on.

"I'm perfect now that I'm with you," she said. "And now we have two whole months of nothing to do."

Cole smiled. "Oh, I'm sure I can think of something."

CHAPTER 40

WARM hands slid sensuously over P.J.'s bare back, and she moaned softly, arching into Cole's touch. Damn but the man was spoiling her sinfully.

His mouth soon followed and he kissed a line up her spine until he reached the sensitive skin at her nape. A full-body shiver overtook her despite the sun beating down on the both of them.

"I'm back," he murmured against her ear.

She rolled on the beach towel, loving how his eyes darkened when he saw her breasts. "I noticed. What'd you bring me back?"

"Mmmm, depends on how good you've been," he teased.

"I haven't shown anyone my boobs but you," she said.

He laughed. "Well, there is that, I guess."

He stretched out on the towel next to her and handed her a yummy, fruity drink with one of those cute little umbrellas in it.

Then he extended his arms upward and made a big show of putting his hands behind his head.

"You know, as suspensions go, this one is pretty damn awesome," Cole said.

P.J. chuckled. "You know as well as I do, they didn't suspend us."

"They're good people," Cole said seriously. He rolled to his side and rested his hand possessively on her naked hip. "So tell me something."

"Something," she replied quickly.

He gave her a light smack on the ass.

She grinned. "Okay, okay, what do you want to know?"

"You going to be okay working? I mean you and me. Same team. Like before?"

For a moment she was alarmed. Was he trying to say he had a problem with it?

He put a finger to her lips. "Don't get all worked up, P.J. You've got to learn to stop jumping to conclusions. This is a conversation. Something two people who love each other have. It's not the end of the world. There are things we need to talk about. Work being one of them."

She let out her breath, feeling like an idiot. "Yeah, yeah, I get it. And yeah, of course I'll be okay working with you. I mean God, you gave me a heart attack. I thought you were going to suggest that one of us transfer to Rio's team since he's a man short."

Cole's expression darkened. "Hell no. I want you right where I can see you all the time. And as I've told you before, I like the idea of you guarding my six. I trust you more than I do anyone else and I know you'll never let me down."

She scooted in close and then rotated so she was staring down at him. Then she kissed him, long, hard and lusty.

"Damn straight I'll never let you down," she said huskily.

"Now on to the other things we need to talk about."

She lifted an eyebrow.

He slid his hand over her ass and up her spine, rubbing back and forth. She didn't even wonder if anyone could see. For one thing they were on a very private beach in Bora-Bora. They'd only run into two other people in all the time they'd spent in this particular little haven, and she knew for a fact Cole had coughed up a lot of money for exclusivity.

Right now she was thinking it was well worth whatever he'd had to pay.

"We've done everything in this relationship pretty much bass-ackward, so I figure a honeymoon before the wedding is pretty much par for the course, and this definitely should count as a honeymoon."

Her eyes widened and she stared down. "Whoa, wait a minute, Coletrane. Are you proposing to me?"

"Well I would if you'd let me finish," he grumbled.

She lowered her mouth and proceeded to pepper every inch of his face with kisses. He laughed and finally pulled her away.

"Okay, okay, ask!" she said.

His eyes went soft and he touched her now-healed face, smoothing some of the sand off. "Will you marry me, Penelope Jane Rutherford?"

"Yes! Yes, yes, yes!"

"I like your enthusiasm," he said with a grin.

But then her face fell and she glanced away.

He nudged her back to look at him, frowning as he caressed the line of her jaw. "What's going through your head now?"

"You said we'd had the honeymoon before the wedding, but Cole, this hasn't been a real honeymoon and you know it."

He looked pissed and so damn loving all at the same time she wasn't sure how he pulled it off.

He grasped her face in both hands, forcing her to look directly at him.

"Do you think love and marriage and a honeymoon is all about sex? Do you think we don't have anything unless we're fucking like monkeys?"

She would have shaken her head but he was holding her too tightly.

"I love you, P.J. *You*. And that's not conditional on us having sex yet, or even tomorrow, or next month. We'll get there. And I plan on having fun every step of the way. But you know, I'm an old-fashioned guy, and I kind of like the idea of having paperwork that says you belong to me and I belong to you. So what do you say we hop a plane to Vegas after we're done here and get hitched before our two months is up?"

She smiled down at him, a sheen of tears obscuring her vision. He leaned up and kissed the scar that ran straight down her midsection.

"I do love you, you know," he said, repeating the words she'd spoken to him after that terrible day when she'd taken Brumley out.

"I do know," she said softly. "And I think Vegas sounds like a hell of a lot of fun."

TURN THE PAGE FOR THE KGI NOVELLA

SOFTLY AT SUNRISE

by Maya Banks

AVAILABLE EXCLUSIVELY IN PRINT
ONLY IN THIS MASS MARKET EDITION.

NOTE TO READERS

Softly at Sunrise takes place in a gap of time that occurs in *Shades of Gray*. Reading this novella will in no way spoil *Shades of Gray*, though there are some brief mentions of events that occur in that book.

With love to every single reader who read and loved "The Darkest Hour" and wanted to know more about Ethan and Rachel and how they were doing down the road. This is for you.

CHAPTER 1

RACHEL Kelly stared back at her reflection and then heaved a sigh before taking her hair down from the loose bun she'd fashioned. She brushed out the long strands and let them fall over her shoulders.

She was over-thinking this too much, and if she couldn't get it together, Ethan would never let her out of the house. He was already worried over the fact that she was returning to work. If he had his way, she'd remain at home, cocooned in his and his family's embrace.

She understood his concern, and she loved him dearly for it. But it was time to move on with her life—a life that she'd once thought was over. After being officially "dead" for an entire year only to be resurrected when her husband and his brothers' special ops group, KGI, rescued her from imprisonment, she was ready to live fully again.

For the last couple of years, she'd tiptoed through life, as if she were afraid to take any risks at all. She'd surrounded herself with family—and it was ever growing with new additions as more of the brothers and team members married—and had contented herself with complacency.

No more.

New house. New start. She was young and had her entire life ahead of her, even if she'd taken that life for granted in the past. She'd never do it again. Every day was precious, and she was grateful for every minute with her husband and her family.

She smoothed a hand over her flat belly, a flutter of nervousness welling up from within. Excitement over her dreams of the future. Of the possibilities that could even now be realized. It was hard to be calm and tell herself the unlikelihood of it happening so quickly.

She and Ethan—after long and careful consideration—had decided that she'd go off birth control a few months earlier. They hadn't even confided in family . . . yet. Ethan had been reluctant, and it had taken convincing on her part for him to agree. Not because he didn't want a child, but because he worried for her.

Once before, seemingly a lifetime ago, she'd been pregnant and had miscarried while Ethan was away with his SEAL team on a mission. That event had been the catalyst for so many things. Ethan had walked away, resigning his commission in the navy because he'd felt guilty that he wasn't there when she needed him.

The decision had made him desperately unhappy, and it had strained their relationship to the breaking point. She'd known things were bad, but she hadn't known just how bad until right before she'd left on a mercy mission with other teachers to South America. Ethan had presented her with divorce papers, looked her in the eye, and told her he was ready to end their marriage.

She closed her eyes, because even now, so many years later, it had the power to gut her.

And then she'd left for South America and hadn't returned until a year later when Ethan and his brothers had come for her.

It had been a new chance, a fresh start, one more opportunity for them to make things right. And they had.

She knew there was no guarantee after all she'd endured

that she could even get pregnant, and if she did manage it, she could very well miscarry again. It could take them months or even years to conceive, which was why she'd wanted to go off her birth control now.

But the thread of hope was there. Alive and burning inside her. She had only to look at her niece, Charlotte, and she was filled with fierce yearning for her own child.

Ethan appeared in the door, and he stared intently at her with those piercing blue eyes.

"Are you sure you want to do this, baby?"

She smiled, warmed by his concern and the love she could see burning in his gaze.

"I'm only substituting for now. It'll be a good test run. If I hold up well, then maybe I'll consider going back full time next year if a position is open."

Wordlessly, he stepped forward and pulled her into his arms. He was damp with sweat from his morning run. He got up every morning for his workout regimen that he did on his own, but he also trained with his brothers at the KGI facility. The compound where she and Ethan would be moving to in just a few days.

She inhaled his scent, the muskiness of sweat and the faint hint of soap from his earlier shower. Hugs were something else she never took for granted. During her captivity, something as simple as human touch had been a craving that had been as crippling as the torture she'd endured.

He kissed the top of her head and gave her an extra squeeze.

"Call me if you have any problems."

She smiled. "I will. I promise."

"Is your cell charged?"

Her smile grew bigger. She was forever forgetting to charge the damn thing. It frustrated Ethan to no end not to be able to get in touch with her. They both still battled their demons in different ways. His fear was of losing her again, and he liked to know where she was at all times. He checked in frequently with her and worried endlessly if he couldn't reach her.

It might annoy some women, but Rachel understood his need for reassurance. He wasn't controlling. He was scared to death. There was a huge difference.

"It's charged, but don't call me during class," she scolded lightly. "I left my schedule on the fridge so you'll know what time my classes are. I'll text you when I can."

Ethan sighed and slowly released her. "I know I'm an overbearing bastard. I can't help myself. If I had my way, you would never go back to work, but I want you to be happy, so if this does it, then I'm okay with it. I'll deal. I promise."

"I love you," she said, moving back into his arms. "Remember that, okay?"

He lowered his mouth to hers in a heated rush of lips and tongue. "I love you too," he said in that low, growly voice that always sent shivers down her spine. "Be careful and text me when you get there so I know you made it safe."

She rolled her eyes and withdrew, checking her appearance in the mirror one last time. "I'll be fine. And don't forget. Your mom and Rusty are coming over tonight to help box up some stuff. Rusty's home for the weekend, and she's volunteered her services."

"I won't be late," Ethan promised. "Light training day today. Working with the new recruits for Nathan and Joe's team."

Rachel's lips turned down into an unhappy frown. "Have you heard anything from P.J. yet?"

Ethan went quiet and then shook his head. "Not a damn thing since she bugged out. It's killing Cole. Steele's not taking it very well either. The team isn't the same without her, and Steele refuses to replace her."

"Good," Rachel said fiercely. "She just needs time. She'll be back. I know she will."

"I hope you're right," he said, his tone somber. "I said the team's not the same without her, but the fact is, *KGI* isn't the same without her either."

Rachel sighed and slid past Ethan into the bedroom so she could get her shoes. P.J. Rutherford was the only female

KGI member. Well, no, that wasn't right anymore. Skylar Watkins was a new recruit, but Rachel didn't know her well. She'd only met her once.

Things had gone terribly wrong for P.J. on a mission, and she'd walked away in the emotional aftermath. Rachel's heart ached for the other woman because she knew how it was to feel like you'd lost a huge part of yourself. To be at loose ends.

"Okay, wish me luck," she announced after she'd slipped on the low heels and picked up her briefcase.

"You'll be awesome," Ethan said, pride evident in his voice. "You were a damn good teacher before. Mom was so proud of you. She was over the moon when you followed in her footsteps. All you did was take a little time off. It'll come back to you in a flash. The kids will love you, just like they all did before."

She went into his arms for another hug. "Thank you. I needed that this morning."

He squeezed her hard and then reluctantly let her go.

"I'm going to jump in the shower again and then head over to the compound. I'll talk to you soon."

Rachel watched as he disappeared into the bathroom, and then she squared her shoulders and walked out of the bedroom and through the kitchen to the garage where her car was parked.

She was terrified. Her palms were sweaty around the steering wheel, and it irritated her that such a small thing as substitute teaching for middle school kids would frighten her after all she'd been through.

Her therapist would tell her all things in time. It was a mantra she'd repeated a lot over the last year. And it was true enough. Everything in good time. She just had to be patient and cut herself some slack.

Moving was a good step. A positive step in the right direction. Ethan hadn't understood why she'd gone in such a different direction with the new house they were building. He'd thought they'd have the same house built inside the compound. The house they lived in now was one they'd chosen together and had incorporated all their favorite things.

As she backed out of the garage and stared at the house that had once been her dream, she took a deep breath. The truth was, she couldn't wait to move away from the house that now represented some of the unhappiest moments in her life.

Her husband had once stood in the living room that she'd painstakingly designed and handed her divorce papers.

She'd never be able to settle back in and just forget that it happened.

She had a new dream now. To stop living in the past. To move forward. New house. New life. New chance to make things right and to leave the past precisely where it belonged.

CHAPTER 2

WHEN Rachel pulled into her driveway a few minutes after four, she was surprised that Ethan's truck was already there. She got out, eager to see him and to tell him about her day.

She hauled her briefcase from the passenger seat and started up the walkway. Halfway there, the door opened and Ethan stood against the frame, watching her approach. One hand was behind his back, and as she mounted the steps, he pulled it around so she could see the gorgeous bouquet of flowers he was holding.

They were her favorite. Roses that were a beautiful shade of peach. Not quite orange and not quite pink. For the longest time, Ethan had been unable to buy them for her because he'd taken them to her grave during the year she'd been believed dead.

"To celebrate your first day," he said.

"They're beautiful, Ethan!"

She gathered them and buried her nose in the fragrant blossoms.

"How did it go?" Ethan asked as he ushered her inside.

She went in search of a vase and, after stuffing the stems

inside and filling it with water, she turned an excited smile on Ethan.

"It went great!

He smiled indulgently at her enthusiasm and then pulled her into his arms.

"I missed you."

She laughed. "No you didn't. You were at the compound. You wouldn't have seen me whether I'd gone to work or not."

He kissed her nose and squeezed his arms around her. God, but she loved the security of being in his arms. There were still nights she woke in a cold sweat and there he was, always right beside her to hold and comfort her. He always knew too. He'd gather her into his embrace and whisper in her ear that she was safe and that he was here and that nothing would ever hurt her again. Then he'd tell her over and over again how much he loved her and how sorry he was for ever making her doubt it.

"Just knowing you're here in our home while I'm away makes me feel like I'm with you."

As they walked into the living room, Ethan's arm still snugly around her, she noticed the packing boxes scattered around.

"You did get home early," she exclaimed. "You've already started the packing, I see."

Ethan smiled. "Yeah, I didn't want you having to do too much. The guys are coming over later to help move the furniture and Ma and Rusty are on their way over now to help pack the smaller stuff."

Just thinking of her family filled her with a warm glow that never failed to vanquish the shadows of the past. She was loved, and she was whole again. The emptiness that had gnawed at her for so long had finally been filled.

"Guess I should get to it then," Rachel said, staring around at the living room.

"Uh no," Ethan said, his voice firm. "First you're going to sit down, put your feet up, and I'm going to crack open a bottle of wine to celebrate your first day at work."

She sighed. "You spoil me shamelessly."

He cracked a grin. "Yup, that's me. Completely shameless. Park it while I go get the wine."

He took her briefcase and carried it with him toward the kitchen while she settled onto the leather sofa and, as he'd directed, propped her feet on the ottoman.

Her gaze wandered over the living room, taking in all the details. Details that hadn't changed since they'd moved in. The piano still occupied the same spot. The framed pictures—of their wedding and of other family times together—were still neatly in their places.

Ethan hadn't changed anything in the entire year she was presumed dead. Nothing had been changed since her return.

She was ready for that next step. Ready to embrace the new and move away from the old. It was a matter she'd only discussed with her therapist in the sessions that Ethan didn't attend, but she firmly believed the last step in her recovery was to remove herself from the house that held so many painful memories for her.

There were still gaps in her memory. Maybe she'd never fully regain everything of her past. A year hooked on drugs and the emotional and physical trauma she'd endured had perhaps altered her mind enough that there were simply things she'd never remember. Maybe it was better that way.

It was difficult for her—since she'd lost her memory of so many events—when they did come floating back, she experienced them all over again. Some were hurtful and vivid, and it took days and even weeks to come to terms with them.

It was hard to tell herself it happened four years ago when it was so fresh in her mind. The arguments. The stony silence between her and Ethan. The miscarriage. Ethan being gone. And the accusations that still stung if she let herself dwell on them.

The man Ethan was today wasn't the man Ethan was in the early stages of their marriage. She knew that. But it was hard when those memories came back to her. New. As if it had happened yesterday.

Her gaze drifted to the bookcase where those damnable papers had been hidden. Immediately the image flashed of that last terrible day when Ethan had stood in front her, his expression impassive as he calmly handed her papers that would effectively end their marriage.

He'd told her not to bother coming back.

And she hadn't.

For an eternity she'd remained a prisoner in unimaginable circumstances, her mind shattered. She'd clung to the only thing she'd known. Ethan. He'd been the one constant. He would come for her. He wouldn't let her die in hell. Thank God her mind had protected her from the awful reality of the way they'd parted, or she would have never survived or held on to the hope that he'd come.

"Rachel? Are you okay?"

Ethan's concerned question drifted through the painful memories, and she blinked, turning in the direction of his voice.

He was holding two glasses of wine, and his brows were drawn together, his sharp gaze peeling back layer after layer until she worried he'd know exactly what she was thinking.

She smiled, mustering all her control to prevent the shaking that usually accompanied the flashbacks. She reached for the wine and nodded. "I'm fine. Just thinking."

Ethan handed over the glass and then settled on the couch beside her.

"Whatever you were thinking, it couldn't have been good. You were pale, and your eyes were so distant that you didn't seem to be here at all."

"It was nothing. I'd rather focus on us. And the move to our brand new house."

She held up her glass, and he gently clinked his to hers.

"I'm going to miss this place," he said. "Lot of memories tied up here. I can understand why Mom and Dad are reluctant to relocate. They've been in that house my whole life. I can't imagine them anywhere else."

She swallowed and then sipped at her wine.

"You sure this is what you want to do?" he asked.

Her eyes widened. "We're certainly beyond that point now. The other house is already built! What on earth would we do with it if we decided not to move?"

He shrugged. "Van and Joe haven't built houses yet. One of them could always take it."

She shook her head. "No. I love that house. It's perfect. I'm excited to move into it."

He studied her a minute as if deciding whether to state what was on his mind. Then he leaned over to put his glass on the end table.

"You aren't happy here, are you?" he said bluntly.

She froze, because she hadn't wanted him to know just how much she wanted to be free of this house and its hold on her. The last thing she wanted was for him to feel guilty. They'd wasted enough time on guilt and anguish. It served no purpose. They'd never move on if they were always dwelling on the past.

The doorbell rang, and she nearly sighed an audible sound of relief.

"I'll get it. You sit," Ethan said as he sprang upward.

He walked to the front door and opened it, and a mere second later, Rusty entered the living room.

Rachel smiled and got up to hug the other woman.

"Rusty! I'm so glad to see you!" Rachel stepped back to examine the smiling girl. "You're looking so gorgeous! How is school?"

Rusty dipped her head a little shyly but beamed at Rachel's compliment. And it was true. Rusty had blossomed into a beautiful young lady. A long way from the scrawny, surly teenager with ragged, brightly dyed hair who'd stolen into Marlene and Frank Kelly's house a few years earlier.

She could definitely still hold her own with the Kelly clan and could be plenty sassy when the occasion called for it, but Rusty had softened under the love and tutelage of Marlene and the rest of the Kellys.

"I heard you went back to work today," Rusty said after offering Rachel her own enthusiastic hug. "How did it go?"

There was worry in the other girl's eyes, and Rachel's heart squeezed. She and Rusty hadn't always had the best relationship. Rusty had entered the Kellys' lives at the precise time when Rachel had been rescued and returned to her family. Rusty had feared that concern for Rachel would overshadow her own existence and that she'd be discarded and sent on her way.

"It was scary and wonderful at the same time," Rachel said. "Hard to believe I can be intimidated by a bunch of junior high kids, but believe me, they're pretty terrifying!"

Rusty laughed. "I remember me at that age so I can well understand why you'd be shaking in your shoes."

"Where's Ma?" Ethan asked. "I thought she was coming with you?"

Rusty turned to Ethan. "She said to tell you she'll be here as soon as she can. Sophie was running late, and Marlene was keeping Charlotte for her."

Ethan's cell rang, and he made a grab for it, turning away from the two women as he answered.

Rachel took Rusty's hand and dragged her toward the couch. "So how are you doing in your classes, and how are you liking college?"

Rusty's eyes glowed with excitement. "I love it. It's as you said. Scary and wonderful all at the same time. There are so many people. Everywhere. And from all over! I'd never been out of Dover my entire life so it was like culture shock. But it's fun, and I've made so many good friends. There's so much to do."

"You're keeping up with your studies, right?" Rachel asked.

Rusty grinned. "You sound just like Marlene. And yes, I'm doing very well. Better than I would have ever thought I was capable of. I have one B, but it's a high B, so I think I can bring it up to an A before the semester is over. I have

As in everything else. Who would have thought that I would ever be an honor student!"

"You're smarter than all of us," Rachel said dryly. "It was always just a matter of focusing your efforts in a positive direction."

"Sorry to interrupt, girls, but I'm going to head over to round up a crew to help move furniture. Sam has a delivery truck he's borrowed, and we're going to bring it over here to load up as much stuff as we can this evening."

Rachel smiled up at her husband. "Okay. We'll work on packing some of the smaller boxes while we wait for Marlene. I should probably put in a pizza order for later. Everyone will be starving."

Ethan dropped a kiss on her lips. "Let us worry about the food. If I know Ma, she's already prepared a feast, and she'll probably come over loaded for bear."

"True," Rachel said ruefully. "Okay, off with you. I'll see you and your brothers in a bit."

Rusty also stood and motioned toward the boxes. "Is there any particular place you want me to start?"

Rachel rose, setting her glass down beside Ethan's on the end table. She'd only had a sip, but her stomach was roiling, and a clammy sweat had broken out on her forehead.

Without saying a word to Rusty, she hurried past her and to the guest bathroom down from the kitchen. She barely made it to the toilet before her stomach heaved and ejected the contents.

A soothing hand rubbed up and down her back as Rusty's anxious question was issued. "Rachel, are you all right? Should I call Ethan back?"

Rachel shook her head as she wiped at her mouth with a towel. "N-no," she said shakily. "I'm fine. Really."

When she lifted her head, she saw Rusty frowning at her.

"You aren't fine. You were puking your guts up. What's going on?"

Rachel swallowed nervously and then went to the sink to wash out her mouth. She gargled with mouthwash, praying it wouldn't send her back to the toilet to vomit again.

She leaned against the sink, her hands braced on the countertop, as she stared at herself in the mirror.

It was time to stop discounting the possibility. Having the wine had been irresponsible. She knew she could be. Even if she'd thought it unlikely that it would happen this soon.

"Rusty?" she said faintly. "Is there any way you could do me a favor?"

Rusty came up behind her and put her hand on her shoulder. "Of course. Just tell me what you need."

Rachel turned, taking Rusty's hand in hers. "I don't want you to tell anyone about this, okay? Promise me."

Rusty frowned but nodded.

"If you leave now, you could get back before everyone gets over here. But you'll have to hurry."

Rusty cocked her head to the side. "What are you wanting?"

Rachel took a deep breath. "Is there any way you could run to the pharmacy and buy an over-the-counter pregnancy test for me?"

CHAPTER 3

RACHEL paced the confines of the living room, the wait for Rusty to return an eternity. She checked her watch and then looked anxiously out the window. She didn't expect Ethan for a while yet. The compound was across the lake, and he'd no doubt get sidetracked talking to his brothers before they made their way back over. But Marlene could show up at any time, and while Rachel loved her dearly, she wasn't ready to tell anyone of her suspicion yet. The last thing she wanted was to build anyone's hopes only for it to be a false alarm.

And she didn't want the inevitable questions and concerns that would surely accompany the knowledge that she and Ethan were trying for a baby. For now it was their own precious secret. Only now Rusty knew, and Rachel hoped that Rusty would keep it in confidence.

Her pulse bounded when she heard a vehicle in the drive. Her gaze jerked to the window, and she sagged in relief when she saw it was Rusty's jeep.

A moment later, Rusty hurried in the door with a plain, brown paper sack in her hand.

"I bought two," she said as she began pulling one out of

the bag. "I figured it would be better to take two no matter what the first result is, just to make sure."

Rachel smiled and hugged Rusty tight. "Thank you. I appreciate you doing this for me."

Rusty pulled carefully away, her eyes dark with concern. "Is this a good thing or a bad thing, Rachel? I mean if you're pregnant."

"It would be a very good thing," Rachel said in a low voice.

Rusty smiled. "Then I'll cross fingers and toes the test is positive. You better hurry, though, if you don't want the entire world to know. If Marlene shows up and finds you peeing on a stick, the entire family will be gathered in short order."

Rachel laughed but took the box from Rusty and hurried toward the bathroom. "You be my lookout," she called back.

"I'll guard the door," Rusty said in an amused voice from just outside the bathroom.

Rachel's hands shook as she hastily tore into the box. They were shaking so badly that she nearly dropped the stick once she freed it from the packaging.

After reading the instructions twice to make sure she did everything accordingly, she forced herself to calm down and focus on the task at hand.

And then, so she wouldn't drive herself crazy waiting for the first test's results, she squeezed out just enough to go ahead and take the second test.

She straightened her clothing, washed her hands, and then checked her watch, all while avoiding the little indicator windows on the sticks lying on the counter.

Then she looked.

"Rachel?"

At first she didn't respond.

"Rachel, is everything okay in there? It's awfully quiet."

"Y-you can come in," Rachel managed to get out.

The door opened, and Rusty stuck her head in and then looked down at what Rachel was obviously staring at.

"They're both positive," Rachel murmured.

Then she looked up at Rusty, a rush of fear, excitement, and pure adrenaline pumping through her veins.

Rusty smiled. "That's good, right?"

"It's wonderful," Rachel breathed.

Tears filled her eyes, and then Rusty was hugging her, holding on tight as Rachel fought the wave of emotion engulfing her.

"Congratulations," Rusty said in a fierce voice. "I'm happy for you, Rachel."

"Thank you," Rachel said, giving her a watery smile as she pulled away.

Rusty shook her head and made a tsking sound. "You so better get rid of the watery, red eyes before Mama Kelly gets here. She'll be on you faster than a duck on a june bug. I'm assuming you want to tell Ethan before the rest of the family."

Rachel grabbed a washcloth and ran cold water over it. "Yes, of course I do. I appreciate you keeping it secret, Rusty. It's such a shock. I mean, it's not completely unexpected. I certainly knew it was possible. It's just that I never imagined it would happen so fast. I figured with everything that's happened, that it could be months or even years after we started trying before I got pregnant. I want some time to get used to it myself, and I want to be able to tell Ethan at the perfect moment before we tell everyone else."

She wrung out the washcloth and pressed it to her eyes and face. When she pulled it down, she grimaced.

"There's also the fact that I miscarried once before, so I don't think it's wise to bust out with the news until a little further along in the pregnancy."

Rusty's face wrinkled in sympathy. "I'm sure you'll be just fine this time. You know the family will close ranks around you. You'll be fortunate if they let you lift a finger at all."

Rachel bunched up her nose. "Ugh. Ethan was already not happy about me going back to work. He'll really flip out now."

Rusty's soft chuckle echoed through the bathroom. "I'm

sure you'll straighten him out in no time. It's not like you
don't have him wrapped around your little finger."

Rachel grinned, and then a giddy rush fizzled through
her veins much like a shaken up soda.

"Oh my God, Rusty, I'm pregnant!"

She wanted to do something ridiculous like squeal and
twirl around in circles.

"Yay!" Rusty shouted.

She grabbed Rachel's hands, and they both jumped up
and down like little girls skipping rope. Rachel dissolved
into laughter, and then Rusty joined her.

"Hello? Rachel? Rusty? Are y'all here?"

"Oh crap, it's Marlene!" Rachel whispered.

Rusty clamped her lips shut and made a show of zipping
them and then winked at Rachel. Rachel impulsively
hugged the other girl and squeezed her in gratitude.

"Thank you," she whispered urgently in her ear.

"No problem," Rusty whispered back. "Now let's go see
what Mama Kelly brought us to eat."

THE evening was a flurry of activity. Marlene had come,
and as Ethan had predicted, had brought enough food to
feed an army. Or at least the majority of the Kelly clan.

Ethan showed up not long after with all his brothers in
tow, plus Swanny, a family friend and member of KGI, and
Ethan's dad, Frank Kelly, as well. Not that anyone was
going to allow Frank to do anything, but he could organize
and oversee at will.

He'd had a heart attack a few years earlier, and it was
still very much on the minds of all the family members.
The mere idea of losing him had them all in terror.

Though Rachel packed her share of boxes, Rusty always
stepped in, making sure she never lifted anything too heavy.
Rachel could hardly contain her smile. Rusty was already
acting fiercely protective of Rachel, knowing she was pregnant, even though she never let on so much as a hint that she
was objecting to Rachel carrying anything heavy.

"How was your first day, sweetness?" Garrett asked as he pulled Rachel into a hug.

She returned the hug and squeezed him tightly. Garrett had always been one of her favorites. He'd been there during her first miscarriage, and he'd been a steadfast friend and shoulder to lean on during her return and recovery.

"It was great. I was terrified and nervous, but it went so well. The kids were terrific. There were several teachers still there from when I taught before, and they all welcomed me back. It was really nice. I loved it."

Garrett smiled and ruffled her hair. "That's wonderful. Glad to hear you sounding so happy."

"Hey Garrett, more working and less talking," Sam called from across the room.

Garrett rolled his eyes but let his arm drop from Rachel's shoulders and ambled toward his brothers.

Rachel smiled as she took in the big, noisy Kelly family. Ethan was right in the middle with three older brothers and two younger brothers. Sam was the oldest. Garrett was a year younger. Then there was Donovan, or Van as most of the family called him. Then Ethan and then the twins, Nathan and Joe.

Of the six, four were married. Only Donovan and Joe hadn't settled down yet and were showing no signs of doing so. Rachel wasn't even sure they had a steady woman in their lives. They were so busy with KGI that it didn't leave them a whole lot of free time, and what time they did get was usually spent with the family.

She placed a hand over her belly, a flutter of excitement deep in her stomach. So far, Sam and his wife, Sophie, were the only ones who'd had a child. Charlotte. An adorable toddler who was doted on by every single member of the family.

Garrett and his wife, Sarah, had only just married as had Nathan and his wife, Shea, and neither couple had voiced any desire to start a family yet.

Of them all, she and Ethan had been together the longest. She often wondered if she hadn't miscarried their first child how different their lives would be. Perhaps Ethan would have never left his SEAL team. Maybe he'd even now still be in the navy. Maybe she wouldn't have gone on the mercy mission to South America. At the time, she'd done it as much to escape the awful reality of her marriage as she had for the cause it supported.

Losing their baby had been the catalyst for so many things. It was foolish to play the what-if game, but she couldn't help but wonder how different things might have been if only . . .

"Everything okay, Rachel?"

She blinked and looked up to see Joe standing in front of her, his eyes dark with concern. Then she glanced rapidly around, hoping that she hadn't attracted attention from the others. To her relief they were too busy loading furniture onto the truck.

"Everything's fine," she said with a genuine smile.

And it wasn't a lie. Everything *was* okay. More than okay. Maybe even perfect.

He smiled, relief edging out the worry on his face.

"Time for dinner break," Marlene called from the kitchen she'd been packing up just moments earlier.

There was a whoop from her sons, and Rachel stood back, enjoying the very normal way of life in the Kelly family. Lots of love, unconditional support, always a helping hand, and plenty of food, thanks to Mama Kelly.

It was a family she'd bring a son or daughter into, and she couldn't wait. How fortunate her child would be to grow up under the umbrella of so much love and loyalty.

Ethan walked up to her, sliding his arm around her shoulders and pulling her into him.

"Hey, you hungry? Let's go grab something to eat before the hyenas get it all."

Rachel laughed, allowing some of the bubbling joy to surge right out of her soul. She caught Rusty's grin from across the room and shared a secret smile with the other girl.

She let Ethan lead her toward the kitchen as she dreamed of the perfect way to tell him he was going to be a father.

CHAPTER 4

IT was late when the truck was unloaded at the new house and everything was set up. Oddly, Rachel had insisted that their bed be moved first so they could stay the night here instead of at their old home.

It felt strange to say old home. Ethan still hadn't adjusted to the idea of a new house. Oh, he agreed with the idea that they should live behind the walls of the compound. He was on board with anything that assured him of his wife's safety. Or at least gave her an added measure of protection.

But Rachel seemed . . . *eager* to move. She showed no outward signs of regret over leaving their old life.

He flopped down on the bed waiting for her to finish in the shower and join him. The thought shouldn't nag him, but there was something he couldn't quite put his finger on. He wondered if everything was all right with Rachel and if she really was taking the move as well as she seemed to be.

He worried endlessly over causing her any upset. His brothers cautioned him not to go so overboard and to lighten up. Not to smother her. He knew they were right, but they'd never lived with the knowledge that the woman they loved beyond all measure had died. That they'd pushed her away. That they'd rejected her. Taken her love and thrown it in her face.

Ethan had done all of that. He'd lived it. He'd had the very heart of him taken away the day he was informed that Rachel had died in that plane crash.

To this day, he still woke in a cold sweat, reaching frantically beside him to reassure himself that she was here. Alive. Next to him.

So if he was a little overbearing, surely it was understandable. Not many people had lost and then miraculously regained a loved one. He damn well was going to make sure he didn't ever lose her again.

The bathroom door opened, and Rachel stepped out, her skin rosy and glowing from the heat of the shower. Her hair was wet, and she was toweling it dry as she walked toward the bed.

She was wearing a teeny, tiny silk camisole set that drove him insane. The shorts—if you could call them that— barely covered her ass, and the cami top plunged between her breasts, damn near baring her belly button.

She may as well not wear anything at all, which would be more than fine with him, but then she did love to tease him mercilessly and then pretend innocence when he tore the little scraps of material from her body.

She'd filled out a lot since the day they'd brought her home from South America. She'd bordered on gaunt. Hell, she *had* been gaunt. A ghost of her former self. Thin. Deep shadows under and in her eyes. Her hair had been lopped off without care, and she'd looked intensely frail. As if the slightest thing would knock her off balance.

How deceptive her appearance had been, because to survive as she had, she would have to have been forged in steel and possessed the will of a warrior.

Now her curves had returned, though she'd always been more willowy. But she'd lost the look of fragility. Her hips were more rounded. Even her breasts were plumper, and she'd gained much-needed pounds.

Her hair had grown long again, and it was thick and glossy and healthy-looking. Her eyes glowed with contentment. He never tired of that look on her. He'd seen her with despair that was bone deep, and if he never had to see such a thing again, it would be too soon. Whatever he had to do to prevent her from ever feeling that kind of hopelessness, he'd do.

"Hand me a comb and I'll brush out your hair," he offered.

She sent him a smile that curled his toes. He knew she loved to have her hair brushed, and it was a simple thing that brought him every bit as much pleasure as it did her. It was an excuse to hold her. To touch her. To simply spend time with her and just . . . be.

He'd taken those things for granted before. He'd never make that mistake again.

She retrieved a comb from the bathroom and then crawled onto the bed and settled between his legs after he'd positioned himself against the headboard.

He started at the bottom, gently working the comb through her tangles. She tilted her head back, and he could see that her eyes were closed, her expression one of deep contentment.

It was automatic for him to smile. His chest tightened and then eased as the knot of emotion formed and then loosened, spreading warmth all the way to his soul.

God, but he loved this woman. He never wanted to be without her.

As he finished detangling her hair, he leaned forward and kissed the side of her neck, inciting a shiver that he felt go down her entire body.

"I have an idea," he murmured suggestively. "I was thinking that we do away with the silky bits you call sleepwear and then we practice making that baby. Practice makes perfect or so they say."

She went completely still, and then she twisted around, positioning herself so that she was on her knees between his legs facing him.

"Speaking of that . . ." she began.

He studied her intently, wondering if perhaps the idea of pregnancy had been occupying her thoughts of late. Perhaps it was why he couldn't quite put his finger on her mood.

"Are you having second thoughts?" he asked. "Because it's absolutely okay if you are, baby. I certainly don't mind waiting as long as it takes for you to feel comfortable with it. I want you to be sure you're ready."

Part of him hoped she was reconsidering. He wasn't certain she was strong enough yet—physically or emotionally— to endure a pregnancy. And God forbid, what would happen if she miscarried again? It would devastate her, and he couldn't bear for her to be hurt like that.

She smiled then, and it was so breathtakingly beautiful that for a moment he couldn't force air into his lungs.

She gathered his hands in hers and pulled them to her chest, her hands cupped over his as they pressed against her skin. He could feel the gentle rhythm of her heart as her warmth seeped into his fingers.

"Apparently you don't need practice at all," she said in a hushed tone barely above a whisper. "It would appear that you're quite the expert. We did it, Ethan. We made a baby!"

His eyebrows went up, and his mouth dropped open. He stared at her in complete befuddlement as he tried to collect his scattered wits.

"We did *what*?" he asked hoarsely.

Her smile grew even broader, and tears shone in her eyes, making them a glossy, rich brown.

He raised trembling hands to frame her face, and he thumbed away the tears as they brimmed over her eyelids.

"We're having a baby?" he whispered.

She nodded, her eyes shining like stars.

He was assaulted by a multitude of emotions all at the same time. Indescribable joy. Gratitude. Gut-wrenching fear. Overwhelming love and tenderness for the woman he was holding in his hands.

"When? How?"

He ended the sputtering before he turned into a blithering idiot.

"Rusty went to buy me a home pregnancy test after she got to the house tonight. I was sick in the bathroom, so she went out for me. She bought two, and I took them both. They both came up positive."

He frowned. "Sick? Are you all right?"

She leaned into him, nuzzling her face into the side of his neck. "I'm fine. Just normal pregnancy stuff. I shouldn't have sipped the wine. I knew . . . I mean I suspected there was a chance. I've felt off for several days. Sick in the mornings and afternoons. Overwhelming fatigue. Tenderness in my breasts. I think I was just afraid to have it confirmed."

He stroked his hands down her body, caressing, just wanting to touch her in some way. He laid his cheek on the top of her head and cuddled her even closer, his heart about to burst right out of his chest.

"Are you okay now? Do you need anything?" he asked anxiously.

He felt her smile against his neck.

"Right now I couldn't be more perfect. I'm right where I want to be."

He pulled her up his body even more until her mouth hovered precariously close to his.

"Have I told you lately how much I love you?"

Her smile lit up the entire room once more.

"As a matter of fact, you have, but I never get tired of hearing it."

"A baby," he said in awe.

It was too much for him to comprehend. Oh, they'd talked about it. Seriously. They'd not made the decision to start trying for a baby lightly. It had taken months for them to talk out all the possibilities, the potential issues that could arise, whether they were ready for parenthood, whether their fragile relationship could withstand the risks involved.

They'd even talked about it in therapy.

Nothing about this decision had been made lightly, and

yet Ethan was gobsmacked now that the reality was staring him in the face.

A baby.

A son or a daughter.

A part of Rachel, a woman who meant the world to him. Who meant *everything* to him.

His own eyes burned, and he blinked away the discomfort. His stomach clenched into a ball, and his chest tightened and flexed uncomfortably.

"Are you happy about it?" she asked anxiously.

He stared up in stupefaction at the worried glint in her eyes. He gathered her more closely, until their noses touched and their breaths mingled.

"Oh baby, I'm over the freaking moon. I don't even have words. Happy? That seems such a pussy word for what I'm feeling right now. God, I'm happy, but I'm also scared shitless for you."

Her smile was gentle, and she reached up to touch his cheek. "I'll be fine, Ethan. I have you now."

That one statement. Just those simple words had the power to undo him. He had to close his eyes to prevent himself from completely breaking down and unmanning himself.

"Yes, you have me now," he said hoarsely, so choked up that he could barely get the words out.

She hadn't had him before. They both knew it. He'd checked out of their relationship early on. He was never there for her when she needed him. And after her miscarriage it got even worse.

He'd very nearly destroyed the one good thing in his life. The one person he loved beyond reason, and he'd tried his damnedest to push her away.

"You'll always have me, Rachel. You and our baby both will have me. I swear it. You'll never have to worry about whether I'm with you or not."

She caressed his cheek with loving hands and then pressed her mouth carefully to his.

"I'm not worried, Ethan," she whispered against his mouth, her words swallowed up when he inhaled.

"When do you want to tell the rest of the family?" he asked.

They'd be so thrilled. Though most of his brothers had gone on to marry, Rachel was still the first. She was dearly loved by his brothers and his parents. By his sisters-in-law as well. Rachel's pregnancy would be greeted with so much love and enthusiasm. He had no doubt that when the day came for her to deliver, every single Kelly would be crowded around at the hospital, all holding their breath waiting for his son or daughter to arrive.

She licked her lips nervously as she pulled away. For the first time, anxiety burned in her eyes.

It was automatic for him to reach for her. To take her hands. To reassure her in some way.

She vibrated with unease.

"I don't think we should say anything yet," she said in a low voice. "It's early yet. I honestly don't remember when my last period was. They were kind of irregular after I stopped taking birth control, and I didn't think anything of it. So I honestly don't know how far along I am. I won't know until I see a doctor."

She took another breath and plunged ahead.

"I'd hate to make this big announcement and for everyone to be so happy and excited for us and then for something to happen. Like last time," she choked out.

He hugged her to him, stroking his hand over her hair. Though her first miscarriage had happened some years ago, for her it was like yesterday because she hadn't regained her memory of the event until recently.

"I don't think I could bear it," she said in a muffled voice. "It would be bad enough that we knew of our loss, but for everyone else to also have to grieve. I'd rather wait until I'm further along before we tell the others."

"I agree," he said firmly.

She swallowed and pulled away to look him in the eye.

"Will you go with me to the doctor? I want so much for you to be with me. For you to share every step of the process with me."

He grasped her shoulders with gentle hands, but his gaze was intent and fierce.

"Rachel, baby, I'm going to be with you every single minute of the way. I swear it. There is *nothing* that's more important to me than you and our baby. Not KGI, not a mission. Nothing. I need you to understand that. No matter what's happened in the past between us, this is the new us, okay? You come first. Always."

Joy flared in her eyes. And relief. It was a painful reminder of his past mistakes. But they were mistakes he'd never make again.

He slid his hand down the silky bodice of her top until it rested over her slim belly.

"Our child," he said in wonder.

She put her hands over his and squeezed. A splash of moisture dripped onto his hand, and he glanced up to see silver trails down her cheeks.

For once, the sight of her tears didn't rip his heart wide open. Because these weren't tears of grief or pain. They were tears of extreme joy. Her smile was as wide as a mile, and it was the most beautiful sight he'd ever seen in his life.

He'd carry to his deathbed this memory of her on her knees between his legs, his hands covering her belly as she cried tears of happiness.

"We did it, Ethan," she whispered huskily.

"Hell yeah, we did," he murmured just before he pressed in to devour her mouth.

CHAPTER 5

IT was typical for Rachel to get up when Ethan did, and while he was out for his run, she'd make breakfast. She loved the early morning routine they'd comfortably fallen into.

Usually she'd brew a pot of coffee because Ethan liked a cup after downing a bottle of water after his workout. But this morning—as with every morning of the past week—the smell of coffee nearly did her in.

Perspiration beaded her forehead, and she swallowed huge gulps of air to try to steady her rebelling stomach. Unfortunately for her, the typical fare she made for breakfast didn't at all agree with her now that she was pregnant.

Eggs made her want to hurl. Bacon nauseated her. Sweet rolls made her clench her teeth and breathe through her nose. The only safe bet seemed to be dry toast or bread products like croissants or biscuits.

She was leaning over the counter, inhaling settling breaths, when Ethan came in from his run.

"Rachel?" he asked sharply. "Are you okay?"

She quickly twisted around, forcing an appeasing smile to her face. The last thing she wanted was for him to worry. He'd do enough of that on his own without her help.

"I'm fine," she reassured him. "Honestly. It's just that certain foods set me off now. Particularly breakfast stuff. I'm super queasy in the mornings. Less so in the afternoons, but I still have to be careful. Eggs and bacon in particular seem to trigger my symptoms."

Ethan frowned and then carefully moved her away from the stove where the bacon still sizzled and the eggs were hardening up and becoming fluffy.

"Sit," he ordered.

Then he returned to the stove and finished the eggs and bacon, plating them while she watched.

"What *can* you eat?" he asked.

"Toast. A croissant. Anything dry."

"What can you drink?"

She wrinkled her nose. "Mainly Sprite but we don't have any. I just got the bare essentials at the grocery store yesterday. I need to do a full-blown shopping trip today."

His frown deepened as he popped bread into the toaster.

"We need to talk about the rest of the move. I know you'd planned to go pack boxes and stuff, but I don't like the idea of you being alone at the house packing around heavier stuff. I know you don't want to tell the family yet, so we can't go to them with why I don't want you doing very much."

She started to protest but he shook his head, his eyes glinting with the stubbornness the Kellys were famous for.

"It's Saturday. We aren't training today so I'll see if my brothers are free to come help pack boxes and get them onto the truck. If we can get it all done in one big push this weekend then we won't be unpacking this crap for weeks."

She nodded her agreement. "I need to go shopping. I have an entire list of stuff we need. I'll call Rusty and see if she wants to go."

"Good idea."

He lightly buttered the toasted bread and slid the saucer across the bar toward her. Her stomach rumbled, and her mouth watered in that icky way it did right before she usually got sick.

She stared cautiously at the bread and then peeked up at Ethan. His expression was worried but even she couldn't eat it just to appease him.

"I can't," she said honestly.

"Is there anything I can do?" he asked anxiously.

She smiled and shook her head. "I'll be fine. I haven't eaten much of anything in the mornings for the last several days. Usually around noon, my stomach starts protesting and demanding something to eat."

"Any particular cravings you have? You name it, and I'll make sure you have it for lunch."

Her chest ached with the love she felt for him.

"Maybe not for lunch, but if someone wanted to break out the grill tonight and dish up some Kelly barbeque, I certainly wouldn't complain."

"I'll get Van on it," Ethan said slyly. "He can't resist anything for you. If I tell him you want some, he'll do it."

Rachel shook her head, stifling her laughter.

"Okay, so you'll have the guys over to get the rest of the stuff from the other house, and I'm going shopping with Rusty."

"Yep," Ethan said. "Unless you need one of the guys to go shopping with you. I don't want you lifting anything too heavy."

She rolled her eyes. "I think I can manage groceries. I'll pick up something for the grill while I'm out too."

Ethan nodded.

Rachel reached for her cell phone just as it went off. She stared at the incoming number and other than recognizing it as local, she didn't have it in her address book.

"Hello?" she said as she put the phone to her ear.

"Mrs. Kelly. This is Principal Talbot at the middle school. How are you today?"

"I'm fine, thank you," she said politely.

"I apologize for calling you on a Saturday, but I have a situation with one of my teachers. Mrs. Ashton was in a car accident last night."

"Oh, I hope she's all right."

"She'll make a full recovery. But she's going to be out for several weeks, and I'm scrambling to try to fill her position. I wondered if you'd be interested in taking over her class while she's on leave."

Rachel's eyes widened. "Yes, yes, of course I would."

She could see Ethan's eyebrows go up in question from across the bar, and she held up one finger to signal that she'd let him know momentarily.

"That's wonderful. We appreciate your willingness to step in. If you'd like to come in a little early on Monday, one of the other teachers will brief you on where the children are."

"That's fine. I'll be there."

"Okay then, I'll see you on Monday, and again, thank you."

"No problem. I'll see you then."

She ended the call and then stared up at Ethan, excitement dancing up her spine.

"One of the other teachers is going to be out for a few weeks, and they want me to fill in."

Ethan was silent for a moment. His words were careful when he spoke. "Do you think this is a good idea? For you to go back to work being pregnant?"

She shot him a look of surprise. It never occurred to her that it wouldn't be okay.

"I'm not saying you shouldn't," Ethan hastily added. "And I'm certainly not telling you I don't want you to work. Even if I don't," he added ruefully. "I just want to make sure this is something that doesn't hurt you or the baby."

Her tension eased and she smiled. "We'll be fine. Pregnant women work every single day. If I have to sit at home for my entire pregnancy, I'll go insane. I'll never make it.

Teaching will give me something to focus on rather than worrying obsessively over the baby."

Ethan nodded. "I just want you to be sure."

"I am," she said resolutely. "Now, I'm going to call Rusty and get going so we aren't shopping the entire day. I've got my heart set on barbeque tonight."

CHAPTER 6

RACHEL checked her text messages and smiled when she saw three from Ethan. Two were checking up on her to see how she was coping at work, and the third was to let her know he'd gotten her an appointment right after school with an obstetrician in Murray, Kentucky, which was not far from where they lived, just across the border.

There was a big women's clinic in Murray, and she preferred to use it rather than the much smaller hospital and clinic in Paris, Tennessee.

She sent a quick text back saying she'd meet him at the clinic and then turned her attention back to the papers in front of her. It was her planning period, and the classroom was empty of students and eerily quiet.

Her first day had gone well. Far better than she'd anticipated. Oddly, she hadn't suffered the attack of nerves she had on the day she'd substituted the previous week.

For now, at least, this was her class. These were her kids.

She frowned when she got to the paper of one of the girls in her class. Rachel knew the child to be particularly bright. Her grades reflected a studious nature and someone who took her classes very seriously.

The test hadn't even been completed. There were doodles up and down the margins. The name had been filled out and the few questions she had answered bore the responses of "I don't care" or "Who cares?" The rest were left blank, and the paper was worn and crumpled as if the girl had fidgeted and toyed with it the entire testing period.

Rachel put the test to the side, determined to delve further into the matter.

She was absorbed in grading the rest of the test papers when the bell rang, startling her from her concentration. A moment later, the students began to file into the room, and she quickly sought out the girl whose paper had been rife with incorrect and unanswered questions.

Jennifer was her name, and she was a beautiful, shy little girl. Not yet up with most of her classmates who were beginning to experiment with make-up and showing mad interest in boys.

Rachel watched as Jennifer took her seat and hunched over at her desk, not looking anywhere but in front of her.

Something was terribly wrong, and Rachel just hoped it wasn't too complicated.

It was difficult to continue casually in class without drawing notice to the fact she was preoccupied with Jennifer. The very last thing she wanted was to make the girl uncomfortable or draw attention to her.

When the final bell of the day rang, dismissing the kids to the respective bus and car lines, Rachel breathed a sigh of relief.

"Jennifer," she called softly when the girl got up to depart the room. "Can I have a moment please?"

Jennifer turned, her eyes wide with alarm. Nervousness radiated from her in tangible waves, and she fidgeted as she approached the desk.

"I won't keep you long so you won't miss your bus," Rachel said gently. "I was looking at your test paper from earlier and wondered what was wrong. It's not like you not to perform well on an exam. You're an excellent student with an A average in all subjects."

Jennifer's face crumpled as tears flashed in her eyes.

"I'm sorry, Ms. Kelly. I know what I did was wrong. I was just so angry and upset."

Rachel put her hand on Jennifer's and squeezed gently. "I'm more concerned about you than I am one test grade. Is everything okay at home?"

"N-no," Jennifer sobbed. "My mom and dad are splitting up and it just sucks. They're so selfish. They fight all the time, and they never think of anyone but themselves. They don't care about me."

Rachel's heart sank as she viewed the devastation in the younger girl's eyes. Thirteen was such a hard age under any circumstances. Let alone when your entire family was crumbling in front of you.

"I'm so sorry, honey," Rachel said. "I know how upset you must be. I'm sure your mom and dad love you very much. Sometimes adults forget themselves and react emotionally, and often they say things they don't mean."

"Maybe," Jennifer mumbled.

"How about you come in on your lunch break tomorrow, and I'll let you retake your exam," Rachel offered.

Jennifer lifted her head, her eyes a little more hopeful than before and not so desolate. "You'd do that for me? I don't deserve a second chance. I screwed up big time."

Rachel smiled. "Honey, we all deserve a second chance."

"Thanks, Ms. Kelly. You're the best. I'll be here. Promise."

"Keep your chin up, okay? Things will get better."

Jennifer sighed but didn't respond. She turned, clutching her books to her chest, and hurried out the door.

RACHEL sat in stunned silence in the exam room, hardly able to process what the doctor had told her. It was shocking enough to find out she was, by the doctor's approximation, at least twelve weeks along, but when he'd done the internal sonogram to ascertain fetal age, he'd found *two* heartbeats.

Twins.

She couldn't even wrap her head around it. Her hands shook every time she pried them away from one another, so she finally gave up and left them clasped tightly in her lap.

Ethan leaned against the exam table where she sat, her legs dangling over the edge, and he seemed every bit as in shock as she was.

His breath was explosive in the small room.

"Holy shit," he breathed. "Twins."

Then he turned to her, his eyes glowing with excitement.

"Twins!" he said again.

A broad smile attacked her face, and then she latched onto Ethan's shoulders all but shaking him in her excitement.

"Oh my God, Ethan. *Two* babies."

She felt light-headed, and for a moment she wobbled like a drunken party girl in four-inch heels. Ethan made a grab for her and held her steady so she didn't fall off the exam table.

"Whoa, sweetheart. Why don't you come over here and sit. I don't want you taking a header."

He led her to the chair against the wall and then eased her down. He knelt in front of her, her hands gathered in his.

"We're so blessed," she whispered. "I can hardly believe it."

He smoothed the hair from her cheek and tucked it behind her ear. There was concern as well as elation in his eyes.

"We're going to have to be careful, baby. You're going to have to take it easy. I don't want anything to happen to you or to the babies."

She leaned into him, touching her forehead to his. "I'm scared out of my mind, but I'm so happy and giddy that I could just explode."

He kissed her softly. "I'm scared too. Terrified is probably a better word. This time is going to be different, Rachel. I swear it."

She looked at him long and hard, love welling from deep within her as she took in the sincerity of his words.

"I lost a lot of my memories," she said in a low voice. "Some have returned. Some have stayed buried. But perhaps the miscarriage should be a memory we both agree to put away and keep in the past where it belongs. It has no place in the here and now and serves no purpose except to make our hearts heavy with regret."

For a long moment he went completely silent. There was a wealth of emotion burning in those blue eyes. His lips were firm, almost as if he were keeping a tight leash on his emotions and keeping himself in check.

"I love you," she said.

He hauled her into his arms and held on so tightly she couldn't breathe. His entire body heaved against her as his breaths tore raggedly from his chest.

"I love you too," he choked out. "God, I love you so much, Rachel. I love our babies."

Slowly he released her and pulled back, a look of awe on his face.

"*Our babies*," he whispered.

Tears slid unheeded down her cheeks, and her face hurt from the wide smile cracking her lips ever upward.

"Well, I guess I don't have to worry about how the news was received," the doctor said from the doorway.

Rachel and Ethan both turned to see the middle-aged obstetrician standing in the doorway, a grin on his face.

Ethan scrambled up, and Rachel started to rise herself, but the doctor motioned her down.

"Sit, sit," he urged. "I won't keep you long. I know this has all been quite a shock for you, and you'll want and need time to soak it all in."

"That's one way to put it," Ethan murmured.

The doctor leaned against the exam table as he studied her chart.

"You've had one previous miscarriage, is that correct?"

Rachel nodded, refusing to allow anything to dampen her euphoria.

SOFTLY AT SUNRISE 325

"Miscarriages are a lot more common than most people realize," the doctor continued. "There's no obvious reason why you won't be able to have a perfectly normal pregnancy and deliver two healthy, squalling babies."

She grinned at the image, and Ethan reached over to squeeze her hand.

"You automatically go into the high-risk category, as anyone pregnant with multiples does," he said matter-of-factly. "That doesn't mean anything more than you'll need to take extra care to rest. Take it easy. Don't try to lift anything heavy. Don't overdo it. Moderate exercise is fine. Nothing too strenuous. Make sure you're eating enough. If the old adage eating for two is correct, then realize you're eating for three."

He chuckled as he said the last.

"For now I'll see you once a month, and later I'll want to see you every two weeks. We'll watch you a lot more closely, and we'll monitor the babies as it gets closer to your due date. In some cases, it becomes necessary to take the babies before the normal gestational period is up, but there are more full-term sets of twins being born all the time. It really depends on mother and babies. But we'll cross that bridge when we get there. For now go home, celebrate, take it easy, and I'll see you back here in four weeks. If you have any problems or questions, don't hesitate to call me."

"Thank you," Ethan said, extending his hand.

The doctor smiled and shook Ethan's hand and then took Rachel's. "Congratulations to the both of you."

"Thank you," Rachel murmured, echoing Ethan's words.

The doctor disappeared, leaving the two alone in the exam room. As Rachel rose from the chair, the nurse bustled in with an appointment card and a prescription for prenatal vitamins.

"We'll want to redo labs when you come in next month just to make sure your HCG levels are where they should be. Nothing to worry about. Just routine stuff."

"Thank you," Rachel said.

The nurse smiled and backed from the room, then gestured for Ethan and Rachel to go ahead of her.

Rachel walked through the waiting room, numb, somewhere between shock and utter elation. She still couldn't take it all in.

"Are you going to be okay to drive?" Ethan asked, a frown covering his face.

She blinked, remembering that they'd taken separate vehicles to the clinic. She shook off some of the fog surrounding her and then nodded.

"I'll be fine. I'll follow you. No sense leaving my car here."

He pulled her into his arms and gave her a long, sweet kiss.

"Twins. I still can't believe it."

She shook her head ruefully. "Neither can I. Oh my God. You realize I'll start showing soon. Like any time. I can't believe I'm already twelve weeks. With two in there, I'll pop out like a beach ball."

"You'll be the most adorable, gorgeous pregnant woman ever," Ethan said, a warm glint to his eyes.

"Oh, Ethan. I can't even take it all in. I feel like someone's going to pinch me any minute and I'll wake up and this will all have been a dream. This has been the most wonderful week. We moved into our new home. I started back teaching. And now we're having two babies instead of one."

His expression became totally serious. He reached up to touch her face, stroking down the curve of her cheekbone with a whisper-soft caress.

"Every single day with you is a dream I always fear I'll awaken from. You're a gift, Rachel. You and the babies are the most treasured gift I've ever been given. I don't deserve it, but by God I'm going to cherish it for the rest of my life."

CHAPTER 7

RACHEL stood outside her old house, keys in hand, staring at the place she'd called home for her entire married life to Ethan.

The realtor had just left, and a brand new "for sale" sign was now mounted in her front yard.

She examined her feelings for some sign of regret. Sadness. Nostalgia even. But the only thing she could put her finger on was . . . relief.

Now that she was pregnant, her relief was compounded by the fact that she wouldn't bring her babies home to a place that still held so much darkness for Rachel.

She took a deep breath and made the effort to let go. Of the past. The memories. The hurt. And the sadness. There was so much joy to replace the sorrows of yesterday. A new house. Precious babies nestled in her womb. A husband and a family who loved her dearly.

She closed her eyes and let the crispness of the fall winds blow over her face. The scratch of leaves on the concrete walkway and the faint smell of smoke in the distance brought home the changing season.

Change was in the air.

Changing seasons. Changing lives. All for the better.

The sound of a car crunching over the gravel drive diverted her from her reverie and turned her around, her brows drawn together as she looked to see who was approaching.

It was her sister-in-law Sophie's SUV, but when it stopped, Sarah and Shea hopped out as Sophie got out from behind the wheel.

"What are you guys doing here?" Rachel asked in bewilderment.

"We're kidnapping you for dinner," Shea said smugly.

Sarah smiled and nodded. "Yep. That's exactly what we're doing. Thought we'd go over to Big Sandy and eat at the Feed and Grain Mill."

"Oh yum. You guys totally know my weakness."

"Thought you could use some girl time about now," Sophie said in a gentle voice. "A lot has been going on with you lately."

"That sounds absolutely perfect," Rachel said, warmed by the friendship in each of their eyes.

She turned one last time and stared at the empty shell of a house. It had no power over her any longer. She was free of it and the memories it housed. She could let go now and focus on the future.

"Why don't we follow you to the new house so you can drop off your car, and then we'll all ride together in my SUV," Sophie suggested.

"Sounds like a plan," Rachel said.

"I'll ride over with Rachel," Shea volunteered. "We'll see you guys in a minute."

Shea climbed into the passenger seat of Rachel's Honda Accord while Rachel slid behind the wheel.

"Is Sam keeping Charlotte tonight?" Rachel asked as they pulled away.

Shea chuckled. "He and Nathan are both on babysitting duty. It'll be interesting to see if Sophie's phone starts blowing up in an hour."

"Speaking of, can you grab my cell and send Ethan a text telling him what we're doing? It'll save time if I don't go in and explain."

"Sure."

Shea picked up Rachel's phone and brought up Ethan in the text messages and promptly froze.

"Uh, Rachel?"

"Hmm?" Rachel made a questioning sound, not looking away from the road as she turned out of the neighborhood and onto the highway.

"Look, I wasn't prying or anything. It's kind of right here and impossible to miss."

Rachel went still. "Oh crap. I completely forgot. I wasn't even thinking."

"Does that mean you *are* pregnant?" Shea asked hesitantly.

Rachel sighed. "Yeah, I am."

Shea sent her a dubious look. "You don't sound happy about it."

Rachel lit up with a smile. Not happy? Never in a million years.

"I'm over the moon," she said softly. "We both are. I just hadn't planned to tell you or anyone else this way. We only just found out. It was quite a shock. When I first suspected, I wanted to wait until after the first trimester in case . . ."

"I understand," Shea said.

"But then we went to the doctor and I'm further along than I thought. And . . ." She glanced over at Shea and bit her lip to keep from shouting it out. "We're having twins."

"Oh my God, Rachel!" Shea screeched. "Holy shit. Twins? Are you serious?"

Rachel nodded, beaming the entire time. "But you can't tell anyone yet. We want to wait for just the right time. And honestly I need a few days to adjust to it myself before I hit the family with something like this."

"Oh Rachel, I'm so happy for you and Ethan," Shea said with a dreamy sigh. "I know how much this has to mean to you. Oh my God, I'm so excited! I'm going to be an aunt!"

"You're already an aunt, dork," Rachel said, laughing.

"Yes, but Charlotte was already here by the time I came along. This will be the first time I was here from the very beginning."

Rachel reached over to squeeze her hand. "I'm glad you're here with us, Shea. I wish Grace could be here more often."

Shea's expression didn't fade a bit at the mention of her sister. Grace was married to Rio, one of the team leaders of KGI, and they lived in Belize when Rio wasn't off on a mission.

What made the sisters so unique is that they both had telepathic abilities and could communicate from great distances.

"I talk to her daily," Shea said cheerfully. "It's almost like having her here. And Rio brings her when he goes out on a mission. He hates the idea of Grace and Elizabeth being alone."

Elizabeth was the pre-teen girl that Rio and Grace had adopted after her father had been killed in the mission that brought Rio and Grace together. Rio was insanely protective of them both. But then all the men of KGI had protective streaks a mile wide.

As they began the drive over the bridge that Rachel had once nearly plummeted over, her palms grew sweaty on the steering wheel, and it was instinctive to accelerate while staying to the far inside lane.

By the time they got across, the steering wheel was damp under her palms.

It was her hope that one day she could conquer her fear of that bridge, but the mere sight of it still sent a wave of panic down her spine.

When they pulled up to the gates of the compound, for a moment Rachel went blank on the security code. She sat there staring at the keypad, feeling like the biggest moron.

"39561*425," Shea supplied.

"Thank you," Rachel said as she punched it in. "I'm still

not used to having to access my house through a security net."

"It makes the guys feel better," Shea said with a shrug. "I guess by the time the children come along, we'll feel the same."

"You're right there," Rachel acknowledged.

And it was true. She wanted her children safe above all else. With the things that had already happened to the family over the past years, it wasn't a stretch to believe that their children would be at risk.

It was a sobering reality of the profession the Kellys had taken on and the missions they were involved with.

She drove toward her house in the distance. The idea of living on a compound with other members of the family sounded a bit hokey and even a little creepy on the surface. But each house was set up so that it maintained its privacy from the other houses. They could see as little or as much of the rest of the family as they wanted. It was no different than living in any other planned subdivision. At least this way they got to choose their neighbors.

The houses were spread out and backed up to the lake so that each one had a magnificent view of the water. The training facilities and the war room where most of the planning and staging went on were well away from the houses so that there was at least a semblance of normalcy to the residences.

So far the only holdouts were Donovan and Joe and then, of course, Frank and Marlene. Sam was working steadily on his parents, but they'd refused to consider moving from the house they'd live in for some forty-odd years.

Rachel couldn't really blame them, but she, like Sam, worried for their safety. Marlene had already been kidnapped once. It had been a sharp reminder to them all how close danger lurked at all times.

Ethan was waiting for them, leaning against his truck, as Rachel pulled up. He offered Shea a smile and called out a hello just as Sophie pulled in behind Rachel in her SUV.

"Girls night out, huh," he said as he dropped a kiss on Rachel's lips.

"Yep. Sam and Nathan are holding down the fort over at Sam and Sophie's. You should go offer them moral support."

Ethan laughed. "More likely I'll watch while Charlotte paints their fingernails, and then I'll get to call them pussies."

Sophie glared at Ethan. "Just wait, Ethan. Your day is coming. Miss Charlotte will corner you, and I guarantee that you won't tell that child no, and you'll be sporting pink, glittery fingernails and toenails."

"God help me," Ethan muttered.

The rest of the women laughed.

"You ready, Rachel?" Sophie asked.

"Have fun and be careful," Ethan said as the women turned to go.

Rachel and the others waved and then climbed back into Sophie's SUV.

Thirty minutes later, they were seated at one of the back round tables at the Big Sandy Feed and Grain Mill sipping iced tea and waiting for their food to arrive.

Sarah cleared her throat. "I propose a toast."

Sophie grabbed up her mason jar mug. "Oh do tell. I'm up for a good toast."

"To a truly eventful couple of years and coming out on top just like the Kellys always do," Sarah said solemnly. "And!" she broke in when the others would have toasted. "To Rachel and Ethan's new beginning."

Shea sent Rachel a secret smile and then raised her glass. Rachel grinned at her sisters-in-law and said, "I'll certainly drink to that."

The rest of the evening was spent laughing and poking fun at the Kelly men, but it was obvious the women adored their husbands beyond reason. It was also evident that the Kelly brothers loved their wives just as fiercely.

Rachel gazed wistfully at her sisters by marriage and imagined them all with children. Holidays and birthdays.

All gathered under one roof with Frank and Marlene looking on at their brood of children, both blood and honorary. Marlene did tend to lay claim to people whether they wanted to be claimed or not.

At that particular random thought, Rachel's brow puckered, and she frowned.

"Has anyone seen Sean lately? With how crazy the move has been and going back to teaching, I haven't seen him in weeks. And he didn't come over to help move, which is not like him. He's always so willing to jump in and lend a hand."

Sean had been there more than once for Rachel when she was still finding her way in the aftermath of her return home. The sheriff's deputy was younger than all the Kelly brothers, but he was as solid and dependable as someone well above his age.

"I heard Sam talking to him the other day on the phone," Sophie piped up. "Sean's been working a case in cooperation with Henry County and the state police. Sounded like a big drug ring. They've pulled in city and county guys for this. He's been working a lot of long hours. Sam sounded worried about him."

Rachel sighed. "There are times when I wish he'd go to work for KGI, but he doesn't have the experience yet, and then I think how silly it is to think he'd be any safer going off on the kinds of missions our husbands do."

Sarah nodded. "I understand what you mean though. It's reassuring to think of him having that kind of back-up system, you know? We know nothing about the kind of men Sean works with currently, but we certainly know our guys would look out for him."

"That's exactly what I mean," Rachel said in agreement. "I was happy when Swanny joined them."

"Oh me too," Shea said in a rush. "My heart just aches for him. He's so . . . alone. If you only knew what he and Nathan endured . . ."

Her voice trailed off and her features went bleak. Rachel reached over to squeeze her hand. Shea had gone through a lot to help Nathan and Swanny escape after months of

them being tortured by the enemy. She more than anyone
knew precisely what the two men had suffered. She knew
because she'd suffered along with them and *for* them.

"Mama Kelly will work him over," Sophie said with a
chuckle. "Do you see how he is around her? It's so cute.
He's completely bemused by her. She pats him and calls
him her baby, and I swear the big man just melts in a puddle
at her feet."

Everyone laughed and warmth filled Rachel's heart.
Life was good. The very best. She was surrounded by people who loved her and whom she loved with all her heart.

There wasn't a single Kelly by birth or marriage who
wouldn't do anything he or she could to help another family member. She thought briefly of Jennifer from her class
and how broken up the little girl was over her family dete-
riorating.

She swallowed the knot in her throat. *But by the grace
of God go I.*

It *had* been her. Only she'd gotten a second chance.
Redemption.

"Do you think P.J. will come back?" Sarah asked in a
quiet voice. "I'm so worried about her."

The others fell silent.

P.J. had been instrumental in each of their lives. She'd
gone on the mission to rescue Rachel from Colombia.
She'd been there when Sophie had traded herself for Marlene Kelly and gone back to her madman of a father. She
had been there when Sarah's brother had died taking a bullet meant for Sarah. And she'd been instrumental in reunit-
ing Shea with Nathan when Shea had been abducted by the
people pursuing Shea and her sister, Grace. For that matter,
she'd been there covering the women's husbands when
Grace had surrendered herself in order to prevent members
of KGI from dying.

P.J. was a fixture of KGI. She was always there, protecting their husbands when they put their lives on the line.
Rachel would never fully be able to express her gratitude to
the other woman. There simply weren't adequate words.

She just hoped she had the opportunity to try one day. P.J. had fallen off the map months earlier and her team was mourning their loss. They weren't the same without her.

"I worry about her too," Sophie said softly.

"She'll be back," Shea said confidently, though her voice lacked conviction. "She's tough and she's a fighter. I don't see her wimping out. She just needs time."

Everyone nodded at that. It was a concept they were all familiar with. Time healed all wounds. Time and . . . love.

Sarah checked her watch and winced regretfully. "We better wrap this up soon. I know the guys have to be up early in the morning for training drills."

"I have to be up early for work," Rachel said in a rueful tone. She sighed. "That sounds so nice to say again."

"Are you loving it?" Sarah asked.

"I really am," Rachel replied. "I didn't realize how much I missed it until I went back that first day. I love teaching. It's a part of who I am, and I'm tired of being a different person."

"Good for you," Sophie said, reaching across to squeeze her hand. "We're all so proud of you, Rachel. You're such an example. I'm so glad my daughter has you to look up to."

Rachel's mouth dropped open in astonishment, and she looked at the other women like they'd lost their minds. Then she laughed because she simply couldn't help it.

"Don't laugh," Sarah said in her quiet voice. "We're all aware of your story. What you endured. How you never gave up. And how resilient you've been. It takes a very strong woman to endure what you did and to not only survive but to triumph over such adversity."

"Oh God, you guys, don't make me cry," Rachel choked out.

She dabbed furiously at her eyes to prevent the flow of any tears.

Laughter rounded the table, breaking the serious tone that had settled over the group. They paid their checks and then headed out to the truck.

As they drove back, Rachel's hand went unconsciously

to her belly, and she marveled that she was shielding two tiny lives deep in her womb.

She couldn't wait to tell the rest of the family. Couldn't wait to bask in the joy of the moment. It would be her moment in the sun after a long sojourn in the shadows.

CHAPTER 8

"DID you enjoy your evening out?" Ethan asked as he pulled her down against him on the couch.

She snuggled in his arms, enjoying the feel of his bare chest against her cheek.

She'd changed into another of the sexy little night outfits she knew drove him crazy, and he was wearing his boxers. She loved evenings like this when they just snuggled on the couch and watched television or even just talked about nothing at all.

"It was fun. It's been awhile since we did anything together. Everyone's been so busy, and Sarah and Garrett and Nathan and Shea were off on their honeymoons."

"And we were moving," he added.

"Yes, finally," she said with a happy sigh.

He went still against her, his breathing soft and even, but he was tense, his muscles firm and unrelaxed. After a moment she pushed herself upward and cocked her head in a questioning manner.

"Is something wrong, Ethan?"

His brow furrowed a moment, and then he pushed up to

his elbow so their faces were more level. He seemed hesitant to say what was on his mind.

"I get the impression you were eager to move," he began. She nodded.

"I mean I know you were excited about the new house. I guess I don't understand . . ."

He drifted off and then closed his lips, almost as if he'd decided not to bring up whatever it was that was nagging him.

"What don't you understand?" she prompted.

"I admitted that I was surprised you went with a design so dramatically different than our old house. It was almost as if you wanted nothing at all to be the same. And then you seemed so relieved when we moved out, and I've noticed that you're happier since we started living here."

She studied him a moment, hating the conversation she knew they were going to be forced to have. "That bothers you."

She didn't pose it as a question because it was obvious that it did bother him.

"Yeah, I guess it does," he admitted. Then he shook his head. "It's stupid of me. I'm just glad you're happy. I *want* you to be happy."

"I am," she said gently.

"But you weren't happy at the old house."

Slowly she shook her head, knowing she couldn't lie to him. She wouldn't lie to him, not even to spare his feelings.

"Why?" he asked, his voice cracking with that one word.

She pushed herself upward until she'd repositioned herself so that she sat opposite him with her knees bent against his chest and her hip firmly nestled into his groin.

"You have to understand what it was like for me," she said in a low voice. "Regaining memories at random times. And each time something came back to me, it was fresh and vibrant in my mind. As though it had just happened instead of years before. Not all of them were happy memories."

She glanced helplessly up at him, knowing there was no way to make it any easier for him to hear.

He flinched but maintained her gaze, as if he were determined to pay his penance and not back away from the reminder of the things he'd said and done.

"Some of the worst moments of my life happened in that house," she said, an ache in her voice. "I just felt that if we were ever truly going to have a fresh start, that we had to begin with a completely clean slate. And we have that now. A brand new home just in time for the precious babies we'll have. A place where we can start over and make new memories to replace the painful ones."

Moisture glimmered in Ethan's eyes before it was blinked away. Then he pulled her down, his hand cupping the back of her neck. Their foreheads touched and then their mouths.

"I love you," he said, his voice clogged with regret and so much pain.

"I love you too," she whispered back.

"This house will hold only happy memories for you," he vowed. "For you and me and the babies. We'll start right."

She smiled. "Yeah, we will."

"We haven't yet christened the new bedroom," he said, his voice husky and laced with suggestion.

"Mmm, however did we miss out on that?"

"It's an error I have to correct immediately."

"I agree."

He sat up and then scooted down the couch so he could get up without sending her sprawling. Then he simply reached down and plucked her from the sofa.

She landed gently against his chest, his arms firmly around her. Protective. And so loving.

He carried her into the bedroom and laid her out on the bed, staring down at her with sinful promise in his eyes.

His hands skittered up her thighs, and he slid his fingers underneath the waistband of the satin shorts. As he began to slowly pull them down, his eyes darkened, and he stared accusingly at her.

"No underwear? You intended to seduce me all along."

She gave him an exaggerated innocent look, widening her eyes as she stared up at him. "Maaaaybe."

He chuckled and then lowered his mouth to the soft juncture of her legs, pressing a kiss to the vee. She shivered and closed her eyes as chill bumps raced each other over her belly and to her breasts.

As he nuzzled deeper into the soft flesh between her legs, his hands wandered upward, sliding the top up over her breasts. Just as his fingers found her painfully erect nipples, his tongue swiped over her clitoris sending another spasm of bone-melting pleasure through her body.

Her palm glided through his hair as her fingers flexed and curled against his head. It was an erotic image, her guiding and directing him, holding him there so his tongue hit just the right places.

She moaned softly and arched into him as she reached for the pleasure he offered.

He lifted his head and then moved up her body to remove the top completely. After he'd tossed it away, he lowered his head to her belly. Framing her waist in his big hands, he bestowed the most tender of kisses right over her womb where their children were nestled.

"Your mama and your daddy can't wait to meet you," he whispered against her skin.

"Ethan, I need you," she pleaded, her heart so full of love she was near to bursting. "Make love to me, please. I don't want to wait. I need you inside me."

He didn't move right away. Instead he pressed a trail of kisses up her midline before moving to her breast. He licked a trail around one puckered nipple and then sucked it into his mouth.

He was exquisitely gentle. He seemed to know just how tender her breasts were as a result of pregnancy. The slightest manipulation had her gasping for breath and her senses screaming for mercy.

His dark head moved to the other nipple, and he lazily traced a similar line around the hard peak before tucking it in his mouth to suckle.

In turns he gave each breast careful tugs with his mouth, increasing her pleasure and weaving delicious tension into her body. She coiled tighter and tighter as his hand slid between her legs to work its magic against her damp, swollen flesh.

"Inside me," she gasped out. "Ethan, please."

She was desperate for that connection. For them to be joined in the most intimate way two people could be joined. She wanted to feel his big body hovered protectively over hers. To feel him driving in and out as she stretched to accommodate him.

Her eyes closed as he rotated over her, his leg moving aggressively over hers as he prepared to mount her.

Oh but she loved how small and delicate she felt underneath his solidly muscled body. The body of a warrior. Lean and hard. No spare flesh anywhere. There was power in his every movement. It was why he always took such care with her. It would be so easy to hurt her with his strength.

"I want you with me," he said in a hoarse, needy voice.

She slid her hands up his arms to his broad shoulders where she let her fingernails dig in, marking him.

"I'm always with you, Ethan," she said softly.

He closed his eyes and groaned as he positioned himself at her opening. She could see the strain in his jaw. Knew how hard he was working to hold himself back.

Then he pushed inward, sliding into her, stretching her and forcing her to accommodate his width.

She sighed and melted back against the mattress. The sensation of fitting so snugly around him was blissful. There was no part of her that was untouched by his possession.

He flexed himself upward to push her legs higher. It forced her to take all of him, angled so he could slide all the way. His hips met the backs of her legs then pressed firmer still as he pushed even harder.

She was on fire. She fidgeted restlessly as he withdrew and thrust deeply again. And then again.

His mouth came down hot and wet against her shoulder and worked its way up to her neck. Breathless, scorching, open-mouthed kisses. His tongue worked over her earlobe, and then his teeth grazed the sensitive skin underneath.

She shuddered uncontrollably as her orgasm swelled, flashing like a sky full of fireworks. Wave after wave of pleasure rippled through her body, faster and faster, tighter and tighter, until it all released in one huge tumultuous burst.

Wrapping her arms around him, she held him close, absorbing his taste, his smell, the feel of him so deep inside her. His steady heartbeat against hers. The warmth of his body as it covered hers.

"I love you," she whispered against his skin. "This is *our* time. Our beginning. You, me, and our children."

He shuddered against her, her words seeming to drive him over the edge. He plunged deep and then went rigid atop her as his body shook and heaved.

He gathered her into his arms, molding her against him as he pulsed within her.

"I love you too, baby," he whispered back. "Always. You're mine. Always mine. I'll never let you go again."

She smiled, hugging him that much harder. No matter what the future held for them, she knew they would face it together. She'd never have to be alone again.

CHAPTER 9

RACHEL ate her lunch in her classroom, hoping that Jennifer would show for her retake. Glancing at the clock, she was ready to concede defeat when the door cracked open and Jennifer peeked in.

Rachel smiled broadly and motioned her inside.

"Am I too late?" Jennifer asked.

"Of course not. You have plenty of time, and I want you to not rush through it."

Rachel picked up the paper and held it out for Jennifer to take. Jennifer smiled shyly, took the test and then went to sit in the first row of desks.

Rachel watched from underneath her eyelashes while pretending to grade other papers. Jennifer's brow was creased in concentration, and she nibbled at the eraser on the pencil as she carefully read through the questions.

Holding back a smile of triumph, Rachel did a mental fist pump.

When the bell rang signaling the end of lunch, Jennifer stood, a satisfied smile on her face.

"I finished," she announced. "And I think I got them all right."

"Very good," Rachel said proudly. "I knew you could do it."

"Thank you, Ms. Kelly. For giving me another shot at it. I won't let it happen again."

"See that you don't," Rachel said crisply. But she softened the statement with a genuine smile. "Go ahead and take your seat. The others will be coming in soon. Do you need a bathroom break before the next class begins?"

Jennifer shook her head. "No ma'am. I'm fine, thank you."

The kids began to noisily file in, the roar from the hall invading the classroom as well.

Rachel stood to clean the blackboard from the previous class so she could begin anew for this period. After wiping it down and drawing up her outline, she turned and was startled to see a man standing in the back of the room.

"Sir, you can't be in here," she said.

He had no visitor's badge. She'd received no call from the office to suggest a parent was arriving. Alarm bells immediately went off, and she reached underneath the desk for the panic button that had been installed the year prior.

Maybe she was jumping the gun, and maybe she was being stupid and overreacting. But when it came to the safety of her kids, she didn't really give a damn if it turned out to be a false alarm.

The silent alarm would immediately send the school into lockdown. The local police would be notified and would converge on the campus with astonishing speed. Everyone took the safety in schools seriously here. And, well, everywhere. School shootings had become so commonplace that no leeway was given, and police were swift to stamp out any threat.

The students swung around to see whom she was addressing. Jennifer went pale.

"Dad! What are you doing here?" she hissed.

But her father didn't look at her. He didn't even acknowledge her. Rachel's heart plummeted when he lifted his hand to reveal the pistol he carried. Her instincts hadn't been wrong.

"Everyone get down!" Rachel yelled. "Under your desks!"

There was a series of screams and desks scraping across the floor as the students scrambled for cover.

"Everyone be still!" Jennifer's father roared.

He waved the gun precariously, and Rachel's heart nearly stopped for fear the gun would discharge and one of the children would be caught in the crossfire.

Only Jennifer remained where she was. She was terrified, completely pale, and staring at her father in utter disbelief.

"Dad, what are you doing?" Jennifer asked in a shaky voice. "Why are you here? Where did you get that gun? You're scaring me!"

For a moment, the man's face softened as he looked at his daughter, and then his expression hardened, and he waved the gun in Rachel's direction.

"Everything will be just fine once she makes a call for me," he muttered.

In the distance, sirens could be heard, and Jennifer's father froze. Then he rushed to the window to peer out and let out a string of obscenities.

Sobs rose from several of the children, but most huddled under their desks too petrified to make a sound.

"What did you do?" he raged at Rachel. "Did you call them? How did they know so fast?"

"Someone must have seen you through the window," Rachel said calmly. "You've had your eyes on me the entire time. I've made no phone calls."

He glared suspiciously at her and then waved the gun in her direction.

"Close the blinds. Do it now!"

Rachel hurried to do as he asked, her heart stuttering like a jackhammer in her chest.

"Daddy, don't hurt her," Jennifer pleaded. "She's nice. Please don't hurt anyone. Let's just go home, *please*."

"Your mother won't allow that," he snarled. "She's issued a restraining order. Stupid bitch is refusing to allow me to see you. Says she's going to get full custody in the divorce. That ain't going to happen. I aim to make sure of that."

"Sir, please listen to your daughter," Rachel said in a soft, appeasing tone. "You'll never be able to see her if you're locked in a jail cell, and if someone gets hurt today, you'll go away for a very long time."

Her words seemed to further infuriate him. He advanced as though he'd strike her, but Jennifer flung herself in front of Rachel, spreading out her arms in an effort to protect Rachel.

Rachel hugged Jennifer to her and then thrust her behind her back. "Stay there, honey," she whispered. "Don't move. Just stay quiet and let me talk to him."

Jennifer let out a whimper but did as Rachel said.

"What's your name?" Rachel asked in an easy tone, almost as if they were exchanging ordinary conversation or that he was a parent who'd come in for a conference.

He looked befuddled and answered automatically. "Kent. Kent Winstead."

"Mr. Winstead, you have an extremely bright daughter. She excels in all her classes. I'm sure you're very proud of her."

He seemed confused by the change in direction of the conversation.

"Well of course I'm proud of her. Inherited my brains. Her mother is as dumb as a brick."

Behind her, Jennifer let out a pained gasp, and Rachel's heart ached all the more for her.

"Work with me on a solution to this," Rachel said calmly. "Tell me what it is you want so I can help you. The children are frightened. Your daughter is terrified. I'm sure the very last thing you want is to scare the students."

He looked torn as he surveyed the kids all huddled under their desks, many of them with tear-ravaged faces.

"I don't want to scare them," he muttered. "But I have to do what I have to do."

"And what is it you plan to do?" she asked.

His brows furrowed as if he hadn't considered exactly

SOFTLY AT SUNRISE   347

what his plan was, but then it was likely he had no clear plan. He'd acted in desperation, and now he'd ruined any chance he ever had of being with his daughter. Not that she'd tell him that now. It would send him right over the edge.

"I want you to call the police," he said firmly.

She nodded. "I can do that. Will you allow me to reach for my cell phone? I assure you I'm not armed. They don't allow weapons in the school."

He raised the gun, pointing it at her, and then he nodded. "Get the phone but don't call anyone yet. I need to tell you what to say. Don't try anything stupid. I don't want to hurt anyone, but I will if you make me."

"We both want the same thing, Mr. Winstead. I assure you that you have my full cooperation."

She reached slowly for her purse, making sure he could see inside the entire time as she retrieved her cell phone. She pulled it out and simply held it so it was in clear view, and then she looked expectantly at him.

"What would you like me to tell the police?"

He rubbed his chin with his free hand, all the while holding steady aim at her. It struck fear in her heart the way his hand shook. He was running on adrenaline, and one wrong move could mean her death. The deaths of her precious babies.

She swallowed hard, refusing to give in to the rising panic. She'd withstood the very worst and survived. She would survive this. Her babies were counting on her. Ethan was counting on her. She wouldn't put him through the hell of her dying all over again.

"Please lower the gun," she said, allowing her voice to shake. "I can't think when I'm terrified that you're going to shoot me. Just lower the gun. I'll do whatever you want."

He was wracked by clear indecision. Jennifer started to move, but Rachel put her hand out, pulling her closer to her back to shield her.

Finally he lowered the gun, but he still kept it away from his body. He trained it on the far wall and then settled his hard stare on her.

"You tell them that I want that restraining order lifted and that I want to be able to have access to my daughter. I want that bitch of my wife up here so she can see how serious I am. If she's not here quickly, I start shooting."

Rachel hastily punched her contacts button and hurriedly scrolled to Sean's number, praying he was on duty. She was taking a huge risk in not dialing 911, but she trusted Sean, and he'd let Ethan and his brothers know the situation.

When it started dialing, she put the phone to her ear and kept eye contact with Jennifer's father so she could be prepared for any sudden mood swing or movement on his part.

"Rachel, fancy hearing from you. How are you, girl?"

Sean's cheerful voice immediately calmed some of her stark terror.

"This is Rachel Kelly," she began as if she didn't know Sean and as though she were calling a regular dispatcher. "Kent Winstead is here in my classroom with a gun, and he has some demands. If his demands aren't met, he said he'll start shooting the children."

More terrified sobs rose from the children crouched under their desks.

Sean was immediately all business. "Simple yes or no, Rachel, are you on speaker phone?"

"No."

"Okay. I'm going to patch this in to the local and state police. Do you know if any police are already on scene?"

"Yes."

"Okay, stay with me here. Tell me what his demands are. Let's keep him appeased. We'll get you out of this, sweetheart."

Kent was already growing impatient, and a scowl had darkened his features. His grip on the gun tightened, so she hastily relayed the demands he'd given her. Kent relaxed some when she began to list all he'd asked for.

"I'm being patched in to the person in charge on scene," Sean said. "I've relayed everything you've just told me. I need you to keep him talking. Throw him a bone and ask him for his wife's number so we can call her."

Rachel let the phone slide slightly from her mouth as she looked at Kent. "They need your wife's number so they can call her. They'll do it now."

"That's good. That's real fucking good," Kent said, nodding his head adamantly. "Let the bitch know what she's done. She'll come crawling back, but I don't want her sorry ass anymore."

"The number," Rachel prompted softly.

As he recited the number, Rachel relayed it to Sean.

"Okay, stall for me, sweetheart. Try to keep him calm. A S.W.A.T. team is getting into position even as we speak. My dispatcher has called Sam and has apprised him of the situation. Let him know we're calling his wife now."

"They're calling right now," Rachel said to Kent.

He nodded his satisfaction, and then he stared toward the windows with a frown. As if deciding he was putting himself at a huge risk, he crossed the room and positioned himself in a corner where there was no clear shot through the window. He wedged himself between two bookcases but kept the gun trained in Rachel's direction.

"Daddy, please don't do this," Jennifer pleaded. "I don't want you to have to go away. They'll put you in jail, and I'll never see you again."

Rachel squeezed Jennifer, hoping she got the message to remain quiet. Reminding Kent of the huge mistake he'd made would only heighten his agitation, and it could make him do a very stupid thing.

Desperate people did desperate things.

Kent's expression hardened. "I'm not going anywhere except home with you. It's your stupid mother who's going away."

Jennifer began to quietly sob and buried her face in Rachel's back.

"What's taking so long?" Kent demanded. "What are they doing? You need to let them know that if I even *think* they're jacking me around, I'll start shooting. If they don't think I mean it, just try me."

Without warning, he pointed the gun upward and shot.

The room exploded and reverberated with the retort. Plaster flew everywhere. Screams rose and utter panic ensued.

"Rachel! Rachel! Goddamn it, Rachel, are you there? Talk to me. Are you all right? Give me the situation."

Rachel had immediately squatted, covering Jennifer's body with her own. They huddled together beside the desk, and Rachel put out her hand to try to calm the other children.

"Stay where you are," she whispered urgently. "Don't move. And be quiet. Don't say a word. Don't do anything to draw attention to yourself."

"Rachel!" Sean roared.

She put the phone back to her ear. "I'm h-here."

"Are you all right?" he demanded. "What the hell just happened?"

"It was just a warning," Rachel stammered out. "He wants to know what's going on and why it's taking so long."

"Damn right," Kent snarled. "You tell those bastards they better not screw around and piss me off."

"Hurry, Sean," she whispered. "He's very unstable."

"Tell him we have his wife on the phone and that she's agreed to drive right over. It'll take her at least twenty minutes."

When she relayed the information to Kent, his lip curled.

"I know damn well it only takes fifteen to get here, and she better be here in that time."

"Fifteen minutes," Rachel said faintly. "He'll give her fifteen."

"Get off the phone," Kent snapped. "You've been on there long enough. You told him what I wanted. Now we'll see if they deliver."

Wordlessly she ended the call, not wanting to risk angering him by saying anything further. By now, Sean would have a very good idea of the threat they were dealing with. She just had to pray that the police would be able to bring about a peaceful end to the standoff and that none of the students would be hurt in the process.

CHAPTER 10

ETHAN, Donovan, Sam and Garrett stood watching the newly formed team comprised of Nathan, Joe, Swanny, Skylar and Edge as they went through their drills at the firing range.

Skylar and Joe were the two standouts and were the most probable candidates for the sharpshooters on the team. Edge was a big son of a bitch, and while he shot well, his specialty was obviously going to be in hand-to- hand. He was a former MMA fighter and brute force was his strong point. Hell, he just looked like a mean bastard. But he also had history in the military, and he was disciplined and had intense focus. A very solid addition to KGI.

Sam went for his phone, looked at the LCD, and then lifted it to his ear.

"Hey, Sean, what's cooking? You getting fat and lazy over there in your cushy office?"

Sam's expression went from teasing to complete business in two seconds flat.

"Oh shit. Give me the rundown."

Ethan, Donovan and Garrett immediately forgot all

about what the others were doing and turned their full attention to Sam.

"Son of a bitch!" Sam swore. "You've got to be fucking kidding me! Is she okay? What the hell's going on? Do you have S.W.A.T. on scene?"

A prickle of unease snaked down Ethan's spine. It had to be family related for Sean to call and for Sam to be so flustered. And most of the family was accounted for. Except for Rachel. But Rachel was teaching. Surely it had nothing to do with her.

Then Sam glanced over at Ethan, his expression grim, and Ethan's stomach bottomed out.

"Rachel," he mouthed.

Ethan forgot to breathe. He crowded in close to Sam, straining to hear everything Sean had to say. He only got bits and pieces because Sam had the damn phone glued to his ear, but what he heard chilled him to the bone.

Gunman holding Rachel's class hostage. Extremely volatile. Threatening to start shooting if his demands weren't met. A fifteen-minute timeline. Holy fuck. It would take at least twenty for them to get to the school, and that was hauling ass and breaking land speed records.

Ethan whirled on Donovan. "Van, can you get the chopper in the air that quickly? We could make it in ten minutes if we haul ass."

Sam hung up the phone, but he was already running toward the newly constructed helipad.

"Get the others. I want every man we've got on this," Sam yelled.

Nathan and Joe and the rest of their team scrambled up without hesitation and fell in behind the others as they ran for the helicopter.

Donovan hopped into the cockpit and began flipping switches to get the engines started.

"What the fuck is going on?" Garrett demanded.

The others were crammed into the chopper and were leaning forward to hear what Sam had to say.

"Some crazy motherfucker, a parent of one of Rachel's

students, is having domestic issues. His wife issued a restraining order and is pursuing sole custody in the divorce proceedings. Husband went batshit crazy and went to his kid's classroom waving a gun around, and now he's threatening to start shooting if his demands aren't met."

"And what are his demands?" Ethan bit out.

"He wants the restraining order rescinded." Sam snorted. "Fat chance of that happening. He wants custody of his daughter. Yeah, like that's going to go over well. And he wants his wife up at the school in fifteen minutes, which can't be good. Even if he doesn't go off his rocker and start shooting kids, you know he'll end up killing her."

"Did Sean say if Rachel was okay?" Ethan asked, fear nearly choking him.

"She's scared out of her mind, but Sean says she's doing a very good job of keeping the guy calm. She's cooperating fully, trying to keep him appeased. She called him instead of 911."

"That's our girl," Garrett said, pride in his voice. "She's smart and she's a fighter. My money is on her."

Ethan rubbed his forehead tiredly. He'd never been so damn scared in his life. "You guys don't understand."

Nathan eyed him sharply. "What don't we understand?"

Ethan sucked in a deep breath. "She's . . . pregnant. We're having *twins*. We just found out. This kind of stress can't be good even if she doesn't get herself shot."

The others looked dumbstruck.

"I'd congratulate you," Sam said grimly, "but right now I'd prefer to get her out in one piece so we can celebrate like hell later."

Ethan nodded his agreement. "I can't lose her. I can't lose *them*," he said with quiet desperation.

Oh God, he'd already gotten luckier than any one person could ever hope for by having her miraculously restored to him after he'd thought she was dead for an entire year. Was he doomed to lose her to fate after all?

Garrett put his hand on Ethan's shoulder. "You aren't going to lose her. We'll go in and kick some ass. Fuck what the local police say. We'll take out this asshole, and then everyone can go home to their parents, and Rachel can come home with us."

Ethan bumped knuckles with Garrett and muttered a hooyah. Garrett rolled his eyes. "Only because this involves Rachel will I let you get away with that navy bullshit."

The helicopter touched down just off the school premises, and Sam was already on the phone with Sean, who was on scene.

"We're coming in," Sam said in a hard voice. "You make damn sure no one gives us any grief."

Ethan's heart was in his throat. Flashbacks of his time with Rachel since her return played over and over in his head.

The memory of those two fuzzy blobs on the monitor that pulsated, signaling life, and the look of incredible joy on Rachel's face as they realized what those two blobs meant was rich in his mind.

He couldn't lose Rachel or their babies. He'd fought too damn hard to get his life back. He wasn't going to let it all slip away now.

They ran onto the paved parking lot of the middle school exactly eighteen minutes after Sean had first placed his call.

"Sitrep!" Sam barked. "Where are we on his timeline?"

Sean looked relieved to see Sam but gestured toward the chief of police and the sheriff. Sean wasn't senior on the scene even if he was the point of contact.

"I bought us a few extra minutes by telling him his wife was almost here. She *is* here but she's scared shitless, and she's going to freak out if we put her on the phone with him," Sean said.

"What about Rachel?" Ethan demanded.

"She's doing okay," Sean said quietly. "Scared, but she's calm, and she's protecting those kids fiercely."

Ethan's pulse hammered up until it was pounding in his head. In a moment of selfishness, he didn't want Rachel to stand in harm's way for those kids, but he also knew it was exactly what she would do. He felt pride and insane fear at the same time.

The chief of police, the sheriff, a lieutenant from the state troopers and the S.W.A.T. commander converged on Sam, and the tone of conversation grew tense and heated. Ethan tried to focus on what was being said, what the plan of action was, but his gaze drifted beyond to the school building, and he imagined Rachel and all those kids inside, terrified, fearing death.

How must Rachel feel to face death again so soon? After being granted their fondest wish. The blessing of not one but two precious babies. He knew how nervous and scared she was to miscarry, how much she didn't want to get her hopes up.

Even if she managed to escape this situation with her life, would the stress cause her to lose their babies?

His gaze carried over the cordoned-off area to where the rest of the students had been bussed and even now were still being boarded to be driven away. There was a crowd of media and hysterical parents being held at bay by an entire line of police officers.

It was chaos.

Nothing like this had ever happened in their small town. Everyone believed it couldn't happen here. They were untouchable. Still innocent of all the bad things that could happen in the world around them.

Today, reality had come.

It was a reality Ethan and his brothers and their teammates were well acquainted with. They dealt with situations like this all the time.

Most missions weren't personal, though, although Sam would argue that all were, just some more personal than others. But most involved people that hired them. Or people wanted by the government.

This involved his *wife*. The woman he loved with every breath. Their two unborn children. New to Ethan, but already so very loved and cherished.

He felt a bond to those tiny lives nestled in Rachel's womb. He was a *father*. Sworn to protect his family.

He turned to Sam.

"Get us the schematics on the building. We can go in through the air ducts. If we're quiet, he'll never even know we're there. He knows the police and S.W.A.T. and every law enforcement officer in a hundred-mile radius is here or is en route. But he won't expect us. We move in, take a closer look at what we're dealing with, and then we go in and neutralize the target."

"You don't make the decisions here!" the chief of police puffed.

Ethan got up in the man's face before Garrett could make a grab for him.

"That's my *wife* in there," he snarled. "This is what we *do*. This is who we *are*. I'm not going to put her life in someone else's hands. My brothers and I will go in. No one else."

"Do you have any idea what kind of publicity nightmare this would be?" the sheriff demanded. "I have every bit of respect for KGI, but the liability is huge here. You fuck this up, and we go on record as letting some off-the-books special ops group with no jurisdiction or authority go in instead of S.W.A.T. or the local police and get a child killed. I'm sorry, Ethan, but I can't let you do this."

"Sir, he's calling again," Sean cut in. "We're not going to be able to put him off for long. We have to act. Now."

Several rounds of curses splintered the air.

Sean picked up the phone, and Ethan looked desperately at his brothers.

"Your plan is a good one," Sam said in a low voice. "We could access the ducts in the gym. It's not far from Rachel's class from the diagram they've drawn, but it's not so close he'll know anything's up."

"Mr. Winstead, please, just calm down for just a minute. We're doing everything we can to get your wife here just like you wanted. I've even personally called the judge who issued the restraining order."

Ethan listened as Sean's voice grew more unsettled. He couldn't hear what the other guy was saying, but judging by Sean's increasing agitation, it couldn't be good.

The distant sound of a gunshot and then screams, from across the parking lot, over the phone and the assembled crowd echoed harshly through the air.

Sean went pale, and then he started redialing.

"He hung up," Sean ground out. "I'm trying to get him or Rachel back now. Goddamn it!"

Sam grasped the chief of police's shirt, his fists balled into tight knots as he got into the other man's face.

"We're going in. Arrest us later. I don't give a fuck. But we're going in to take this guy down."

CHAPTER 11

RACHEL cowered against her desk, clutching Jennifer to her side. Glass had shattered everywhere. The idiot had aimed at the window. Had his aim been off even a little, he could have easily shot one of the children. As it was, there was a good possibility he could have hit someone outside the school.

"Mr. Winstead, please," she pleaded. "Please listen to me. I understand how upset you are. I would hate the possibility of being separated from my child, but this isn't going to help your case any. You have to listen to me before it's too late."

"Stand up so I can see you," he barked. "And leave my daughter down. You tell her to stay down."

"Stay down," she whispered fiercely to Jennifer. "You have to do as he says. Don't do or say anything to upset him. You stay down and out of the way so you don't get hurt."

After Jennifer nodded, her eyes wild and huge against her face, Rachel slowly rose, her breath escaping in tight squeezes from her chest.

She faced the gunman, praying she had the courage to withstand whatever was to come.

"What do you know about what I'm feeling?" he demanded belligerently. "Do you have kids? Jennifer said you didn't have none."

The cell phone began to ring again. It had already gone through two series of rings before kicking to voicemail. The ring tone was loud in the small room and sounded abrasive.

He scowled and motioned toward it with his gun. "Turn the damn thing off. Don't turn it back on until I tell you. Understand?"

She hastily complied, holding it up so he could see the blank screen. He nodded for her to put it back on the desk, and then he pursed his lips.

"Answer my question. You got kids?"

"Not yet," Rachel said softly. Praying she wasn't making a huge mistake, she said, "But I'm pregnant. With twins. I only found out this week. My husband and I have been wanting a family for a very long time."

For a moment, the gunman's expression softened, and then, as if reminding himself of his purpose, he raised his gun again and waved it menacingly.

"You're lying. Trying to get in my head!"

Rachel shook her head but didn't try to argue with him. His emotions were already all over the board.

"You get on the phone, and you tell the cops that I'm going to start shooting kids if they don't start taking me seriously. I'm tired of being jerked around."

Sobs rose. One of the girls started screaming, a high-pitched, shrill, hysterical scream that sounded raw and terrifying. It sent chills up Rachel's spine, and the gunman swung in the child's direction.

"Shut up! Quit the screaming!"

Jennifer burst from beside the desk and ran to the screaming girl. She faced her father defiantly, her eyes blazing in anger.

"Stop it, Daddy! She's my friend. She's scared. *I'm* scared. Why are you doing this? I just want to go home. We all want to go home."

Jennifer's father looked torn. Clear indecision tracked over his face, and the gun lowered a fraction. He stared back at Rachel as if he had no idea what to do. Rachel began to realize that he regretted his desperate act but saw no way out now. He was trapped in a nightmare of his own making.

Thinking quickly, she stepped forward to focus his attention back on her and away from the girls.

"Mr. Winstead, I have an idea," she said quietly.

He seized on it immediately. "What? Tell me."

"Let me call the police back and tell them that you're going to let the children go."

His face darkened. "Are you crazy? And lose my bargaining power?"

Rachel adamantly shook her head. "Hear me out. We'll call it an act of good faith. It will show them you can be reasonable. I'll tell them you're letting the children go because you don't want them harmed. You can keep me as your hostage. I'm pregnant with twins, Mr. Winstead. I'm your perfect hostage. They won't want to screw this up. The media will be all over it. A pregnant woman as a hostage will be a news sensation."

He looked befuddled. "That won't work. Will never work."

"You'll still have a hostage," Rachel gently pointed out. "But you'll make them realize that you don't intend to harm the children. Right now they're likely thinking that the only way to rescue the hostages is to force their way in and kill you."

It was another huge gamble for her to make him feel threatened, but she knew he was afraid and nervous, and she hoped that knowing he could very well die would make him more willing to make that first move.

"Jennifer stays," the gunman said resolutely. "I won't turn her over to her mother. Stupid bitch would take Jennifer and run. She wouldn't care about you or anyone else. She only ever thinks of herself."

Rachel met Jennifer's gaze, and to Rachel's surprise, Jennifer nodded.

"I'll stay," she said in a quiet, tense tone. Her voice trembled the slightest bit, but she notched her chin up and then fixed her stare on her father. "If you'll let the rest go, I'll stay here with Ms. Kelly and you."

Rachel watched him, holding her breath, every part of her body held in anticipation of this huge victory. The children stared anxiously, their expressions hopeful. The entire room went silent.

The gunman thought a moment longer and finally turned back to Rachel.

"Do it. Pick up the phone and call them. Tell them I'll let the kids go, but if they don't deliver what I expect, I'll kill you."

Rachel's hand shook as she reached for the cell phone. The wait for it to turn back on and find a signal was interminable. Finally the indicator flashed on, and she punched Sean's number from the list of recent calls.

"Rachel?" Sean demanded as soon as the phone rang. "Tell me what's going on. Are you all right?"

"I'm okay," Rachel said calmly. "Listen to me. This is very important. Mr. Winstead is going to let the children go."

"What? How the hell did you get him to agree to that? What's going on, Rachel?"

"He's going to keep me as his hostage, and his daughter is remaining with him as well."

She was careful not to piss Jennifer's father off by suggesting that Jennifer, too, was a hostage. Even if that's exactly what she was. In his own twisted way, he cared a great deal for his daughter, and if that love was called into question, who knew how he'd react? At this point, Rachel was doing nothing to jeopardize the release of her students. She just wanted it done as quickly as possible.

"Oh hell no, Rachel. You can't stay there with him. Tell him you have to come out too."

"I'm his hostage, and he's releasing all of the students," she said, stressing the fact that all of the children were being released. "In return, for this act of good faith, he wants his demands met immediately upon the release of the kids. If his demands aren't met, he'll kill me."

Sean swore softly. "I don't know how the hell you got him to do this, sweetheart, but we'll take it. Tell him it's a done deal. I'll get some damn document from the judge and have him sign it. The wife is here, but we've kept a lid on her because it's likely he's going to kill her the minute he lays eyes on her."

Rachel agreed but she remained silent. She wanted to ask Sean what was being done, but she couldn't.

"Ethan's here," Sean said in barely a whisper. "Hang in there, honey. They'll get you out."

Bolstered by the news that Ethan and his brothers were on the scene, she lowered the phone and looked at Mr. Winstead.

"They've agreed to give you signed legal documents from the judge who issued the restraining order, and your wife is here now. Let the children go, and then they'll talk to you again to make the arrangements."

Once more she held her breath. He paused for what seemed like an eternity as he grappled with the decision. He glanced at his daughter and then back to Rachel. He leveled the gun at her once more, his hand much steadier, almost as if the longer this went on, the more comfortable he got with holding a weapon.

He dipped the barrel toward the door and then back at Rachel. "Get them to the door. Single file. Line them up. I'll open the door and let them out. When the last one's out, the door closes, and you and Jennifer stay with me."

Then he motioned for Jennifer to go stand by Rachel.

Rachel hastily nodded her agreement. "Let me line them up but I'll stay back. I promise. I can do it from the back of the room. Can I call to let the police know the children are on their way out so that no one gets hurt?"

Grudgingly, the gunman nodded, and Rachel turned her attention on her terrified students.

"Listen to me, boys and girls. I want you to line up single file. No pushing. I need you to remain calm. Line up quickly. Once you leave the door, go straight to the bus ramp exit. Someone will be waiting for you and tell you where to go from there. Do you understand?"

There was a mad scramble as desks were shoved out of the way and children sprung up to hastily form a line.

Rachel picked up the phone and hit Sean's number.

"Talk to me, Rachel. What's going on?" Sean asked.

"They're coming out," she said calmly. She nodded in Mr. Winstead's direction.

He pointed the gun squarely at her as he opened the door. She leaned her hip into the desk, positioning herself between Jennifer and her father.

"Go now," she told the children while she kept the line open. "Someone will be waiting at the bus ramp exit."

"You got it," Sean said. "We'll have officers there to guide them out safely. You're amazing, Rachel. Sit tight, sweetheart."

Rachel hung up so she wouldn't anger the gunman and watched the last of the children hurry from the classroom.

When the last child was through the door, Mr. Winstead firmly shut it and then turned back to Rachel.

The ceiling above them exploded, plaster pelting down over their heads. Men dropped down onto the floor, forming a barrier between her and the gunman.

The gunman's expression turned from initial shock and befuddlement to one of fury as he realized what was happening.

"You fucking bitch! You lied!"

He raised the gun, and in that instant, Ethan took a step sideways, maneuvering himself in front of Rachel, and took the bullet right to the chest.

CHAPTER 12

"NO!" Rachel screamed.

Sam and Garrett both dove for the gunman, taking him down hard. Jennifer screamed and tried to run to her father, but Joe swept her into his arms and turned, holding her so she wouldn't see what was going on.

Rachel dropped to the floor, sobs welling from her throat in ragged, raw bursts. She covered Ethan with her own body, screaming for him to wake up, to be all right.

She wiped her hands frantically over his body, searching for the source of the blood she knew would be covering him. But her hands came away clean.

The scuffle went on around her. Jennifer's sobbing rose with Rachel's own. And then there was a gentle touch on her shoulder as Donovan moved in beside her.

"Rachel, honey, it's okay. It's all right. I promise."

"No," she sobbed. "He shot Ethan. Oh my God, he shot Ethan. Help him, Van. Please. Don't let him die." She pushed at Ethan again. "Please don't die, Ethan," she begged.

Please don't die.

The cry welled from her very soul. Ethan let out a low

groan, and relief blew wild and hot through her veins, making her light-headed in the process.

The door flew open, and the police poured in. There were exclamations, demands for answers, information. It all blurred into one insane litany. She didn't care what else happened. She only wanted Ethan to live.

"Rachel, sweetheart. Listen to me," Donovan said calmly. "He was wearing a vest. He took the bullet in the chest. He'll be okay."

She stared uncomprehendingly at Donovan, her eyes and mind blank. Then she gazed down in bewilderment at Ethan, whose eyelids fluttered open at that precise moment.

"A vest?" she echoed.

Donovan cut Ethan's shirt open and pushed the remnants aside. His hands slid down the face of the Kevlar vest, and then he pointed at the bullet lodged in the middle.

"See?" he said to Rachel. "Vest did its job. He's going to be bruised, and he'll be sore as hell for a few days, but he's fine."

She threw her arms around Donovan's neck and clung fiercely as her sobs poured out in one relieved, forceful rush.

"Oh God, I was so scared," she whispered.

Donovan hugged her back, rubbing his hand soothingly up and down her spine.

"You were fierce," Donovan said. "I'm so damn proud of you, Rachel. We were in the ducts planning to drop in, and then we heard you negotiate for the release of the children, so we waited until they were out of the room."

"Mr. Winstead?" she asked fearfully as she still clutched at Donovan.

She didn't want to turn around. Didn't want to see what had happened.

"And Jennifer?"

"They're taking the father away now, and Joe has Jennifer," Donovan said in a low voice.

She sagged against Donovan, but then the sweetest sound she'd ever heard rose from her husband.

"Rachel?"

She pulled away from Donovan and pressed her body down over Ethan's so her face was level with his.

"Are you all right?" she demanded. "Do you hurt anywhere?"

"I don't give a fuck about me," he said gruffly. "I want to know how you and our babies are."

Her heart filled with so much love that she thought she might burst from it. Relief had weakened her until she bobbled and nearly toppled over on top of him.

Donovan gripped her shoulders, giving her much-needed support as she hung there over Ethan. She stared down at him, tears making her vision all shimmery.

"Me and the babies are fine," she whispered. "Especially now that I know you're going to be okay. Don't ever scare me like that again, Ethan. God, I thought you'd been shot. I didn't know you had a vest on. I thought I'd lost you."

"Never going to let you go again," he muttered. "Stuck with me, baby. You and our babies."

Two teams of paramedics rushed in and went to Ethan and Rachel separately. When she realized their intention, she turned pleading eyes on Donovan.

"Don't let them do this. I don't want to be separated from Ethan. He needs to be checked out, but I'm fine. I'm not hurt."

Donovan cupped her face. "Do this for us, okay? We're all frantic with worry over how all this stress and the huge scare has affected you. Just let them take you in, run a few tests. You'll be home before you know it. But if you don't go, then Ethan's going to get all surly, and he'll refuse treatment because he'll be worried about you. We need to be sure he didn't break any ribs."

"I don't want to go alone," she confessed.

"I'll go with you, sweet pea," Garrett said as he joined Donovan by Ethan's side.

"Go with him," Ethan prompted. "Garrett will watch out for you while I get checked over. My brothers aren't going to rest until we're both given a clean bill of health. It's better to just go with it so we can get it over with quickly."

"He's learning," Donovan said with a grin.

"Joe and Nathan are taking Jennifer out to be reunited with her mom right now," Garrett said in a low voice.

"Can one of you carry her out into the hall?" one of the paramedics asked. "We can only get one stretcher in here and we're going to load up her husband first."

"Not a problem," Donovan said. He rose and scooped her up in her arms.

Rachel clung to Donovan's neck as he carried her into the hall and eased her down onto a stretcher. As he arranged the sheet over her, she glanced earnestly up at him.

"Don't let anyone break the news that I'm pregnant," she said. "This isn't the way I want Frank and Marlene to find out."

Donovan smiled and brushed a kiss over her forehead. "Don't worry. Our lips are sealed. But congratulations, little mama. I'm so damn proud for you and Ethan."

His smile was gentle, and there was a wealth of emotion in his eyes. "You've come a long way, Rachel Kelly. I never doubted you for a minute."

"Damn straight," Garrett said in a gruff voice as he came to stand beside the stretcher.

He reached down to squeeze Rachel's hand. "I've called Sarah and the others. I didn't want them freaking out and worrying when they heard what was going on. They're on their way to the hospital, so be prepared for the whole damn family to be there. Sophie was gathering the troops. They'll probably beat you there."

Rachel smiled and squeezed Garrett's hand back. She loved this big, messy, noisy family with all her heart and soul. She wouldn't change a single thing about them.

Of course, she worried every single time the guys went out on a mission. There was the reasonable fear that one or more wouldn't return. She could lose Ethan after fighting so hard to get back to him.

But they were the best of men. They had a strong sense of family and justice. It didn't surprise her at all that they'd been the ones to drop down from the ceiling and to end the standoff. She would have been more surprised if they hadn't been involved.

Ethan's brothers crowded around her stretcher, all demanding to know if she was all right.

"I'm fine," she stressed. "Just shaken up. Please make sure Ethan is all right. He's the one who was shot."

"He's a tough bastard," Sam said with a chuckle. "Though he did give me a damn heart attack when he stepped in front of that bullet."

Rachel shuddered and felt the blood drain from her face.

Nathan stroked his hand over her head. "Don't worry about Ethan. They'll load you both up and get you to the hospital. If I know the grumpy bastard, he'll raise so much hell that they won't be able to wait to get rid of him. He'll probably show up in your exam room and be done before you are."

Rachel glanced anxiously over at Ethan, who was predictably protesting the need to go to the hospital at all. Then he seemed to have lost her in the crowd of people crammed into the room and hallway, and he let out a bellow of displeasure.

Sam glanced up as a grim-faced older man stalked toward him. He let his hand briefly touch Rachel's shoulder.

"I'll see you at the hospital. There are things here I need to take care of. Garrett will ride with you and stay until Ethan is cleared."

"Is everything okay, Sam?" she asked in alarm.

He smiled and leaned down to kiss her forehead. "Nothing that won't work itself out. I have to smooth some ruffled feathers, and then I have to call my wife. She's been blowing up my phone, and she's not very happy with me because I didn't tell her the entire story. I'm sure she'll be waiting at the hospital to light into me."

Rachel grinned, relief so sweet in her blood that she was intoxicated. Her family would be waiting at the hospital.

Her sisters by marriage. Ethan's brothers would all be there soon. Frank and Marlene would rush in and take over.

She closed her eyes and leaned back on the stretcher, emotionally exhausted by the stress of the morning.

As soon as her stretcher was pushed into the bright wash of sunshine, the world dissolved into chaos. The media was shouting questions. Parents were demanding answers. People asked if she was alive.

She opened her eyes just to answer that particular question, but she remained quiet, the buzz of questions swimming in her ears until she wanted to cover them to shut out the cacophony.

She and Ethan were loaded onto waiting ambulances, and she stared through the open back doors at the sea of police, media and general public. It looked as if half of Tennessee was gathered on the middle school parking lot.

Then the medic attending her climbed into the back and shut the doors, obscuring her view. The ambulance pulled away, leaving the flashing lights and mob of people behind as it headed toward the hospital.

"You okay?" Garrett asked. "Sarah's texting me wanting to be sure I'm taking good care of you. If she gets it in her head I'm falling down on the job, she'll kick my ass."

Rachel laughed and put her hand out for the phone. Garrett relinquished it with a grin, and Rachel quickly sent a text to Sarah telling her she was fine and then affixed her name to the bottom of the text.

Barely seconds later, the text came back from Sarah. Just two words.

Thank God.

"I'm so lucky to have all of you," Rachel whispered.

Garrett gave her an indulgent smile and then ruffled her hair affectionately. "We've been friends a long time, sweet pea. I think it's safe to say that we're lucky as hell to still have you. Ethan knows it too. He may be stubborn as hell, but he's not dumb."

Rachel closed her eyes, no longer able to keep her head up. It was plenty warm in the ambulance, but a chill had settled bone deep, and she shook from head to toe.

She heard Garrett's worried demand to the medic and the medic's reassurance that it was just shock. A warm blanket slid over her body and was tucked around her neck. Garrett's hand curled around hers, gripping it tightly.

Now that she allowed herself to think of all that had happened that morning, she was ready to completely lose her cool. She could have died. One of the children could have gotten hurt or killed.

Ethan could have died.

It was more than she could hold up under any longer.

CHAPTER 13

"I don't need goddamn X-rays!" Ethan roared. "What I need is to see my wife!"

Donovan put his arm out to push Ethan back onto the bed. "Look, if I go check in on her and get a report from Garrett, will you shut the hell up and get the damn X-ray? You're making things worse by raising so much hell. If you'd just let them do the X-ray, you'd be done and out of here, and you could go be with Rachel."

Ethan pushed up from the bed, holding his chest where the bullet had bruised his ribs through the vest.

"Just give me a damn shirt and not one of those fucking hospital gowns either," he said in a testy voice.

He wasn't in the mood to play nice. The very last thing he cared about was whether he'd cracked a rib. It was obvious that he hadn't broken one or done serious damage. If the X-ray showed minor fractures of his ribs, what the hell could they do about it anyway? All they'd do is tell him to take it easy and give him something for pain.

The best thing they could do to ease his pain was to let him get to Rachel.

Donovan sighed in exasperation and then tossed him a T-shirt from his pack.

"Get your dumb ass dressed while I find out where they put Rachel. Swear to God, if you so much as move before I get back, I'll hold you down while they sedate you. You can't go barging through the ER scaring the shit out of the other patients."

"Then hurry the hell up," Ethan snapped.

He yanked on the T-shirt, wincing when his knuckles brushed over the tender spot on his midsection. Not that he'd admit it in a million years, but he hurt like a son of a bitch. Taking a bullet close range, even with the vest on, wasn't exactly a walk in the park.

A bruise the size of a softball had already formed.

But that's all it was. A bruise. Hell if he was going to be sidelined over a damn bruise. He'd endured worse, and nothing was going to keep him from Rachel.

He was getting fidgety when Donovan finally walked back into the tiny cubicle. He lunged up from where he had been leaning against the bed and confronted his brother.

"So where is she? And is she all right?"

Donovan held up his hands. "Garrett's with her, and Ma just got here. The wives are in the waiting room, and Dad's on his way to see you right now. Just settle down. Let Dad see that you're okay, and then we can all go down and see Rachel. The ER is a madhouse, and they've had to position police officers to keep the media out. Getting home is going to be interesting."

Ethan sighed and leaned back against the bed again. He was going to go out of his mind if he didn't get to Rachel soon, but he also didn't want his dad worried about him. The last thing Frank Kelly needed was more stress. He'd already had one heart attack, and Ethan wasn't going to be responsible for giving him another.

The door burst open, and his dad barreled through it. As soon as his gaze lighted on Ethan, his entire body sagged in relief.

"See, I told you, Dad. He's fine and cranky as ever," Donovan said.

Frank Kelly didn't respond. He hauled Ethan into his beefy embrace and damn near squeezed the life from Ethan. Ethan winced but held on to his dad.

"I'm fine, Dad," Ethan said in a low voice. "It's Rachel I'm worried about."

His dad held him for another long moment and then pulled away, his eyes suspiciously bright.

"Your mother and my daughters-in-law are checking in on her now," Frank said gruffly.

"I'm heading down there. Was just waiting on you once I heard you were here," Ethan said.

Frank frowned. "They're already finished with you?"

Ethan cleared his throat, and to his relief, Donovan came to his rescue.

"Told you nothing was wrong with the ornery bastard. He's too much like Garrett. He's worried about Rachel though. It would calm him down if he could just see her, so let's move down there so he can put his mind at ease."

Ethan shot Donovan a grateful look.

"You scared me, son," Frank said gruffly. "I swear you boys are always getting up to something. You're going to make an old man out of me yet."

Ethan grinned. "Nah. Just keeping you on your toes." He slapped his dad on the back. "Come on. Let's go see, Rachel."

IT was hard to keep her pregnancy secret when the medical personnel were ensuring that all was still well with her. Garrett stayed off to the side and out of the way, but then Marlene Kelly arrived, and hell no was anyone keeping her from her baby.

Disregarding medical staff objections, Marlene pushed her way to the bedside, sat down and gathered Rachel into her arms, hugging her so tightly that Rachel felt smothered.

It was the very *best* kind of smothering.

"You scared the wits out of us all," Marlene said even as she held Rachel closer to her. "I've never been so scared in my life, baby. It was all over the news, and then I saw you being carried away on a stretcher, and I made poor Frank break every speed limit getting here."

"I'm fine, Marlene," Rachel said, a smile in her voice.

She pried herself away and leaned back, taking in Marlene's anxious gaze.

"Ethan's the one who was hurt," Rachel said, the smile fading. "He was shot. He had a vest on, but it still hurt him. I wish someone would let me know how he is."

"He's fine," Garrett said from the corner. "Van just came down a second ago. They're coming in just a few minutes."

Marlene shook her head as she stared helplessly at Garrett. "I can't even fuss at my boys for getting into trouble because they got you out, but I swear they put more gray hairs on my head with every passing day. And now that Nathan and Joe are back home and joined up with the rest of their brothers, I'll never sleep another night through."

Garrett stepped forward and squeezed his mother's shoulders. "Now, Ma. You worry too much. You know we look out for each other. And we look out for this family. No way we were going to leave things with Rachel to chance with the local police. No telling how they would have f— uh, screwed it up," he amended hastily.

"Can we come in?"

Rachel glanced up to see Sophie peeking inside the doorway. Just behind her were Shea and Sarah. Rachel smiled and motioned them inside. Her sisters-in-law hurried in and quickly enfolded her in big hugs.

"Oh God, we were so scared," Sophie said as she stood back with the others. "How is Ethan? We heard he was shot!"

Garrett had looped his arm around Sarah, pulling her into his side, and he was quick to alleviate the worry in the women's eyes.

"He's fine. He was wearing a vest. He'll be down in just a minute."

"Thank God," Shea breathed.

Shea stared anxiously at Rachel, her eyes brimming with worry. Rachel gave her a reassuring nod so she'd know that all was well with the pregnancy.

The door flew open, and suddenly Ethan was at her bedside, his intense gaze burning over her. Everyone hastily moved so Ethan could have access to Rachel, and then Rachel was in his arms, firm against his chest.

She closed her eyes and clung fiercely to him. "Thank God you're okay," she whispered. "I was so worried, Ethan. Please don't ever scare me like that again. I'll never forget hearing the gunshot and seeing you go down. I'll never get that out of my head."

"Shhh, baby," he soothed. "That's why we wear vests. I was never in any danger. You, however, had no such protection, and that asshole would have gunned you down in cold blood."

"Take me home," she begged. "I just want to get out of here and be in our home where it's quiet."

He stroked her hair and kissed her forehead as she lay nestled in his arms.

"I'll get you home soon. I promise."

She pulled away to see that Marlene and the others had backed discreetly toward the doorway where Donovan and Frank were standing.

"They don't know," she whispered. "This isn't the way I want to tell them. I want to go home, and then I want to tell them properly, when the family is together and all the worry and stress is gone."

"Is everything okay with you?" he whispered back. "The babies?"

The fear in his eyes made her stomach knot and she hastened to ease his worry.

"I'm fine. Just reaction. They gave me a shot to help calm me down, and I'm okay now. I just want to go home."

He flashed a rueful smile. "I can't even argue with you

because I was bound and determined to get the hell out of that room I was in too. I understand how you feel."

She pulled him down even closer so she could whisper without being overheard.

"Tell them I'll make a follow-up appointment with my obstetrician in a couple of days and make sure everything's okay, but I want to leave now."

He pressed his lips to her forehead and left them there a long moment.

"I'm so proud of you I could burst," he murmured. "You kicked ass today, Rachel. Even if you scared the shit out of me in the process. Those kids owe their lives to you."

She shook her head and frowned.

He smiled and gently nudged her cheek with his knuckle. "Yeah, they do. Now, let me go see what I can do about springing you. It's going to be tricky to get you out of here without the media swarming."

She made a face and shuddered. "Can't Van land the helicopter here?"

Ethan glanced over at his brother, his expression one of surprise. "Van? I hadn't even thought of that. What do you say? Can we give Rachel the KGI VIP treatment and land the helicopter up top and get her home that way?"

Donovan cracked a grin. "For Rachel, hell yeah. Give me half an hour, and I'll be back. Then I'll need to go make sure Sam hasn't gotten his ass arrested."

CHAPTER 14

IT was quiet, and the room was darkened, with only a lamp burning by the bed when Rachel entered the bedroom from the bathroom.

Ethan was sprawled on the bed, shirtless but still wearing his fatigues. Even his boots were still on, and he looked too tired to take them off.

Her heart softened as she stared at his closed eyes, and then her gaze drifted down his lean, muscled chest to the bruise that darkened his already tan skin.

He'd been so worried for her, but in fact, she hadn't come close to injury. Certainly not as close as he'd come. That he'd been so willing to put himself between her and their children and harm's way told her more than words how much he loved her.

She went to where his feet hung off the bed, and she took one boot to prop it on her thigh while she unlaced it. Ethan came awake immediately and lifted his foot free of her grasp.

"Don't baby, I'll get them. Crawl into bed and get comfortable."

She shook her head and pulled his foot back. "Just lie still and let me get your boots off. You're exhausted. It's been a tough day for both of us, but I'm not the one who got shot."

He put his hands behind his head, watching as she wrestled with one boot and then transferred her attention to the other.

His lips parted hesitantly, as if he grappled with what to say and how to say it. There was torment in his eyes, and deep shadows lurked, making his gaze appear haunted.

There was an ache to his words that touched the deepest part of her soul.

"From the minute I knew what was going on, I kept wondering if this was where it would all be taken back. I guess some part of me has lived in fear that I was living on borrowed time and that people just don't get handed what I've been given without having to give it back at some point."

Her heart throbbed at the vulnerability in his voice. She tossed aside the boot and then crawled onto the bed, her hands smoothing up his chest until she got to his shoulders.

Her mouth hovered just over his, her dark hair falling like a curtain onto his skin.

"I hate to tell you this, but you're stuck with me," she teased, hoping to lighten the darkness in his eyes. "You can't get rid of me that easily. I think I've proved that already."

He wrapped his arm around her waist and anchored her firmly against him. "I don't want to ever lose you, baby. You're my life. The babies are my life. Our family means everything to me, and I'll always fight to keep you safe and happy."

She kissed him then. Warm and melting, their lips fused together.

"You make me so *very* happy," she whispered. "I can finally sleep at night without fear that I'll wake up in hell or that I dreamed you coming for me. I can see past today and get a glimpse of our future when our children are older and we have a lifetime of loving behind us."

He ran his fingers through her hair, toying with the strands in a tender gesture.

"Do you want me to quit KGI?" he asked in a serious tone.

She blinked in surprise. Then she studied the earnestness in his expression and sighed.

"I never wanted you to quit your SEAL team. That was your decision. What I want is for you to be happy, and working with your brothers makes you happy. I can see it in your eyes when you come home from work. We're older and wiser now, Ethan. We're stronger than we were when you were in the navy. I have a solid support system when you're away on a mission."

"I just want you to know that nothing is more important than you and our children. And I mean that. If it would make you happy, I'd walk away from KGI tomorrow and have no regrets."

"But it wouldn't make *you* happy, and if you aren't happy, I certainly won't be happy," she said.

He kissed her again, and she molded her body to his. She reached down, sliding her hand between them until she cupped him intimately, stroking him through his pants.

He groaned. "God, woman. I'm cut to my knees, weak with relief that you're alive and well, and you're acting the temptress, like you didn't almost get yourself killed today."

She smiled against his lips as she kissed him again, and then she drew away, propping her elbow on his upper chest, above where he'd been bruised.

But then she sobered as she took in the worry in his eyes. She touched his face, tracing the hard lines and then smoothing a finger over his lips.

"I made peace with death a long time ago. I'm not saying I want to die, but I don't *fear* it anymore. There were days that I wasn't strong during captivity, and I actually hoped for death. That they'd grow tired of keeping me on a leash and would give me an overdose and that I'd slip away."

Tears glittered in Ethan's eyes, and his jaw hardened. His entire body was tense. She knew it was difficult for him to hear, but she didn't hold anything back. She was honest if nothing else.

"I think it's why I could be relatively calm and not lose it today. One, I didn't want those kids to get hurt. And two, after everything I've endured, I've come to the conclusion that when God is ready for me to go, I'll go, and not a minute before."

"I'm just grateful He wasn't ready for you and that you're back home with me where you belong," he said, his voice husky with emotion.

She adjusted her body so she could turn and unfasten the fly of his pants. He lifted his hips upward and helped her push them down over his thighs. She got to her knees to finish removing the rest of his clothing until he was fully naked beneath her roving hands.

Tonight she was going to make love to him. So many times he'd been the one to handle her so gently. Always offering her reassurance. Telling her with more than words that he loved her and would always be here.

She wanted to be that person for *him* tonight. To show him that she loved him every bit as much. That she valued the sacrifices he'd made and was willing to make for her and their children.

Easing from the bed, she took only long enough to slip from the gown she'd put on after her shower, and then she crawled back onto the bed and positioned herself between his muscled thighs.

She leaned forward, pressing her mouth to his taut abdomen. Not a spare inch of flesh could she find. Gently she pressed tiny kisses to the bruise that marred his flesh, and then she moved lower again, teasing a trail down to the apex of his legs.

He sucked in all his breath when she licked from the base of his cock to the very tip. It twitched and bobbed underneath her lips, allowing her to suck the head inside her mouth.

In a warm, moist glide, she took him all the way in and

then slowly released him, inch by agonizing inch, exerting firm suction the entire time.

He stirred restlessly, fidgeting, unable to remain still as she stroked up and down, squeezing him with her mouth.

His hands twisted in her hair, holding her then pulling her to meet his thrusts. It was as if he had no control over his movements and he was frantic for more.

Already, she knew exactly what she wanted. How she wanted to make love to him. She teased and toyed with him until she tasted the first spill of pre-cum on her tongue. Then she slowed her movements and let him slide down from his impending release.

When his breathing slowed, she shifted upward again until she straddled him, arched up as she carefully fit him to her opening.

His big hands closed over her hips, offering his help as she angled over him. But he let her do as she wanted, never forcing the action.

Closing her eyes, she sank slowly down, taking him deeply inside her until she came to rest over his groin.

"God, you're so beautiful," Ethan said, his voice full of awe. "The most beautiful thing I've seen in my life. This is the way I want to remember you. Naked and lush, astride me, my dick so deep inside you. Your head thrown back and all that gorgeous hair flowing over your shoulders."

He slid his hands from her hips up to her breasts, cupping the small mounds and rubbing his thumbs over the peaks.

She fidgeted and then leaned forward into his grasp, savoring the feel of his hands on her breasts. She braced her palms against his arms and eased upward, allowing him to slide out of her.

Then she let herself down again, engulfing him until they both let out soft moans of appreciation.

"I want you with me, baby," Ethan whispered. "Together. Let's go together. Tell me what you need."

She sighed again. "Touch me. I'm so close."

He moved one hand between them, sliding a finger through the curls covering her mound to the sensitive nub of flesh sheltered in her slick folds. As soon as he stroked her, she tightened all over, which caused him to grow even more rigid inside her.

Needing more, she picked up the pace and began a steady rhythm that caused the most exquisite friction she'd ever experienced. He was so tight within her.

His free hand curved over her ass, and then his fingers dug into her flesh as she rode him.

"Come baby," he gasped out. "Get there."

He didn't have long to wait. Her body tightened into a taut coil, and then she snapped, suddenly releasing all the pent-up tension in one explosive burst.

Her soft cry was lost in his roar as his own orgasm flashed over him. She went warm and slick, the snugness eased by his release. Euphoric satisfaction wafted through her veins, infusing her with a drugged, hazy sensation.

She settled over Ethan, allowing her body to blanket his. He wrapped his arms around her so she was surrounded by him. Completely content, she snuggled more firmly into his embrace and let out a long sigh.

Life had taught her that nothing worthwhile came easy, but everything was all the more sweet for the sacrifices made.

"I love you," she said against his skin.

"I love you too, baby," he said, his voice fierce and possessive. "Sleep now while I hold you. I just need some time to hold you and remind myself that you're okay."

"I'm sorry to have scared you."

He slid his hands warmly over her back. "I know, baby. I know."

CHAPTER 15

RACHEL had never been so grateful to live behind the gates of the compound. She was extremely thankful for the timing and that she and Ethan had moved from their old house before the incident at the school because the media had camped out in their old neighborhood ever since she'd been released from the hospital.

It was a complete zoo in the small town where Frank's hardware store was, and he'd had to close it down after only one hour in operation the day he reopened after the gunman's arrest.

Once again, Rachel found herself in the media spotlight, only this time she hadn't returned from the dead. She'd merely flirted with death once again.

The only article she'd glanced at had mentioned that she had nine lives. Maybe it was true, but she wasn't going to waste time dwelling on all the ways she'd cheated death.

For the past few days, she and Ethan had sequestered themselves in their new home. Marlene and Rachel's sisters-in-law had taken turns bringing them home-cooked meals, and so Ethan and Rachel had remained indoors, soaking up the fact that they'd survived a close call and Rachel was suffering no ill effects from the scare.

"Baby, Ma just called," Ethan said as he ambled into the living room.

Rachel had kept the television off ever since they'd gotten home because they couldn't flip through the channels without coming across a mention of the shooting.

The police had made multiple trips to the compound because Ethan refused to take her out where they'd be mobbed by media.

She'd told her version of the incident so many times her ears were numb from listening to herself.

"Oh?" Rachel asked, turning her attention from the book she'd been reading.

"She informed me that they've given us enough alone time to recover and that they're converging tonight for the housewarming party they'd already planned."

Rachel froze, sure she had a deer-in-the-headlights look. "Tonight?" She glanced around the living room in horror. Nothing was clean. There were boxes everywhere.

Ethan held up his hands. "Don't freak. Ma wouldn't do that to you. I mean just come over when she knows we've been moving and stuff's not clean. She's rounding up the daughters-in-law and they're coming over in an hour to clean and cook.

Rachel stared at him, utterly appalled. "And that's supposed to make it better? I'm supposed to sit and watch them clean my house and cook for a party we're having here *tonight*?"

"That's precisely what you're going to do," Ethan said sternly. "I don't want you overdoing it."

Rachel sighed, and Ethan plopped down on the couch and wrapped his arm around her shoulders.

"Everyone's worried about you. They just want to do something to make you happy and to celebrate our move. I think they think you're sad over leaving the old house."

She pressed her lips together and puffed her cheeks out before allowing the air out in an audible pop.

"Does it still bother you that I'm not bothered by leaving?"

Slowly he shook his head. "Your reasons made sense. How can I fault you for being honest? And I want you to be happy. If having a new house in a safer location makes you feel content and secure then I'd have to be a complete asshole to begrudge you that."

She turned into his chest and hugged him fiercely. "We're going to make some great memories in this house, Ethan."

He kissed the top of her head and ran his fingers through her hair. "Yeah, we are. Starting tonight."

THE house was alive with chatter, laughter and the warm smiles that only came from being with family.

All of the Kellys were present and accounted for. Even Rusty and Sean, honorary members of the Kelly clan, were there.

Rusty had cornered Rachel as soon as she'd arrived, concerned for Rachel's pregnancy. Rachel had assured her she was fine, but she hadn't shared the fact she was having twins. She'd save that surprise for when they made the official announcement.

She knew Ethan's brothers knew, but they were keeping it quiet, not wanting to ruin the big surprise.

It was as if the entire family had made a pact prior to arriving at Ethan and Rachel's that no mention of the incident at the school would be made.

There was no conversation about the gunman, the media or even KGI's involvement in ending the standoff.

Wanting her curiosity—and her fears—appeased, she cornered Sam while the others were piling food onto their plates.

"Did KGI get into trouble over the hostage situation?" she asked anxiously. "Ethan said they didn't want you going in and that you did anyway."

Sam smiled, a rueful glint in his eyes. "Let's just say

that we exchanged quite a few words. But because of the way it all went down and where the media was confined to, S.W.A.T. was already making a move in after the children were released, so they got the credit for taking Winstead down. Which is fine. It keeps KGI out of the picture. The chief wasn't happy. The mayor was pretty pissed. The sheriff looked like he'd swallowed an egg. They were probably all shitting their pants, worried that we'd screw up and they'd take the fall."

Rachel shook her head. "I'm sorry."

He blinked. "What the hell do you have to be sorry for? Did you honestly think we'd sit on our asses while you were at the hands of some deranged ass hat?"

She grinned. "No, I'm sorry that people are so stupid. But I'm glad you didn't get arrested or anything. It would suck to have to visit you in jail."

His soft chuckle rose, and then he took her elbow and turned her toward the table where Marlene had set up the food buffet style.

"Let's go get something to eat before my brothers devour it all."

He didn't have to tell her twice. She took a plate and piled it high with food. Truth was, she was starving, and she hadn't felt queasy for two whole days. It was enough to make her want to take a chance and enjoy every single bite she had tonight.

As everyone ate and conversed, Ethan found his way closer to Rachel until the two were standing side by side. When she finished with her plate, he took it from her and set it aside before lacing his fingers through hers.

He gave her a look so filled with love that she could scarcely breathe. She was warmed to her toes by the contentment that rested so comfortably on him.

It was time. Everyone who mattered to them was here. In their new home, a place that would be the foundation of their future.

Ethan cleared his throat and then called for attention. Conversation hushed, and all eyes were directed at Ethan

and Rachel. Butterflies—excited butterflies—danced around
Rachel's belly. A belly that would soon expand to accommodate the two tiny lives nestled there below her heart.

"Rachel and I have something we'd very much like to
share with the people who mean the most to us."

He glanced down at her, his brow raised in question as
to whether he should tell or if she wanted to. She smiled
and squeezed his hand before nodding that he should tell.

He took a deep breath, his smile growing so broad that
his teeth flashed.

"After much thought and consideration, endless soul-
searching, finally being at peace with the decision and feeling that Rachel was ready for such a step, we decided to
start trying for a baby."

The smiles were instantaneous. Marlene leaned over,
punched Frank on the arm, and whispered in a loud voice,
"I told you!"

Rachel smiled and jittered in Ethan's grasp. She was as
giddy as a kid at Christmas. She loved the way Ethan was
drawing it out for maximum effect. She wanted to savor
this moment for as long as possible.

"What we didn't count on was it happening so fast,"
Ethan added with a grin.

Everyone went silent. Eyes were wide. Knowing smiles
were on Ethan's brothers' faces. Shea smothered her own
reaction, clenching her fingers into excited fists. She looked
as though she'd start bouncing up and down on Nathan's lap.

Frank's brow furrowed. "Does that mean what I think it
means?"

Ethan chuckled. "Yes, Dad. Rachel is pregnant."

A chorus of whoops went up, and Ethan let it go for a
minute, but when the family started to get up and swarm
toward him and Rachel, he held up his hands.

"Just a minute. There's something else you should
know."

Marlene's mouth flapped open, and she stared between
Rachel and Ethan as if trying to decide if it was good news
or bad news. She stopped halfway over to where Ethan and

Rachel stood, and Frank came to a halt beside her, sliding his arm around her.

Ethan glanced down at Rachel, love warm and alive in his gaze. He squeezed her to him, and in the background, Rachel could hear the soft sighs from those who stared at the two of them. But her focus was on Ethan and the promise in his eyes. The promise of a wonderful future so bright she could barely imagine it.

Then he looked back up at his family, his face about to crack under his enormous smile.

"We're not just having one baby. Last week we learned that we're having . . . twins."

A series of gasps, exclamations and sounds of complete surprise echoed across the room. Excited babble. Joy and enthusiasm danced tangibly in the air.

Marlene could no longer contain herself. She converged on Rachel, her hand waving excitedly in the air as squeals of excitement burst from her lips.

"Oh baby," Marlene exclaimed as she pulled Rachel into her arms. "What wonderful, *wonderful* news. I'm so happy for you and Ethan."

"Thank you," Rachel said, returning her fierce hug.

"How frightened you must have been through all of this," Marlene said, sympathy shining in her warm, brown eyes.

Frank pushed his way in and gathered Rachel into a huge hug, but he was extremely gentle, careful not to crush her. He kissed her cheek, and when he spoke, his voice was clogged with emotion.

"I couldn't be prouder," Frank said. "What a blessing two more grandchildren will be. You take good care of yourself, young lady. I'll be watching."

Rachel grinned. Oh but she was about to burst from the joy of it all. "I know you will."

"This calls for a toast," Sam called out, holding his glass high.

The room went silent again as the oldest Kelly son smiled in Rachel and Ethan's direction.

"You've long been special to us all, Rachel," he said.

Everyone was quick to agree, their smiles as bright as the sun. She basked in those smiles. At the love and acceptance that shined as brilliantly as a million stars.

"You're also one hell of a kickass woman. I don't know of many other people as resilient as you. And even after all you've endured, you've still remained the sweet and loving Rachel that we all fell in love with all those years ago."

Tears burned her eyelids until she gave up trying to hold them at bay. Sam was so serious, giving her no doubt he meant every single word.

Donovan broke in, looking directly at Ethan.

"If your children—Rachel's children—inherit even one half of their mother's spirit and determination, then you'll have yourself two children who'll never be beaten down in life."

"Hell, they'll rule the damn world," Garrett muttered.

Laughter swept through the room, relieving some of the solemnness.

"Thank you," Rachel said, her voice as watery as her eyes were. "I'm so grateful for you all, and I don't know what I'd do without you."

She looked directly at Marlene and Frank, her love for the older couple so powerful that it was hard to even put into words all she felt and all she hoped for.

"My hope for my children is that I can be the kind of parent that you are to your children and to the people you offer that unconditional love and support to."

"I'll second that," Ethan said, wrapping his arm around Rachel.

Rachel looked around the room, at every single face. "My babies will be the luckiest children who ever lived to have such a wonderful family. I'll never forget how much you've helped me overcome in the past few years."

Sean cleared his throat. "Rachel, honey, just do me a favor, please? Given all that you and I have gone through together, when you go into labor, make sure I'm nowhere in the vicinity."

The room burst into laughter, and Rachel laughed along with them. She closed her eyes, simply absorbing the vibration of so much joy.

She was no longer a victim of the past, held prisoner by the demons who haunted her mind. She was moving beyond that, into a future filled with the promise of brighter days and happier times.

She was a Kelly. And she was *loved*.